D0708348

THE WIMBLEDON POISONER

by the same author

fiction
MY LIFE CLOSED TWICE
JACK BE NIMBLE
STAR TURN
WITCHCRAFT

plays
MY BROTHER'S KEEPER
COUNTRY DANCING
BREAKING UP (*for television*)

THE
WIMBLEDON
POISONER

Nigel
Williams

faber and faber

LONDON · BOSTON

First published in 1990
by Faber and Faber Limited
3 Queen Square London WC1N 3AU
Reprinted 1990 (three times)

Phototypeset by Input Typesetting Ltd, London
Printed in England by Clays Ltd, St Ives plc

All rights reserved

© Nigel Williams, 1990

Nigel Williams is hereby identified as author of this work in accordance with Section 77 of
the Copyright, Designs and Patents Act 1988

A CIP record for this book is available from the British Library

ISBN 0-571-14242-7

For Suzan

'It is forbidden to kill; therefore all murderers are punished who kill not in large companies, and to the sound of trumpets.'

Voltaire, *Philosophical Dictionary*

PART ONE

Innocent Enjoyment

'When a felon's not engaged in his employment
Or maturing his felonious little plans,
His capacity for innocent enjoyment,
Is just as great as any honest man's!'

W. S. Gilbert, *Pirates of Penzance*

CHAPTER ONE

Henry Farr did not, precisely, decide to murder his wife. It was simply that he could think of no other way of prolonging her absence from him indefinitely.

He had quite often, in the past, when she was being more than usually irritating, had fantasies about her death. She hurtled over cliffs in flaming cars or was brutally murdered on her way to the dry cleaners. But Henry was never actually responsible for the event. He was at the graveside looking mournful and interesting. Or he was coping with his daughter as she roamed the now deserted house, trying not to look as if he was glad to have the extra space. But he was never actually the instigator.

Once he had got the idea of killing her (and at first this fantasy did not seem very different from the reveries in which he wept by her open grave, comforted by young, fashionably dressed women) it took some time to appreciate that this scenario was of quite a different type from the others. It was a dream that could, if he so wished, become reality.

One Friday afternoon in September, he thought about strangling her. The Wimbledon Strangler. He liked that idea. He could see Edgar Lustgarten narrowing his eyes threateningly at the camera, as he paced out the length of Maple Drive. 'But Henry Farr,' Lustgarten was saying, 'with the folly of the criminal, the supreme arrogance of the murderer, had forgotten one vital thing. The shred of fibre that was to send Henry Farr to the gallows was – '

What was he thinking of? They didn't hang people any more. They wrote long, bestselling paperback books about them. Convicted murderers, especially brutal and disgusting ones, were followed around by as many *paparazzi* as the royal family. Their thoughts on life and love and literature were

3

published in Sunday newspapers. Television documentary-makers asked them, respectfully, about exactly how they felt when they hacked their aged mothers to death or disembowelled a neighbour's child. This was the age of the murderer. And wasn't Edgar Lustgarten dead?

He wouldn't, anyway, be known as the Wimbledon Strangler, but as Henry Farr, cold-blooded psychopath. Or, better still, just Farr, cold-blooded psychopath. Henry liked the idea of being a cold-blooded psychopath. He pictured himself in a cell, as the television cameras rolled. He wouldn't moan and stutter and twitch the way most of these murderers did. He would give a clear, coherent account of how and why he had stabbed, shot, strangled, gassed or electrocuted her. 'Basically,' he would say to the camera, his gestures as urgent and incisive as those of any other citizen laying down the law on television, 'basically I'm a very passionate man. I love and I hate. And when love turns to hate, for me, you know, that's it. I simply had no wish for her to live. I stand by that decision.' Here he would suddenly stare straight into the camera lens in the way he had seen so many politicians do, and say, 'I challenge any red-blooded Englishman who really feels. Who has passion. Not to do the same. When love dies, it dies.'

Hang on. Was he a red-blooded Englishman or a cold-blooded psychopath? Or was he a bit of both? Was it possible to combine the two roles?

Either way, however he did it (and he was becoming increasingly sure that it was a good idea), his life was going to be a lot more fun. Being a convicted murderer had the edge on being a solicitor for Harris, Harris and Overdene of Blackfriars, London. Even Wormwood Scrubs must have more to offer, thought Henry as he rattled the coffee machine on the third floor, than Harris, Harris and Overdene. It wouldn't be so bad, somehow, if he was any good at being a solicitor. But, as Elinor was always telling him, Henry did not inspire confidence as a representative of the legal profession. He had, she maintained, a shifty look about him.

'How could you expect anyone to trust you with their conveyancing?' she had said to him, only last week. 'You look as if you've only just been let out on parole!'

Glumly, Henry carried his coffee along the dark corridor towards the stairs that led to his office. 'Office' was a grandiose term for it really. 'Cupboard' would have been a better description. It was a room about eight to ten feet square, offering, as an estate agent with whom Henry was dealing had put it, 'a superb prospect of a ventilator shaft'. It was, like so many other things in Henry's life, more like a carefully calculated insult from the Almighty than anything else.

He would give himself a treat today. He would go up in the lift. He stabbed angrily at the button. Mr Dent from the third floor, who was waiting by the lift doors, looked at him narrowly. 'Can't you tell – ' his eyes seemed to say, 'that I have already pressed it? Surely you realize that when the button is illuminated someone has pressed it?' Henry, before Dent was able to start talking to him about lifts, weather, the Law Society or any of the other things that Dent usually talked about, headed for the stairs. He pushed open the door and, as he put his foot on the first step, experienced a revelation comparable to that undergone by Newton in the orchard or Archimedes in his bath.

He could kill Elinor, very easily and *no one need know*. The implications of this were absolutely breathtaking. No one need know. He said it aloud to himself as he trudged up the stairs. No one need know. Of course. No one need know. Every minute of every day people were being murdered. Hundreds of people disappeared without trace every year. No one ever found them. The police were all, as far as Henry could see, totally incompetent. They spent their time hiding behind low stone walls and leaping out at motorists travelling in bus lanes. They liked people like Henry. People like Henry, white middle-aged men who lived in Wimbledon and had one daughter, were their idea of what British citizens should be. One young constable had come to the house last year when they had been burgled and, very laboriously, had

5

written the details of the crime into a book. He had looked, Henry thought, like a gigantic blue infant, a curious cross between cunning and *naïveté*, a representative of an England that was as dead as the gold standard. Henry had tried to tempt him into making a racist statement by announcing that he had seen a black person outside the window two weeks ago, but all the constable had said was 'You don't see many coloureds in this part of Wimbledon.' He said this almost with regret, in the tones of a disappointed birdwatcher searching for the great crested grebe.

Nobody would ever suspect Henry. Because – he was well aware – most people thought he was something called a Nice Bloke. Henry was never quite sure what being a nice bloke entailed – it certainly wasn't much to do with behaving scrupulously well towards one's fellow man. If it meant anything at all it probably meant other people thought you were a bit like them. To most of those who knew him Henry was just eccentric enough to be terrifyingly normal, and even his carefully calculated bitterness, the quality of which, on the whole, he was most proud, had become, in early middle age, a Nice Dry Sense of Humour.

I'll give them nice dry sense of humour, he thought savagely as he came out on to his floor and lumbered towards room 4038, I'll give them nice dry sense of humour and then some. I'll give them the real Henry Farr, and he won't just be making witty little remarks about the London orbital motorway either.

Of all Elinor's friends he was the least likely to be suspected of her murder. She had, even at their wedding, surrounded herself with people, nearly all of whom were interesting enough to warrant the close scrutiny of the police. Many of them, to Henry's horror, openly smoked drugs. One of them wore a kaftan. Two wore sandals. And they still trooped in and out of his house occasionally, looking at him pityingly, as they talked of foreign films, the latest play at the Royal Court and the need for the immediate withdrawal of armed forces from Nicaragua. Sometimes they sat in the front room reading aloud from the work of a man called Ian McEwan, an author who, according to Elinor, had 'a great deal to say' to Henry Farr.

Oh yeah, thought Henry grimly as he passed 4021a, his coffee threshing around dangerously in its plastic beaker, and Henry Farr had a great deal to say to Ian McEwan as well.

The trouble was, of course, that among Henry's sort of person, a rugby-playing surveyor, for example, or the kind of dentist like David Sprott who wasn't afraid to get up on his hind legs at a social gathering and talk, seriously and at length, about teeth, he was considered something of a subversive. At their wedding, all those years ago, his friends, all of them even then in suits and ties, had nudged each other when he rose to answer his best man. 'Go on then,' he could see them thinking, 'be a devil!' But as his eyes travelled across to Elinor's crowd, with their frizzy haloes of hair, their flowered dresses and carefully arranged profiles, he realized that there was nothing he could think of to say that would persuade them he was anything other than a boring little man.

But there were certain advantages in being considered boring. And if they wanted him to be boring then that would be the performance that he would offer. He would be so stunningly boring that even the bankers, account executives, product managers and stockbrokers he counted as his friends would start to back away from him. He would play up to Elinor's friends' idea of what he was. He would play the part of the upright citizen, the dull wounded little man whose horizons were bounded by the daily journey to the office, the suburban garden and the suburban sky, set around with suburban roofs and neat suburban trees. He cut a little caper as he walked along the corridor that led to his office, recovering a quality that had suddenly become important to him – his drabness. He would be drab. Drab drab drab drab. He would be as drab as Crewe railway station. As drab as a not very important mayor. He would blend into Wimbledon until he was indistinguishable from the trees, the homing children, the lollipop ladies, or the gables on the red brick houses.

And they would never, never find out that he had done it.

When he came into the office, past Selinda his secretary, an elderly woman who was constantly asking him to give her 'something interesting to do' (How could he? Henry himself never had anything interesting to do), he squeezed close to the wall and coughed to himself in an extra drab way. He left his office door opened and, for the next hour, treated her to a stunningly drab conversation about the searches on a leasehold flat in Esher. When she put her head round the door and asked in her usual, conspiratorial manner if he wanted tea, Henry said, 'Tea would be a delight, my dear!' He said this in a high-pitched monotone that was intended to convey boringness; he was, however, he could tell from Selinda's expression, trying a little too hard.

He pulled out a correspondence file between a landlord and tenant in Ruislip – nearly eighty pages devoted to conflict over responsibility for a dustbin area – and tried to concentrate. How was he going to do it?

Murder should not, he felt, be unnecessarily complicated. It should have a clean, aesthetic line to it. It should involve as few people as possible. Oneself and the victim. If it was like anything, thought Henry, it was probably like the art of eating out.

His first thought was to do something to the Volkswagen Passat. That would have the advantage of getting rid of both car and wife at the same time. If there was anything that Henry hated as much as his wife, it was the car they had chosen and purchased together. He had hated the little brochure that described it – the pathetic attempt to make it look glamorous, the photographs of it, posed, doors open, doors shut, desperately trying not to look like what it was – a square box with hideous speckled seats. The Volkswagen Passat was about as glamorous as a visit to the supermarket, which was what it was principally used for. The people in the photographs in the brochure – a man, his wife, his two children and his stupid, stupid luggage, his folding chairs, his folding table, his hamper, his sensible suitcase packed for his sensible holiday – were exactly how Henry imagined the advertisers thought of him. A man called Frobisher-Zigtermans – a person who insisted on not remaining anonymous during the transaction – had described it as 'all car'. 'It's all car!' he had said. 'I'll say that for it!' And, as Henry smiled and nodded damply, he thought to himself, Is that all you can find to say about it? 'It's all car.' Can't you talk about its roadholding? Its incredible power over women? You can't, can you? Because you think I wouldn't respond. Because you think I'm as boring as this car. Which is why I'm buying it.

Just thinking about his car made Henry want to hire an electric hammer and run with all convenient speed to Wimbledon, to fall upon its bodywork with screams of rage.

He would saw through the brake cable. Not right through. Almost through. He would do it tonight, Friday, just in time for the weekly trip to the supermarket. Elinor would turn left up Maple Drive, left again into Belvedere Road, left again on to the hill . . . and then . . . oh then . . .

Except she didn't go to the supermarket, did she? He did. Which was one of the many reasons, now he thought about it, why he was planning to kill her. How did one saw through a brake cable anyway? It was no good chopping the thing in half, was it? Your victim would catch on before accelerating to a speed likely to be fatal. You had to saw it halfway through, didn't you? Henry wondered where the brake cable was, what it looked like, whether it was the kind of thing to which you could take a saw. The trouble with this sawing-halfway-through lark was that you had no control over where and when the thing was likely to break. Christ, it might even be when he was driving! Even if she was sitting next to him, complaining about his driving, her own imminent decease would not compensate for the depression generated by his own. Ideally, of course, Elinor would be driving her mother somewhere. Somewhere a little more interesting than Wimbledon Hill. Somewhere, well, steeper . . .

Henry sat for quite a long time thinking about the conversation between Elinor and her mother as they hurtled down the Paso della Lagastrella, brakeless. 'Darling, *do* something!' 'I'm *doing* something, darling!' 'Oh darling, we're going to die, oh my *God*!' 'I *know* we're going to die it's not my fault, oh my *God*!' He thought about the soaring, almost optimistic leap the Volkswagen would make as it cleared the edge of the cliff (from Henry's memory of it there was no safety barrier on that particular stretch of the Apennines). He thought about the long, long fall and then the flames, way below. About the immense difficulty that would undoubtedly be experienced by rescue teams.

It was five twenty-nine and fifteen seconds. In just forty-five seconds he would get up from his desk, take his coat and walk past his secretary. He would say 'Goodnight all' (although she would be the only other person in the room), and then he would take the lift down to the chilly autumn street and Blackfriars station, all soot and sickly neon. And from there he would rattle back to Wimbledon and his wife of twenty years.

Henry sat in his chair as the seconds ticked away. But when the large hand of his watch passed the twelve, he did not move. He sat and stared at the desk in front of him, the creamy whorls in the wood, the tanned grain. And he thought about the endless mystery of objects.

CHAPTER TWO

It was dark by the time Henry reached home. The lights were on in all the houses up Maple Drive. At number 23 the Indian was seated, motionless, in his bay window. On the top floor of 32, Mrs Mackintosh stared nervously out at the dark street. Mrs Mackintosh had Alzheimer's disease. 'Has my husband gone out now?' the expression on her face seemed to say. 'Or is he due back at any moment? Or perhaps he's here somewhere in the house, lurking behind a chest of drawers, waiting to spring out at me.' Only last week she had told Henry (who had lived in Maple Drive for twelve years) that she wished to welcome him to the neighbourhood. On Wednesdays she was driven by her sister to something called the Memory Clinic, where Henry imagined some ghastly psychiatric version of Kim's Game being played. Not that Henry's memory was getting any better. Only the other day . . . Only the other day what? . . .

At 49 all the curtains were drawn and at 51 Mrs Archer had left the front door open, perhaps in the hope that Mr Archer would return. Mr Archer had left her four years ago for a married man with a beard who lived, people said, in Shepherds Bush.

In his own house the curtains were open, the light was on and he could see a young girl with a pigtail, seated at the piano. She was playing 'Für Elise', very, very slowly and cautiously. Next to her was a woman with long black hair, a stubby nose and the kind of jaw found on actors playing responsible sheriffs in cowboy films. As the girl played the woman dilated her nostrils and rose slightly off the piano stool, as if someone was drawing her up by an invisible wire attached to the crown of her head. When the child reached the bottom of the first page the woman darted forward, black

11

hair swinging across her face, for the kind of effortful page turn that would have upstaged Paderewski himself. 'Behold!' the gesture seemed to say. 'I turn the page!' The child struggled gamely on to page two but seemed to suspect that, after a page turn of this quality, anything else was liable to be an anti-climax.

Henry watched the woman for some time. Her broad shoulders. The determined set of her upper torso. Her grim concentration on her child's performance. Mrs Elinor Farr. The mother of his child.

Should he, perhaps, push her off a cliff? They could go down to Beachy Head. Wander along the edge of the cliff. Some remark, along the lines of 'Oooh look! Over there, dear!' And then a smart shove in the small of the back.

But how to persuade her to go to Beachy Head? Let alone to stand near the edge of a cliff. And suppose, as she fell, she clutched on to him? Or, suspecting what was up, dodged smartly to one side when Henry made his move? Henry saw himself in the air, high above the sea and the shingle, spread out like a starfish, Elinor above him, cackling wildly.

She was going to be difficult to kill, no question about it, thought Henry. She had that dogged look about her. Sighing, he let his key into the lock. His daughter was see-sawing, inelegantly, between E natural and D sharp. Maisie had managed, somehow, to make Beethoven's tune sound like a tired police siren; when it dropped a fourth to B natural she paused, fractionally, before playing the note; it sounded, as a result, like a burp or a fart. At the cadenza, she stumbled down the keyboard with something that had elements of a flourish but ended up sounding more like a digital coronary, an awful, shaming collapse of the fingers that, at the last minute, recovered itself and looked as if it might turn into something like the chord of A minor. Such was not its destiny. As Henry removed his coat and set his briefcase down, Maisie's fingers, like demented spiders in a bath, ran this way and that, in any direction, it seemed, that might lead them away from the wistful logic of the melody. All Mrs

Craxton's pencilled annotations on the manuscript (*Sudden drop!! Fingering here, Maisie!!!*), all of O. Thurmer's revisions, phrases and fingering, all four hundred and sixteen pounds-worth of tutorials suddenly slipped away and Maisie Farr hammered the keys of the piano like a gorilla on amphetamines.

Henry paused on his way upstairs. He loved music. Why was Elinor in charge of Maisie's piano lessons?

He had never really been allowed near his daughter. She had been presented to him, rather in the way she had been presented to her mother, ten years ago, by a Jamaican mid-wife, in Queen Mary's Hospital, Roehampton. Served up, thought Henry, and not always graciously. Sometimes she was served up garnished with prizes, a certificate of excellence in swimming or a merit card from a teacher, but more often than not she was slapped down in front of him like a British Rail sandwich, garnished with a series of medical complaints. 'She needs grommets!' Elinor would squawk, pointing at her daughter in the gloom of the kitchen. Or else, 'Her chest! Listen to her chest, Henry! It's awful! Listen to it!' And Maisie would stand like some artist's model, exhibiting her diseases as if they were her only claim on him.

Perhaps a few blows to the side of the head with an axe? Or an electric fire tipped into the bath one afternoon? Henry liked the idea of his wife dying in bath gear. The thought of her twitching her last in a plastic hat, face covered with green mud, carried him through to their bedroom (a room Elinor had taken to calling 'my' bedroom) and shored him up against Maisie's rendition of the second subject in 'Für Elise'. F major did not help her any, he reflected, as he struggled out of his ridiculous businessman's shoes.

The trouble was, all these methods were now the staple diet of Radio 4 plays. Just as cliché haunted Henry's daily journey to the train, his socks from Marks and Spencer's, his regular nightly bedtime, his fondness for a cup of tea at ten thirty in the evening, just as he seemed to be destined to be as remorselessly English as the plane trees in the street outside or the homecoming commuters clacking through the twilight towards the village, so his one existential act (hadn't someone called it that?) seemed destined for suburban predictability. Why couldn't he roast her in oil? Hurl her into a pit of snakes? Inject her with a rare South American pois –

The word 'poison' had scarcely formed itself in his mind before Henry knew, with the sweet certainty that accompanies most forms of conquest, that he had found his *métier*. He wasn't, clearly, the Mad Axeman of SW23. He was not, could not be the Southfields Strangler or the Rapist of Raynes Park. But the Wimbledon Poisoner! He stood up, walked across to the mirror and there studied his reflection. Then he said, aloud – 'The Wimbledon Poisoner'. First ideas were always the best. He removed his jacket, trousers, shirt, tie and underclothes and studied himself in the mirror. A fat man of forty with an improbably long penis and a dense mass of wiry pubic hair. A face, as Elinor was often telling him, like a deviant grocer's. A few thin strands of black to grey hair and a nose that looked like badly applied putty. An out-of-date Englishman.

At the thought of the word 'Englishman' Henry stiffened to attention. He straightened his shoulders (straightened one of them anyway. It seemed to be impossible to straighten both at the same time) and thrust out his chest. Don't be down! There was some go in him yet! By stealth and devotion to his craft he might yet give something back to the class and the country that produced Crippen. What did England produce now, by way of criminals? Louts who could go no further than ill-thought-out violence on street corners. Where were the classic murders that had once held the attention of the world? The patient, domestic acts performed in this country of fogs and mists that had made English murderers the doyens of the civilized globe. These days, the average Brit's idea of a crime was a drunken assault on a Pakistani grocer. He would do it, and he would do it slowly, exquisitely. He grasped his penis firmly in his right hand and agitated it. It stiffened with blood and, like a dog sighting its lead,

14

throbbed with anticipation. Henry removed his hand and wagged his index finger at his member.

'Not yet!' he said. 'We need all our energies for the task ahead!'

He had remembered (how could he have forgotten?) that the suburb had once boasted a poisoner almost as celebrated as Henry intended to be. A really first-grade monster. A beast. A ravening wolf in sheep's clothing. Everett Maltby. Chapter 24 (Appendix), Volume 8 of his book.

Where was the section on Everett Maltby? It was always going missing. Sometimes you would find it wedged next to 'Witchcraft in Stuart Wimbledon' and, later, it would appear in the middle of 'The Impact of the Black Death on South West London'. He padded through to the room that Elinor described as his 'study'. Henry thought of it more as a shrine. It was here that he completed income tax forms, read carefully through the property pages of most of the local newspapers and, most sacred of all, worked on his *Complete History of Wimbledon*. The title alone had cost him two weeks' work. It couldn't be simply *The History of Wimbledon* (there was a book with that title – it didn't matter that it had been published nearly two hundred years ago). It had to be something that would give the prospective punter some idea of the staggering depth and scope and thoroughness of Henry's work. Suggest to them the fact that when they had finished this one they would know absolutely bloody everything that could be possibly known, now and for always, about Wimbledon. That there would be no escape from the great wall of knowledge Henry was propelling in their direction.

He opened the desk drawer and took out a page at random. It was from a rather combative chapter somewhere around the middle of 'Wimbledon in the Ninth Century after Christ'. 'We read', he read, 'in Richard Milward's unreliable, tendentious and often plainly wrong book *Early and Mediaeval Wimbledon* that "in 878 a Danish army took up winter quarters just across the river at Fulham. Nothing is known of its activities, but Vikings normally maintained themselves by raiding the country within a wide range of their base. *So Wimbledon would have been very fortunate to have escaped without some damage.*'' (My italics.)'

He had hit Milward pretty hard, thought Henry, but he had been right to do so. Standards were standards. The thought of Milward cheered him up, and he got up and went over to the bookcase where the offending pamphlet was stored. He opened it and chose a sentence at random. He was not disappointed. 'During the Bronze Age – 2,500 to 750 BC the first metal objects appeared in Wimbledon.' What did the man think he was doing? Had he no notion at all of historical method? The sentence conjured up, for Henry, bizarre images, ancient and modern. He seemed to see men in winged helmets lounging around Frost's, the late-night delicatessen, or peering oafishly into the windows of Sturgis, the estate agent. From there, he allowed the Vikings more licence. They swarmed up Parkside and boarded buses bound for Putney, shouting unpleasant things at the driver-conductor. And then they surrounded Milward's house and pillaged and put to the sword Milward and other members of the Wimbledon Society who simply did not understand that –

'You look as if you're going to have a thrombie!' said a voice behind him.

Henry wheeled round, the pamphlet in his hand.

'You're naked!' she said accusingly.

Henry lowered the pamphlet and stood in what he hoped was a coquettish manner. She looked at him stonily. He gave her his best smile, a greeting he normally reserved for waiters. It was going to be important not to arouse her suspicions during the planning stages.

'I'm sorry!' he said, adding in a tone that was intended to be gentle, but came out wheedling, 'Do you find me repulsive?'

Elinor's answer to this was to slam the study door. Henry scratched his crotch reflectively and stared down at his *History of Wimbledon*. Down below the piano started up again.

She was playing slightly better this time, but the effect was still markedly sinister. She sounded just perfect for the Wimbledon Poisoner's Daughter.

CHAPTER THREE

The next morning was Saturday.

Once, a long time ago, Henry could recall being alarmed at the emptiness, the ease, the sheer possibility offered by Saturday. This was no longer the case. On Saturdays Maisie now followed a routine as carefully planned as a day in the life of a nun in a particularly strict order. She went to piano. She went to ballet. She went to drama classes. She went to lessons in drawing, ice-skating, junior aerobics and many other skills which she had absolutely no hope of acquiring. She did not, thought Henry bitterly, as he dragged himself out of bed and weaved his way to the bathroom over Elinor's discarded knickers, go to classes in being thin, or classes designed to allow the participants to hold one idea in their heads for more than five minutes.

My daughter, he told himself as he brushed his teeth and stared down at number 47's red Mitsubishi, is like me, fat and untalented. Opposite him, the net curtains of number 47 parted and number 47 peered out. Henry did not have to see his thin anxious face, his nervous nibble at his lower lip or the furtive glance to left and right to know that number 47 was performing the ritual known as Is the Mitsubishi Scratched Yet? Ever since the pharmaceutical company for which he worked had given him the vehicle (*given*, thought Henry grimly) number 47 had been watching over it in a manner that suggested an emotion deeper than motherhood, more desperate than romantic love. It was as if he feared the car would suffer from some mechanical equivalent of cot death, would suddenly buckle and blister and bend, hideously out of shape, there before his eyes, at berth, peacefully parked at its usual angle. Sometimes, Henry thought, it would be kindness itself to rise one night between three and

18

four when the suburb slept and drag a sharp stone across the Mitsubishi's flanks. At least it would end the awful suspense. At least number 47 would know, instead of suspecting, that even expensive objects get old and dirty and die.

Die.

Elinor, now asleep in the bedroom, her square jaw up like a tombstone, her mouth as wide as a new grave, her light snore ticking fitfully, like some tired machine. Elinor was going to die. Henry brushed and spat into the basin, noticing the blood darken the snow-white saliva.

He would get the poison today.

Humming to himself, he went back into the bedroom and put on a pair of grey corduroy trousers, a red shirt and a bright turquoise jumper, stained with food. He looked, he thought as he examined himself in the mirror, more than usually hideous. He rather hoped his wife would wake and catch him like this, unshaven, hair greasy and uncombed, and as he stood beside the bed he farted quite loudly, as if to remind her that she deserved someone as awful as him.

But she did not wake and for a moment Henry was flooded by helpless rage, a feeling that made him want to run to the bedside table, snatch up Elinor's nail scissors and twist them into her neck, this way and that, gouging out blood and veins. 'Excuse me!' he would scream as he slashed at her throat, 'I am here! I exist! Excuse me! Excuse me!'

Giving himself dialogue seemed to calm him and he stood for a moment, arms idle at his side, breathing slowly and heavily. He felt as if he had just run fifty yards, rather quickly. Calm, Henry. Calm. The great thing about poisoners is their control. You don't dash into breakfast and slop paraquat over the wife's Frosties, while hurling abuse at her. You are quiet and slow and methodical. And when she clutches at her side and complains of a slight ache you lean forward solicitously and ask, 'Are you all right, my darling?' You are gentle and considerate. And inside you are the Wimbledon Poisoner.

He was OK now. He bent over, kissed the least precipitous

19

bit of her chin that he could find and went downstairs to find his daughter.

Maisie was sitting in front of the television, glaring sullenly at a man in a pink tracksuit. Getting her out was clearly going to be a problem.

After 'No' her favourite word was 'Why'.

Henry's ploy was simply to lie. 'I thought of going out for some choc bars,' he would say, adding *sotto voce* as his daughter ran for her anorak, 'and I thought we might drop off at the gym/piano teacher's/library on the way . . .'

He promised her a sight of Arfur this morning. He had remembered that Donald, Arfur's father, was liable to be waiting, with other fathers, in his parked car outside the Wimbledon Young Players' rehearsal. Unbelievably, he had actually christened his only son Arfur. Even more unbelievably Maisie thought Arfur was, to use a word too much on her lips these days, 'cute'. Even more unbelievable than either of these details was the fact that Donald was a doctor.

All the men in the suburb had jobs. Henry didn't know any unemployed people. He read about the unemployed in newspapers and saw films about them on television, pacing across photogenic sections of contemporary Britain and muttering darkly about waste and emptiness. The curious thing was that the lawyers, dentists, opticians, salesmen and accountants he knew didn't seem to do much work. Perhaps, he thought as he followed Maisie down the front path, it was that he knew them only as fathers, as people whose primary function was to stand at the edge of swimming pools, dank gymnasia or football fields, their collective manhoods bruised by nurture, blurring with age and helpless love.

Or perhaps they didn't actually do any work at all. Perhaps they only pretended. Perhaps the unemployed were the only people who did any work these days.

Once you knew Donald was a doctor, of course, it was impossible to forget it. His manner, over the years, had come to seem eerily medical. If Henry offered him a drink, Donald would compress his lips, lower his eyes, as if in the middle of a difficult diagnosis, and nod, slowly, responsibly, like a man burdened with some ghastly secret about the state of Henry's insides.

'Thanks, Henry,' he would say, in a tone that indicated this might well be the last drink he would be accepting from his friend, 'thanks!'

The phrase Henry wanted to use whenever alone with Donald's permanent bedside manner was *How long have I got, Doctor?* There was something about the care with which he looked into your eyes that was truly frightening.

The only time that Donald didn't look like a doctor was when people at parties asked him anything about health or physiology. Then he looked like a frightened animal. His composure would vanish, his grey eyes would shift around the room and, muttering something about antibiotics, he would disappear to the other end of the room, where some hours later he would be discovered at some local worthy's side, discussing parking problems at Waitrose with the quiet authority of a great physician.

Maisie had gone round to the passenger door of the Volkswagen and was standing, one hand poised to open it as soon as Henry should unlock it. Henry lowered himself into the driver's seat and stood looking out at her for a moment. It was amazing how little time children wasted. How they went on to the next thing with such satisfaction and certainty. How they went on from being carried and put in things to sitting in the front seat of cars, opening things for themselves, unlocking the tame mysteries of life. She'll be bloody driving soon, he thought, as he clicked open the lock and his daughter settled in beside him. She had her mother's knack of occupying space around her. She snapped the seat belt into position and stared out through the window as if in search of something else to organize.

'Elsie Mitchell says I stink!' she said, as if opening this topic for theoretical debate.

'Who's Elsie Mitchell?'

'A girl in Class Two of course,' said Maisie, 'with a nose like a pig!'

Henry drove.

He turned right into Caldecott Road, left into Howard's Avenue, right on to Mainwaring Road and up the wide thoroughfare that led to Wimbledon Hill. In all these streets, thick with lime trees, estate agents' boards and large, clean cars, there were no people to be seen at all. Henry knew all the houses – the double-fronted mansion with the Mercedes in the driveway, the row of early Victorian workmen's cottages, fastidiously restored, the occasional bungalow or mock Gothic affair with turrets – he knew what each one was worth, and he followed their fortunes, decay, repair, sale, in the way a countryman might watch the seasons. At 29 Howard's Avenue the builder's skip was still outside and the rusty scaffolding blinded its shabby windows. At 45 Mainwaring Road the upper maisonette was still advertising itself for sale – no less than six boards competing for the passerby's attention. Henry noticed all these things with something like affection while Maisie pressed her nose (very like a pig's, Henry thought) to the window of the Passat.

How was he going to turn the conversation round to the subject of poison? Henry could not imagine, when it came to it, the beginning, middle or end of a conversation in which Donald would tell him how to get hold of an untraceable poison.

He could steal some leaves from Donald's prescription pad. But were doctors allowed to order poisons? Why should they be? What were the medical applications of, say, arsenic? Henry realized he had absolutely no idea. He was as pathetically unqualified in the art of murder as he was at golf or philosophy. The problem with this poisoning business was that the preliminary research was horribly incriminating. One minute there you were asking casual questions about arsenic and the next there was your wife throwing up and having her hair fall out. People would put two and two together.

Christ, what were the major poisons?

There was arsenic, cyanide, prussic acid and – the list stopped there. Nobody much used poison any more; that was the trouble. Or if they did it was so modern that nobody got to hear about it. Henry couldn't think of any celebrated poisoners apart from Maltby and Crippen. And after Crippen, what? The line died out, didn't it? And while we were talking about Crippen, it would probably be unwise to choose as a role model someone who had been topped for the offence. He wanted someone who had got away with it.

He was drawing up outside the hall when he thought of Graham Young.

For the moment he could think of nothing apart from the name. Young had, as far as Henry could remember, been sent to Broadmoor. But hadn't he been a state-of-the-art poisoner? A man who approached the subject with some finesse. Even if it wasn't quite enough finesse to keep him out of the loony bin. From Henry's recollection of the trial, which was, admittedly, not all that clear, Young had been some kind of chemist. There was probably no better way, if one was going to do this thing properly, than to study a celebrated practitioner. It wouldn't be enough to find a poison that would finish her off. He needed to know how to play it when the abdominal pains got started. Was there, for example, a poison that created symptoms that looked like a fairly recognizable disease? And if so, why wasn't every red-blooded English male using it?

Graham Young, yes. Graham Young. Henry had an image of a quiet man in a suit. A man not unlike himself. Something wet and heavy hit the side of his head. He realized Maisie was kissing him. He turned and watched her run up the path and into the hall. Where, though, was Donald? His white Sierra was parked just ahead of Henry, the door open, but there was no sign either of him or Arfur.

Henry got out of the car and sauntered over to the Sierra. No one around. The passenger door was open. And there, on the top of his open bag, staring straight at him, was the white notepad he used for issuing prescriptions. Henry

23

pulled open the door, yanked off the three top sheets and scuttled back to his car. Only when he was safely inside the Passat did he look round to see if he had been observed. He was safe he was safe he was safe.

As he groped his way under his seat, seeking somewhere to stow the paper, his fingers met something cold and hard and sharp. The jack. He'd been looking for that for ages. And if all else failed it would probably be an effective, if unsubtle way of letting his wife know that something rather more serious than Marriage Guidance was required to get them out of their marital difficulties. He wrapped the prescription paper round it and started the engine. He had an hour to get to the library, do his research and return for Maisie. A whole hour. What better way to spend one of those rare breaks in the suburban day than by studying methods of getting rid of one's wife.

CHAPTER FOUR

There were no fewer than four books in the Wimbledon
Public Library that dealt with the Graham Young case. One
of them – by a man called Harkness – was 400 pages long,
contained twenty-four black and white photographs, three
appendices and several maps and diagrams. It was eighty
pages longer than the standard biography of Antonin
Dvořák, the composer, and only seventy pages shorter than
the definitive historical account of Rommel's North African
campaign.

There were pages and pages of psychoanalytic rubbish,
Henry noted, and endless, dreary character sketches of the
people Young had poisoned. But there was also a fairly con-
cisely written chapter entitled 'Thallium Poisoning: Odourless, Tasteless and almost Impossible to Detect'. This was
just the sort of thing Henry wanted to read.

Most poisons, it seemed, tasted unpleasant. (Elinor did
not drink either tea or coffee and only the occasional glass
of mint tea. She drank no alcohol and thought most forms
of seasoning depraved. Her diet was, in a sense, poison
proof.) But thallium, it appeared, was quite tasteless.

Its effects, however, were sensational. Your hair fell out.
You had hallucinations. You lost the use of your limbs. You
went on to do sterling work in the diarrhoea, headaches and
vomiting department and you ended up coughing out your
last in a way that Henry thought would be entirely suitable
for Elinor. It wasn't just that. Thallium poisoning created a
set of symptoms exactly matching a series found in a type of
polyneuritis known as the Guillain-Barré syndrome. The first
post-mortem on one of Young's victims – Fred Biggs – had
found no traces of thallium in the body, although later micro-

scopic analysis revealed there were several hundred milli-grams, more than enough to kill him.

It was the polyneuritis that Henry liked. Two years after they had been married, Elinor had suddenly, mysteriously, developed a weakness in her legs, and Henry, who, equally mysteriously, in those days wasn't trying to kill her, had hurried her to the local hospital where the doctors had diag-nosed – wait for it – polyneuritis. Polyneuritis was clearly a word like morality that meant so many different things as to be absolutely meaningless. If it meant anything at all, thought Henry, it was something along the lines of *We haven't got a clue*. Henry could imagine the conversation with Donald now. Elinor on the bed, hair falling out, vomiting, losing the use of her limbs and he and Donald, over by the window, voices low, faces discreetly grave. Donald would issue a death certificate for any cause you suggested to him; this case, Henry felt, might be so staggeringly self-explanatory as to allow him to come to a diagnosis off his own bat.

'It's the . . . polyneuritis . . .' he heard himself say, as Donald sneaked towards the medical dictionary, his big handsome head bowed with concern, his grey eyes looking into the distance, in the direction of the local tennis court.

He might even sob. That would be good. If only to observe the embarrassment on Donald's face.

Where should he have her cremated? Somewhere rather low-rent, Henry thought. There was a particularly nasty crematorium in Mitcham, he recalled, with a chapel that looked more than usually like a public lavatory. And, from what he remembered of the funeral (his grandmother's), the ushers looked like men who were trying hard not to snigger. Or should he go completely the other way? Hire a small cruiser and slip her coffin over the side in some ocean that might have some special meaning for her? (The Bering Straits, possibly.) He could . . . but Henry was almost too full of good ideas for her funeral. She wasn't even dead yet.

Half an hour left.

The chief problem with thallium was that it didn't seem to

be used for anything much apart from the manufacture of optical lenses of a high refractive index – camera lenses, for example. Henry stared for some moments at the word 'optical'. Why should he need stuff for making lenses? He didn't make cameras, he wasn't an optician –

No, but Gordon Beamish was. Gordon Beamish was a real live optician. He was all optician. He was probably always nipping down to Underwoods for a few grams of thallium. Susie Beamish probably drank it for breakfast. There would be an especial pleasure in using Gordon Beamish's name. If anyone deserved a few years in an open prison it was Beamish.

Like many people who wear glasses, Henry hated opticians, especially opticians with 20/20 vision. Gordon Beamish was a man who made a fetish out of being lynx-eyed. He could be seen most mornings at the door of his shop in Wimbledon Village, arms crossed, mouth twisted in a superior sneer, just waiting for the chance to decode the small print on the front of buses.

'I saw you in the High Street the other day,' he would say, in a tone that suggested that it was quite impossible for Henry to have seen him. Henry had lost count of the number of times Beamish began a sentence with the words 'I notice . . .' or 'I observe . . .' Things were always crystal clear to Beamish; he was always taking a view or spying out the land or finding some way of pointing out the difference between his world – a universe of sharp corners and exact distances – and the booming, foggy place in which Henry found himself every time he took off his glasses. When suffering eye tests in the darkened cubicle at the back of his shop, almost the only thing Henry ever managed to see was the pitying smile on Beamish's face as he flashed up smaller and smaller letter sequences, all of them probably spelling 'You are a fat shortsighted twerp'!

Beamish, thought Henry, could be the fall guy. He liked to think of Beamish in the dock at the Central Court, his counsel blustering on about his client's perfectly normal,

27

acceptable need for heavy metal poisons ('But how do you explain, Mr Beamish, your ordering a quantity of thallium from a perfectly reputable chemist's . . . ?') He closed the book, replaced it in the cookery section of the open shelves, and walked briskly to the car. There was no time to lose. It was entirely possible, Elinor being the way she was, that somebody else would try to kill her before Henry got in with his bid.

Indeed, he reflected, as he joined the queue at the traffic lights opposite the library, it was such a blindingly simple, brilliantly obvious idea, it was very difficult to think why everyone wasn't doing it. Why, while they were about it, wasn't she trying to kill him?

Henry drove cautiously up the hill. He tested the brakes when he reached the top. They seemed OK.

Maisie looked, as always, subtly different after her piano lesson. She looked more aware of the world, brighter, more optimistic. This was some compensation for the fact that she was almost certainly no better at the piano.

Donald's son, Arfur, was there, a small, fat six-year-old, who stared at Henry and said: 'I played the plano!'

'Good!' said Henry, through compressed lips. He seized Maisie by the hand and walked back to the car. If he could get hold of something from Beamish, he might be able to lay his hands on some thallium by lunchtime. She could be dead by the time children's television started or, if not dead, at least well on the way to it. He chose a route back down the hill that did not involve too many serious gradients, moving from Roseberry Road to Warburton Drive to Chesterton Terrace and, from there, doubling back along a series of streets with an offensively tangible air of *esprit de corps* – Lowther Park Drive, where people called to each other over their Volvos and, even worse, Stapleton Road, a place that seemed almost permanently on the verge of a street party.

The brakes still seemed OK.

Gordon Beamish was not in his shop – instead, under a gigantic spectacle frames stood a small, rat-faced girl called

Ruthie. Ruthie, as if to compensate for her boss's powers of vision, seemed to have every known complaint of the eyes short of blindness. Astigmatism, squints, premature presby-opia, short sight, long sight, tunnel vision, barrel vision, migraine, Ruthie had the lot, and her glasses resembled some early form of periscope; they were a circular, heavy-duty affair, with catches and locks and screws. Somewhere under-neath the pebble lenses, tinged both grey and pink, the steel traps and the wires were, presumably, a pair of eyes but they were only, really, a flicker, in the depths of the optician's *pièce de résistance* that towered above Ruthie's nose.

Henry liked Ruthie and Ruthie liked him.

'Is Gordon about?'

'No,' said Ruthie, 'he took Luke to Beavers.'

Beavers. That was a new one on Henry. What the hell was Beavers? Some neo-Fascist organization perhaps? From what he could remember of Luke, the boy would have fitted well into the Waffen SS. Leaving Maisie on the street he went into the shop.

'I'll leave a note for him!' he said.

Ruthie folded her arms, as if to emphasize her lack of responsibility for the shop she was minding. Her eyes, or something very like her eyes, moved in the thick depths of the glass. 'Fine!' she said.

Henry went through to the back of the shop.

On Gordon's desk was a pile of headed notepaper. Henry picked up two sheets. Then he saw something better. In a square, steel tray at the back of the desk was a notepad, the kind of thing given away by small businesses in an attempt to register their names with the public. A. M. Duncan, it read, Lenses, Photographic and Ophthalmic. And under-neath the heading, an address. After a quick glance back through the shop (Maisie and Ruthie were staring out at the street in silence) Henry slid one sheet of the printed paper into Gordon's typewriter. What he really wanted to write was:

29

Henry Farr wishes some thallium to administer to his wife. Please give this to him. He is desperate.

But instead he told whomsoever it might concern that he was Alan Bleath, a researcher employed by the above company and he needed to buy 10 grams of thallium for research purposes. Was that going to be enough? She was quite a big woman. Shouldn't he order a kilo? Two kilos? A lorryload, for Christ's sake! The trouble was, he thought, as he signed the paper, indecipherably, with his left hand, folded it and put it into his jacket pocket, he didn't know much about thallium poisoning, and even less about the making of lenses with a high refractive index. A really thorough murderer would have boned up on both subjects more intently.

Ten grams would have to do. He took a sheet of Gordon's notepaper and typed a short note to Alan Bleath, thanking him for his recent contribution to the stimulating seminar on lenses of a high refractive index, signed this with a fair approximation of Gordon's hand and put it in one of the 'Gordon Beamish: See?' envelopes, addressed to Alan Bleath, 329 Carradine Road, Mitcham. ('Do you seriously expect me to believe, Mr Beamish, that someone came into your office and, without your knowledge, used your typewriter to address a letter?' 'Well, I – ' 'I put it to you that you had always loved Elinor Farr. Your lust for her knew no bounds and when this loyal woman spurned you for her husband of twenty years you wreaked a terrible revenge!' 'No no no! You've got it wrong!')

Actually, thought Henry, as he checked himself in the mirror, no one, not even the police, would be stupid enough to imagine that Elinor could be the victim of a *crime passionnel*. The only passion involved in this operation was an overmastering desire to see her nailed down in a brown box.

He looked, he thought, fairly Bleath-like. Apart from the glasses. He slipped these off and saw a blurred, red disk of a face which resembled a Francis Bacon portrait. Alan Bleath.

'Hurry up!' said Maisie. 'What are you doing?'

'Leaving a note for Gordon,' said Henry.

Let's have a jar! he wrote on Gordon's pad. 'Jar' was the sort of stupid, hail-fellow-well-met word that Gordon would appreciate.

He decided not to go to a chain chemist's. Those sort of places made so much they could afford the luxury of high standards. He wanted an old-fashioned, grubby place with old-fashioned glass bottles in the window. Somewhere run by an elderly couple with no commercial sense. The sort of people who cried with relief when you went in to buy a piece of Elastoplast.

He needed the sort of chemist's he had gone to as a child. If he could remember that far back. These days he had trouble recalling the troublesome fragments of his education he had bothered to memorize in the first place; the names of new acquaintances were jumbled together with old verb forms and things he thought were childhood haunts turned out to be places he had only just discovered. But there was somewhere, wasn't there, where once, years ago, he had gone with his mother, or someone fairly like his mother, anyway? Wealdlake Road. That was it! Wealdlake Road!

At the corner of Wealdlake Road, four streets north of Wimbledon station, was the ideal place. A heavy wooden window frame, dusty glass and three big-bellied bottles, coloured with the bright, mysterious fluids Henry remembered from his childhood. He couldn't remember quite when he had first visited the shop but, like Wimbledon itself, it had always been there. Henry had lived in Wimbledon all his life. They would, Henry thought, be glad to see anyone, even a prospective poisoner. They were probably desperate enough to offer a comprehensive after-sales service ('Thallium not right, sir? Try antimony perhaps? Or potassium chlorate . . .').

He parked the Passat and told Maisie he was going to buy some aspirin.

'Can I come?'

'No!' said Henry.

Before she had time to protest he had locked the doors and, removing his glasses as he went, walked briskly over the road. He narrowly missed what he thought was a lamp post but turned out to be a tree, and reached for where the handle was usually to be found on a front door. To his surprise it was there.

He felt perfectly calm as he entered the shop. Not only calm. He felt Bleath-like to a surprising degree. Perhaps this was because he could hardly see more than a yard in front of his face.

'Hullo, sir!' said a blurred, white shape. It sounded old and incompetent.

'Hullo!' he replied, moving cautiously towards it. Then, with the air of a man asking for twenty cigarettes, he said, 'I need 10 or 15 grams of thallium. Do you keep it or should I go to a larger store?'

The blurred white shape came closer. It seemed to be smiling. Why was it smiling? *You are Henry Farr the Wimbledon Poisoner and I arrest you in the name of* – Hang on, hang on. He wasn't the Wimbledon Poisoner. Yet.

In the face of the shape's silence, he continued, breezily. 'I don't know whether a place as small as this keeps registered poisons but I've just moved labs . . .'

Moved labs! Brilliant!

'And I don't know this neck of the woods . . .'

The shape was close enough for Henry to see that it was male.

'Thallium,' it said, in a frankly sinister tone, 'thallium . . .'

Henry wished it would not say the word quite so loudly. And was it necessary to repeat it like that? Or, in so doing, sound like that man in *Journey Into Space* who was born in 1945 and died in 1939? Yes, thallium you old berk, thallium, the heavy metal poison that makes your hair fall out and gives you diarrhoea and you die screaming. That one. Thallium.

'Not Valium,' said Henry briskly, 'but thallium!'

'Yes,' said the shape. 'I remember . . .'

It sounded, Henry thought, as if all this had happened before. As if, on this very spot a hundred years ago . . . what? Some thought, some fragment of memory was tugging at him but he could not quite catch it, as so often these days. Something he had said or somebody had said, something . . . There was, anyway, an atmosphere in this shop, an unpleasant feeling, as if he had just walked through a gateway into a world parallel to our own, where huge and unpleasant moral choices are offered, fought over and discussed.

The shape seemed to be looking through a book, although what the book was Henry could not tell. *How to Spot a Poisoner* perhaps, or *Some Common Excuses Used by Murderers*. Or perhaps he was just trying to find out what thallium was.

'The heavy metal . . .' said Henry, in what he hoped was an offensively knowledgeable tone.

'What do you require this for?' said the shape.

'Work on optical lenses,' said Henry, adding, smartly, 'with a high refractive index!'

'Oh yes . . .' said the shape.

Maybe he was looking at a book that told you things like that. Or maybe people were always popping in here for 10 grams of thallium. Or maybe he was bluffing. He was going to look it up, whip down to Boots and, having bought a few quidsworth, sell it to Henry at ten per cent over the retail value. He was probably willing to sell anything, the glass jars in the window included.

It was spooky, though, thought Henry, it was a spooky shop. Or was it just that what he was doing was spooky?

He moved up to the counter with the air of a man who doesn't like having to go through a routine *once* again but is *prepared* to do so, *all right then here's my card if you insist*! He took out the letter and tossed it on the counter.

'There's my authority,' he said, 'if you need that.'

Bleath was clearly a man impatient of bureaucracy, anxious to get back to his lenses. The shape seemed impressed.

'Do you have any identification, Mr Bleath?'

33

Bleath put a hand into his breast pocket. Then he transferred the same hand to the back pocket of his trousers and did some not very good patting of both flanks.

'I seem to have mislaid my driving licence!' he said tetchily and then, 'Here's a letter addressed to me!'

It was the way he handed the old fool the letter, Henry decided afterwards, that had done it. He had long ago noticed that if you stared at a customs officer when going out through the green channel, the customs officer stopped you. You had to be careful with officials. And he handed over the letter (which had creased beautifully in his pocket) with just the right note of impatient politeness.

'You'll have to sign the register!' said the shape.

He had done it.

CHAPTER FIVE

The Poisons Register was, like the rest of the shop, a piece of England's past. It was in a thick blue binding and its antique look – the paper was ruled in the way Henry remembered books of his childhood being ruled – gave it the air of a family bible. 'There you are, Mr Bleath.'

He went on to name a sum that Henry thought very acceptable. It was a cheap and easy way of murdering your wife, thought Henry. Very reasonable. Very reasonable indeed. Mind you, in any area of domestic life it was more sensible, in budgetary terms anyway, to Do It Yourself. Some of these types who went in for murder as a professional thing would probably take you to the cleaners as soon as look at you.

He went out, slowly, calmly, ready for the catch question at the door . . . 'Best of luck with the poisoning!' 'Thanks!' *Shit!* Henry replaced his glasses. But the shape, who was now revealed to be an amiable-looking man of about thirty, remained silent.

The air outside smelt good. Up the hill from the southwest a gentle breeze was blowing, and opposite him a huge chestnut tree, already infected with the beautiful rust of autumn, stirred in sympathy with the wind. It was good to know that Elinor would not be breathing this sweet, suburban air for very much longer.

In the car Maisie was studying her music. She looked old and serious. She had scraped her hair back from her forehead and tied it in a ponytail with a pink ribbon. Maisie was always doing things with her hair. Sometimes she piled it up, sometimes she pulled it forward in a fringe, and sometimes she let it hang straight, like her mother's. But whereas Elinor's hair fell, as she herself put it, 'like a great, calm waterfall', Maisie's hair just hung, like old socks on a washing line. And whatever she did with her hair, it still, thought Henry, didn't do anything for her face – Maisie's face was still there, round as a dinner plate. The kind of face one saw on children by roadsides in Connemara.

He leaned over and kissed his daughter on the forehead. She continued to study her music. After Elinor was dead, he and Maisie could really get to know each other, thought Henry. As he intended to behave extraordinarily well, she would grow to like and respect him (he wasn't entirely sure she did at the moment). One of the advantages of scheduling one's own bereavement was that it was far easier to respond in a mature, caring way to one's partner's decease. Henry had read an article in *The Times*, which said that partners who lost a loved one often blamed the departed for the death. Henry did not intend to do this. He was going to be a tower of strength to all concerned.

'You've been ages,' said Elinor, as he and Maisie trudged up the steps.

'Sorry!' said Henry.

His wife came towards him menacingly. When she walked she moved each hip separately, like a gunslinger moving towards an opponent down Main Street. She drew her right hand out from the folds of her apron and thrust a piece of paper at him, averting her eyes as she did so. It was as if, thought Henry, she wished to have nothing to do with the dispute she knew this word would provoke.

'Waitrose!' she said.

'I thought you went yesterday . . .' said Henry. His voice, he noticed, made him sound frightened. Why was this?

Elinor narrowed her eyes and swung her straight black hair out behind her like a scarf. She moved, as she often did, from pure, concentrated malice, to a vaguely girlish mode, as if she was looking for someone (not Henry) to put his arms round her and tell her everything was all right. A fatherly sort of chap. Henry grabbed the paper and backed away down the path.

'You go to Waitrose now!' she barked.

Was this a command or a statement? It felt like a command, as did so many of Elinor's remarks – but it had the menacing power of a scientific law.

'It isn't my turn!' said Henry.

'It is!' said Elinor.

'It isn't!' said Henry.

'Oh yes it is!' said Elinor.

Henry kicked the side of the kerb viciously. She was being more than usually assertive. Things weren't helped by the fact that he had remembered, in the course of this not very elevated argument, that it was actually his turn. He kicked the kerb again hard and set his lips in a scowl. Why did he always choose to lose his temper over issues in which he was in the wrong?

She's been seeing her therapist again, thought Henry, as he stumbled towards the Passat.

'Can I go?' said Maisie.

Elinor drew herself upwards and outwards. Then, with the fluidity usually only displayed by cartoon characters, she swooped down and around her daughter; her arms cradled each shoulder and her face slid down next to Maisie's. Her voice changed too. It acquired an impossible sweetness, a tenderness that was almost sinister.

'Darling,' said Elinor, 'shall Maisie stay with Mummy and do her cello practice while Mummy helps her?'

Maisie looked trapped. She liked Waitrose. In Waitrose there were Twix bars and Breakaways; there were chocolate digestives and huge jumbo packets of crisps and giant, plastic bottles of Coca-Cola. Sometimes she and Henry sat together in the car, a few streets away from their home, munching chocolate bars, while in the back of the Passat huge cardboard boxes of grains, wholewheat cereal, low-fat spreads and calorie-free, taste-free things to stop you dying of cancer awaited Elinor's approval. She would not have sweets in the house. Simply to smell Coca-Cola made her, she said, violently sick.

'See you later, Maisie!' said Henry.

'We were going to Elspeth's !' said Maisie.

37

Christ yes! He started to mouth the words 'I'll bring you a choc bar,' but before he was halfway through this soundless sentence his wife's face levelled up towards him. She had the clear gaze of an experienced poker player.

'No sweets!' she said.

'No dear,' said Henry.

Clutching the phial of thallium in his pocket he got back into the car. It was curious. The last place he wanted to be was in the car. Why, every time he got out of it, was he forced back into it?

Today, of course, it suited him to be doing the shopping. What went well with thallium? Curried things? Chicken Dopiaza Thallium Style! But she wouldn't eat curry, would she? Anyway the stuff had no taste. Just give her thallium! Thallium *à la mode de* Wimbledon, served in a little china pot with a spray of basil and a clean table napkin. Elinor might almost accept that. *Nouvelle cuisine* methods of preparing thallium . . . a drop of thallium on a piece of seaweed, chilled thallium, served garnished with a single *radicchio* leaf . . . down home thallium . . . thallium and beans . . . big, tasty, hearty, man-sized thallium burgers served with french fries, pickle and thallium on the side . . . 'It's so *versatile,*' said Henry, aloud, as he drove back down the hill, '*There are so many things you can do with thallium!*'

Shopping with death in mind made shopping almost bearable.

Henry was by far the most cheerful-looking person in Waitrose, as he scanned the loaded shelves for his wife's last meal. Elinor's favourite food was yoghurt. Yoghurt and thallium? Not really. Ahead of him a morose-looking man in a cardigan was sorting through slabs of meat in plastic containers. Once again Henry was struck by the enormity of supermarkets . . . those millions of dead animals, butchered, arranged in parcels, labelled with a SELL BY or a BEST BEFORE date, grouped, not by species or sub-species, but by parts of the body. Whole rows of chicken thighs, galleries of boneless

38

chicken breasts, chicken escalopes coated with breadcrumbs, ready seasoned, free-range, corn-fed chicken that –

Hang on. Ready-seasoned, free-range, corn-fed chicken. Henry pulled one towards him. In a way, he thought, it was a cleaner life being a battery chicken than a free-range, corn-fed chicken. At least the battery chicken knew what it was up against. Stuck in a cell, the light on twenty-four hours a day, at least the battery chicken wasn't going to be fooled into thinking well of people. But the free-range, corn-fed chicken was the victim of a cruel joke. Given a little hope, a little patch of ground . . . so that it would taste better. Soon, thought Henry, feeling, as he often did, a sense of solidarity with chickens, they would label one with THIS FOWL HAS BEEN HAND-REARED AND TALKED TO NICELY. IT DIED PEACEFULLY.

Elinor liked ready-seasoned, free-range, corn-fed chicken. And the fine dusting of the seasoning – the green of the parsley, the black of the pepper, would be a perfect cover for thallium. Even more importantly, Maisie didn't like chicken, especially free-range, corn-fed, humanely killed chicken that had been through Jungian analysis. She liked great slabs of chicken in crispy batter. It would also be comparatively easy – he was getting excited – to sprinkle the thallium on the breast, because Elinor liked breast and he liked leg.

'A little white meat, darling?'

'Of course, my darling!' Elinor would squawk, brushing her mane of black hair away from her forehead. And then the plate, piled high with sprouts and potatoes and gravy and topped with succulent slices of perfectly roasted breast of chicken, coated with a crispy surface of parsley, pepper and thallium, would land before Mrs Farr. And she would spear a piece of chicken and carry it high in the air towards that great black hole of a mouth and, still talking about her therapy, her plans for the future, his inability to understand her as a woman, his crude, male-orientated sexuality, she would munch, munch, munch . . .

'Are you going to make love to that chicken?'

Henry jumped.

39

It was Donald.

'Oh. Hi!'

'You look miles away.'

'I was.'

Donald peered into Henry's trolley in a companiable fashion. All it contained was a small jar of capers.

'You're a bit behind, Henry.'

'Indeed.'

Donald had got four sponge rolls, three jumbo packets of cornflakes, five loaves of bread, some digestive biscuits, a square packet of something called Uncle Sam's Chocolate Chip Cookies, a Battenburg cake and two mixed, assorted crisps, in bags that were the size of a small dustbin. Donald approached Waitrose with military precision, working his way steadily through Farinaceous, Vegetables (Salad), Vegetables (Root, Loose and Packed), Poultry, Game, Continental Cuts and Mince, and from there by way of Fish (Frozen) and Fish (Fresh) to Spices, Pickles and Non-refrigerated Ready-packed Sauces, through to Pet Food, Pet Accessories and Household Cleaners.

He nodded his big, handsome head still thick with greying curls.

'Keeping well, though?'

'Fine,' said Henry, 'fine.'

Donald narrowed his eyes very slightly and nodded once again. His perfect profile looked off down the rows of brightly coloured packets. 'Should I tell him now?' his expression seemed to say, 'Or would it be better to let the disease take its course? It won't be long now anyway . . .'

'Elinor's a bit off colour, though.'

'Yes?'

'Well . . . it's a funny thing. I don't know whether I told you . . . but some years ago she was diagnosed as having . . . polyneuritis . . .'

Donald's perfectly formed lips began to tremble.

'I was wondering whether . . . maybe . . .'

Donald looked away, longingly, towards Refrigerated Delicatessen, his clear doctor's eyes, moving expertly from Ready-packed Gravadlax, through Hand-sliced, Oak-smoked, Ready-interleaved Salmon Slices, along the twelve varieties of German and Polish sausage, the pre-packed slices of Waitrose Pastrami and Salt Beef until they reached the orderly rows of Fresh Tortellini, Cappelletti, Paglia e Fieno and Tagliatelle (Green and White).

'Well,' he said finally, 'must get on!'

And with one more nod of that perfect head he was off, working his trolley through the morning crowd with the air of a great surgeon.

Henry put the chicken back in the pile. He paused, then from the back took one that seemed to have got separated from the rest. Its polythene wrapping looked vaguely torn and grubby, as if members of the Waitrose staff had already been playing catch with it. It was past the SELL BY date too. It would do perfectly. It seemed wrong, somehow, to poison a piece of meat in pristine condition.

He threw it in the trolley and went off to look for things Elinor didn't like.

CHAPTER SIX

Once he had decided on Free-range chicken *à la* Thallium, it was fairly important not to buy anything Elinor might choose as a substitute. If she were to insist on veal goulash, for example, all would be lost. Maisie liked veal goulash. She had heard it was bad for you.

If only she drank something other than herb tea.

Trying not to think about her possible reaction, Henry loaded cured fish, offal, red meat and a bold assortment of vegetables he had never even heard of, let alone eaten. All they had in common was a potential for repelling Mrs Farr. Bags of kohlrabi and okra, sweet potatoes, chillies, Chinese-leaf lettuce and three pounds of a very peculiar thing called an edenwort, which looked like a beetroot going through a severe identity crisis. There was a little plastic notice next to it which read EDENWORT: SLICE IT OR BAKE IT OR USE IT IN CASSEROLES. Or just throw it at the neighbours, thought Henry grimly, as he tipped the edenwort in next to the water-chestnuts and the giant yam.

Checking his purchases against her list as he approached the checkout, he was pleased to find that at no point did the two coincide.

Then he saw Donald, trolley piled high with middle-of-the-road food.

'Hullo there!' called Henry.

Donald nodded, briefly.

'How about a pint?'

Donald considered this offer; his features rippled with thought. If he were a picture his handsome, regular cheekbones and serious eyes would probably be titled 'A Doctor Decides'.

'OK,' he said, in the end. Imaginary nurses sighed with

42

relief. The hours of waiting over! At last they had a diagnosis! 'A jar would be very nice.'

If Henry arrived back after three, Elinor would be at therapy. Maisie would be at ballet. He would have time to stow away the kohlrabi, the offal and the edenwort. And by the time she returned it would be six or six thirty. Teatime!

Time, now Henry was forty, did not proceed in the way it had previously done. Once upon a time, there was waking, which was slow and painful, and then quite a long period, replete with chances and triumphs and defeats and risks, which sometimes, though not always, ended in lunch. Afternoon, Henry remembered, used to be as prolonged and arid as Arizona, and they were followed by things called evenings, which were entirely different and separate from nights. Now – you woke up with a sense of relief and surprise that you were still there, you got up, brushed your teeth, and before you knew it you were watching television. It was dark outside and well past your bedtime. You were also, probably, drunk, but how you got drunk, or where you had been between that first moment of reacquaintance with yourself and now, was a mystery. Apart, of course, from the shops. You had almost certainly been to the shops.

'We could go to the Rose and Thorn!' said Donald.

'Great!' said Henry.

Donald began to place his groceries on the moving counter.

Henry tipped out the edenwort and looked at Donald's back. He looked like a man who would sign a mean death certificate.

What to do with the chicken after the meal? Assuming he phoned Donald as soon as she began to vomit and have headaches, wouldn't Donald ask what they had eaten for dinner? Maybe not, since Henry, unless he got the thallium anywhere near the chicken leg, would be feeling fine.

It was vital, though, to include Donald in the diagnosis of Elinor's condition. He was not only a close personal friend, he was also, to Henry's knowledge, one of the worst doctors in the south-east of England.

43

'Some bloke came into the surgery,' he would say, sourly, 'complaining of headaches. "What do you expect me to do about it?" I said. "I get headaches. We all get headaches. Piss off out of it!" I said, "You're giving me a headache!" '

'Good for you!' Henry would reply. 'Send him away with a flea in his ear. Psychosomatic, I suppose?'

Donald would pull on his pint (he had to be fairly drunk in order to even start discussing medicine) – 'In fact,' he would say, 'turned out to be a bloody brain tumour, didn't it?'

'Christ!' – from Henry.

'Can you beat it? Can you beat it?'

'Indeed not,' Henry would reply.

And the two men would shake their heads over the inconsistent, bloody-minded civilians who swarmed through a general practitioner's surgery, deliberately misleading qualified men about the nature of their fatal diseases.

Over the pint Henry would make a few more casual references to Elinor's polyneuritis. When Donald examined his wife in the last stages of the illness it might be necessary to lead him to a medical textbook and steer those calm, grey eyes in the direction of the chapter headed 'The Guillain-Barré Syndrome'.

The Rose and Thorn, on the edge of Wimbledon Common was, in the eighteenth century, a favourite spot for highwaymen. The infamous Tibbet, executed at the roundabout at the top of Putney Hill, is reported to have stabbed a man to death there; it has literary associations also. In the nineteenth century, Swinburne, having been thrown out of his local, the Green Man, on the west side of Putney Hill, walked over the common to the Rose and Thorn, where, according to a letter of Watts Dunton, he drank eight pints of strong ale and was violently sick over the landlord's daughter, a woman called Henrietta Luce who later married a distant relative of Trollope's.

Henry told Donald some of this, as he did every time he and Donald used the pub, and Donald nodded and smiled and said: 'Really! How extraordinary!' As he did every time Henry told him these things.

He had got to the point, now, of sometimes saying, 'Yes. I read somewhere I think there was a landlord's daughter called Loo or Loup or . . .'

Thus giving Henry the chance to reply, 'In fact her name was Luce . . . perhaps I told you . . .'

To which Donald would reply, a little too swiftly, 'No, no . . . I don't think so . . .'

And then . . . 'Fascinating, really!'

And the two of them would discuss, with some enthusiasm, where Donald could have acquired this information. Their conversations were, Henry felt, the sweeter for having a core of known fact which they could then decorate and refine, like old men in some village discussing last year's harvest.

'Of course,' he said on their third pint, 'the Wimbledon Poisoner used to use the back bar.'

'Is that right?' said Donald.

'Everett Maltby,' said Henry, 'who lived off Wimbledon Hill. He poisoned his wife and his mother-in-law and any number of other people, including some of the regulars at his local.'

'Christ!' said Donald. 'Why?'

'Liven things up a bit, I suppose,' said Henry.

Donald took a deep swig of his beer. He ran his tongue round his lips, as if assessing the taste.

'Can get pretty dull, I suppose . . .' he said.

Pretty dull, thought Henry, I should say so.

'I think I've heard of Everett Maltby,' said Donald.

'It's possible you have,' said Henry. 'He's a well-known local story!'

That must have been where he got the idea from, of course. That was why Everett, suddenly, seemed more real, more frightening than usual. Not that Henry believed in any of that rubbish about possession or reliving history or the power of the myth. That was all so much fashionable garbage, wasn't it? History was what happened to dead people. It didn't act on the living, like yeast. Although . . .

'Wasn't he hanged?' Donald was prompting him.

'Yes, yes,' said Henry, 'in 1888. The mystery really, is why he did it. He was a quiet, apparently happily married man with no enemies. He stood to gain nothing. A complete mystery man. He was a model citizen.'

'Like you Henry!' said Donald.

They both laughed. Then they drank a little. Then Donald said: 'How did they catch him?'

Well, he had confessed, hadn't he? 'Burdened' as he put it at his trial, 'with the intolerable knowledge of my own beastliness!' That wasn't going to happen to Henry though, was it? If a chap hadn't the guts to stand up for his own beastliness where was he? There was, Henry felt, something rather unsavoury about Maltby. Perhaps that was why he had never worked up the notes he had made on the case. At one time he had intended a whole chapter of *The Complete History of Wimbledon* to be devoted to the issue of Maltby, but somehow the chapter had never materialized. For a start, he kept losing the notes, and then, when he had managed to find them and set them out on his desk, he seemed to lack the will to start work on them. There was something decidedly spooky about Maltby. And as they talked the image of the man became clearer and clearer, until Henry wanted to say to Donald, 'No. Don't let's talk about this, shall we? It's too . . . dangerous.' He could see the stuffy front room and the hideous green plant. The heavy oak furniture, the unused piano, the not very attractive daughter . . . He could see Everett's trips up to London, in the days before the electrification of the Wimbledon Railway. He could see Everett sitting at a tall stool, in an office not unlike Henry's, helping to build the wealth of the empire. But there was some detail he knew he didn't want to remember. Why didn't he want to remember it? And why did thinking about it, yes, it did, frighten him?

'How did they, though?'

He had been silent too long. Henry took the route often taken by historians faced with a tricky historical problem. He made something up.

'He confessed,' said Henry. 'It all got too much for him. Guilt. You know? And he broke down. In this very pub, one night, and told everyone that he was the Wimbledon Poisoner. It took him some time to convince them, apparently.'

'I don't think you've ever told me that!' said Donald, sounding peeved to have elicited an original statement from Henry while on licensed premises. Henry, too, felt somewhat alarmed to find himself using his imagination. He tried to steer the conversation back to theory.

'Your typical poisoner,' he said, 'is a drab, quiet creature seeking to call attention to himself by his crimes. But often, so drab is he that even when he barges into the pub waving a bottle of paraquat and shouting *I dunnit*, people just don't want to know. No one could believe that Everett Maltby had done the appalling things he had done. He had to convince them.'

He drank some more.

'Murder,' he said, in the tones of someone who knew a bit about the subject, 'is something we try and classify. Try and put beyond the pale. But we all have a murderer in us. It's just that most of us are not honest enough to admit to the fact. And there are more ways of killing people than by killing them. If you know what I mean.'

'Not sure I do . . .' said Donald.

Henry looked at the clock. It was two thirty. Donald had had enough local history. Like many people, he thought that local history was dull. You could see him wanting to talk about the controversy over the redevelopment of Wimbledon town centre (Greycoat versus Speyhawk, or Caring Architects versus Greedy Planners). Henry did not want to talk about the redevelopment of Wimbledon town centre. As far as Henry was concerned they could fill the whole thing in with concrete.

If he wasn't careful they would get on to the subject of the motorway. Someone, it appeared, was planning to run a motorway through Wimbledon. There were even rumours that it was going to go straight through the middle of Henry's house, a thought that, somewhat to his surprise, filled him with savage pleasure. It was the past that inspired Henry, not the present.

Up at the bar he saw Everett Maltby and, beyond him, Tibbet the Highwayman and beyond him Cicely de Vaulles, who held the fief of the manor house, 250 yards from where he and Donald were drinking. And he touched the thick-ribbed beer mug, brought it to his lips and drank again, sour, brown English beer. History. He had read somewhere, possibly in one of the books Elinor was always reading, that people under totalitarian regimes had no access to their past. This happened in Wimbledon, too. People were simply too lazy to try and remember.

Henry's memory, of course, seemed only defective in matters that immediately concerned him. Who he had had dinner with the night before, and what, if anything, he thought about them. But he was starting to lose track of the things that had made him what he was as well. Where he had been to school, what kind of degree he had got at university. Once upon a time he had read a quite terrifying number of books and accumulated an equally terrifying number of opinions about them. But now his intellectual horizons had shrunk to debates about motorways or endless conversations about the right school for one's child, it was as if he didn't want to remember the Henry who had once promised a little more than that.

To his surprise, Donald was talking about disease. Perhaps he was drunk. Henry felt rather drunk.

'Tell me . . .' Donald was saying, 'this . . . polyneuritis of Elinor's . . .'

'Yes . . .' said Henry.

'Was that when I was treating her?'

'I should think,' said Henry, 'you would have noticed if a

patient of yours was diagnosed as having polyneuritis. I mean, I should think you would have something to do with it, wouldn't you?'

'Not necessarily,' said Donald gloomily. 'I might not have noticed it. I might have said . . . "pains in the legs sort yourself out sort of thing." I sometimes do. And she might have gone to a specialist to have it diagnosed. Or perhaps I did diagnose it but I've forgotten. These days I forget what I prescribe and what people have got when they walk out of the surgery. It just goes. I forget everything. I forget where I'm supposed to be and what I've done the day before and whose round it is . . .'

'It's yours!' said Henry quickly.

'You see?' said Donald, with an air of triumph, 'you see? The old brain is cardboard. Complete and utter cardboard these days.'

He got to his feet and walked stiffly to the bar.

Perhaps you only forgot things you didn't want to be there in the first place. That was certainly how Donald felt about his patients. And maybe that was how Henry felt about himself. And Maltby. Why should he not want to remember Maltby, though? Back to the matter in hand. Come on. Come on. Elinor.

Elinor. All this stuff about polyneuritis was handy, thought Henry, but perhaps a little too neat. One minute, there they were talking about polyneuritis, next minute, there she was dying of it. But Donald's first remark, when he returned with the drinks, was even more eerily appropriate to what Henry had in mind.

'Tell you what,' he said, 'I'll pop up and have a look at her, shall I?'

Henry gulped. Donald drank.

'Most likely,' he said, 'it's stress. She's feeling stressed. She has what we doctors call . . . stress. She's probably in a . . . stressful situation. And so she imagines she has . . . this . . .'

'Polyneuritis,' said Henry.

49

'That's the one. Well . . .' Donald went on, 'who knows what polyneuritis is? Really? Really? Medicine makes a lot of claims, you know, but basically all of us doctors are pretty well in the dark on most things medical . . .'

Donald was about the nearest he was likely to find to a Murderer's Doctor. But he wasn't too keen on the idea of Donald arriving just as Elinor was wiping the last traces of chicken thallium off her lips. One of the chief requirements of a poisoner was a quiet domestic life. One needed few visitors, an oppressive routine, long silences, broken only by the tick of the clock and the groans of one's victim. It was not a public crime. Everett Maltby had . . . But no. Henry didn't want to think about Maltby any more.

'Are you with me?' Donald was saying.

'Sure,' Henry was saying.

'So I'll pop up about half nine,' went on Donald. 'I'm very fond of old Elinor. I think she's a sweet, no nonsense, old-fashioned girl. She's such a gentle person!'

Henry goggled at him. This remark, it seemed to him, was on a par with 'Stalin was quite a nice guy, basically'. And what had he agreed to anyway?

There was no chance that Donald would diagnose thallium poisoning. Donald couldn't diagnose a common cold. Having him there at the beginning was simply a stroke of luck so colossal that Henry's natural pessimism was trying to turn it into a disaster.

'Make it half ten!' he said.

They ate supper at eight. By half past ten the thallium would be creeping round Elinor's bloodstream. She would be suffering from pins and needles. Stomach cramps perhaps. She would be pleased to see a doctor.

CHAPTER SEVEN

When he got back the house looked empty. The autumn afternoon was paling and the ivy that covered the façade of number 63 dripped with yellows and browns. Opposite, number 47 in huge green wellingtons and baseball cap was talking to number 60. Number 60's wife was shouting something at number 60's children. Or were they number 58's children? Henry pulled the plastic bags out of the boot of the Passat, and lowered his eyes. Number 47 looked as if he were in a conversational mood.

As Henry got through the front gate, number 60 went back up the street towards his wife and number 47 dropped, suddenly and dramatically, on to his knees in front of the red Mitsubishi. For a moment Henry thought that this might be a genuine act of worship, a public act of love towards the vehicle (*I am not ashamed of what I feel about this car! It's the most beautiful thing that ever happened to me!*). But, somewhat to Henry's disappointment, number 47 did not start necking with the bodywork. He started to spray the hubcaps with what looked like toothpaste. Henry was safe anyway. Number 47 was either talking to you or the car; he was incapable of socializing what he felt about the Mitsubishi.

Henry was rather drunk.

How had he got back? Had he gone via Windlesham Avenue and the comprehensive? Or up Abacus Road, where the only black man in their part of Wimbledon lived? Had he gone down to the bottom of the hill and worked his way up to Belvedere Road from the south-east? The suburb was beginning to play tricks on him, to lie about itself. He should never have started making up stuff about Everett Maltby. Few things were sacred to Henry, but local history was one of them.

As he stowed the edenwort and the kohlrabi at the back of the cupboard, he saw his mother's strained, pale face as she boasted, unconvincingly, of her son's prowess to a neighbour. 'Henry's got a real gift for history!' she would say. After he got his lower second at the University of Loughborough, she told Mrs Freeman at 82 that Henry was 'on course for a Nobel Prize'. Could it be, thought Henry, as a shower of yams, bottled gherkins and packets of pastrami disgorged themselves on to the red-tiled floor of the kitchen, that his present bouts of cultural amnesia were a response to his mother's extravagant hopes for him?

'Why have you gone into the law?' she used to say to him. 'You're better than that, aren't you?' In fact, Henry's real problem with the law was that he wasn't quite up to it. Even after eighteen years at Harris, Harris and Overdene he was, he reflected, about as much in the dark on legal questions as Donald was on medical issues. Which was saying something. Henry's mother had, he recalled bitterly, thought that he could 'do better' than Elinor as well. 'It all depends,' Henry had said, 'what you are looking for in a relationship!' In those days Henry had talked like that. Well, if you were looking for the qualities Elinor had displayed in their years together, you could probably only have done better by marrying a man-eating tiger.

But of course, once Mrs Farr Senior had expressed doubts about a woman, it meant Henry was almost duty bound to marry her, just as, as soon as she expressed a political or aesthetic opinion, he immediately experienced a passionate surge of enthusiasm for the view most directly opposed to it. He was almost as hostile to his own mother as he was to Elinor's, even though the politesse observed by his family meant he had not yet worked out a way of expressing it. In the thirty-six years of which he had conscious memory of Mrs Farr Senior, their relationship had never developed beyond the 'isn't it a nice day?' stage. They had never had an argument, apart from one occasion in 1956, when Henry

52

refused to wear a pair of short trousers. Henry's mother still referred to this argument.

'You remember . . .' she would say coquettishly, 'when you made that awful fuss about the trousers . . .'

Thinking about his mother brought Henry back to the matter in hand and, grim faced, he went out to the car to retrieve the chicken. He had left it on the passenger seat, where it lay, legs in the air, headless rump deep in the upholstery. It was only when he was reaching across for it that he remembered. Those three stolen sheets from Donald's prescription pad. All it needed was someone to go looking for the jack, find their hands curling round them and start asking *why* . . .

You couldn't be too careful. Everything had to be very, very carefully done indeed.

Henry yanked out the jack, groped for the papers and stuffed them into his pocket. Just as he did so, a voice behind him said, 'I've got an awful headache!'

Elinor. Headache. How to respond. Henry tried out a little gasp of sympathy. 'Oh no!' he said. He sounded, he thought, almost openly satirical. 'One of your headaches again!'

This was supposed to be said in the tone of one dealing with news of some immense natural disaster. It came out as positively offensive disbelief. Henry turned to her and held up the jack. Appealing for clemency.

'Look,' he said, 'I found the jack!'

She sniffed.

'Put it in the shed!' she said.

Henry leered at her.

'And I got a chicken,' he said, 'the kind you like!'

And kohlrabi and okra and chili and pastrami and *thallium*!

She frowned at the pavement.

'When you've put the jack away,' she said, 'could you get in the car and go and get Maisie from ballet?'

'Yes!' said Henry.

She thrust her white face towards him. She looked as if

53

she was in pain. Her eyebrows, Henry noted, were curiously thick. Black and bushy. Like a gorilla's, he thought.

'You block me,' she said. 'You block my creativity!'

'Sorry!' said Henry.

She swung her bottom south-south-west and steered herself off up the path. As Henry watched her retreating buttocks, grinding out yet another dismissal, he tried to remember if there had ever been a time, years ago, when he had desired her. Or had she just seen him one day, walking around the suburb where he had been born, and said to him, in that sharp voice she used for all commands: 'Marry Me!'

There was probably a man, somewhere, who could cope with Elinor. Ten feet tall and eight feet wide. With no nerves.

Henry went to the front hall, put the chicken and the jack on the table by the front door and trudged back out to the Passat. It looked smug, Henry thought, about the fact that he was going to have to drive it again. As he drove off down the street he saw the curtains of the front bedroom close. Elinor was going to have her sleep. She always needed a sleep after therapy. An hour or so spent talking with other women about how weak, cruel, uncaring, lazy and insensitive their husbands were always made her tired.

'Oh Maisie,' thought Henry, 'you who are, even now, longing to get your fat little feet out of the ballet pumps that you will never wear gracefully, soon we will be free of her. Soon we will not have to go to ballet or piano or junior aerobics. We can go wherever we like.'

Actually, if he were offered the choice of going wherever he liked in the world, he would probably choose Wimbledon. The tribal customs of Wimbledon were, in Henry's view, as worthy of study as the totems and taboos of the Aborigines of the Northern Territory. The stories of the suburb, the tales that gave number 24, 59, 30 or 47 their right to their homes, these were, in their way, as substantial as the creation myths of the Eskimos. Passats, BMWs, dormer windows, back extensions, wooden garden sheds, all meant something more than at first appeared – white wooden railings, gold nameplates on doors, stained-glass windows in bathrooms, net curtains, numbered dustbins, unnumbered dustbins, sash windows, plate-glass windows, windows with double glazing, windows without double glazing, walls painted white, all of this was part of a body of myth as strange and mysterious as the *Epic of Gilgamesh*. What was the relationship between new roofs and marital discord? Why did people who put adverts for local fêtes in their windows so often neglect the paint on their woodwork? The codes of Wimbledon were too strange and complex to be understood by its inhabitants. It needed some stranger to unlock it, to explain it to itself, to see behind that apparent silence and quietness.

Wimbledon. Its architecture compared favourably with that of northern France (bar one or two cathedrals). Its cuisine was as varied as Hong Kong or Bangkok (you could eat as well at the Mai Thai restaurant, Wimbledon Broadway, as in anywhere around the Gulf of Thailand). Its history, if you skipped a thousand years, was as violent as Phnom Penh's or Smolensk's. The things the Vikings had done in Raynes Park were, let's face it, unspeakable.

Why, Henry wondered, was he getting defensive about Wimbledon? Who was attacking it? Perhaps it was that letter from that bastard up in town. That –

Dear Mr Farr,

Thank you for your letter and thank you for letting us see your nine-volume Complete History of Wimbledon. *It's a massive work and has obviously taken a great deal of your time and trouble.*

I fear, however, that a detailed analysis of a suburb, especially a not particularly well-known one like Wimbledon, would not 'travel' well in our terms. I'm sure you'll understand what I mean when I say that a reader in, for example, Moscow would find your book very difficult to relate to. For a book to have truly international appeal, it must have, well, truly international appeal!

We all loved the chapter about Victorian Wimbledon though.

55

Might not this make a pamphlet of some kind? Perhaps for your
local historical society?
Best wishes,
Karim Jackson.

Henry's hands tightened on the wheel as he thought about
Karim Jackson's letter. There were people in Moscow, New
York, Rome, Paris, Oslo and Naples who were absolutely
dying to find out about Wimbledon. Wimbledon was as much
a mystery to them as was the Orinoco to Henry. All he had
to do, he knew, was get the thing in print.

Why had this Pakistani – if he was a Pakistani – got it in for
him? Why did he take this extraordinarily negative attitude to
the most important suburb in the Western world? Was it
something to do with tennis? They played cricket in Pakistan,
didn't they? Was that the problem? And more importantly
than that, what was a Pakistani doing in a position of power
and influence in a publishing house? The man (if it was a
man) was probably a fairly junior member of the firm; if only
Henry could find a way of getting past him to the people
really in the driving seat.

He mustn't think about his book. Thinking about his book
was almost worse than thinking about Elinor. He would
think about what his mother always used to call 'nice things'.
'Think about nice things!' she would say to Henry as she
tucked him into bed at night. And, as he coasted towards
Maple Drive through the suburb's still deserted streets,
Henry thought about nice things. He thought about thallium
and the Guillain-Barré syndrome and whether it was or
wasn't too late to have Elinor heavily insured.

CHAPTER EIGHT

Everything happened very quickly after he had got Maisie back to the house.

Elinor was still asleep. Before she should have a chance to wake and discover the edenwort, Henry got to work on the supper. Maisie sat in the corner of the kitchen with one chocolate bar in her mouth, another in her right hand, another in her lap and a fourth beside her on the draining board, in case anything should happen to the other three.

Henry paused over a half-dismembered edenwort. He had better catch up on Elinor's latest batch of instructions.

She wrote him notes. Notes saying what to get for supper, notes telling him not to leave his shoes by the bed . . . sometimes she left him notes telling him how she felt. About life, about the world, and above all, about him. Since she had started going to therapy, these notes had got longer and more articulate. They didn't start 'Dear Henry', or 'My Dear Husband', but simply began, picking up (as her therapist had taught her) at 'the moment of rage'. There was one, now, lurking in the vegetable basket and Henry moved towards it as one might move towards an unexploded bomb.

Why do you not understand my needs as a woman? You do not commit to the home, do you, Henry? You are (I have to say) intensely judgemental. You block and deny my aspirations to creativity and permanence.

Elinor attended art classes at Wimbledon School of Art. She was particularly keen on pottery, a skill she had, in Henry's view, even less hope of acquiring than her daughter.

You deal death to the need in me to grow and change and become myself. Like a huge wall that shields tender shoots from the light,

57

you do not allow my passions and sensations their scope. I am afraid of you, Henry!

Not half as much as I am of you! thought Henry, as he ran his eyes down the rest of the manuscript (she must have written it before going to sleep).

I am afraid of the male violence that is in you. In a world run by men, for men . . .

Maybe, thought Henry, but, if so, run by other men for other men. I am not one of these men!

A world of cruel greed, rape, nuclear war, phallocentric control, where women are pushed to the sidelines, how can I not be afraid of you? With the fierce hatred that I know is in you? Like a mugger you leap out at me from the dark, and my rights as a woman are violated by your obscene masculinity!

Henry looked at himself in the kitchen mirror, as he crumpled up the other three pages of this latest missive and threw it in the swingbin. He looked, he had to admit, the very picture of obscene masculinity. Glumly, he began to pull out okra and edenwort. If she didn't eat the vegetables, she was almost sure to eat the meat.

Elinor was a star pupil in her therapy class. Having been taught, first at an expensive public school and then at Oxford University, to express herself to order, she found the poor creatures who shambled along to 23 Dorman Road every Saturday, Thursday, Monday and Wednesday absolutely no competition at all. Most of these women had been in what they called 'the therapy situation' for years. Elinor's difficulties were, at least from her description of the classes, bigger and better than those of her fellow therapees. She was a kind of Stakhanovite worker in the field of female suffering, setting new targets for pain, finding each week some new emotional cross to bear. The main topic on the agenda of the therapy class was, to start with anyway, Henry. They all sat around in a circle agreeing what a swine Henry was.

But as the therapy continued, Henry had observed, others were found to be guilty of the capital crime of blocking Elinor's creativity. There were other saboteurs and wreckers, Trotskyists and double-dealing spies, who, sneakily and shamefully, crept about, blocking Elinor's rightful place as an internationally acclaimed oil painter, star newspaper columnist or opera singer. Her mother for a start.

At first, Henry had not been able to believe that her therapist had got it so right. If anyone had prevented Elinor from being an oil executive, or a leading novelist and short-story writer, it was Elinor's mother, a small, heavily built woman with a squint, who lived very near the Sellafield atomic reactor. Principally because Elinor's mother was completely without talent for anything apart from giving men a hard time and had, presumably, passed on her genes to her daughter.

The therapist, apparently, while finding her mother guilty of the hideous and anti-state offence of blocking Elinor's creativity, took the view that she had managed to do this by getting Elinor to love her too much. How she worked this out was a mystery to Henry, since her mother's role in Elinor's life was confined to twice-yearly visits in which she sat in their front room and listened to Elinor telling her how awful Henry was.

He put the chicken in a roasting bag and felt in his pocket for the vial of thallium.

'Ugh!' said Maisie. 'Chicken.'

'It's OK,' said Henry, 'you can fill up on choc bars and then pretend to eat it and when she isn't looking I'll sling it in the bin.'

'Good!' said Maisie.

'I wouldn't touch a mouthful of it myself,' said Henry, 'it's that healthy free-range chicken that she likes . . .'

'Yuk!' said Maisie.

While she was munching her way through her third chocolate bar, Henry took the chicken through to the scullery and carefully anointed its breast with the thallium. On top of the thallium he sprinkled salt, a very little pepper and a coating of tarragon leaves. It was six thirty.

Back in the kitchen, he cleaned the edenwort and the okra and chopped them up small enough to be unrecognizable. He whistled as he chopped and, as he tipped the vegetables into the frying pan, he sang, to the tune of Candyman Blues, the following song:

> Thallium
> Thallium
> Guillain-Barré
> Thallium
> Thallium Thallium
> Thallium Guillain-Barré.

Underneath the frying pan was another note.

You hate women, don't you? Why do you hate women? Why are you so frightened of them? Why do you seek to destroy them? To caricature them? Is it their creative potential that frightens you? Their menstrual power? Their child-bearing power? Is it their fund of womanliness you hate? Don't you hate women, Henry?

Henry couldn't think of a woman he disliked apart from Elinor. And, of course, Elinor's mother.

How would Elinor's mother react to her daughter's death? Henry had a feeling that she would take it well. She had taken her husband's brain tumour like a . . . well, like a man. 'OK,' her square jaw seemed to say, 'Derek has a brain tumour. That happens. We can deal with it!' And she and her daughter had dealt with it. They had coped. They had certainly coped a lot better than Elinor's father, a man Henry had always liked. The news of his impending death had badly ruffled his composure. He had talked wildly about the meaning of life, the emptiness of it all, the lack of scope offered by the Guardian Building Society. Elinor and her mother had clearly found all this in bad taste.

'Daddy is depressed,' they would say, narrowing their

eyes and tilting their square chins downward, 'very, very depressed. About the fact that he is dying.'

They clearly felt he should have taken a more manly approach to the brain tumour. A man who had such a positive attitude towards Do It Yourself could surely have used some of that energy to combat the decay of his central nervous system. Henry thought about his father-in-law's funeral, as he placed the Chicken Thallium in the oven, and then checked his watch again. He thought about the dignified posture of Elinor and Elinor's mother, about how good they looked in black, about how they retained their composure even as the oblong box containing Derek slid off through a gap in the crematorium wall. About how, as Elinor and Elinor's mother stood by the flowers in the rain at Putney Vale Crematorium, someone had said to him, 'They're taking it very well!' Of course they were, thought Henry, they couldn't give a toss about the poor bastard.

He would wear his black leather jacket at Elinor's funeral. And the green socks. And the red shoes. He would deck himself out in the kind of clothes that would give most offence to her were she alive. And if Elinor's mother should break down he would sob operatically and people would say to each other, as he stood by the flowers afterwards, 'My, my. He is taking it badly.'

It was six forty-five. He turned the oven on to 250 and put the okra and the edenwort on to a low heat. In approximately one hour she would be getting her chops round the first succulent mouthful of Chicken Thallium. By midnight she would be experiencing severe abdominal discomfort.

Whistling to himself, Henry laid the table, while, in the corner of the kitchen, Maisie finished her last chocolate bar and got to work on a packet of crisps, a tube of Rollos, half a pound of jellybabies and a jumbo bar of Turkish delight. As she ate she cast worried glances up towards the cupboard by the stove, where lay a small sack of potato crisps, some Liquorice Allsorts and two packets of biscuits. Sometimes Henry wondered whether the junk food industry was going

61

to be able to take the kind of demands Maisie was going to make on it in the years ahead.

Occasionally, for some obscure reason of her own, Elinor was pleasant. Henry could not quite work out why, since her pleasantness was not always followed by a request for money or some other favour; perhaps she was remembering something he had quite forgotten, an incident during their courtship perhaps (they must have had a courtship) or a Henry, now lost to Henry himself, who could have inspired feelings such as pleasure. Or perhaps this was part of some internal clock of hers and, at some moments, often weeks or months apart, Elinor was programmed to be briefly but definitely pleasant.

It always threw him.

'Hullo, darling!' she said, as she came round the kitchen door in her black trouser-suit, her black hair swept back under an Alice band. 'I've had a lovely sleep!'

Henry looked at her suspiciously. Why is she saying this? he thought. What has she got in mind?

She crossed the kitchen floor and pecked him on the cheek.

'Sorry I was cross!' she said. Her voice was light, tremulous. Perhaps she was planning to murder him!

'You're making supper!' she said.

'That's right!'

With just a hint of normal, workaday Elinor, she pointed a stubby finger at the vegetables.

'What's that?'

'It's edenwort, darling,' said Henry. 'It's a new vegetable!'

Elinor did not pick up the pan and hurl it across the room. She scooped up a little on her forefinger and nibbled at it.

'It's rather nice!'

'And I've done chicken!' said Henry. 'Free-range chicken. How you like it. All crispy in the oven. Topped with . . .'

'What's it topped with?' said Elinor suspiciously.

'Lovely herbs!' said Henry. 'Lovely fresh herbs from the garden picked all fresh and with no chemicals on!'

'Mmmm!' she said.

And skipped off towards Maisie who, at the first sound of her mother's footsteps, had concealed her cache of sweets under her jersey.

Perhaps, thought Henry, she was appealing to his better feelings. She was making herself difficult to kill on humanitarian grounds. He watched her as she danced a few larky steps with her daughter, singing in an effortfully pure soprano while Maisie shuffled along trying to keep the sweets safe under her jumper.

'Love-lee chicken!' she was singing. 'Love-lee chicken!'

Still in a larky mood, she began to lift her daughter up off the floor. Maisie, like Henry, did not like being lifted. She held herself quite still, staring seriously at her mother, thinking, quite obviously, Henry thought, about Turkish delight. Elinor put her down.

'You two,' she said, 'are so stiff!'

Henry looked across at Maisie. Was Elinor perhaps going to try and top her as well? Never mind. In a very short space of time she would have her feet under the table and those huge jaws would be munching their way into the breast.

And then the doorbell rang.

CHAPTER NINE

It was Donald.

Elinor was pleased to see him. She it was who opened the door and Henry heard a high-pitched giggle followed by a lengthy squawk of pleasure.

'Donald,' she said, 'it's Donald.'

Henry wondered whether she was having an affair with Donald. WIMBLEDON DOCTOR IN POISON LOVE TRIANGLE, he thought to himself. Or possibly, DOCTOR IN LOVE PACT POISON DEATH WISH PATIENT HORROR.

No. Donald would never do it with a patient. His offence against those who came to him for medical help was less easy to punish. But he was certainly guilty, thought Henry, of liking Elinor and, as he came into the hall, nodding his big head as Elinor fussed round him, Henry wondered whether his wife might not be, *au fond*, quite a pleasant woman. Numbers of people seemed to like her. Neighbours, friends, colleagues. People bought her lunch and rang her up and sent her birthday cards; it seemed a particularly cruel joke that one of the few people who really did dislike her should be married to her.

'You must stay to supper!' Elinor was saying.

'Oh, Elinor,' Donald was saying, 'I couldn't . . .' But he was saying it in a way that implied possible assent. Elinor went to the stove, singing in a high soprano voice 'Donald's coming to supper . . . Donald's coming to supper . . .' When this song failed to make the impact she clearly expected it to make, she turned to Henry as if she was addressing some Yugoslav peasant and did a lot of the kind of lip and tongue work she had used on Elke, their one and only au pair.

'Donald's staying to break bread with us!' she said.

Henry managed a smile. Once again, Lustgarten was on

the line to him. 'It was when the friend of the family, Donald Templeton, the trusted and valued doctor who attended both Farr and his wife, came to call that the plans of the man who came to be known as the Wimbledon Poisoner came badly unstuck. Suddenly, to Farr's consternation and disappointment, it wasn't a cosy, deadly meal for two by the fireside, but Chicken Thallium for three!'

Lustgarten stopped by the fire, his hand on the wall, and glared, menacingly, at the camera.

Lustgarten had a point. Did Donald like breast meat? If he did, was Henry going to be able to avoid serving him with any? He tried to readjust his face to make him look less like Macbeth.

'Oh,' he said again, 'great!'

Donald looked at Maisie. 'Only ten!' his big, grey eyes seemed to say. 'Ten years old, and less than a month to live!' Maisie grinned.

'Hullo, Donald!' she said.

Henry attempted to gain some control over the situation. 'Well,' he said, 'we've got a nice, juicy chicken leg for you!'

Donald did not seem unresponsive to this notion. He did not say, 'Actually – I'm a breast man myself!' But then, it was early in the game for such delicate negotiations. Soon, carving etiquette might well be as developed and intricate a ritual as chess and, when it did get that advanced it would probably be in Wimbledon but, for the moment, Henry was faced with the unattractive prospect of involuntary double murder. Was polyneuritis infectious?

'I don't understand it, Doctor! They both started throwing up and seeing flashing lights! Might it be some form of . . . I don't know . . .' (rapidly) '. . . infectious polyneuritis?'

The trouble with this, of course, was that it might lead to another doctor, one more competent than Donald, examining their evening meal. No – he would have to make sure that no breast meat came Donald's way. It shouldn't be too difficult.

'Henry tells me,' Donald was saying in a carefully conversational manner, 'that you've had a touch of the old . . . polyneuritis!'

He said this as if amused by the thought. There was nothing terrifying or frightening about polyneuritis, his half-smile and gentle nod seemed to say, it was just an illness . . . like . . . cancer . . . or coronary thrombosis . . . or Alzheimer's . . . or leprosy! Pretty soon they would all be laughing about it.

'He what?' squawked Elinor.

She shot him one of her more mainline, Elinor-style glances. The standard who-is-this-jerk-and-why-am-I-married-to-him expression. Which, for some reason, then turned into a laugh.

'Silly old thing!' she said, and cuffed him affectionately.

Henry looked at Donald. 'She's a brave little liar!' he tried to make his eyes say. 'She doesn't want to bother you with it.' Donald, who was still nodding his head, did not seem to notice any of this. Perhaps he was just in the kind of trance he went into as a matter of course every time illness was discussed. He had a faraway, Buddhist look in the eyes – a kind of stillness and peace that denoted the complete absence of any mental process.

'I've been a bit depressed,' she said, 'that's all.'

Bit depressed? Bit depressed? You've been behaving like a commodity broker on Black Thursday, haven't you?

'Let's have a drink!' said Henry as he thought this.

'Sherry,' said Elinor swiftly.

A pint mug, my dear? Or shall we decant it into a bucket?

'Surely, my love,' said Henry lightly.

Donald chose Scotch. Maisie had a lemonade. Henry poured himself a Perrier water. He was going to have to keep calm and steady for the task ahead.

'For Farr,' said Lustgarten, 'as he laughed and joked with his old friend in the front room of their Wimbledon home, was already planning exactly where his carving knife would skirt the edge of the poisoned breast meat, digging deeper and deeper away from the tainted flesh, so that neither he

66

nor Templeton would suffer. Farr's doctor was no part of his murderous plan. His venom, both actual and metaphysical, was held in reserve for his wife!'

Henry went to the oven and looked through the grease-stained glass window. He could just make out the chicken. It was still oatmeal-white around the fleshy part of the thighs. But the breast was turning a golden brown – the herbs, the black pepper and the thallium were crisping up nicely. He turned back to Elinor and Donald.

Donald looked, thought Henry, like a perfect blend of Doctor Kildare and Gillespie, the older, wiser doctor of the partnership. Donald was perfectly poised on the edge of middle age – greying curls, the big, sculptural ears, the solidly Roman nose all suggested power, maturity, certainty. Henry concentrated on Donald's face and, as so often these days, found it easier to look as if he was listening by doing the reverse. He timed his nods and yesses and 'Indeeds!' on an entirely mathematical basis, interspersing them with a sort of pucker-cum-squint that could be mild disagreement or the preface to some statement of his own. Sometimes he helped along this impression of participation by opening his mouth and shovelling his chin forward until someone interrupted him.

'Actually,' Elinor was saying, 'we were going to Portugal, but I think we'll be staying in Wimbledon this year. I can't see myself getting out of Wimbledon at all.'

Unless you count the ride up to Putney Vale Crematorium, thought Henry, that'll be a nice little outing for you, won't it? He got up again and went back to the oven. Donald and Elinor had been talking for thirty minutes. Henry marvelled once again at time. Its passage seemed, nowadays, to be the only event in his life. Nothing happened in it any more. It just went. It wasn't the flying thing described by poets. It was the only thing on the horizon, shouldering aside achievement and sensation with attention-seeking roughness, and nothing, not conversation, wine, sexual encounters or the search for knowledge or fame could prevent it. What had they actually done while this chicken was cooking? Bugger all.

Maybe murder was the only way to make all this meaningful. Maybe that was why he was trying to poison Elinor? For a moment he could not quite think why he was trying to poison Elinor. It was just another thing he did – like dealing with wills and conveyancing at Harris, Harris and Overdene, or shouting at Maisie to go to bed. Then he pulled down the oven door, smelt the sweet, fatty smell of the meat and knew that it was probably this very fact that accounted for his decision to go through with the business.

He was poisoning Elinor because she was there.

'Lovely chicken,' said Henry, 'coming up!'

She was smiling at him. My God, thought Henry, perhaps the therapy is beginning to work. Perhaps she is going to turn into a quietly spoken, normal human being. Perhaps that is the point of therapy. For the first year or so it turns you into a kind of psychopathic animal and then suddenly, like a butterfly emerging from the pupa, you sprout wings, your heart opens, you become . . . charming. He looked at Elinor as he brought the chicken to the table.

No. Not yet, anyway. Killing Elinor was, Henry felt, still an ecologically sound thing to do. It would take at least another seven or eight years to turn her into a recognizable human being. Maybe even longer. In fact (Henry went back to the fridge and took out two bottles of wine), if she kept on with this present therapist there was absolutely no hope for her at all. If there was any hope for her, it was indisputable that the outlook was grim for anyone with whom she might come in contact. The woman kept telling her she needed assertiveness training. Elinor needed about as much assertiveness training as Napoleon.

'Lovely chicken!' said Henry. 'Tasty free-range chicken.'

They were looking at him oddly. Elinor took another swig of sherry and Henry arranged wine glasses at each place. Then he went back to the cutlery drawer and, with a skill born of long practice, lobbed knives and forks over to Maisie, who set them down in her customary eccentric manner. Sometimes forks would appear on the right and knives on the left, sometimes (Henry always felt this was Maisie's way of telling people they were not welcome) two knives or only a spoon. Elinor, who usually took it upon herself to criticize all aspects of her daughter's behaviour, was into her third sherry. She and Donald were discussing cars with great enthusiasm. They talked of the Nissan Cherry, the Volvo 740, the Granada Ghia, the Renault 5, the XJ6 Jaguar.

People in Wimbledon, these days, always talked about things as if they were people, and people as if they were things. They lacked confidence in their own values.

Henry was going to add a chapter towards the end of *The Complete History of Wimbledon* in which he planned to deal with the failure of nerve he sensed in the place. Some creature he had met at a dinner party recently (he was, it had to be said, from East Finchley) had had the nerve to tell him that New York was 'more vibrant' than Wimbledon. He had gone on about lofts. People in New York, apparently, lived in lofts, presumably because they couldn't afford houses. 'You have to go there,' he had said to Henry, pressing his face forward, 'it's so alive!' And another man, who should have known better even though he was from Southfields, had announced that Wimbledon was 'on the dull side. It's all accountants and solicitors, isn't it?' What was wrong, thought Henry, with being a solicitor? He thought about Harris, Harris and Overdene. He thought about how Harris smiled at Harris, whenever Henry passed his office door. He thought about the way that Overdene looked at him from his glass cubbyhole whenever Henry was twenty minutes late from lunch. And found to his annoyance that he was grinding his teeth.

Henry breathed deeply. Sooner or later something was going to snap.

'Are you all right?' said Elinor.

'Fine, darling!' said Henry.

The plates were on the table. The group was seated. Henry

69

was carving. Ladies first. Two, three, four huge chunks of Chicken Thallium. Smothered with gravy, garnished with unspeakable, uneatable edenwort and okra. Ladies first. If you don't like the vegetables – have the meat! Ladies first! The plate was on its way to Elinor.

'Leg OK for you, Donald?' said Henry.

'Actually,' said Donald, 'I fancy a bit of breast!'

'Have this!' said Elinor, thrusting her poisoned meat towards him. 'I'm not hungry all of a sudden. Have this!'

CHAPTER TEN

Of course, in all the books, poisoning was a comparatively simple affair. You made them Horlicks or Ovaltine or tea or coffee. You added the arsenic, the antimony or the heavy metal. And they took it down dutifully. Henry might have known that in his case the operation would prove a little more complicated. He watched, open-mouthed, as Donald beamed down at his Chicken Thallium.

'Well,' said Donald, 'I'd better get abreast!'

Elinor seemed to find this very funny. It was the kind of joke that went down well in Wimbledon. Normally, Henry would have joined in the laughter. Now he watched in horrified silence as Donald cut himself a giant slice of poisoned meat.

'Won't you have any?' he said, desperately, to Elinor.

'No,' she said, 'I might eat later.'

'It's lovely!' said Henry feebly.

'Mmmmm,' said Donald, swallowing a mouthful, 'it is!' He chewed it very thoroughly and, as Henry watched, began to swallow. 'You could die for this!' he said.

Too right you could, thought Henry.

Things were now going very, very slowly. As Henry watched (no one else round the table was eating) Donald lifted another laden fork towards his mouth. Halfway through the trip he decided to make the mouthful even more exciting. He smeared the chicken with edenwort, okra and gravy, rubbed it round the plate and set it off once more in the direction of his wide, beautifully moulded mouth.

The edenwort and the okra would do it. Surely. Unlike thallium, Henry felt, they were probably odourful and tasteful in the extreme. Enough to make you gag on first crunch, surely. Donald would choke and spit and deposit the whole

71

mouthful back on to the plate. But, as Henry watched, Donald broke into a smile. And not just any smile. It wasn't simply that he was managing to smile with his mouth full – a difficult enough task at the best of times – it was that his smile expressed so many real, positive qualities that it must be designed to sell something. It seemed a shame to waste it on friends.

'Mmmm,' said Donald, 'mmmm!' And then, after a bit of Christ-this-is-so-delicious-it-seems-a-shame-to-go-on-about-it-but-I-feel-it-is-my-duty acting, he went on, 'So chewy. So chewy and fresh!'

He was even beginning to talk like an advertisement. He really liked Chicken Thallium and he wanted people to know that he did. Feeling like an accomplice in this business ('Tell me – how did you get it so chewy?') Henry said, 'Yes. It is. It is chewy. It's a bit tough, the meat. I – '

'What is it?'

'Edenwort and okra.'

Even this did not make Donald crane his neck forward and start retching all over the table. He just nodded and smiled and went on chewing Chicken Thallium, slowly and methodically

Henry tried to think of a remark that would go with an expansive gesture. The sort of gesture that might, reasonably, allow a chap to knock over a bottle of wine and make sure at least half of it got all over Donald's plate. 'But what does it all mean?' perhaps, or, 'For God's sake, we're all going to die!'

He was unable to think of a suitable gesture. With a violence born of desperation, he swung at the bottle nearest to him and the mouth of a bottle of Tavel Rosé landed neatly in the pile of Donald's chicken, allowing pink liquid to pulse on to the plate.

'Henry!' said Elinor. 'What on earth did you do that for?'

'Sorry,' said Henry, 'I slipped!'

Donald was looking foolishly down at his plate. 'Oh . . .' he was saying, 'oh. . .'

72

He wanted more Chicken Thallium, you could tell. Henry was so infuriated by the childlike look of loss on his face he had half a mind to give him some. Then, getting to his feet, he scooped up the plate. Before he could head off for the dustbin, Elinor gripped his wrist firmly. She had strong hands, and the pressure she put into her grasp felt as if she was about to throw him over her shoulder or come out with some menacingly appropriate comment.

'Hang on! Shall we just run a lab test on this chicken!'

In fact she said: 'Give it to Tibbles.'

Tibbles was Henry's cat. Or, more accurately, she was Maisie's cat. Or, even more accurately, she was no one's cat. Responsibility for Tibbles was a free-floating affair, mainly consisting of whoever didn't want to feed her saying to whoever they thought should be feeding her, 'She's your cat!' She was, of course, in the way of cats, no one's but her own. A small, thin tabby, she spent her life trying to work out the central dilemmas of her life – how to get in and out of the house, and why the fat man called Henry tried to kick her every time the two other people in the house were out of the way. Henry hated Tibbles. He had fantasized about her death almost as much as he had fantasized about Elinor's. Why, now her end was so imminent, did he feel a desire to avert it?

'Why not?' he said, and taking both plate and chicken he hurried out to the scullery. 'I'll cut you some leg!' he called.

How much had Donald eaten? Enough to kill him? And, if he had, what was the antidote?

He very much did not want Donald to die. Donald was boring, sensationally incompetent at his job, complacent, vain, narcissistic, almost aggressively narrow-minded. But he was a forty-year-old Englishman. He was someone to drink with, for Christ's sake! He did not deserve death by heavy metal poisoning.

There was a poisons unit at Charing Cross Hospital, wasn't there? Some years ago Maisie had swallowed a whole bottle of vitamin pills and, although Henry had suggested that in

73

his view Maisie's stomach could probably have stood a diet of broken glass, aspirin and raw steak, Elinor had insisted on ringing Charing Cross Hospital. As far as Henry could remember they gave advice over the phone. But he couldn't possibly phone from the house. He could go to a phone box. '. . . Er . . . I seem to have swallowed a bit of thallium . . .' How could he put it? 'I'm doing some work on optical lenses with a high refractive index and I seem to have got some . . . er . . . thallium on my sandwiches . . .' They would want to know where and how, wouldn't they? They were probably in close touch with the police. Oh, Jesus Christ, how long had he got? How long had Donald got? Not long, from the look of the chicken. One thing was for certain. Tibbles had got hardly any time left at all. She was bum up in the air, small head to one side, gnawing her way through Donald's portion and then on to the rest of the poisoned carcass of the chicken, which Henry added to her plate.

If she was well enough to formulate a view on the question – and at the present rate of progress it looked as if she might be – Elinor would take a dim view of the poisoning of Tibbles. Cats did not rate quite as high on her scale of things worth fighting for as, say, dolphins, but their stock certainly stood higher than that of the middle-aged, white, heterosexual male. She seemed unable to appreciate the fact that Henry himself was one of a threatened species, even though that threat was treated with contempt by most ecologists and nearly all women. Perhaps this was why, increasingly, Henry saw life as a struggle between him and the things his wife cared for so passionately – whales, seals, Aborigines, dolphins . . . If it came to a straight choice between a dolphin and Henry (and in Henry's view things had already got that serious) he would go for Henry every time. Would Elinor though?

He stood looking down at Tibbles, breathing heavily. Blood pressure, Henry. Blood pressure. Don't think about animals. Don't think about anything that disturbs you. Think about what your mother used to call 'nice things'. Think about

74

Wimbledon. Think about the rows of quiet houses. Think about the rattle of the electric trains on their way to South-fields and Putney. Think about the neatly kept front gardens and the commuters clacking their way back in the twilight towards the carefully assembled innocence of home.

He was all right now. He cut Donald a generous slice of untainted leg, and went back to the dining table. Now. How was he going to make this phone call? He could not think of a single convincing excuse that would get him out of the house. He would have to use the phone in the hall. Now, while they were eating. He got to his feet.

'Just got to . . . er . . .' Elinor and the doomed man looked at him oddly.

'Make a call,' said Henry with a crispness that surprised him. 'It's a work problem. Tricky conveyancing thing. I think a tort may be involved.'

Elinor was looking at him with what might have been respect. He almost never discussed his work with her, while she, like many other progressive people, regarded the law as a sinister conspiracy to defraud the laity.

'It all hinges on Prosser v. Prosser,' went on Henry, in a world-weary voice, 'as usual . . .'

And, with the purposeful stride of a great barrister on his way to a confrontation in the Old Bailey, he went out into the hall.

It was curious. His attempt to murder her seemed to have given him a new strength in the relationship. He was, suddenly, almost decisive. And that was what was needed. Even as he closed the door behind him, the thallium was on its way down through Donald's oesophagus, slithering towards his stomach and digestive tract, where his body chemicals would turn it into a disease Donald would have difficulty in recognizing. There was no time to lose.

CHAPTER ELEVEN

Henry dialled the number of Charing Cross Hospital and asked in low tones for the Poisons Unit.

'The what?' said the girl on the switchboard.

'The Poisons Unit!' hissed Henry, in what he realized was a distinctly suspicious manner.

'Can't hear you, caller . . .'

'The Poisons Unit!' said Henry, as loudly as he dared. He tried to say this in a way that suggested that he was always ringing up for a natter about arsenic and thallium, that there was nothing odd about his request.

At that moment Elinor came into the hall. She stood in the darkness, looking at him curiously.

'Hullo,' said a voice at the other end, 'the Poisons Unit.'

'Hullo,' said Henry breezily, 'Henry Farr here from Harris, Harris and Overdene . . .'

'Yes,' said the voice cautiously. Elinor was still looking at him.

'I've got a problem,' said Henry, 'with the conveyancing papers on 56 Northwood Road. I have a real difficulty in locating who has responsibility for the dustbins.'

'This is the Poisons Unit,' said the voice, cautiously.

'I know,' said Henry, 'and I am sorry to bother you at this time of night but my client has given me to understand that this is when you would be available. Tell me, in the lease as originally drawn up would you be able to let my client know whether there was specific reference to the controversy over the dustbins or did this develop after the Maltese took over?'

Elinor folded her arms.

'Tell your client,' said the voice at the other end of the phone, 'that he or she would have a better chance of establishing who is or is not responsible for his or her dustbins if he or she employed a lawyer who didn't address his inquiries to people whose principal concern is pharmacology.' The line went dead.

'Thank you very much indeed!' said Henry with what sounded like genuine enthusiasm. 'That really is most helpful in our terms. I will of course let my client know that Mr Makaroupides takes full responsibility for this and that will take a weight off his mind. Have a nice day!'

He put the phone down and stared coolly at Elinor. 'It's four o'clock in New York!' he said.

'So what?' said Elinor.

'That's where I was phoning. Glyn, Harwood and Schmeiss operate almost entirely out of New York.'

Elinor goggled at him. She had never heard Henry talk like this before. Neither had Henry. But desperation could do strange things to a man. Donald was dying in there, for God's sake. Hadn't there been something in that book about Graham Young? Graham had got him into this. He could get him out of it. Young had, as far as Henry could remember, suggested the antidote for one of his victims himself. Dyner— something . . . dyner—

'Are you all right?' said Elinor.

'I'm fine,' said Henry, 'but this means I'd better just pop out for a second.'

Elinor's eyes were wide with concern. Henry never popped out anywhere. Especially after nine o'clock at night.

'I'll have to go and see Martin Rubashon. He's only just down the road, but this is a face-to-face matter, I'm afraid.'

Who, Elinor's expression seemed to be saying, is Martin Rubashon? And why have I never heard his name before?

'What's a face-to-face matter?' she said.

'The dustbins, of course,' said Henry testily, 'this is a nine-million-dollar contract. I'm not letting it slip over a few measly dustbins!' And with a calm purpose that he did not feel he went out into the street.

As the autumn air met his face, he remembered. Dynercaprol and potassium chloride. That was it. Young had actually

77

suggested its use to the police at one stage of their investigations. All he had to do was stroll down to Underwoods and pick up a bit of dynercaprol and potassium chloride. He didn't fancy another trip to the chemist's he had visited that morning. There was something scary about the place, something, well, Maltbyish . . .

He had, of course, still got a few sheets of Donald's prescription pad. With a quick glance back at the house he ran to the car. Once inside he groped for the sheets in his pocket. He must be careful to disguise his handwriting. Wasn't doctors' handwriting supposed to be hard to read? Henry normally wrote a neat, italic script; it was, according to the more malicious of his colleagues, his only real legal qualification. How much though? How much would Donald need to get him back on the road? And how, come to think of it, was Henry going to get him to absorb the stuff, short of creeping up on him while he was asleep and forcing it down his throat or up his arse? He stopped for a moment, the crumpled sheet of prescription pad on his knee, and wondered whether Donald was really worth all this effort. Might it not be simpler just to let him go? He had had a pretty good life. A pleasant wife (in his terms anyway), a nice house in the suburbs. He had had six glorious years with Arfur.

No. He couldn't do it to Donald. Henry filled in the form and drove down to Underwoods.

Although the pharmacist seemed to have some trouble deciphering the prescription, and Henry had to go through a nerve-wracking pantomime of ignorance about the nature of the chemicals he required, it wasn't long before he was standing once again on the doorstep of 54 Maple Drive.

It might be possible to slip the antidote in some pudding or dessert wine or *digestif*. He had a few hours anyway. And Elinor was just going to have to wait for her merciful release. Henry wondered whether dynercaprol and potassium chloride taken without thallium might be poisonous. He could slip some to Elinor as well. But no, even as he thought this, he realized the hopelessness of the task ahead of him. Killing

Elinor was the kind of thing you would need years of study to accomplish. You couldn't just walk into it casually, as he had done, drop home from the office and decide to eradicate her on the spur of the moment. As her mother was fond of saying – it had taken a lot of trouble to get her this far, and this last little step was going to take a deal of organizing as well.

On the doorstep of number 54, Henry stood for a moment in the gloom, flexing his fingers. The Wimbledon Strangler. Inside he could see Elinor talking, with some animation, to Donald, her long hair falling across her face. Donald was nodding eagerly as she talked. She was gesturing about something now, some issue that had excited her, dolphins probably, and as she waved her arms Donald gave her an admiring smile. She was, undoubtedly, in good physical shape. She had a fairly thick neck and her forearms, well, the only way to describe them was meaty.

You could use tights of course. Or piano wire. Like the SAS.

With this comforting thought Henry rang the doorbell, hard, and watched his wife heave herself out of the chair and stump through to the hall. Go for it, Henry! he said, once again to himself, Go for it! The evening has a new agenda. Detoxification followed by strangulation. Go for it, Henry! he said, for the last time, Go for it!

CHAPTER TWELVE

Both of them refused all offers of food and drink.

The conversation had turned to law and order. Elinor had begun, Donald told him, by discussing her problems. It appeared she had something called the Madonna Complex. Either she was a Madonna and people didn't give her credit for being one, or else she was trying to be one and people were trying to stop her or possibly she was being forced to be one against her better judgement. Henry couldn't work out, from Donald's description, which of these alternatives was best described by the Madonna Complex, indeed he didn't really listen to a word either of them said. All of his energies were devoted to bringing the conversation round to the topic of food and drink, but Donald, once he had explained, or failed to explain, the Madonna Complex, moved swiftly on to what he described as his problem, which turned out to be law and order.

'Say what you like!' he said. 'Say what you like. If a yobbo attacks my home and family. If some coloured youth breaks into my house and tries to rape my wife . . .' Henry goggled at him. 'I'd strangle the bastard with my bare hands. I don't see why coloured youths should have *carte blanche* to steal my stereo and shit all over my compact-disc player and rape my wife. I don't see it.'

Elinor was looking at Donald, her mouth open. There was, Henry knew, an unspoken contract between them. She was allowed to talk about herself if he was allowed to rave on about black men. The fact that he was soon going to die, thought Henry, gave his words a special poignancy.

'England,' he was saying, 'used to be the most civilized country in the world. Say what you like, you were safe in Wimbledon. Right?'

'Right!' said Henry.

'But now,' said Donald, 'England is a country run by yobbos for yobbos. A country in which respect for law and order takes second place to the problems of some illiterate chocco.'

Henry wasn't sure how to answer this. Hadn't Mrs Thatcher solved this kind of problem? Wasn't it OK to be racist these days? Donald seemed to be describing the bad old days before Mrs Thatcher, as far as Henry could see. Perhaps his memory, like Henry's, was buckling under the strain of being forty. Or else, possibly, the thallium was starting to affect his brain. It would be difficult to assess things like that with Donald. Whatever was the case he, Henry, had better get something down him.

'Whisky, Donald?'

'I won't, thanks.'

'Beer? Brandy?'

'I won't.'

'Cup of tea? Coffee?'

'Not for me.'

Wine? Ouzo? Vodka? Mead? Mineral water? Hot chocolate? Dynercaprol? Potassium chloride?

'Bugger off, friend chocco, I say. Bugger off, friendly neighbouring Paki. And bugger off, Greek and Arab while you're at it. We don't need you. England used to be a country with red pillar boxes and policemen with red noses and decent law-abiding citizens you could eat your dinner off. Now it's a refugee camp!'

Elinor looked pained. Her anguish, Henry noted, went down rather well with Donald.

'Shouldn't we,' said Elinor, 'welcome the refugee? Shouldn't people of all races and nationalities be welcomed by a caring country?'

Donald chose not to confront this vague, if morally positive statement. He was grinning, in a fatherly sort of way, and wagging his hands at Elinor.

'My point, Elly, is this – ' (*Elly? Elly?*) 'Where is the space

81

in all this for the little man? The ordinary, average Englishman. What I would call the little man. Me and Henry, say,
who just want a mortgage and a little house and get on with
it!'

Elinor started to make more anguished noises.

'How about a cool glass of orange juice?' said Henry. 'Or
a sandwich?'

They both looked at him oddly. Elinor narrowed her eyes.

'Washing up, Henry!' she said.

'Yes, m'love!' said Henry lightly.

Oh well. Donald had had a good innings. His time had
quite obviously come.

'How about some mineral water?'

'No thanks, old man,' said Donald, 'we're setting the world
to rights here.'

Henry started to pack the plates into the washing-up
machine. Smeared with grease, fragments of chicken and
edenwort, they reminded him, as so often, of his life. Quite
decent things, hopelessly botched, needing to be made clean
again. That awful doubt came at him again. Maybe Wimbledon wasn't such a great place. Maybe *The Complete History*
was what that publisher said it was – a boring load of old
rubbish. Maybe – but these were the kind of thoughts that
kept Henry awake sometimes at four in the morning, longing
for the dawn. They were not to be contemplated. That way
lay madness.

Even as a poisoner, not, you would have thought, the
most demanding of professions, he seemed to be a complete
failure. Seeing him engaged in domestic activity, Tibbles
came up to him and began to rub her harsh fur against his
legs. In a curious way he would miss Tibbles. Who was going
to go first? Her or Donald?

'What the English have given the world,' said Donald, 'is
a respect for law and order and decency. I'm talking about
justice, you get me? A people who care passionately about
fair play, whose legal system is – Christ!'

Henry jerked round.

'You OK?'

'Just got a blast in the gut.'

'Oh,' said Henry, 'have a drink of something!' But Donald was doubled up on the sofa.

Henry rushed through to the kitchen, poured the dynercaprol and potassium chloride into a small glass of water and hurried back to Donald.

'Here,' he said, trying to keep his voice jolly, 'some new tummy thing for you. It'll set you right in no time.'

Donald looked at him suspiciously.

'The best thing for a gyp tum,' he said, 'is – '

'Quickly – ' said Henry, raising the glass to his lips.

Donald spat back the liquid. 'Christ, old man – ' he muttered, 'what are you trying to do? Poison me?'

It was clear that Donald extended his brutal, no-nonsense attitude to medical care to himself.

'No,' he said, 'I'll be all right. Sort myself out in no time at all. I'll be – Oh my God!'

Henry made one more attempt. Putting his left arm round Donald's shoulder, he took advantage of his first relaxation from the spasm of pain, to raise the glass to his lips, push his head back and, as if he were administering medicine to Maisie, roll the fluid past the perfectly kept teeth. There was a gulp and a yell and the rest of the glass (he had drunk at least some) flew up and out and on to the sanded floor of the dining area.

'Henry – ' said Donald, 'what the fuck is that?'

'It's called . . .' Henry paused. 'Globramine.'

The sound of the name seemed to reassure Donald. 'I think I know it,' he gasped, 'though I'm not very good on drugs. I'm rather against a lot of these medicaments . . .'

He was wheezing now, as if in the grip of an asthma attack.

'Let the bastards sort themselves out.'

It was difficult to know, though, whether he had had enough to save him. But at least, thought Henry, the man had a fighting chance. If only Elinor hadn't refused her portion. She must have some radar, he thought, that at the last saved her from the worst effects of his anger and frustration. Which is why it all came back on him. It's a war, thought Henry, between men and women. It's a war, a long, bitter and pointless war, in which towns are burnt, cities taken, allies betrayed . . . and at the end of the war, as after all wars, there is no victory, only the shabby compromise of peace.

He could have murdered her then, in front of Donald and Maisie and the cat. He could have run at her, forced her to the ground and banged her stupid, glossy head until her brains spilled out on to the stupid, glossy floor.

But he didn't. He stood there, clenching and unclenching his hands, trying not to twitch. Am I going crazy? he thought. And when I do, will all this get easier?

'I'll run Donald home!' Elinor was saying, 'you get Maisie to bed!'

'Yes, dear!' said Henry.

As Elinor and Donald shuffled towards the door, Tibbles shouldered her way into the room. She looked left and right and approached the pool of dynercaprol and potassium chloride in a carefully stylish manner. She looked round the room, as if to check that no one else wanted it and then, watched by a sullen Henry, began to lick it up greedily.

Women and cats, thought Henry, women and cats . . .

While Elinor and Donald were gone, Henry practised strangling.

The whole problem was going to be catching her off her guard. And Elinor was never off her guard. Now Henry thought about it, she seemed to enter rooms which he was in carefully, keeping her back to the wall; if he got close to her, she nearly always moved away quickly, usually making sure their bodies did not touch. Henry had always assumed that this was due, on her part, to an entirely natural physical repugnance for him; she moved away from him as one might move away from a bad smell or a dangerous horse. And up until now, the effortless ballet of their lack of encounter had come, in a way, as a relief. He, after all, found her quite as repulsive as she found him and, as the two of them waltzed from oven to sink, from window to cutlery drawer, staring up, down, sideways, anywhere but at each other, Henry had always assumed that this was no more than the usual politesse of a failed English, suburban marriage.

But now he thought about it, weighing up different locations in the house as possible strangling areas, there was a definite pattern to her movements. She was – in the bedroom and the kitchen anyway – quite definitely trying to get behind him, and in clearer ground, the hall, stairs, lounge or garden, she moved fast, certainly too fast to be strangled. This had to be deliberate. Didn't it?

About the only safe areas were the lavatory or the bathroom.

Henry went up to the landing and sized up the lavatory. The chief advantage here was that the door was never locked. Elinor's only defence system was to say, in a tone fractionally the right side of panic – 'I'm in here!' – if ever she saw the door move. It might also be the case, too, that if he timed the attack carefully he might be able to give the verb 'caught short' a transitive sense. They would, however, be facing each other. There was, presumably, a sound evolutionary reason for the fact that no one had yet designed a lavatory in which the occupant faced away from the door, some relic of the time when primitive man was most at risk when at stool, but it did mean that the lavatory user was finely tuned to the approach of strangers.

Henry gave a short run and shouldered his way past the door.

It wasn't entirely satisfactory. She might get her head down and then butt it upwards into his stomach. She had, to hand, the lavatory brush, three toilet rolls and the hardback edition of a very long novel by a Peruvian author with an unpronounceable name. She had her teeth and her two strong arms.

Her teeth. Brushing her teeth. That would be the ideal

activity to interrupt by strangulation. It would be late at night, she would have her back to the door and, when brushing her teeth, Elinor went into a kind of trance. He stood at the door of the bathroom, visualizing this most familiar of her rituals. Her left arm by her side, her right elbow out at an angle and her forearm shaking like a pneumatic drill. Her head motionless as her hand moved up, down, side to side, up, down, side to side, the only sound the scritch scratch of the bristles against her perfect ivories. He would do it tonight. He would have to do it tonight. You fell off the horse, you got straight back on and did it again. Go for it, Henry! he told himself. Go for it!

'The deadline,' (this time he spoke aloud) 'is midnight!'

CHAPTER THIRTEEN

Maisie came into the bathroom as he was standing slightly to the right of the basin, arms outstretched, thumbs interlocked, squeezing an imaginary neck.

'Are you practising strangling?' she said.

Henry jumped. 'You should be in bed!' he said.

'Pozzo is depressed!' said Maisie.

Pozzo was a small black furry creature that, years ago, had belonged to Henry. Before Henry it had been Henry's father's. Whether it was a zebra, or a panda or a bear or a seal, cat, ocelot or kangaroo was unclear, but whatever it was, on the grounds of its appearance, it had every good reason to be depressed.

Henry decided to out-twee her. 'Was it sad because its mummy was nasty to it?' he said. 'And shall we make it a pwethent to make it happy?'

Maisie looked at him in disgust. 'Don't be stupid!' she said. He grabbed her, propelled her towards the basin and began to brush her teeth.

'Well, don't you be so disgustingly arch!' he said, brushing her teeth vigorously.

Maisie put out her tongue at him (no easy task for someone who is having their teeth brushed) and made a farting noise. 'You hate Mummy, don't you?' she said.

'Of course I don't!' said Henry. 'I love Mummy. I love Mummy very much and she loves me and we both love you and we all go diddledy diddledy dumpling through the heather on a hot sunny day, like a bunny rabbit with the clap.'

Maisie laughed coarsely. Then, a shade of nervousness entering her voice, she said: 'You do love Mummy, don't you?'

'Oh yes,' said Henry (he sounded, he thought, incredibly sincere as he said this), 'deep down. Incredibly deep down. Millions of miles down in the black, twisted heart of me I do. It's just that I am so evil and perverted and encrusted with slime that it's rather difficult for me to remember the fact.'

Maisie laughed. She was one of the few people in the world who genuinely found Henry funny. Other people, he thought, probably found him funny, but funny for the wrong reasons. Funny because he was forty and not very clever and lived in an English suburb called Wimbledon. Funny laugh-behind-your-hands, thought Henry, funny the way Karim Jackson –

'You're hurting me!' said Maisie.

To his horror Henry saw that as he had been brushing her teeth he had started to grip her neck, hard. There was a brutal, red thumb mark just at the point where her shoulders met her neck. He bent down and kissed it, overcome suddenly with remorse. It was thinking about that publisher that had done it. Why did that bastard have the right to say 'no' to him? Just like that. To ignore something that could (Henry was prepared to admit that *The Complete History* might need work) be one of the most exciting developments in social history this century. It seemed, somehow, monstrously unfair that a decision of such importance to England's cultural future should be left to a person from Pakistan.

Henry wasn't a racist. He just didn't want the bastards to get the upper hand. Didn't they have enough? Couldn't they just ease up a little? Why did Karim –

'Ow!' said Maisie.

He was squeezing her neck again.

'Sorry!' sad Henry.

'I won't have any teeth left.'

England was owned by other people these days. After years of greatness it was just a place like any other place. That, somehow, was the worst insult of all.

'Ow!' said Maisie again.

'Sorry!' said Henry.

She turned her plate-like face up to him. 'Can I have my story?' she said.

'Of course, my love,' he said.

Maisie was the only person to whom Henry ever talked these days. She was certainly the only person to whom he started to describe his feelings. In the stories he told her were roads and trees and houses and mountains and monsters and rivers and magicians; but at the centre of the story there was always Henry. Henry, in the story, lived in Wimbledon, but not the same Wimbledon. It wasn't even the Wimbledon of *The Complete History*. It was Wimbledon with some things left in and some things left out. Wimbledon at once grotesque and matter of fact. The suburb became, under Henry's hands, like a vacant lot in Hollywood – full of cardboard houses under an artificial sky. And yet, almost against Henry's will, the real suburb kept breaking in until among the paper houses you could smell the decaying leaves, the acrid exhaust of cars and hear the children shouting to each other under the huge sky on the common.

'What's this one about?' she said, as, holding his hand, she climbed the short flight of stairs that led to her attic room.

'It's about the time I turned into a pig!' he said.

Maisie bounced into her room. 'What kind of pig?' she said.

'A male chauvinist pig!' said Henry.

'Is that a good sort of pig?' she said.

'No,' said Henry, 'it's an awful, rude, wicked, cruel sort of pig.'

'Why did you turn into it?'

'Because,' said Henry, 'I was depressed.'

He lay next to his daughter on the bed and put his arm round her. She looked up at him.

'Why were you depressed?' she said.

'Because,' said Henry, 'my pig wife was going to be made into bacon.'

'Why was she going to be made into bacon?'

'Because,' said Henry, 'she had caught a very serious disease.'

'What disease?'

'It's called feminism,' said Henry, 'and I hope you never get it, because it is absolutely awful and it makes you swell up to an enormous size and when you have it really badly you go round bonking men on the head and blaming them for everything. And your arms grow all hairy and muscly like a man's and you get very keen on boxing and tossing the caber.'

Maisie showed worrying signs of interest in feminism.

'It sounds fun!' she said. Then she looked at Henry suspiciously. 'Anyway,' she said, 'I know what feminism is. It's thinking girls and women are good. What's so wrong with that?'

Henry's stories quite often developed into debates of this kind. In fact, on many occasions, Maisie talked more than Henry.

'There's nothing wrong with that,' said Henry, 'and some feminists are quite nice. But some of them are bad-tempered ratbags who should be locked away in a cellar with a lot of other feminists. I'm not saying that women and girls are bad. I think they're nice. I just don't like being told that boys and men are bad. I think it's stupid and unfair.'

Maisie thought about this. Then she said, 'Well. Boys and men are all right, I suppose. Anyway. Go on with the story.'

'So,' said Henry, 'my pig wife . . .'

It was curious. Here he was, as usual, telling Maisie her story. And a few streets away, Donald was probably in his death agony. Or if not actually in it, well on the way to it. What was so attractive about poison (and Henry had, with some regret, more or less reconciled himself to Donald's death) was that it acted so independently. It was like a good secretary. The sort of secretary you couldn't get hold of at Harris, Harris and Overdene. 'Thallium,' you said, 'job for you!' and thallium picked up the papers, simpered, and went out into the world to do your bidding.

Strangling was not like that.

'You're squeezing again!' said Maisie. 'Why are you squeezing?'

'Because I love you,' said Henry.

'Go on about the pig now!' said Maisie.

'Well,' said Henry, 'my pig wife – '

'What was her name?'

'Her name,' said Henry, 'was Elinor.'

'Oh,' said Maisie, 'like Mummy.'

'Yes,' said Henry, 'but my pig wife wasn't like Mummy. Mummy is sweet and good and kind. But this pig was odious and conceited and impossible to live with.'

'Because it was a feminist!' said Maisie, with a touch of satire.

'That's right!' said Henry. 'Which is not to say that it was odious and conceited because it was a feminist. I repeat. Not all feminists are odious and conceited. But they are not automatically right about everything. And the ones who see life purely as a battle between men and women – which, of course, it is, I suppose, are . . .'

He stopped. Maisie was looking at him doubtfully. He wasn't getting the story right. It was infected with doubt. Somehow the outside world had intruded and broken up the fabric of the tale. What were usually asides, about life, religion, art, politics, had come to dominate the story. He saw himself suddenly, a fat man on a bed, haranguing his daughter about feminism. Was that what he was? Did he, perhaps, really hate women? Maybe Elinor was right. And if she was, perhaps he ought not be trying to murder her?

No. It was just a difficult, demanding task to perform. That was all. It interfered with your peace of mind. From the outside, murder looked like a quiet, sensible alternative to divorce. When you were actually involved in it, when you were down there at the murder coal-face, it could be as complicated and unsatisfactory as marriage.

He had better get Maisie to sleep, though. He didn't really want her to hear her mother being strangled.

'Actually,' he said, 'this story is really about this pig's father.'

'Oh,' said Maisie.

'In fact,' said Henry, 'it's about my father. Who was, of course, in the story, a pig. And although I didn't like my pig wife or my pig mother come to that – I was very fond of my pig father. Because he, like me, was a male chauvinist pig. We all lived in this sty, just off Wimbledon Hill. It was a very expensive sty and like all the other pigs in the street we were very heavily mortgaged – '

He saw Maisie start to open her mouth and, before she had time to ask the inevitable question, said, 'We had borrowed money from the pig bank. Anyway, one day the farmer who owned the street knocked on the door and told us that my pig father was due to be made into *bacon*. There was no way to avoid it. The next day we had to report to the huge, ugly, frightening, hideous abattoir man who, in case you didn't know, lives, actually *lives* three streets away from us! He is tall and cold and sometimes he doesn't only come for pigs he comes for greedy little girls who make pigs of themselves, with too many sweets!'

Maisie was now bug-eyed with fright. Henry leaned across and tapped her on the chest.

'But,' he said, 'my pig wife, Elinor, decided to save my pig father. She decided he was one fat pig in Wimbledon who was not, could not, should not be brought under the knife of the evil abattoir man who lives, in case you need to know, in Clifton Road just off the common, and the story of how she fought off his terrible friend Farmer Dune, and rallied all the pigs of Wimbledon is the greatest story ever told. You will hear how Farmer Dune was himself eaten by a group of pigs. You will hear how pigs decided to own their own houses, and how pigs like me who worked for Harris, Harris and Overdene openly ate legal documents in the street. And you will hear most of all about the abattoir man, the evil, cold-hearted villain who knows no pity!'

Maisie was still bug-eyed. Her chin trembled with anxiety and her big, blue eyes looked far beyond Henry and the bright patterned curtains, at something only children see. He hugged her tightly, unburdened of some inner horror, suddenly carefree.

'I'll tell you the rest,' he said, 'tomorrow night!'

When we will be a single-parent family.

Henry liked the idea of being a single-parent family. There would be programmes about him on the television. Support groups would flash their telephone number at him late at night on Channel 4. He would, he realized, for the first time in his life have a socially acceptable problem. Being fat and forty and hating one's wife and job were none of them socially acceptable. Murder was to make him something he had always suspected he might be, but had never dreamed of becoming – interesting.

For a moment, he wished he could tell Elinor these things. To talk to her, reason with her, confide in her, as people are wont to do when confronting their victims with loaded guns. 'You see, Inspector, you have to die because – ' 'Elinor,' he could see her white anxious face now, 'you have to let me strangle you. I need to grow and change and develop as a person in my own terms. My therapist, Elinor, a man called Graham Young, suspects that the only way forward for me emotionally is to fasten my fingers round your windpipe and squeeze and squeeze and squeeze until your face turns black . . .'

He was squeezing. But not Maisie. This time he was squeezing the bedhead. And his daughter, her big head lolling across his chest, was fast asleep.

Down below, the front door opened and then closed quietly. Henry loosened his fingers from his daughter's shoulder, tucked her under her duvet and, walking lightly on the balls of his feet, moved with a new precision on to the darkened landing. He smiled to himself at the head of the stairs. Not long now. Not long.

CHAPTER FOURTEEN

'Donald is desperately ill!' was the first thing she said, as he met her in the hall. As soon as she had announced this fact, she pushed past him roughly, on her way to the kitchen. This wasn't as bad, Henry thought, as post-therapy hostility. It was more like plain, straightforward dislike. He felt able to deal with this. One just had to be manly about it.

It was a shame. Strangling really needed a more co-operative partner than Elinor. One of those kittenish creatures he remembered from the films of his childhood in the fifties, clad in waist-high, baby-doll nightdresses, women who seemed to enjoy nothing more than lying back among the yellow nylon sheets and allowing themselves to be strangled.

It was feminism that was to blame. Nowadays women carried everything short of CS gas; all of them – at least, all of the women Elinor knew – were fairly well up on the martial arts. He followed her through to the kitchen where, as far as he could see, she was still in operatic mode.

'Desperately, desperately ill!' she said, over her shoulder, then swooped down to the dishwasher, picked up a handful of plates, and marched off towards a cupboard. As she marched she threw remarks over her shoulder, as if in some climactic race with a large orchestra. 'He is in a very critical state, Henry. He is in the throes of this awful thing, can't you see?' Then – 'Chest pains! Dry skin! Pulse slow! Headache!' and finally, 'Poor, poor Donald!'

Well, it was his own fault, thought Henry. If he would go around pinching other people's food! If only he had managed to force down a little more dynercaprol and potassium chloride! Elinor turned to him.

'We've called in Roger From the Practice!'

Roger From the Practice, eh? thought Henry. Well, that should finish him off in no time.

'Poor old Donald!' he said, limply.

'I don't think you care about Donald!' she said, pushing off from the cupboard, like someone striking out in a swimming bath.

Henry felt this was unfair. He liked Donald a great deal; and the prospect of the man's imminent death did nothing to dispel this feeling, since he was the person directly responsible for this state of affairs. Well, perhaps not directly responsible. This business of being responsible for people had to stop somewhere, didn't it? All Henry had done was poison a chicken which the berk had then insisted on eating. There was no way this made Henry 'directly responsible' was there? We had, thought Henry, gone beyond such primitive notions of morality.

'You don't care about anyone! You don't care about anyone but yourself and your narrow little world.'

'Well, what do you care for?' said Henry.

Elinor thrust her square jaw at him. 'Art!' she said, 'Feelings! People! The world around me!'

She didn't, of course, thought Henry, mean the world around her. The world around her was largely made up of Wimbledon. She meant quite a different world. A world of giving women and strong but equally giving men, a world of Bengali dancing, passionately held ideas and seventeen different kinds of psychoanalysis. A world that existed only in her head.

Henry thrust his hands deep into his pockets, glumly. He wondered which row to select from the library of disputes available to him. It was going to be an important row. He could see it now, tucked up in a cassette case. *Last Row Before Strangulation*. Was it going to be the You Are Cold and Unfeeling Row, the Why Are You So Feeble Row, the Fat Row, the Racist Row, the Right-Wing Row, the Left-Wing Row, the Merits of Jane Austen Row, the Driving Row, the Looking After Maisie Row or the Why Are You so Bitter and

Twisted Row. After some moments' thought, Henry selected the Sex Row. The Sex Row was always the best. It was so beautifully, predictably ugly. It followed the track it had followed for so many years, awakened the parties to rage, apathy and contempt in precisely the usual places and ended, as it always did, in a drawn game. Henry stuck his lower lip out and in an uncouth voice, said: 'How about a bit of sex?'

Elinor looked at him, blankly.

'A bit of sex,' said Henry, 'you know. We take our clothes off and I stick my penis into you and pull it in and out for a few minutes and white stuff comes out and you say "Is that it?" And I say "There isn't any more where that came from." And you say "Why can't you be more tender?" And I say "Search me, squire." You know. A fuck. You must remember. We had a fuck, didn't we once? A few years back.'

Elinor's mouth had dropped open. She looked now like some domestic cleaning device, mouth open for household filth. Henry gave her some more.

'Or buggery,' he said, yawning, 'that buggery sounds good. I read about it in *Knave* magazine. And that magazine *Hot Bitch*. You have to go to Holland to get it but it's well worth the trip. It's very informative. Or oral. You could suck my cock if you liked. We could turn on the artificial gas fire!'

Here he leered in a conspiratorial fashion. By way of answer Elinor's mouth dropped another few notches.

'Or spanking!' went on Henry brightly. 'I fancy spanking.'

Elinor gave a choking sound. For a moment he thought she was going to hit him, and then her face turned crimson, her mouth started to bang to and fro like a door in a gale force wind and a sound came down her nose that suggested she had just swallowed a quart of White's Cream Soda. Elinor was laughing. It was primarily a Display Laugh, something to indicate that she could rise above Henry, but (this disturbed him somewhat) at the back of her he caught a glimpse of something that could only be genuine amusement.

'Oh, Henry,' said Elinor, now blocking her mouth with

the palm of her hand and moaning elaborately, 'you're trying to be funny! Aren't you? Is that the idea?'

Her laughter dropped away suddenly. It was obviously a ploy. She said then, very quickly, like a trick question to someone in the Yes/No interlude on the Michael Miles Quiz Show: 'Marriage Guidance didn't do much for your need to dump, did it?'

Henry was beginning to enjoy this. 'Marriage Guidance,' he said, 'didn't understand my need for brutally climaxing into tight white bottoms.'

Marriage Guidance had been a bloke called Kevin who, in Henry's view, had had designs on Elinor. She, skilled in the ways of therapy, had after the first few sessions begun dissecting his own motives for him and Kevin, like an obedient dog, ended up nodding slowly as she told him clearly, fully, frankly what he meant when he said what he thought about what she or Henry felt, and how what he thought he thought about what they felt, or said they felt, probably wasn't what he really felt any more than what they said they felt was really deep down what they really felt. Except of course, in her case. Because what she thought she felt was what she actually did feel and she said it, loud and clear and everyone else could go and fuck themselves. This was called 'being in touch with your feelings'.

'At Marriage Guidance,' went on Henry, 'I didn't feel able to discuss my need to tie you to the bed and whip you with my pyjama cord. But that wasn't on the agenda, was it? On the agenda was something called Tenderness with a capital T. Well – ' Henry thrust his face towards her, allowing a small fragment of saliva to trickle down his chin. 'Tenderness is just another aspect of female control. Tenderness is just something that women like because it gives them the upper hand. Tenderness is that hideous, cooing voice you hear mothers using to their children as they get them to do this, go there, stay here. I am so pissed off with being told how men own and control the world. I tell you they don't. They all start out doing what some woman wants them to do. And you know the weapon she uses? She uses Tenderness with a capital T!'

Elinor folded her arms and, shaking her head in the way Henry sometimes did at the motorists who cut him up, she began to pace up and down the red-tiled kitchen. She did quite a lot of snorting, quite a lot of brittle laughter and a very great deal of what Henry took to be assumed inarticulacy.

'Basically . . .' she said, 'basically . . . I think . . . I don't know, but I think . . . I suspect . . . I feel . . .'

Here she raised her square white face up to his and sought his eyes. Then she said, according a miraculously even level of stress to each word in the sentence: 'We're-at-the-end-of-the-road.'

At this point the telephone rang. Henry answered it. It was Donald's wife. Henry could never, would never be able to remember her name.

'It's Donald . . .' she said.

'Yes!' said Henry. He sounded curt, businesslike. Perhaps a little too businesslike, he thought. He sounded like a man whose next line would be 'I'm in a meeting'.

'He's . . .'

'Yes?'

Her voice suddenly swooped into hysterics. For a moment, Henry thought she was going to laugh, and then came a sudden explosion of sobbing.

'He's . . . dead!'

At this moment Tibbles came into the room.

'Roger From the Practice is here!'

Well, I'm not surprised he's dead. I'm surprised you're not all dead!

'He's dead, he's dead, he's dead, he's dead!'

Henry wished Mrs Donald (what was her name?) would stop behaving like an extra in *Oedipus Rex*. So he was dead. Plenty of other people were going to be dead before the night was out. Tibbles for one. She was looking a bit like she had the morning of her hysterectomy. She prowled and paused and placed her feet carefully, all as if she were a normal feline, but there was something woefully uncatlike about her performance. She looked as if she was not entirely sure she was a cat, as if, thought Henry, one, two, three, four, five, six, seven, eight of her nine lives were oozing out of her like blood from a wound.

Henry looked up at Elinor smartly. He said: 'Donald's dead!'

'Oh my God!' said Elinor. 'Oh no! Oh no! Oh no! Oh my God!'

Christ, thought Henry, he's only your doctor!

At the other end of the phone Mrs Donald (what was her name?) was grieving with similar bravura.

'Respiratory failure at 11.30 p.m.,' she said (why did women have to be so scrupulously exact as to detail?) 'and before that he couldn't swallow. He said that he had a violent head pain. And then he had hallucinations. He thought there was a pig in the room.'

'What kind of pig?'

'I don't know. Just a pig. Oh my God! Oh my God! He was so sweet. I loved him so much.'

'I . . . Christ . . . I liked him. He was a nice bloke. A damned nice bloke actually.'

'And oh my God my God just like that! Like that. He's dead he's dead he's dead he's dead he's dead. He'll never come back. He's dead.'

A pause.

'Roger From the Practice is here!'

'Good.'

'He was so good and loyal and honest and brave and sweet and kind. And . . . he was such a good doctor.'

Henry thought this was depressingly typical of the way in which people talked about the recently deceased. Inaccurate would be a charitable way of describing Mrs Donald's description of her husband. He held the receiver a yard away from his ear. Tiny strangled sobs floated out of it and across the room. Elinor swung towards him. For a moment Henry thought she was going to hit him, and then, instead, she

100

seized the receiver from him and, sweeping it down to the floor with her she poured love, support, tenderness and quietness down the line.

'Billykins,' she said (surely this could not be the woman's name?), 'Billykins, this is so awful.'

Henry wandered to the other end of the room. Elinor sat on the floor, allowing her long black hair to fall around her and started saying 'Yes . . . yes . . . yes, I know . . .' and 'Of course . . .' a lot. She listened, thought Henry, the way some people figure skated. Presumably Billykins was telling her about Donald the Gourmet Cook, Donald the Great Fighter for Social Change, Donald the Novelist. He can't only have been Donald the Great Doctor.

If Roger From the Practice was doing the post-mortem, thought Henry, he should be OK. Roger From the Practice couldn't tell emphysema from the common cold.

'. . . Yes yes, my darling . . .' (Uh?) '. . . my darling, yes . . . we're with you . . . we're with you . . .'

Elinor put down the phone. She stared bleakly across at Henry.

'My God,' she said, sounding a bit like a vicar who has just discovered the Third World, 'this makes one's own problems seem pretty small, doesn't it?'

'Does it?' said Henry.

He sucked on his lips. She put her head on one side.

'I think,' she said, 'that you have instincts and feelings that are not really human at all. I don't think you are human, actually. I think you're like some disgusting little animal, some creature from another planet. I'm sorry for you, Henry. One day you'll wake up and realize how utterly ghastly you are, and I don't think you'll find that very easy to live with. I'm going to bed.'

Flexing his fingers, Henry followed her up the stairs. Behind him, pathetically, Tibbles mewed in the hall. Henry hoped she wasn't gong to make a fuss about dying. Ahead of him Elinor was pulling her dress over her head. She was wearing, as usual, a sack-like dress, one that hinted coyly at pregnancy. Underneath it was, as usual, Elinor's body. It wasn't, actually, if you could forget who it belonged to, a bad body. The thought occurred once again to Henry that someone who wasn't him might have a sexual interest in his wife. If not Donald, then perhaps one of the women from the therapy group. Was he, could he, be married to a lesbian? Such things had happened to more eminent lawyers than he. He heard the sound of the tap running, and then the sound of bristles against gum, ivory and lip. Arms out in front of him, Henry ran up the stairs, thinking, as he ran – She has three minutes to live.

CHAPTER FIFTEEN

She turned out to have rather longer than that.

For a start, when Henry rounded the bathroom door it seemed, to use a phrase of Elinor's, 'inappropriate behaviour' to run at her. He found himself walking at a steady pace towards those meaty shoulders. Her head, which was rotating at a different speed and a contrary motion to her brushing arm, reminded him of a duck in a shooting gallery. It had a difficult-to-hit quality about it, an almost larky imperviousness to attempts to interfere with it.

Still flexing his fingers, he started to dig them into the base of her neck, or rather, in the area where her neck might be assumed to begin. He found his hands full of dry, papery skin which, as he worked his way closer to her windpipe, came up and away like a curtain of strudel dough. Tossing this first layer of skin aside, he attempted to burrow deeper, only to discover yet more skin, though whether this was the outer skin that had slithered back through his advancing fingers, or a whole new layer was not apparent, but it was pretty clear that finding her windpipe, let alone getting hands round it and squeezing it, was a two-person job.

'What are you doing, Henry?' she squawked. 'Do you want sex again?'

'What do you mean, "again"?' said Henry.

'You only ever touch me when you want sex,' said Elinor. And started to brush her teeth again.

'I don't,' said Henry. 'I sometimes put my arms around you because I need to feel your closeness. I need to touch you tenderly and feel the warmth of your body.'

As he said this, Henry pulled at his nose and raised his upper lip to expose his gums. He looked, he thought, like a nasty species of rodent.

'Shut up, Henry!' said Elinor. 'You just grope my fanny and expect me to respond. Sex isn't just about an animal urge. It isn't like going to the lavatory.'

Henry started to slide down the wall. It looked as if strangling her was not going to be possible. Tonight anyway. Maybe he should go for a contract killing.

'It's a bit like going to the lavatory!' said Henry. 'Anyway, what's so wrong with going to the lavatory? I like going to the lavatory.'

'We had noticed!' said Elinor archly and, shaking out her black hair behind her, she placed the toothbrush, emphatically, in the plastic cup and marched out of the bathroom. On the landing a new thought occurred to her and she re-entered, her long arms swinging, her face screwed up with anger.

'How can you, though?' she said. 'How can you? Your best friend lies dead. Dead. And all you think about is . . . that!'

Here she pointed dramatically at Henry's flies. Henry found he was grinning foolishly. Any sort of attention to his genitals, even if it was the sort of gesture usually used by particularly aggressive barristers, was welcome.

'And stop smirking!' she barked. 'Christ! Anyone'd think from the way men carry on that their . . . things . . . are somehow clever and funny.'

She was down to its level now, her finger jabbing at the zip of his trousers.

Sex between Henry and Elinor had come to a halt some four or five years ago and, from what Henry could remember about it, it was something that was better discontinued. Elinor had spent most of their congress complaining. There were pains in her back, her right arm had gone to sleep, she was stiff, he wasn't stiff. It was lasting too long. It was over too quickly. He was too tentative, too assertive, too submissive, too dominant.

Following her into the bedroom, he decided to continue on the plainly offensive tack.

'Maybe,' he said, sitting on her side of the bed as she reached for a woman's magazine, 'maybe I'm gay!'

She looked at him oddly. 'Don't be silly, Henry!' she said, in a slightly querulous tone. Then she started reading a recipe.

'I often think,' he went on, 'about having sex with men.'

Elinor looked at him over the rim of her magazine.

'Well,' said Henry, 'it would make a pleasant change from having sex with you. Or rather, from not having sex with you.'

Elinor snorted.

'You are just being silly,' she said, 'and offensive!'

'Getting down on all fours,' went on Henry, 'and being rogered by a complete stranger in the open air. On the common. Melting back into the undergrowth, your trousers by your ankles – '

'Henry,' said Elinor, 'I think you are sick. I think you are ill. I think you need treatment.'

'What kind of treatment?' said Henry, licking his lips, 'corrective treatment? A good lashing?'

'Donald,' she said, 'is dead. He's gone. We've lost him. Doesn't that mean anything to you? Don't you have any human feelings?'

If he had hoped that a row might spur him on to a direct, hands on approach to murdering Elinor, Henry was disappointed. Talking to her, as so often, left him demoralized and confused. She seemed to have such endless resources of anger, so many obviously right, sincerely held opinions.

The more he thought about it, the more it became clear to him that this was a job for a real professional. A man with a hatchet face in a blue suit. Elinor would step out of her therapy class one morning, wave goodbye to Anna and Linda and Susie and Tatiana and Ruth and *wham* – several hundred rounds from an M16, the screech of tyres and the howl of brakes as the saloon car roared off down Makepeace Avenue.

'Did you know anyone who had a grudge against her?'

'I . . . can't, officer . . .' Henry would sob, 'she was just a quiet, ordinary housewife . . .'

The trouble was, he thought as he pulled off his trousers, where did one find contract killers? They didn't stick their cards through your letter box or advertise in the Yellow Pages. And very often they were unreliable people, demanding payment in advance or trying to blackmail you. A bit like builders. He had had a lot of trouble with builders last year. As had Donald. They had talked it over in the Rose. If something went wrong with his contract killer perhaps he would talk it over the way he talked over his builder.

'OK, mate?'

'Not so bad. But we've got one of these . . . contract killers on and . . .'

'I had one of those for Billykins. She – '

Donald.

Donald was dead. He had killed Donald. He was a murderer. Henry lay back against the pillow and closed his eyes.

'Sorry, Donald,' he said, in his mind, 'really sorry.'

Donald was very nice about it.

'Look, mate,' he said, 'it happens. Come to the funeral.'

'I will,' said Henry. 'I wouldn't miss it for the world.'

Elinor was looking at him curiously. 'Are you thinking about Donald?' she said.

'Yes,' said Henry, 'I was. I was thinking about what a nice bloke he was.'

'Oh my God!' said Elinor. 'He leaves a great gaping hole in the community.'

'He does,' said Henry.

And indeed he would, very shortly, be going in to a great, gaping hole in the community. In the Putney Vale Crematorium to be precise.

'One minute,' said Elinor, who seemed to have cheered up considerably, 'there he was laughing and joking and having a good time. And the next minute there he was, writhing around on the floor in agony!'

'I know!' said Henry.

'It was like he'd been . . . I don't know . . . poisoned or something!' said Elinor.

Henry coughed. 'I don't think,' he said, 'that that remark was in very good taste.'

It was long after she had gone to sleep and he had prodded her in the ribs to stop her snoring and was, himself, lying awake, staring into the darkness, thinking about Donald that it occurred to Henry that this was the longest conversation he had had with Elinor for about a year and that, after a bad start, she had, once or twice, come dangerously near to amiability.

CHAPTER SIXTEEN

Donald's funeral was, in the planning stages anyway, a magnificent thing.

Billykins, everyone agreed, was magnificent. She was dignified, pale, but, in the playground at least, composed. Arfur seemed positively cheerful. She wore a fetching, knee-length black dress and a kind of Spanish headdress that made her look a little like a sherry advertisement.

'I just want to carry on,' she said, 'as if all this had never happened.'

There were moments when Henry thought she would not turn up for the funeral, so magnificent was she about the whole thing, but as the date approached he noticed she was wearing more and more black jewellery, black scarves, capes, cloaks and jerseys, stockings, blouses and hats. She would deliver Arfur at eight fifty a.m., magnificent in a black coat, black ankle-length dress and black leather boots, and reappear at three fifteen, leaning against the climbing frame in the same ensemble, garnished with a scarf or a single piece of jewellery.

The neighbours, all the neighbours agreed, were magnificent. They called round. They went in and out of Billykins's house, and did something everyone described as 'sitting with her'. Mr and Mrs Is-the-Mitsubishi-Scratched-Yet went up to her in the street and pressed her hands between theirs. They baked cakes and meat pies and wholemeal loaves and they ordered flowers and hoovered the carpets and stairs; in fact, thought Henry, Donald was getting more (and higher quality) attention dead than he ever had alive.

His death, people said 'pulled the street together'. Even Nazi Who Escaped Justice At Nuremberg, at number 42, was seen talking to people in a high, jovial voice, that only increased his resemblance to a Gestapo officer. Mr and Mrs Is-the-Mitsubishi-Scratched-Yet smiled and nodded at people who passed them and tried not to flinch every time anyone went within ten yards of the Mitsubishi. There was, too, at first anyway, wild talk of the honours to be done to Donald. Dave Sprott, the northern dentist at 102, whose carefully preserved northern accent had always seemed to Henry a way of criticizing the London suburb in which he found himself, suggested that they 'hire' St Paul's Cathedral.

'I think 'e's owed that,' said Sprott, 'I think 'e's owed a generous tribute.'

From St Paul's Cathedral to Putney Vale Crematorium did not seem such a short distance to the neighbours, such was their generous enthusiasm for Donald's interment, and when they heard there were plans for a memorial service at Wimbledon Parish Church, some people said it was even better to do it this way. 'Donald', they said, 'wouldn't have wanted St Paul's. What did St Paul's mean to Donald?' This was a fair question, although the same could have been asked about his relationship with Wimbledon Parish Church. But the fact that no one seemed to know where Wimbledon Parish Church was, that no one in Maple Drive had seen the vicar, even at Christmas or Easter, seemed to make little difference. It was, as Nazi Who Escaped Justice at Nuremberg pointed out, the thought that counted. And everyone in Maple Drive, as they cooked, consoled, took out their best suits and thought of even nicer things to say about Donald than the last nice thing that had been said about him, were privately so astonished, so relieved, so savagely glad to be alive that if someone had proposed to bury him upside down in a bucket of horse manure they would probably have agreed it was all for the best.

Two days before the funeral Henry was asked to give a short speech, and although he began by saying he would not be able to talk, didn't think he could get the words out, was no orator, ended, of course by accepting. At the Harris, Harris and Overdene Christmas party three years ago he had made what some considered to be the funniest impromptu speech anyone had ever heard inside the office. At the University of Loughborough there were several people who went on record as saying that you could always get a laugh out of Henry. He didn't see why he shouldn't have a stab at the more serious mode of public address. After all – the man was one of his best friends, wasn't he? It was the least he could do. In one of his private talks with his late general practitioner he said: 'Look old son. It won't bring you back. It won't, you know, make up for the fact that, let's face it, I poisoned you!'

'No no no,' said Donald, 'for Christ's sake, mate. It happens.'

'No, I mean . . .' said Henry, 'I did. I poisoned you. And I'm very, very sorry I did. It was an accident but that doesn't excuse it. And the least I can do is tell them all what a great bloke you are!'

'Were,' said Donald, 'were . . .'

'Christ, mate!' said Henry. 'You see what I mean?'

He wrote his speech several times.

When it actually came to writing rather than vaguely thinking about his address, Henry found it more difficult than he had expected. He had not written much since *The Complete History of Wimbledon* and that book's rejection by ten publishers (he had still not heard from The Applecote Press, Chewton Mendip) had made him a little nervous of putting pen to paper, but he found that if he emptied his mind of everything and forced his hand to fist a biro and then forced that biro across a sheet of paper, some pretty profound and interesting thoughts resulted. He ended by writing twenty-five pages, some of which he read to Elinor late one night. There were also two longish poems in free verse, which he didn't yet feel quite ready to expose to the world. When he had finished the third page she put her head to one side and said in her cross-but-trying-to-be-helpful voice, 'I like the bit about Donald.'

'How do you mean?' said Henry. 'It's all about Donald, isn't it?'

She became assertive-in-spite-of-herself, and marching rapidly from one end of the kitchen to the other, which she always did when entrusting him with a home truth, said, 'It's not, Henry. It's mainly about you.'

'Is it?'

Henry looked at the pages of script he had written in praise of the man he had helped on the way to eternal bliss, and found this to be true. There was a very long story about him and Donald in the Rose and Thorn, a short, rather vulgar anecdote about something that had happened to Donald's wife while crossing Wimbledon Common and a boastful piece about how he, Henry, had amused some French sailors in the bar at the Mini Golf, Boulogne sur Mer. The whole thing was, he had to admit, in very dubious taste.

He started again. He decided to write out a list of Donald's good qualities. *Charity. Skill in Medicine. Standing his Round. Qualities as a Father and Wit.* But the headlines seemed to paralyse him completely. When he got down to *Punctuality* and *Considerateness as a Driver*, he decided to give up and improvise.

'Well, for God's sake,' said Elinor, 'try and make sense. You only make a fool of yourself when you try and speak in public. You were embarrassing at our wedding.'

'Was I?'

'Oh my God, yes,' said Elinor, 'you just sort of dribbled!'

Henry folded his arms over his chest. 'I might, of course,' he said, 'be overcome by emotion.'

Elinor wheeled round, a look of horror on her face. 'How do you mean?' she said.

'I may be in tears,' said Henry, 'I may just . . . you know . . . blub!'

She made the kind of face she made when tasting sour milk. 'For God's sake, Henry,' she said. 'If you do that I shall leave you.'

Henry found such moments of unpleasantness between

them almost reassuring. She had been so pleasant since Donald's death that there were times when he could not believe that he was planning to murder her. The trouble was that it seemed almost unfair to Donald not to have another go. Had the man died in vain?

He had probably been trying something far too fancy. Thallium was an Alfa Romeo among poisons, its charm being the fact that it was almost impossible to detect. But was detection such a problem? No one seemed at all interested in how poor old Donald died; he had just keeled over one night. Arfur spoke for everybody when he said, a wondering expression on his face: 'My Daddy just felled over and died!'

What was needed was something down home and businesslike. Something you could buy over the counter at a supermarket. It didn't have to be colourless, tasteless or odourless, it just had to be got, somehow or other, past Elinor's front teeth, down her oesophagus and into her digestive system, even if to do so it should be necessary to hold her down and clamp a funnel between her jaws. If there was a single reason, thought Henry, why he was once again determined to poison her, it was probably her stubborn refusal to go along with his earlier attempt. There must be something she ate that would act as a cover for paraquat or whatever he was going to use. Some particularly disgusting form of health food, some heavily unbleached flour that could be rebleached.

Bleach. He would start by looking at bleach, and then think of something to go with it. When he went to Waitrose to buy the food for their contribution to what everyone in the street was calling 'Donald's funeral breakfast' Henry spent hours browsing through the domestic cleaners, all of which sounded pretty lethal. *Domestos kills all known germs – Dead!* Their names were harsh, aggressive, Vorticist in tone – *Scour! Blast! Zap!* – and the one Henry most favoured, which seemed from looking at the label to be a sexier version of raw bleach – *Finish 'Em*. It came in a huge blue bottle on the side of which was a picture of something that looked like a bluebottle with twelve legs keeling over, while a housewife in rubber gloves looked grimly on.

There would be especial pleasure, thought Henry, in using a household cleanser against a feminist. Women like Elinor refused to channel their aggression in the direction of household germs. Keeping your house clean was now seen, probably rightly, as a plot by men to stop you doing anything more interesting. No, it was Henry who, on Saturday mornings, scrubbed the kitchen floor, wiped down the surfaces, hoovered the carpets, poured bleach down the lavatories and sinks. But now, a few litres of Finish 'Em would be put to the service of a more crucial domestic task, the elimination of Mrs Farr.

The trouble was – how to conceal the taste? Even hot sweet tea, a favourite refuge for poisoners, would not sweeten the flavour of Finish 'Em and in order to kill Elinor he would need at least half a bottle. And – even assuming he could persuade her to drink it – wasn't it, well, out of the ordinary to find half a litre of bleach in someone's stomach? It was not possible. She would have to eat a bucket of chicken vindaloo to get the stuff down her and, although there had been publicly expressed doubts about the kitchens of the 'Tandoori' Tandoori, Wimbledon, they hadn't, as far as Henry knew, got around to using bleach to liven up their menu.

He had decided to give up, had, indeed, spent several hours trying to think of one thing he actually liked about Elinor when, two days before the funeral, she looked up from a quiche Lorraine ('Billykins says it's about all she could face') and barked: 'What are we going to drink?'

'Uh?'

'At Donald's thrash,' said Elinor, 'we're going to have to drink something. I know it's awful but what? People do like alcohol at a funeral.'

Henry goggled at her.

There had been much discussion in the street on this very topic. Dave Sprott the dentist had suggested a barrel of draught Guinness. Sam Baker QC (almost) from number 113a had suggested that he 'bring along a few bottles of my Australian Chardonnay' but no one could face the prospect of being talked through another glass of uniquely flinty, resonantly expressive Murray River Chardonnay by Sam Baker QC (almost). Vera Loomis, the ninety-two-year-old who lived at number 92 and was known for some reason as Got All the Things There Then? had offered plum wine or home-brewed lager and Susan Doyle, who was reported to watch *News at Ten* while her husband pleasured her, had suggested lemonade shandy. Detective Inspector Rush from 38, known to Henry as Neighbourhood Watch, was of the opinion that alcohol at funerals was disrespectful. He stopped Henry, as he so often did, in the street one afternoon and said, as he so often did,

'Drinking and driving, Henry, wreck lives.'

Someone said that they had heard him suggest that all guests should be breathalysed at the door, for Rush had the reputation locally for being a more than usually dedicated policeman. Henry had been involved in many of these discussions, had indeed had a pint with Dave Sprott to debate the issue, but when Elinor put the question to him he saw, suddenly, how he could not only perform a helpful, neighbourly act, and another last tribute, but also serve something that would, in all senses of the word, Finish 'Em.

'Punch,' he said, throatily, 'I'll make a punch.'

CHAPTER SEVENTEEN

Henry started making the punch the evening before the funeral. He got grape concentrate, sugar, cooking brandy and a large bottle of bleach and put the mixture into a large saucepan Elinor used for making marmalade. He didn't boil it, for fear the bleach might evaporate; after the mixture was warm he added twenty bottles of Yugoslav Riesling, two bottles of Guinness and a pound and a half of oranges cut into segments.

Then, reasoning that a little bit of bleach wouldn't harm him, he sipped, nervously, at a teaspoonful of the mixture. It tasted unequivocally of bleach. In fact though, Henry argued to himself, punch usually tasted of bleach. He was simply responding to the fact that he knew there was bleach in the mixture. He was thinking bleach. His toast in the morning tasted of bleach, his pint at the Rose tasted bleached. He would simply add more sugar.

He added three more packets of brown sugar. It still tasted of bleach.

The beauty of it being a funeral was that no one ever complained about the quality of the food and drink at a funeral. You ate what you were given and tried to look as if you couldn't really bear to think about food. Even when things warmed up, it wasn't really done to comment on what was provided. There was, Henry had noticed, a specially reverent way of saying 'thank you' when accepting a cheese and tomato sandwich at a funeral reception and he did not see why people should develop critical faculties just because they were swigging back a wine glass containing a fair quantity of the domestic bleach known as Finish 'Em.

The apparent disadvantage of the scheme – the fact that he was going to end up poisoning not only Elinor and Donald but also most of the inhabitants of Maple Drive, including what remained of Donald's family (Arfur was notoriously fond of 'Daddy's 'Ine') was outweighed by its brilliantly direct character.

One of the main problems about person-to-person poisoning, Henry had found, was its very intimacy. You had to go to such trouble to persuade the subject to accept the poison and when (or rather, in his case *if*) you managed it, your very intimacy made it all too clear to everyone that you were the one who was slipping them the doctored crumble, the dodgy spaghetti bolognese or the potato salad unusually rich in mineral salts. This way, it was going to be fairly obvious that someone had emptied a bottle of bleach into the punch but, since Henry could not possibly have a motive for murdering the whole of Maple Drive (as far as the police were concerned, anyway), it would be relatively easy for him to gasp in horror and dismay and to take the Wimbledon CID around the places where he had left the bowl of punch unattended. He intended leaving the bowl in as many places easily accessible to a psychopath as possible.

As he mixed away happily (Elinor had retired to bed early) Henry began to see the headlines. WIMBLEDON POISONER – PSYCHOPATH MAY STRIKE AGAIN SAY POLICE! He, of course, would have to take a glass or two, enough to make him moderately sick, but that would be a small price to pay for finishing off Elinor, not to mention Mr and Mrs Is-the-Mitsubishi-Scratched-Yet and Nazi Who Escaped Justice at Nuremberg.

THE BLEACH PRANKSTER: NEW FACTS! They would never trace it to him. Even if he was noticed forcing glasses on to his wife, no one would suspect. Because one of the beauties of this crime was his apparent (or indeed real) lack of motive. Not many people murdered their wives out of dislike. They usually did it for more obvious, sordid reasons; they wanted money, they had fallen in love with someone else or lost their temper. Henry's dislike was a more rational, delicate emotion than that. It was much more, he thought as he

116

moved the boiling pan off the stove and on to the floor, trying to ignore the unholy smell of bleach that came off it as it sloshed against the sides of the vessel, that he had simply woken up one morning and realized, to use a phrase a friend had used about someone else's wife, 'what he had got hold of'. And once he had realized that . . .

To the left of the gas ring was a note. For a moment, Henry thought it would be another few thousand words on the subject of his obscene masculinity, but to his surprise he saw it began 'Dear Elinor . . .' A lover. She had got a lover! Well, this made his activity all the more comprehensible, didn't it? He was picking the letter up when he noticed that it was in Elinor's own handwriting.

Dear Elinor,
  Mean that! Because you are dear! Listen! Listen!

Henry detected the influence of therapy here.

Do not despair! You are Elinor! Talented cook, linguist, dancer, mother, opera singer and interior designer! Love yourself! Doesn't Irma Cauther have something to say about this?

(Probably.)

Oh, cast off the glooms! Be! Be womanly! Escape from the heavy hands of Patriarchy! But there is one, not far from here, who feels for you as a woman! There is one who would know you, is there not? One who would speak your name and seeks to know the woman in you! Cast off the glooms!

Really she was getting off lightly with a few glasses of bleach. If there was any justice in the world he should really decapitate her with a spade on Wimbledon Common in full view of her therapy class. *Pour encourager les autres.* And what was all this about one not far from here who knew the woman in her? This sounded, to Henry, dangerously like illicit bonking. And the not far from here made it pretty certain it was a neighbour. He screwed up the note into small pieces and looked around for others. There were, as far as he could see, none. When the punch had cooled he took it out to the garden shed, within easy reach of Tibbles who, since her dose of chicken thallium, seemed to have improved in every conceivable way, and went upstairs to the bedroom. Elinor had woken up and was trying on a black dress that looked more like a kind of solo tent than anything else. With it, she had chosen a pair of black sneakers and a huge black bracelet. She was looking at herself in the full-length mirror by the side of the bed, pulling great lumps out of her stomach and grimacing at her own image.

'I'm fat!' she said, as Henry came in.

'I know,' said Henry, loosening his trousers, 'so am I.'

'God!' said Elinor, and again, 'God!'

Henry did not wash his face or brush his teeth. Instead he pulled off his green boxer shorts, given to him by Maisie last Christmas, and farted in what he hoped was a reasonably light-hearted way. Elinor did not bother to respond. Instead, she said, 'Donald's death has made me think!'

'Has it?' said Henry.

'Yes, darling,' said Elinor.

Why is she calling me darling? thought Henry. What does she want? Did she see me pour the Finish 'Em into the punch?

'I know we're going through a bad patch at the moment.'

Not at all. I think we're developing along the right lines, Elinor. I think there are many positive aspects to our relationship at the present time, not the least positive of which is now out in the shed in a large copper bowl!

'I know sometimes you're almost brutally male, Henry. And unresponsive. But in a way I think this may be a defence mechanism. Because underneath . . .'

A long, long way underneath.

'. . . you are probably quite sensitive. But you are out of touch with that human part of yourself. You've grown a protective skin, a sort of . . . carapace of crudeness to help you deal with the world. And at the moment you've become

118

that outer self. You have no room for good and gentle feelings. Whereas I – '

I am opera singer, talented linguist, cook, mother, feminist!

'I have feelings of tenderness towards people. People I
meet as part of my role as mother. People from nearby. There
is someone – I'm not going to say his name, but there is
someone who I think . . . admires me.'

Henry goggled at her. This was, presumably, a pathetic,
almost touching illusion on her part. He decided not to
pander to it by asking for the admirer's name.

'It's helped me through this depression, actually. And yes,
I have been depressed. I don't deny that. I don't deny that
I have some problems of my own,' she went on, although
from the tone of her voice it was clear she had no idea
what those problems might be. None the less the brisk, no-
nonsense manner implied that once she had found what, if
any, they might be, like the good feminist she was, she
would be out there dealing with them. In fact she might even
just dream up a few to even up the score a little. It must
be difficult, thought Henry, when you were living with an
obscenely masculine, fat, not particularly talented patriarch
like Henry. Especially if you were a quote talented linguist
gourmet cook and opera singer unquote.

'What problems could you possibly have?' said Henry.
'You're a feminist. Feminists by definition do not have problems. They are simply corrupted by patriarchy, aren't they?
All we have to do is to do away with fathers and we're fine,
aren't we? Isn't that the idea?'

'Don't be silly, Henry!' said Elinor, in the style of a primary
teacher, which once, years ago, she had been. 'We're thinking about our problems. Aren't we?'

She sat up very straight on the side of the bed and continued to address him as if he were sitting on a mat in the Top
Infants, wrestling with difficult, dangerous new concepts
like add-ups and take-aways and the precise whereabouts of
Australia.

'We're thinking about how we can be better as a couple

and live in harmony as man and woman. Male and female principle. I believe, you see, that Womb and Phallus must be reconciled in some way!'

'We could do a project on it,' said Henry. 'We could cut out pictures of penises and wombs and – '

'Henry!' said Elinor, in a voice that suggested that if he didn't shut up he might get a clip round the ear. Then she continued in the sort of I'll-be-reasonable-if-you'll-be-reasonable tones adopted by the Russian government to, say, the Lithuanians.

'You seek to control,' she went on, 'it's perfectly natural. It's a very masculine thing. It goes with a whole package of your attitudes. You're very reactionary, politically. You are racist, as poor darling Donald was. And you are frightened of the world. Frightened of the liberation movements. The movements that seek to free black people, American Indians, Nicaragua and so on. Whereas I seek to go with the flow. To change and grow. To progress, Henry!'

Why was it, thought Henry, that Elinor felt so in tune with the poor and the oppressed of the world? And why was it that this deep empathy with the hard done by inspired her to give him such a hard time? Henry had absolutely no consistent views about anything that did not directly concern him; in his opinion, such views were a rather revolting luxury. Why . . . but Elinor was talking again.

'I was reading this book the other day. About this urge to control experienced by males. Men seek control over women apparently. Whereas women – '

'Seek total world domination!' said Henry, under his breath.

'What?'

'Nothing, dear!'

Elinor looked at him suspiciously. 'The world arms race, for example. Is a product of this urge to dominate, isn't it? And if you look around at the world and try and find the women in positions of power, you have to say, where are they? Where are they?'

Henry started to mutter, into the duvet, the names of women in positions of power. 'Mrs Thatcher,' he hissed, 'Mrs Gandhi. Golda Meir!' OK two of those were dead but they had certainly caused a lot of trouble when alive, hadn't they? When he couldn't think of any more women in government, he added a few authors, actresses, athletes – 'Jane Fonda,' he muttered, 'Chrissie Evert, Dusty Springfield, Adriana Rich!' They were all women, weren't they? They were all doing all right. They were doing a lot better than him. 'Ella Fitzgerald,' he mouthed, 'Kate Millett, Nancy Reagan, Benazir Bhutto . . .'

'What?'

'Nothing, darling.'

Elinor turned to him and laid a hand on his head. 'I just felt,' she said, 'since Donald had that terrible thing happen to him, we have been a bit closer. The horror has brought us together. We haven't dumped so much. We've accepted each other for what we are.'

Talented cook, linguist and opera singer and fat, patriarchal slob.

Henry climbed under the duvet. 'I think,' he said 'I feel – '

These two words brought Elinor out in a kind of rash of solicitude. She swung her whole body round and fixed her eyes on Henry's face as if he were a dying spy with some vital secret to impart.

'I feel,' said Henry, 'that – '

Elinor nodded vigorously. This was clearly the way to get her to shut up and listen.

'I feel,' he went on, 'as a man – '

What did he feel as a man? Nothing much really, apart from pretty fucking confused. He felt he probably didn't know what feelings were any more. What feelings were OK and what were obscenely patriarchal and what merely irrelevant. He had more or less given up feeling, thought Henry, when his mother got started on him.

'Yes,' Elinor was saying, 'yes?'

'Well . . . if we could . . . share more . . .'

'Yes?' said Elinor.

'If once or twice,' he looked up at her soulfully, 'we could share a . . . drink, say. You know? Get really drunk together. Have a few glasses of beer or Scotch or . . . you know . . . punch! The way we used to!'

Elinor smiled, a tight, maternal smile. And patted his hand. 'I know,' she said, 'I know . . .'

She wouldn't have to get very drunk, thought Henry. Four or five glasses of Henry's Stomach Cleanser should do it. Finish 'Em. Finish 'Em all. Her, Dave Sprott the dentist and Sam Baker QC (almost), Inspector Rush, 'Neighbourhood Watch', and Mr and Mrs Is-the-Mitsubishi-Scratched-Yet and Nazi Who Escaped Justice at Nuremberg. By tomorrow night Wimbledon was going to be an easier, cleaner, emptier place in which to live.

CHAPTER EIGHTEEN

It was, to start off with anyway, a moving and impressive funeral. It was, as Vera 'Got All the Things There Then?' Loomis, the ninety-two-year-old from 92 pointed out, the best funeral that she had ever attended. It was, she said, adding that she had been to over fifty funerals in the UK alone, the funeral of a lifetime.

She was, she told everyone, particularly impressed with Henry's speech.

At one stage Dave Sprott the northern dentist had suggested they hire a black charabanc and people in Maple Drive, used now to his carefully preserved northern humour, had managed deliberately weak smiles of the kind they managed when Sprott backed them into a corner at someone's Christmas party.

But as Henry remarked to Elinor as the cortège moved away from Darby's, the undertaker in the village, a charabanc might have been a more decent way of moving the extraordinarily large number of people who turned out for what Sprott referred to as 'the big goodbye' for Donald Templeton MD. There were so many limousines and lesser limousines and cars in attendance on the lesser limousines that the queue of cars stretched from Volley's Pizza and Pasta House down to the Polka Children's Theatre on the frontiers of Wimbledon. Some of the delayed motorists were distinctly lacking in respect, one going as far as to say that if he were going to get buried he'd have a bit more consideration for other road users.

In spite of this, to start off with anyway, everyone felt the event was going well. Mr Darby himself, a professionally miserable man in his late sixties, handed Billykins down from the car and into the chapel and, as the mourners crowded in after her, as politely unaggressive as only mourners can be, there was a real, though muted feeling of loss in the air. Inside the chapel there were white flowers, piled almost to the ceiling and, in a brown box a little to the right of a bargain-basement cross, was Donald.

The first sight of the coffin made Henry feel distinctly uneasy.

'Look, Donald,' he said, 'I really am incredibly sorry about all of this.'

'Mate,' said Donald, 'we've all got to go sometime. I'm going today. Very soon you'll be on your way as well.'

'Sure,' said Henry.

'And so,' said Donald, 'will all these people.'

'Very, very, very soon,' said Henry.

Billykins had decided to 'dispense with the burial service as such'. Which, everyone in the street had agreed, was a bold and generous gesture on Donald's behalf.

'What does it mean?' she had asked Henry, a day or so after Donald's death, 'what does it mean?'

'Indeed,' said Henry feelingly, 'what does it mean?'

She had chosen three hymns: 'Say Not the Struggle Nought Availeth', 'Ye Holy Angels Bright' and 'Now Thank We All Our God'. And at the cemetery the vicar, a man who looked as if he needed far more consolation than he would ever be capable of dispensing, had agreed to say a few words before Henry's address. Henry's address, Billykins had said, would be the centrepiece of the occasion. Much, much better to have the sincere words of a family friend than some vicar who didn't really know Donald.

In Henry's hands was a crumpled piece of paper on which was written: 'Skill at medicine 2 mins. Wit and tolerance 3 mins. Father and husband 8 mins. Golfing ability? Tennis serve? Value of house? Poss. tell Biarritz anecdote here (too crude???). Remember: don't be tasteless, Henry!' Lower down the page he had scribbled a quotation from Shelley: 'Life stains the white radiance of Eternity'. This, as Henry looked at it, the piped organ music swelling through the chapel, seemed to sum up the complete irrelevance of English literature. 'Stains the white radiance of Eternity', eh? What did that mean when it came down to it? How many pints would that buy you? In case of trouble, underneath that, Henry had written – 'Death is Nature's way of telling us to slow down'. And, below that – 'Death comes as the end. The everlasting friend. Sophocles.'

In his researches at Wimbledon Public Library he had not been able to find any really cheering quotations on the subject of death. There were a few of the I-am-not-really-dead-but-just-popped-out-for-a-packet-of-fags sort of lines, which all went on a little long for Henry's taste, and quite a number of death-as-a-viable-alternative-to-life stuff, much of it from the fathers of the early church. Henry had thought of taking this line, but the trouble was, he found, one became almost too jolly at Donald's expense, the implication being that he, the jammy bastard, was well off out of it, while they, the real sufferers, were condemned to a few more years of the horrors of living in Wimbledon.

> The worms crawl in
> The worms crawl out
> The worms play poker on your snout
> Be merry my friends be merry! (Trad.)

was also to be found on Henry's scrappy sheets of paper. Next to it he had written: 'Use this if golf joke goes well!' And on the next page a long, uplifting sentence from a French sociologist, the gist of which was that dying was something we needed a lot of help with. The French sociologist, whose sentence was more like a paragraph, went on to argue that death was something that we needed to share – it needed to be seen publicly. The dying man should be surrounded by his friends and family, should make, as it were, a day of it. To Henry, the idea of being cheered on as you croaked, by Elinor, Mr and Mrs Is-the-Mitsubishi-Scratched-Yet, his mother, her mother, Maisie and anyone else with a few hours to spare was almost completely repul-

sive. But Donald, to judge from the size of the congregation
– they were three deep in the aisles and old Mr Donovan
from 21b ('I fought two wars for you lot') had to wait outside
the double doors – Donald was not experiencing what the
French sociologist called the Lonely Death. He was having,
rather, the Oversubscribed Death.

At the end of the second hymn – Ye – Holy – Angels –
Bright – Who-o-o-o wait at God's right hand! – Henry found
himself being tugged forward by Elinor. He looked up and
saw the vicar carrying a book that looked more like an illus-
trated part work from W. H. Smith's than Holy Writ.

'Not yet . . .' he hissed.

'Donald Templeton,' the vicar began, 'was a man loved,
and I mean loved, by all who knew him.'

Which did not, thought Henry, include you, chum.

'Those who followed his career in television, from the
role of humble assistant film editor, up through the features
department of Granada Television, through to his incredibly
successful period as editor of the BBC magazine programme,
Holiday '76, knew him to be resourceful, keen, and deeply
aware, not only of the problems of travel – his chosen speciality – but also of such things as cuisine and interior design.'

Henry looked along the row. Billykins's jaw sagged under
her veil. Most of the other mourners were listening to this
with the same rapt attention they might have accorded a
vaguely accurate account of Donald's life. It didn't really
matter, their expressions seemed to say, he might as well
have been a short-order cook or a deep-sea diver or a male
prostitute. He was just another wally like anyone else. In
some ways, thought Henry, the man with whom Donald had
been confused seemed to have had a better time of it.

'Later,' went on the vicar, 'Donald Templeton showed himself a skilful cross-country skier, on and off piste, a witty
raconteur and an enthusiastic do-it-yourselfer. But, when we
think of him today, which I can assure you we do, we think
of those left behind. Of Norman, of Jean-Paul and of little
Beatrice who feels this as deeply as anyone, including the

Sussex branch of the family who, because of the railway accident you all know about, cannot be with us here today. Donald Templeton – '

Whoever he may be.

'Smiles down at us today. His conversion to Islam, his rejection of that faith and the subsequent, troubled period, when the disease had made him all but unrecognizable to any but a few close friends, are things we may wish to pass over today, but – '

Here the vicar raised his eyes to the congregation and a look of panic passed across his face. Perhaps, thought Henry, there was another Donald Templeton. Perhaps . . . But whatever the reason, whether it was that everyone had been so busy reassuring everyone that no one had bothered to talk to the crematorium, whether they had got the time wrong, or whether the vicar had simply had a brainstorm, he now, you could tell, was dimly aware that he had not given an exemplary performance. Whatever the reason may have been, the vicar had no direction in which to go but forward.

'But,' he said, his voice challenging his audience to rise and refute him, 'death, as someone said, is the great leveller. And in my father's house are many mansions. And if ever a man sleeps well after a day's work done well that man is, and I pray God give him rest, Donald Templeton!'

Here, overcome by a mixture of shame, embarrassment and some genuine fellow feeling for whoever it was inside the box some yards to his left, the vicar turned to the coffin and said, in a Shakespearian voice, 'Goodbye, Donald!'

At which point Billykins, perhaps mindful of the more glamorous, civilized life she could have had as the wife of the editor of *Holiday '76*, burst into tears and was comforted by Elinor.

Somehow or other, the vicar got off stage, and disappeared behind the altar, perhaps off to hurl himself into the flames that would shortly be consuming Donald. It seemed, thought Henry, the least he could do. As he left, Henry, pushed from behind by Elinor, crept up in the direction of the coffin.

CHAPTER NINETEEN

Afterwards he blamed the vicar. Everyone blamed the vicar who, fortunately for him, was nowhere to be found. But Henry knew, however much he might blame the vicar, it was really his fault.

In picking up his notes, he glanced over in Donald's direction. And it was only then that he understood that Donald was actually dead. Up to that moment, Henry had not been quite able to understand the connection between the chicken *à la* thallium he had accidentally served to his old friend and the thing everyone was calling a 'tragic loss' or a 'shocking bereavement'.

At any moment, he had felt, Donald would crop up somewhere in the suburb. He had simply gone missing, somewhere between the Rose and Thorn, the library, the swimming pool or any of the other places where suburban fathers waited for their children. But now he realized with a sense of horror that Donald was actually in the box. That, over there, was Donald. And that woman in the front row, looking up at him severely, was Elinor. It seemed unfair.

The silence in the chapel, broken only by Billykins sobbing, lengthened. Should he, thought Henry, make some mention of the ghastly mistake that had been made? Should he just throw away his speech and talk, as one should, from the heart? Yes, thought Henry, I will. He crumpled the paper in his hands into a ball and fixed the congregation with a stern, preacher's eye.

'I didn't recognize,' said Henry, 'the man that has been described here today.'

This, he thought, went down pretty well.

'I don't know which Donald Templeton he was talking about,' went on Henry, 'but it wasn't my Donald Templeton.'

I'm not saying that that Donald Templeton wasn't a nice bloke. Fair play to him. I'm sorry he's obviously in the same situation that Donald finds himself. But no way. No way was my Donald Templeton the producer of *Holiday '76*. I can't think how this . . . cock-up has occurred and I'm deeply distressed by it. Distressed but also, in a way, glad. Because it shows us, I think, that death is a universal thing. It happens to us all, even if we are a producer on *Holiday '76*, whatever we are, however famous and glorious and so on, death comes for us. We are all going to die. Fairly soon. Today, tomorrow, this afternoon. Pretty soon anyway. Pretty fucking soon!'

He had said 'fuck'. At a funeral. He had sworn. At a funeral. Oh my Christ! Oh my sweet Jesus! Oh God! And it had been going so well. He had had them. There, in the palm of his hand. He had been direct, forceful, tough, compassionate, blunt, and then he had said the F word. Why had he done this? He seemed to be still talking and Billykins, doubled up with grief, was sobbing even harder. She looked, thought Henry, like someone who has just run the 800 metres rather faster than they had intended.

'Donald,' Henry was saying, 'was a doctor. He was a doctor. Of Medicine. Not of Law, not of English, not, thank God, of Sociology. But of that art of healing which we all know that his widow, Mrs Donald, needs so much as do we all after the scene that we have here witnessed today. Yes – '

He was back on course now. 'Yes, Donald was a doctor. Not a brilliant doctor. Not a high flyer. Not always, well, right! Often, as we know, to our cost, completely, hopelessly wrong in diagnostic terms. Way off the mark. Quite frequently.'

Billykins gave a juddering sob and started to bang her head against her knees. Elinor was signalling something to him. To stop, perhaps? But Henry couldn't stop. Thinking about Donald in that box, he knew he had to go on, to try and find, in the middle of all this gibberish that was coming out of his mouth, one coherent sentence that would stand as a tribute to someone he had, yes he had thought, was a bloody nice bloke. A wee bit of a racist –

'A wee bit of a racist,' he was saying, *out loud*, 'a wee bit of a racist. But who, I may say, when it comes down to it, and it does come down to it, isn't? Who isn't, in England, these days, fed up to the back teeth with hearing about Mad Mullahs chopping off people's hands for blasphemy and – '

Why was he talking about Mullahs? He must get back to the matter in hand. He found he was looking straight at Sam Baker QC (almost) whose arms were folded and whose face bore a look of intense, sceptical concentration, as if he was listening to his opposing advocate.

'Lawyers,' said Henry, 'like doctors, are the kind of people who live in Wimbledon and this is the kind of person Donald Templeton was. Not, as I say, a lawyer – '

Sam Baker QC (almost) shifted elaborately in his seat. 'But a doctor. And people like Donald, as I say, are used to slurs that are cast at them. They're not ashamed of being English, of being the people they are, of being the quiet, hard-working middle-class people who make up the backbone of England and indeed of America and – '

He caught sight of Sylvie le Perroquet from 109 (Non Merci ce Soir Sylvie). She looked almost frenzied with concentration.

'Of France. But France, America, England, these aren't the issue here. What is the issue is something that unites all those three countries, something that they all have in common, something that is as true of New York as it is of Wimbledon. I am talking, of course, about the situation which Donald finds himself in, the . . . er . . . dead situation.'

They had gone quiet again. He could pull it back. He knew he could. He found he was looking straight into the eyes of 'Neighbourhood Watch'. Inspector Rush normally struck Henry as a dull little man but today his eyes seemed as bright as a squirrel's.

'But death, even in suspicious circumstances, is something that creates a bond between us. Because all of us, of course, are united by death. Death, as someone said, is no laughing matter. It's not a subject for comedy. Except, of course, in the sense that we, all of us here today, English people here today to mourn a loved friend and colleague . . .'

Loved friend and colleague. That was the sort of thing, wasn't it?

'Here to mourn his passing but also, of course, yes, also to have, well, to have a laugh. To laugh because as Sophocles said – laughter is our only response, sometimes, to things. We laugh because the grief is too great, too deep, and that laughter can be as profound and meaningful an emotion as the tears that sometimes come with it, although they come, of course, out of amusement and not out of sorrow. I think comedy is as vital and meaningful as tragedy and I think Donald, if he were alive, which he isn't, would agree, because Donald, like all of us, like all of the English, whether from the north – '

Henry caught sight of Dave Sprott's grey hair and glasses bobbing up and down like some toy hung in the back window of a saloon car.

'Or the south, was an Englishman. Yes. He was an English doctor and I think there are people in the world who think such people are not, intrinsically, interesting. They would rather hear about Aborigines or people who have it away with gorillas because they don't care about the ordinary, decent people. They don't give a fucking stuff about Donald Templeton.'

He had said fuck again. He had said fuck, twice, at a funeral. He glanced down at his notes and caught sight of the words 'Death is Nature's way.'

'Death,' said Henry, 'is Nature's way!'

Nature's way of what? The rest of the quotation was obscured by a fold in the paper. He looked along the row of faces in front of him. They were now devoid of any clue that might guide him. If he could think of a way to stop this he would. But like a man at a party who simply cannot leave, he could not think of a reason why he should step back into the congregation. Was this his punishment? thought Henry.

'I used to drink with Donald,' he said, 'in a pub called the Rose and Thorn. Not a bad pub. A place where you could go to get away from the wife, the "old rat" as it were, although of course Billykins . . .'

Billykins! That was her name! Of course!

'Billykins and he were as devoted a couple as you will find anywhere and Donald loved her with an almost childlike devotion, could not bear to be parted from her, followed her almost everywhere, almost to the extent of hampering her freedom of movement – '

Elinor was looking at him. She seemed to be trying to say something. Stop, presumably. This was all very well. But how did you stop? Once you'd started how did you stop?

'Look,' said Henry, making one last, desperate effort to get this speech airborne, 'look. Donald was my mate. And if Donald was here today, which in a sense he is, although he's . . . er . . . in that box . . .'

Billykins gave the kind of wail familiar to connoisseurs of Greek tragedy. 'Ay ay ay ay!' she said, and then, 'Aieee-ou!!' It was, thought Henry, a primal grief that seemed to have no place in Wimbledon. His speech, ragged and confused though it obviously was, was having some effect. Christ, he was in the box and Henry was talking about him, a man talking about a man. It was simple.

'Look, he's in the box and here I am talking about him as a man, which I am and Donald was, if you hadn't noticed. A man. Yes, one of those phallic monsters, one of those patriarchal blokes that feminism – and Donald of course was no feminist – yes, an ordinary English, forty-year-old male. And what did he want? Really. With his outdated attitudes and his, well, frankly, penis, what did he want? With his mortgage and his little horizons and his contempt for all the fucking rubbish that gets talked these days?'

He had said fuck three times. But they were listening to him. They were actually listening to him. They were leaning

132

forward in their seats, mouths open, hanging on his every word. Henry didn't care any more.

'He wanted,' he said, 'what any man wants anywhere on the globe. A loyal wife, a bit of land to call his, a job that put food on the table, a child that would grow up to love him and that he would raise properly. He didn't want to go to prison or be involved in a war, although I'm sure if it had come to that he would have been on the right side, although, as I should make clear, you never fucking know what the right side is until a long time after. Right? It isn't Tehran though, is it? It might be, it might just be that life in Wimbledon has developed to a higher pitch than anywhere else in the globe. What I am trying to say – '

What was he trying to say? Whatever it was he felt they wanted him to say it. To say it and then leave the platform.

'What I am trying to say is that no human life form, not even Donald Templeton, is completely beneath contempt!'

He realized, as he said this, that it sounded incredibly rude. He did not mean it to be.

'Look mate,' said Donald, 'go on through. Tell it like it is. Go on.'

'I mean by that,' said Henry, 'that I sometimes feel beneath contempt. I'm the sort of ordinary husband and father with not very many views about the world who's led a very simple quiet life and wanted to do good and brave and dangerous things but just never got the chance. And Donald was like that, I think. He was a romantic, you know? He was a wild fucking romantic. He was a man who dared, who wanted more. And I think that's why I liked him, because like him I look up at the sky above Wimbledon and I say "Oh my God. Oh my God, you bastard, I love you!" '

Henry found he was pointing, dramatically at the coffin. They're with me, he thought, they're getting my drift at last.

'That's me and you in there,' he said, in a kind of shriek, 'that's us. That's the next day of our lives. Let's try, shall we, and let that bit that lurked in Donald Templeton out of us. Let's be wild and ridiculous and free, shall we, in memory

133

of him? Let's do it for Donald. Let's go for it. Because he's dead and we'll be dead soon and I think we owe him something, ladies and gentlemen. I am speaking the truth of my heart here because underneath this rather boring exterior I care. I'm not quite sure what I care about but I care. And one of the things I care about that isn't Nicaragua or Poland or anywhere else but right here and part of the country I love and that I am afraid I don't want to see change too much is people like Donald Templeton. Because Donald Templeton is me! I'm in that box with him, feeling what he's feeling, going through what he's fucking going through, man. Thanks Donald! Thanks for everything.'

Here Henry raised his arm in a kind of quasi-Fascist salute in the direction of the coffin and said, voice husky with emotion, 'It's your round, old son!'

Suddenly his eyes were blinded with tears. Convulsed with sobs, he made his way back to his seat where, to his surprise, Elinor, instead of hitting him in the face, put her arms round him. Other people in the chapel were sobbing too. Dave Sprott was leaning forward, his hands over his face, wailing like a child who had walked into his surgery for the first time. Even Sam Baker QC (almost) was white and nervous-looking and his professionally immobile upper lip was dangerously near to quivering.

It was not what Henry had meant to say. Or rather, it was not what he had meant to say at Donald's funeral. But it was, he felt, as he rose to his feet and the strains of 'Now Thank We All Our God' began to filter through to the chapel, something that needed saying.

CHAPTER TWENTY

'Come and get it!' murmured Henry under his breath as he carried the bowl of punch into Donald's house. 'Finish 'Em! This should help you forget your troubles!'

To give it some more go, he had added some milk and a carton of orange juice as well as a small plastic container of something called Kleeneezee. It was now the colour of strong tea.

No one actually mentioned his speech, but Dave Sprott grasped his hand and said: 'I know how you feel.'

Billykins just stared at him as if he was a creature from another planet. Only Elinor, when he had put the punch next to the glasses in the hall, barked, *sotto voce*: 'How could you do that, Henry?'

'I'm sorry,' said Henry, 'I was just very upset.'

'It was embarrassing,' went on Elinor.

'Have a drink!' said Henry.

'No,' said Elinor, 'I couldn't.'

'I'm having one!' said Henry.

She set her jaw at him. Over in the corner, Billykins, her head still between her knees, was moaning something. Henry caught the words '. . . awful . . .' and '. . . end the nightmare . . .' but whether she was talking about him or the vicar or Donald was unclear.

'You said you would have a drink!' said Henry.

'I won't!' hissed Elinor. 'I couldn't!'

Then she scuffed her foot on the carpet. An expression appeared on her face that at first Henry could not identify. As she spoke he realized with some surprise, that it was doubt.

'Oh, I don't know,' she said, 'at least you spoke out.'

'Yes!' said Henry.

Why is she saying this? What does she want?

'Grief,' said Elinor, 'is so buried with us, isn't it?'

'Yes!' said Henry.

She gave him a searching glance. 'We repress our feelings, we bundle up into a ball and don't talk about how we really feel. Deep down you probably do care, as you were saying today. Deep down you do care about the environment. About what we're doing to whales and dolphins and the North Sea and the inner cities, and the whole unleaded petrol thing.'

Why bring unleaded petrol into this? thought Henry. I have not formulated a view on unleaded petrol.

'What matters,' said Elinor, 'in anyone, is a spark of caring. Just something that tells you they're still alive. That they're still there. That other people can, well . . . touch them. Don't you think?'

Henry narrowed his eyes. He felt more than usually trapped.

'You feel threatened by my feminism, for example. You feel frightened by my growth as a woman. You feel . . .'

'I feel . . .'

Elinor stiffened with attention.

'I feel . . . frightened by you!'

'What about me frightens you, Henry?' said Elinor, laying a hand on his arm. 'Is it me, my physical presence as a woman, my needs and powers as a mother? Or are you frightened of me as an intellectual?'

'I'm frightened of you as a . . . thing,' said Henry, 'by the way you look at me, by the space you take up. By you. When I hear your step on the path I . . . I just cower!'

Elinor threw back her head and gave a braying, mannish laugh.

'Oh, Henry,' she said, 'you are funny!'

And she cuffed him, amiably, about the shoulder. Henry found this curiously erotic.

He looked around for Maisie. She had been very quiet during the service, although a few days before she had been heard asking what people usually ate at funerals and if there was usually a lot of it. Eventually he saw her in the garden with a whole bowl of rice salad and what looked like a new garden trowel. Black did not seem to have its customary slimming effect on Maisie's figure. She looked, if anything, bigger.

Over in the corner Dave Sprott was, to use his own words, 'settling in' to the punch. Next to him, Inspector Rush stood, glass in hand, peering at it suspiciously. But then Inspector Rush peered at everything suspiciously. Even small children on tricycles. Sprott took a sip, shook his head violently and started to bang himself on the back of the head.

'Wow!' he said. 'Wowza! Got a kick to it, eh?' Mrs Is-the-Mitsubishi-Scratched-Yet, a thin, girlish, fluffy woman, in an even fluffier mood than usual, grinned up at Henry girlishly. 'What have you put in this, Henry?' she said. 'Paint-stripper?'

Henry was beginning to have second thoughts about the punch. What had possessed him? He didn't want to poison the entire population of Maple Drive, did he? Well, at least not in a way that would lead so directly to him. He wasn't even sure any more that he wanted to poison anyone. But as so often in the murdering game, it was a bit late for doubts.

'Let me try it,' said Henry. 'I left it out in the front garden this morning. I hope no one's interfered with it!'

He sounded, he thought, like a character in a Victorian melodrama. Several people, including, he was concerned to note, Inspector Rush, were looking at him oddly. He sipped a glass.

It tasted of almost nothing but bleach.

'I think,' Sprott was saying, 'it has quite a resonant, flinty finish!'

Sam Baker QC (almost) was rolling the punch around his glass and wincing at it. He introduced a minute amount into his mouth and rinsed it around his gums.

'Extraordinary!' he said. 'A very positive nose and plenty

of body. It reminds me of a New World wine, aged in the barrel. With a hint of . . .'

'Bleach!' said Dave Sprott.

Everybody laughed.

'Actually,' said Henry, 'if there is anything wrong with it I don't think we should drink it. I left it out in the garden.'

'And put a rat in it!' said Sam Baker QC (almost), accenting as he always did the concrete noun in the sentence. Did he do this, thought Henry, because he favoured anything that might possibly be regarded as evidence? Was it a tic, acquired through long afternoons in the Court of Chancery, where the only way of enlivening sentences might be to stress the wrong word? Or was it simply that Sam Baker QC (almost) was (as usual) trying to make you feel awkward?

'Elinor, love,' said Henry, 'you try it!'

'No no no,' said Elinor, 'it tastes like bleach!'

Sprott drained his glass and smacked his lips. 'It goes down a treat after a while,' he said, in his carefully preserved northern accent. 'It has a nicely balanced quality of well-orchestrated fruit. What have you put in it, Henry?'

'Bleach!' said Sam Baker QC (almost). Everyone (apart from Henry) laughed again. Detective Inspector Rush, who had been rocking to and fro on his heels, started to peer into the bowl.

'I'm a bit worried about this!' said Henry. 'I think we should take a look at – '

'No no no!' said Sprott, dipping his glass in the mixture and taking a deep draught of Yugoslav Riesling, brown sugar and assorted domestic cleaners. 'It's good. It's a bit on the aggressive side. But basically it's good. Has it got Slivovitz in it? Or is it some form of regional tequila?'

'I think,' said Henry, who was starting to sweat with the enormity of his offence, 'that someone may have . . . I don't think we should drink . . .'

But, as so often, people were ignoring him.

'What do you think?' Sprott was asking Mr Is-the-Mitsubi-shi-Scratched-Yet. Mr Is-the-Mitsubishi-Scratched-Yet made nervous little movements with his hands. He sipped a little, smiled prettily and, casting a nervous glance out to the street towards the Mitsubishi, said: 'It's not unpleasant!'

'Can't we – ' Henry began.

But now everyone wanted to get at the punch. Even Elinor consented to have half a glassful. Henry tried to scrape the ladle along the bottom of the bowl when he served her, reasoning that Impact and Start and Finish 'Em would probably sink through the wine, milk and orange juice, but he was not sure that half a glass would be enough. He was not, to be honest, sure that the solution was going to have any effect whatsoever. The only person who did not accept any of the punch was Detective Inspector Rush who, whenever Henry caught sight of him, was looking down into his glass, suspiciously.

'I'm a little cautious about taking drinks I'm not sure about,' he said to Henry.

'Is that right,' said Henry.

'One never knows,' said Rush, smiling thinly, 'you can't be too careful.'

As the friends, relatives and neighbours of Donald Templeton MD crowded round the punch-bowl licking their lips and holding out their glasses like children in a lunch queue, Henry, who took a couple of glasses himself, peered anxiously round the gathering looking for signs of collapse. There seemed, as far as he could tell, to be a fair amount of that. But then, people in Maple Drive were usually in that kind of state at parties. Part of the trouble was that the subtle blend of Yugoslav Riesling and assorted domestic cleaners was proving astonishingly popular. People said they had never had such a punch. It took a couple of glasses to get you going, they said, but when you got going, they said, you went. Vera 'Got All The Things There Then?' Loomis, the ninety-two-year-old from 92, had to be rescued from tipping the bowl up to her lips with her third glass, and Henry and several others remarked that they had never seen such animation among mourners.

'It's always that way at a funeral,' said Vera 'Got All the Things There Then?' Loomis. 'Once it gets going it really goes!'

Dave Sprott seemed totally desperate for the mixture. He stood by the bowl and making a pretence of serving the other guests managed to drink more than anyone else in the room. After a while it became impossible for Henry to discover how many people had actually had more than three or four glasses. He went out through the french windows into the garden. Would the local crematoria be able to cope with the influx of customers, a day or so from now?

When he returned there were only two or three hardened drinkers standing by the bowl, although Henry was disturbed to note that Inspector Rush was still there, standing just clear of the wall, his glass still full, looking across at Sprott as if he was just about to ask him to come along quietly. Sprott had stopped smacking his lips and muttering that it had a refreshing directness and an unambiguous honesty – but had decanted the punch into a small vase and was tipping it back into his throat, pausing only after each mouthful to slap himself on the back of the neck and shout 'Wowee!' and 'Wowza!'

He showed no signs of frothing. He was distinctly unclammy. And from where he was standing, Henry could observe no signs of cyanosis. It was Rush he didn't like. The detective kept peering over the lip of the bowl and pursing his lips, and then looking back at Henry, and though he kept close to the side of the punch, Henry never saw him drink any.

'I remember – ' he was saying as Henry came into the room, 'dealing with a poisoning case once, which made a great impression on me.'

No one, however, was listening to him. They were listening to Dave Sprott.

What Dave Sprott did do – as he always did, when drunk – was to start to talk, loudly and aggressively, about teeth. 'People's teeth,' he said, his carefully preserved northern accent astonishing the artificial gas fire, the Heal's sofa and the watercolours above the mantelpiece collected by the late Donald Templeton MD over a period of twenty years, 'people's teeth are the expression of their personality. For example, a fact not very well known to those outside the profession is that the Romans considered the teeth were the seat of all the most basic human emotions. Was it the Romans, Edwina?'

Edwina Sprott, six foot two, built like a prop forward, hair on the back of the hands, huge nose, voice like Vincent Price, no breasts to speak of, said, 'No, David! I don't think anyone considers the teeth the seat of all the most basic human emotions. Apart from you.'

Sprott, who always saw in his wife's remarks a wit not at first appreciated by others (until Sprott pointed it out to them) laughed hysterically. 'It is, though,' he said, 'it is. Take anyone's teeth and look at them, and you will find the key to their personality. Take that politician I do. The Labour one. His teeth, in my view, say a great deal about his policies!'

Edwina Sprott towered above him. For a moment Henry thought she might be about to scoop him up in her arms, as a mother gorilla might draw her baby to her, but although she looked as if she might like to do this, she did not. 'It's David Steel!' she said instead.

'It's David Steel you do, David!'

'Christ, so it is!' said Sprott. 'So it is!'

A sure test of their marriage's durability was their capacity to be surprised by each other's anecdotes.

'Christ, he come in for a clean t'other week,' said Sprott, 'and I said to 'im, "Clean?, Clean? This isn't cleaning. This is a restoration job, this is," I said. I told him my theory about teeth and personality and I think what I said may have an impact on the future development of the Liberal Party!'

'David,' said Edwina Sprott, her huge hands dangling in front of her, looking down on her man as if he were a particularly tasty snack in some pastrycook's window, 'you say the weirdest, weirdest things!'

141

Teeth and celebrities were Sprott's two main obsessions in life. Once started on the subject of celebrities' teeth he was unstoppable. He talked of the role of teeth in history, their importance in the shaping of the modern world, their influence on great events. As he spoke more about teeth he claimed more and more for them. He spoke of his South African cousin whose entire life had been changed by the clumsy insertion of a bridge. He spoke of the relationship between capped teeth and business success, of the obvious link between loose fillings and feelings of sexual inadequacy.

'Aren't you having any?' said Inspector Rush to Henry with a thin smile.

'I won't, thanks!' said Henry. 'I'm driving!'

Rush's enigmatic expression seemed to hint at the absurdity of this excuse. Sprott, meanwhile, tipped the last of the bowl down his throat.

'Teeth,' he said, just before he hit the last of it, 'teeth, the whole of oral hygiene really, is the expression of a society. Britain today is a society in which we have ceased to care about teeth, in which we have ignored the real nature of what we are because – '

And on the edge of what might have been a truly global *aperçu* about teeth and British society, without any trace of cyanosis, frothing, soiling of the air passages, pneumonia, or wrinkled, greyish, leathery hardening of the oesophagal mucous membranes, he whirled round in mid-gesture, clawed at his throat and fell, headlong, on Billykins's carpet.

CHAPTER TWENTY-ONE

No one was very sympathetic.

Most of the guests were shouting for more punch and Henry, who was dispatched by Elinor to Thresher's for twenty more bottles of Yugoslav Riesling, added it to the more corrosive elements of his recipe, only to be told that the new blend 'lacked fizz'.

Sprott lay face down on the carpet, while Mrs Sprott (who was more drunk than anyone had ever seen her) shouted obscenities at him in a voice that sounded as if it were coming from an even deeper grave than usual. By this stage Henry was back in the room and the group round the punch-bowl had split up; it was Henry who found himself prodding the body with his foot and giving his opinion as to Sprott's state of health. As far as he could tell, Sprott was still breathing. Henry went out into the hall and looked through the open door at the chestnut trees on the green.

Behind him the noise of the party went on. He could hear Billykins shouting something. 'Who wants a widow?' was what it sounded like. Someone, probably Derek Bloomstein, the Other Optician, had started playing the piano.

At least Sprott wasn't exhibiting any of the symptoms of acid poisoning. There was nothing clammy about him. Had Sprott, Henry asked himself, swallowed the stuff in such quantities that it was acting independently of his digestive system? Sloshing around his immaculately cared-for mouth, cannoning into the walls of his gullet and smashing straight through them into the bloodstream?

If it had, he was probably well beyond cyanosis, frothing, or soiling of the lips. He was probably in deep shock. He might, thought Henry, have only minutes to live. If things went on like this there would not only be no one to take his blood pressure or check on his wisdom teeth, there would be no one to sort out his eyes, check out his conveyancing problems or tell him which roofing company to avoid. He had better go back in and get Roger From the Practice to look over Sprott. Except, of course, he couldn't possibly tell the man what was wrong with the dentist. Could he? That would incriminate him, wouldn't it? Could he?

Henry was not particularly fond of Sprott. He had never, for example, liked the mechanical, almost threatening way the man said 'Rinse!' There had also been a nasty incident some years ago, known as The Capping of Elinor's Teeth, in which, in Henry's view, the dentist had steered dangerously close to extortion.

But when it came to it, could he do it? Could he let the man die? Was it fair?

He had already murdered Donald of course. Henry had expected, in the days after hearing the news, to feel some of the things murderers were traditionally supposed to feel. Guilt, for a start. At any moment, as he went between Black-friars, the Rose and Thorn, St Michael and All Angels Primary School, Wimbledon, and Waitrose Ltd he half expected Donald to leap out at him from behind a tree, gibbering, covered in blood and chains. Sometimes, very late at night when he could not sleep, he saw him coming up the garden towards him, blood on his face, soil round his lips and in his right hand a cracked vase in which was, of course, a few drops of fatal thallium . . . But on the whole, having become a murderer did not seem to have altered his life. If anything, he felt slightly better than usual.

He had no particular urge, either, to murder anyone else, a thing he had noticed happening to quite a few murderers. Once they had tasted blood, some characters seemed to get a nose for chopping up people into easily manageable portions and leaving them in left-luggage compartments. A slight lowering of their moral standards seemed to bring on an uncontrollable urge to be beastly, an urge Henry did not feel. Even his urge to be rid of Elinor was not, he noticed, as keen as it once was. If he was still wedded to it, it was in the spirit of 'I've started so I'll finish', rather than the almost romantic fervour with which he had first embraced the notion.

He sighed and went back to the denuded front room. Elinor and Inspector Rush were in the middle of what looked like a rather intense conversation, which seemed, like so many intense conversations, to fail upon Henry's approach.

'You see,' Rush was saying, 'I'm a naturally suspicious man. It's my job. I'm paid to be suspicious.'

He stopped and looked at Henry narrowly. Sprott was still lying face down on the carpet. There was no sign of Roger From the Practice. Mrs Sprott was leaning against the mantelpiece, her mouth open, exhausted enough for silence. Mr Is-the-Mitsubishi-Scratched-Yet was kneeling on the tiled surround to the gas fire. He appeared to be being sick. Glumly, Henry went out into the hall. Some mourners, but not all, were looking clammy. Some were singing. Quite a few were being sick out of windows. On the landing on the first floor, Billykins, veil askew, was sobbing into the arms of Peter 'Where is the Upfront Money?' Furgess from 65.

'Death,' Furgess was saying, 'is certain. You just have to face it, there's no point in moaning about it. It's part of life. It's something that happens. It's . . .' Furgess's face furrowed with the effort of self-expression. '. . . it's . . . par for the course!'

Billykins seemed to find this thought comforting.

Well, death was par for the course, wasn't it? It wasn't such a great event. Perhaps that was why he felt no urge to confess. Henry had never understood why it was that Raskolny-whatever-his name-was had bothered to turn himself in to the police when no one had anything whatsoever against him.

'Oh!' came a voice from the floor. 'Oh my God! Oh!'

It was Elinor, and something in the basso contralto of her tone, the thrusting, stagy grief of it all reminded Henry of why it was he was trying to end her life some thirty or so years ahead of schedule.

'Oh!' she said again, sounding as surprised as she did when approaching sexual climax (in the days when she approached sexual climax). 'Oh! Oh!'

Henry looked down.

Elinor was sitting astride Sprott's chest, jerking her hips up and out and then allowing them to crash down on his lower ribs; she had both hands outstretched in front of her, made into two fists. She had converted herself entirely to piston action, so that as behind rose, arms descended, thumped on chest and then rose again as behind descended for the next assault. No one else in the room was paying much attention to her. Mr Is-the-Mitsubishi-Scratched-Yet was staring at the contents of his evacuated stomach like an archaeologist contemplating some mystery in the soil. As Henry stared down at Elinor, number 61a (Unpublished Magical Realist) zig-zagged towards him. He looked like a man about to make an awkwardly close relationship with the numinous. Behind him came Vera 'Got All the Things There Then?' Loomis, who looked if anything worse, and the two disappeared out into the hall, presumably to be sick all over 32 and 48 (Ecology-Conscious Pensioner in Green Anorak and Publisher Going Through Identity Crisis).

Sprott did not appear to be paying much attention to Elinor's ministrations. Christ, thought Henry, if Elinor was dropping her arse on to my stomach and then bashing me in the chest with her fists I'd want to make a statement on the subject. Sprott was just lying back, neck up, chin ridiculously forward. Was he, Henry wondered, showing off his teeth? Wasn't there some law against dentists opening their mouths as wide as David Sprott was doing? Wasn't it tantamount to advertising?

It was only when he got close enough to see his eyes that Henry realized that David Sprott was not going to be mending any more teeth for a while.

Dave Sprott was dead.

146

'He's dead!' shrieked Elinor, as she continued to hit him in the ribs. 'He's dead! He's dead! He's dead!'

This was all getting depressingly familiar, thought Henry. But, to his surprise, this time the news did strike him as genuinely shocking. Perhaps it was the sheer scale of the carnage he seemed to have provoked in his attempt to get through to Elinor. Outside in the hall he could hear people being sick, wailing and calling on God, and found himself saying, 'My God! How awful!'

Roger From the Practice crawled out from behind the sofa. 'Who's dead?' he called. 'Is someone dead?'

He belched and crawled on towards the hall door. Henry put his foot on the patch of carpet directly in front of the newly promoted GP. Roger From the Practice stopped and looked up at him pathetically.

'Yes,' said Henry sternly, 'someone is dead.'

'Who is it?' said Roger From the Practice.

Henry did not answer. Roger From the Practice rolled over on his back like a Labrador waiting to be tickled in the stomach.

'Who is it?' he said. 'Who's dead? Is it me? Say it's me. Oh God, say it's me. Oh God, please, please let it be me!'

CHAPTER TWENTY-TWO

It very nearly was. But, after a bout of vomiting that would have done credit to a party of schoolchildren going round the Bay of Biscay in February, Roger From the Practice recovered his composure enough to start handing out death certificates the way Napoleon handed out medals.

There were two (Roger From the Practice said) dead on the first landing. One had got as far as the shed before keeling over, and in the downstairs back lavatory, number 61a (Unpublished Magical Realist) had breathed his last in a manner worthy of one of his characters. He had died with his head deep in the Armitage Shanks bowl and his feet at a bold angle. He may not, as someone said later, have turned into a giant ostrich or begun to improvise verses from the Koran, but it was a step in the right direction.

Henry disliked most species of fiction writer but of them all considered magical realists to be the most suspect – perhaps because Elinor was always going on about them at such length. And this particular magical realist was a particularly difficult customer. But however prone the man was to double-park his own neighbours, Henry would not have wished this end on Rufus Coveney, as he was called. Neither would he have wanted Denimed Lout Who Voted Labour and Boasted About It from 129 to have leapt crazily from an upper bedroom and broken both legs in Donald's flower bed.

Henry could honestly have said, as he and Roger From the Practice made a body count, that he had not wanted any of this to happen. And Elinor, who accompanied them, was magnificently human. She consoled, she comforted, she leaned over number 43 (Widower in Blue Suit Who is Rarely in the Country) as he frothed and cyanosed, and with skills presumably acquired in her therapy class persuaded him to think positively about his situation, to enumerate his own personal strengths and maximize 'the plus side of being him' until the ambulance arrived. She gave cardiac massage. She put her fingers down people's throats. She treated the inhabitants of Maple Drive with almost as much care and concern as if they had been Nicaraguan peasants. Henry, looking at her, could not imagine why it was he had wanted to poison such a strong, useful, friendly woman.

This was the whole trouble with murder. On Monday it seemed a clear-cut, straightforward affair. But, by Wednesday, your victim had lost all traces of the things that had made them so eminently killable and, although you felt sure that tomorrow or the next day you would be up to steering them towards a vat of liquid metal or leaving them alone with a naked flame and a mains gas leak, today you just couldn't feel it the way you should. Your resolve weakened.

The real trouble, Henry decided, as he and Roger From the Practice carried another borderline case out into the garden, was people. You just never knew what they would do next. They were so difficult to classify. Sometimes it seemed as if there was no such thing as people, just an endless series of tricks of the light, a history of false impressions.

'Oh my God!' said Elinor, as the first ambulances arrived. 'This is absolutely terrible!'

'Yes,' said Henry, 'yes!'

In the end, only three people actually died at Donald's funeral, and one of these, Vera 'Got All the Things There Then?' Loomis, from 92, was ninety-two and therefore, everyone agreed, didn't really count.

People didn't seem very interested in asking why. There had been, everyone said, 'something not right' about the punch. People had, of course, drunk too much of it. There was talk of analysing what was left of it. But the trouble was – there wasn't any left, which only served to emphasize quite how much the mourners had managed to put away. The person who might have been expected to haul Dave Sprott's remains in to Wimbledon police station and begin the task of cutting him into little pieces was, of course, Detective Inspector Rush. One neighbour had the temerity to ask him whether he intended to do so, to which Rush responded with an enigmatic smile. Mind you, he responded to most questions with an enigmatic smile.

This ought to have reassured Henry. But it didn't. Something about the man's manner made him suspect that he was biding his time. There was something about the way he tipped his hat to Elinor, too, that . . . No. That thought was impossible. Rush was, in the words of Jaspar Cecil, the wine merchant from 83, 'married to the Wimbledon police force'.

That was why his silence was so frightening.

It was two or three days after the funeral that Henry started to study books on toxicology, as a sort of retrospective research effort. He had, he decided, made such a hash of his career as a poisoner that he had no real way of even telling quite how badly he had done. And, in the inquiry that he expected daily, he would have to have some line of defence. All the books he read made him feel a lot worse. But of all of them, from *Lives of the Great Poisoners* to *Some Toxicological Aspects of Pathology*, none made him feel worse than Keith Simpson's *Forensic Medicine*, which he obtained from Wimbledon Public Library.

1. *In a previously healthy subject, the onset, sudden or slow, of symptoms which do not correspond to ordinary illness, should raise suspicion.*
2. *If the source is suspected to be food, endeavour to obtain some of it: trace other persons who partook of it.*
3. *Keep any vomit, stomach wash-out, faeces, units of CSF which come to hand. Seal them and affix labels.*

As far as Henry could see, there were no faeces or stomach wash-outs lying around in Billykins's house, but there was enough vomit on her carpets to keep a team of pathologists in business for a year, and it only needed one person enterprising enough to start picking up bits of it for them to be on to Henry. For several days he went in and out of Billy-kins's house, offering to take things to the cleaners and watching anxiously for strangers equipped with clear plastic bags and sticky labels. In particular he looked out for Detective Inspector Rush: but he saw no sign of him.

But after a week or so, he grew calmer. People in Wimbledon, thank Christ, didn't think like Keith Simpson. They didn't go round rifling through people's faeces and affixing labels to them. Poison (this is its beauty) is part of everyone's diet. People were always pouring poison down their throats. Looked at in this light, Simpson's work became a comfort rather than a threat. On page 322, he read:

Ethyl Alcohol (C_2H_5OH)

Three forms of poisoning occur:
1.   *Acute (fatal) alcohol poisoning.*
2.   *'Drunkenness' (insobriety).*
3.   *Chronic alcoholic poisoning (chronic alcoholism).*

Further on he read:

Stupor – this is the 'dead drunk' stage at which the patient is roused into response only by the strongest stimuli. To be 'anaesthetic' or unfeeling to injury, to lie in a snoring stupor with flushed face and dribbling lips, is the last stage of helpless inebriety. This is the stage which is likely to be simulated by cerebral disease or head injury.

Even the words used to describe drunkenness, thought Henry (who was by now becoming rather censorious of people who abused their bodies, who subjected them to poison when there was so much healthy, life-giving sustenance around), were a giveaway. *Headbash. Braindeath. Wipe out.* And, if he felt guilt, which somewhat to his surprise he did, it was about the fact that he had not tried hard enough to stop the bastards drinking the stuff. He had even, on the evening after the funeral, suggested to Roger From the Practice that someone had 'got to' the punch but Roger From the Practice, true to his late master's instincts, was unkeen to investigate any theory other than that his neighbours and friends had keeled over as a result of alcohol and stress in fatal doses.

Donald, thought Henry, would have been proud of him. His medical knowledge seemed to be largely derived from reading the colour supplements of newspapers, and his analysis of the party was born out by the local journal, whose banner headline read: 'THREE DIE AFTER DRINKING SPREE FUNERAL HORROR. "MY SHAME!" SAYS WIDOW.'

People did not meet each other's eyes in the street. Nazi Who Escaped Justice at Nuremberg met Detective Inspector Rush at the golf club, and suggested to him that someone should inform the coroner. Rush, apparently, had smiled with enigmatic bitterness, and replied, 'My dear Gunther, I would like to inform the coroner. I am a policeman, am I not? But my hands are tied in this matter. You understand? I am not a free agent in this affair!'

And he had looked, people said, so steely and enigmatic that Nazi Who Escaped Justice at Nuremberg had had to go out and play another round of golf, to get over it. Anyway, nobody had any idea where the coroner was. Even if they had been able to find him he was probably out moonlighting, or had been cut or privatized like everything else in Britain. The fact was that nobody much cared that three more people had croaked. They were all too busy trying to sell their houses at a profit or worrying whether higher interest rates would lead to a slump.

Henry, to his surprise, was getting rather left wing.

Murder, of course, changed you. It sharpened you up, made you less provincial. It gave you an interest. And Elinor, who in the days after Donald's funeral might have been expected to go on even more about his grossness, his obscene masculinity and his record-breakingly loutish behaviour at the funeral of a close friend, seemed positively amiable. There was, of course, nothing like surprising people.

'Really, Henry,' she said one evening, 'you're a mystery, aren't you? You're . . . peculiar!'

She screwed up her eyes as she said this. But from her expression Henry gathered that being peculiar was a better thing to be than obscenely masculine. It might, in the end, be almost attractive. Henry had become a question mark, some difficult, unclassifiable quantity, and his behaviour only intensified her interest. After all, it was not habitual for Henry to jump every time the doorbell rang or give a low cry whenever he heard a police siren heading down the hill ('Good evening, Mr Farr. We'd like to ask you a few questions about a quantity of *bleach* we have found in the stomach of the late David Sprott . . .').

Goaded on by her curiosity about the man she had married, Elinor began, in the evenings, to go over the early history of their relationship, much of which, as she described it, bore no relation whatsoever to anything Henry remembered.

'Do you remember,' she would say, 'that little hotel in Switzerland?'

Henry would look at her glumly across the supper table. What was she talking about? They had never been to Switzerland. Had they?

'That funny little man with the alpenstock,' went on Elinor, 'and the beard. And we went up to that waterfall!'

Here she leered suggestively. Did she mean to imply that they had had intercourse? Henry could not even remember going to Switzerland, let alone having intercourse by a waterfall in that country. Not with her anyway. Perhaps she had done all this with someone else. Some teacher from her primary school days. Or possibly – Henry didn't like this thought – with whoever her secret admirer might be.

Maisie was also, for some reason, a great deal more quiet and submissive. Donald's funeral seemed to have impressed her. She even asked Henry on one occasion whether Mars Bars gave you cancer, to which Henry replied: 'If they do – I recommend we begin chemotherapy on you right away.'

Dave Sprott's funeral, a double date with 61a (Unpublished Magical Realist) was a low-key affair, only enlivened by the sight of Unpublished Magical Realist's family, all of whom remained dry-eyed throughout the proceedings. The person who spoke on his behalf, a cadaverous man with a strong Welsh accent, actually waved a copy of his manuscript (*Decay of the Flying Wolves*) and attempted to give some résumé of the plot to the now somewhat blasé mourners of Maple Drive, SW19. 'After this extraordinary mythical character,' he said, 'half tortoise, half publisher, returns to the mythical country of Rumalia, Rufus is, I think, trying to tell us that the victor, ultimately, is not death and, similarly, in this great, this very plangent image of a toothless wolf alone in the deserted Stock Exchange, Rufus is saying that the struggle goes on, to be ourselves, whatever we may be. And I think when this manuscript is published it will be a testament to the positive thing in all of us.'

But people get bored with death, even in Wimbledon. Vera 'Got All the Things There Then?' Loomis was scattered in the scattering area, Coveney was taken in a small urn down to Hastings and cast into the sea by one of his relatives (in death he remained unpublished), and the suburb forgot them. Henry became involved in a rather messy divorce in Aldershot and, in spite of what he regarded as one of the most closely argued letters in British legal history, failed to resolve the issue of the dustbin shelters. It seemed for a while as if no more was to be heard from the man who called himself the Wimbledon Poisoner.

'But at number 54 Maple Drive,' said Lustgarten, pacing the length of the quiet street in a long, dark coat, 'Henry Farr, quadruple murderer, planned his next crime. His poisonings may have been the result of bad planning. He tried to tell himself, in the long, lonely nights that followed the tragic deaths of Templeton, Loomis, Coveney and Sprott, that he was not as guilty as he felt. But the fact was that he was now stained not only with the blood of his doctor but also with the blood of his dentist, a respectable widow and a young man whose only crime, apart from the writing of magical realist novels, was to have drunk the lethal cocktail that Farr had prepared for his wife. Although he felt the Furies close in round him, although he was almost sure that vengeance, that justice was about to descend, Henry Farr saw no way back.'

/

CHAPTER TWENTY-THREE

Often, as October, sunny and cold, starved the leaves along Maple Drive, Henry Farr thought about not poisoning his wife. He thought about not poisoning her as much as he thought about poisoning her.

As Maisie and Elinor and he walked one afternoon across the common to the windmill, he found himself reflecting that, if he stopped now, there was no question of his ever being discovered. Whereas if he continued, who knew who would be the next to get it in the neck? There seemed to be no easy relation between the people he wanted to die and the ones who copped it. He thought about this as the three of them stood in the wet grass to the south of the windmill, and he read from the local guide, sadly lacking as it was in detail.

'It is difficult to understand why Charles March should have built the windmill in this way. But Wimbledon Windmill bears a striking resemblance to one or two other post mills. It is possible – '

Here he tapped Maisie on the chest, 'Listen, Maisie – it is possible that he simply copied this building out of ignorance of normal windmill practice. Do you see? Isn't that amazing?'

'No,' said Maisie.

'I mean,' said Henry, trying to breathe some life into this subject, 'what an amazing dumbo. Just . . . copying a windmill like that. Not knowing anything about normal windmill practice!'

'A windmill,' said Maisie, 'is just a windmill. Isn't it?'

Henry sighed. It was true that since Donald's death he had been making more effort with his daughter; there were times, as a result, when he wondered whether she, not Elinor, was the problem. There were even moments when it occurred to him that he was the problem. He looked across at Elinor.

OK, she was a feminist. That was a harmless eccentricity, wasn't it? She was a feminist, but when it came down to it she put the things in the dishwasher like anyone else. She mowed the lawn. These days she sometimes even listened to him.

'I'm bored of this windmill,' said Maisie. 'I want to go to the café.'

'Yes, my darling,' said Elinor. 'Yes, of course. Salt and vinegar crisps? Or a sticky bun?'

At the worst point in her therapy (she didn't seem to go quite as often these days) she would never have allowed such words to pollute her lips. The women in the therapy group were of the opinion that poisons in foodstuffs were a direct cause of many emotional and psychological difficulties, one of them having gone as far as writing Henry a note to tell him to lay off the salami, and once the mere mention of the word 'salt' would have brought her out in the kind of rash experienced by someone suffering from a dose of atropine methonitrate or a crafty snort of alkaloids of calabar.

It was Henry who saw the world as under the sway of poisons these days. Poisons, like ugly shapes emerging from a Rorschach blot, were there, behind things, and as he read more and more on the subject, he found himself chanting their names like a litany as he rode the train to Blackfriars, or walked up the hill alone to the Rose and Thorn.

> Ecgonine . . .
> Ergot . . .
> Pomegranate . . .
> Stavesacre . . .
> Papaverine . . .
> Thebaine . . .
> Apomorphine . . .

From acetyldihydrocodin, its salts, to zinc phosphide, from tartar emetic to bismuth, Henry rolled the syllables round his tongue until he felt he was eating the names. He planned delicious meals, which would have as their centre some ragout of veal *à la* alkaloids of sabadilla, followed perhaps by a little side salad of homatropine; he thought about poison as something sweet, something that would be easy to swallow, that would lull you to sleep, get you out of all this. And, if he was honest, the poisons he dreamed about were no longer anything as vulgar as a weapon, they were not aimed at anybody, not even Elinor.

'I'll have some crisps too!' said Henry.

'Fatty!' said Elinor, almost amiably.

As the three of them waddled across the car park, pitted with puddles, from the woods facing the windmill, where once Henry had dreamed of burying Elinor in a shallow grave, couples walked in the October sunshine.

The couples wear each other on their faces, thought Henry. The Spanish say that the wife wears the husband on her face, the husband wears the wife on his linen. But in England it isn't like that. People simply grow into each other, the way ivy grows into English walls or roses grow into housefronts in any suburb in this quiet island. Perhaps he and Elinor were growing into each other in that way, as they walked, now, towards the steamed-up glass front of the café where couples sat in a silence he might, a week or so ago, have construed as hostile, staring out at their limited, peaceful horizon. Perhaps he and Elinor had just been going through a crisis. They had 'displaced their aggression'. They had, rather spectacularly, 'dumped'. And if four people had had to die, well . . . according to a woman in Elinor's therapy class, you had to 'die to grow'. They had obviously simply persuaded others to go through this part of their therapy for them.

'I want salt and vinegar, chilli beef and cheese and onion!' said Maisie.

'Yes, darling!' said Elinor, with just the faintest trace of strain in her voice.

If there was one thing that made Henry feel he should do away with her, it was Donald.

He really missed Donald. He was surprised quite how much he missed him. He often found himself wanting to say the kind of thing he always said to Donald, things like, 'I don't know, squire . . .' or 'Whichever way you slice it, mate . . .' or even 'Mine's a light and special!' and halfway through enunciating them, turned to find the doctor absent. And, in a way, it was Elinor's fault. If only she hadn't forced her chicken thallium on him, if she had only eaten it up, like a good girl, at the very moment when his hatred of her was as pure as the best poison. And now it was sometimes hard to remember why he was poisoning her; poisoning her wouldn't bring Donald back. Although, thought Henry, as they joined the queue for food, if his death had brought them together perhaps her death would bring him back to life.

'Mmm,' said Maisie, biting into her bun before it was paid for, 'this is yum!'

'Mmm!' said Elinor.

They moved to a table. The Farr family ate in a briskly competitive, albeit communal style. No one spoke while eating; all that was to be heard was grunting and wheezing until the last crisp, the last drop of tea and orange juice and the last fragments of white icing had disappeared down one or other of the Farr family throats.

Someone was prodding Henry in the ribs. Looking down he noticed that it was Elinor. He mouth full of crumbs, she said, 'What are all those books on poison doing in your study?'

Henry belched and looked at his boots. 'What books on poison?' he said.

'Oh,' said Elinor, '*Great Poisoners of the World, Death Was Their Business, Encyclopedia of Murder, Forensic Medicine, Exit a Poisoner, The Life of "Apple Pip" Kelly the Strychnine Killer, Six Hundred Toxic Deaths* – '

'Oh, those,' said Henry, 'I – '

'*Strong Poison, A Life of William Palmer, the Notorious Stafford-shire Poisoner, Hyoscine; Its Uses in Toxicology* by Adolf Gee Smith, *Some Applications of Arsenic in Industry* by –'

She broke off and peered at him. 'Are you trying to poison me, Henry?' she said, and then, looking round the café, in a humorous voice – 'I say, everybody – Henry wants to poison me!'

Then, because it was such a ridiculous idea, she threw back her head and gave a booming, confident laugh.

'I couldn't do that, darling,' said Henry, 'I love you!'

Elinor's eyes narrowed. 'Do you?' she said.

'You're the sun and the moon and the stars to me,' said Henry, 'you're the reason why I get up in the morning and go to bed at night. You give meaning to my every breath. You are my rationale!'

Elinor folded her arms. She looked, Henry thought, like an off-duty policeman listening to some suspect political opinions in his local pub.

'Am I?' she said.

'Yes, yes,' said Henry, 'deep down. You know. Really deep down. Of course you are.'

She didn't look very convinced by this. Did she, he wondered, really suspect him? And if she did, was it the kind of thing she might mention to Detective Inspector Rush, assuming that she and Rush were . . .

'Actually,' Henry found himself saying, 'I just got really interested in poisons. It became a bit of a . . . well . . . a . . . hobby. You know?'

'Well, I always said,' said Elinor, 'that you should have more interests.'

Henry gulped. 'That's right!' he said. 'And I was trying to look at our relationship in the light of that. To make it, you know, grow . . .'

She still did not look entirely convinced. Henry talked more rapidly. 'Did you know,' he said, 'that alkaloids of pomegranate are a deadly poison? Or that the poisoner Neil

Cream handed out strychnine to young girls for no apparent motive!'

Elinor's brow furrowed. 'Actually,' she said, 'I am very interested in food additives of any kind.'

'Precisely!' said Henry wildly. 'This is all part of it, you see. I've been trying to . . .' He groped for the word. 'Rethink my attitudes!'

She shook her hair out and for a moment looked like someone he remembered liking, years ago. Why was it that they no longer had a common language?

Henry blundered on, trying to use the words she used. 'I've been thinking about poison as . . . as a mode of communication!'

She looked a little doubtful about this. Picking at the crumbs on the table, she said, 'It is odd though, isn't it?'

'What is?'

'Those deaths. All those people at Donald's funeral. And the punch . . .'

'What about the punch?' said Henry.

She didn't answer this question but continued to trace little circles on the damp plastic of the table.

'I was talking about it all to John Rush,' she said, 'I think he knows something. But isn't saying. You know?'

'I know!' said Henry.

'Mind you – ' said Elinor, 'the police never do, do they?'

'No, no . . .' said Henry.

What was all this about *John* Rush?

'They could,' said Elinor, 'be biding their time.'

'I know!' said Henry.

There was a long silence. Henry filled it with a boyishly enthusiastic speech about Mrs Greve, who had poisoned her husband with ground glass in Dublin in the early 1920s. Elinor watched him as he spoke with a kind of sadness he did not understand.

'Actually,' she said, 'it's nice to see you excited about something. There were times when I thought you'd . . . you know . . . given up. There were times when I thought . . .'

She laughed, a little nervously. 'You know . . . you'd . . . poisoned the chicken or something . . .'

Then she clasped his hand, firmly. 'But you wouldn't do a thing like that. You're a confused man. You're a sad man in many ways. But you're not a bad man, are you?'

Henry tried, not very successfully, to look deep into her eyes. 'No,' he said, 'not really!'

'Why would you ever want to poison me anyway?' went on Elinor wistfully. 'What have I ever done to you? You'd be lost without me. Wouldn't you?'

And, with those words, she took Maisie's hand and walked out to the rain-soaked car park.

CHAPTER TWENTY-FOUR

Indeed.

What, when you thought about it, had she actually done to him? Why was he trying to poison her? Didn't this approach to their marriage need a complete re-think?

As they trudged across the common towards the village, Henry realized that few, if any advantages, financial or social, would accrue to him on her death. He would have to get an au pair – some Swedish or German floozy who went out till four in the morning and brought men back to her room. He would have to do even more domestic work than he did at the moment. There would be another funeral to organize. He might even have to speak at it (Henry shuddered slightly at this thought).

Then there was her mother. She would want to help. She would take the train down from Cumbria and sit in the front room and want to talk about her daughter. She would hold Henry's hand and look deep into Henry's eyes and say 'Let's talk about Elinor!' She would go on about how wonderful her daughter was, she would probably describe her talent for opera singing and gourmet cuisine. She might even – Henry started to shake uncontrollably – ask to stay.

There was quite a lot to be said for leaving Elinor alive. From the administrative point of view alone. Where, now he thought about it, was the salt kept for the dishwater? How often did you have to put salt in it? When you put salt in it – where did it go? Did you just chuck it over the dishes like seasoning, or what?

How would he tell Maisie about periods?

They stopped outside a bookshop in the village High Street. Maisie pressed her nose to the glass. Elinor did the same. Then they squashed their lips against its cold, clean surface. They started to laugh.

'Can I buy a book?' said Maisie.

'Of course, darling!' said Elinor.

She wasn't all bad, thought Henry. When the three of them were like this, it almost felt good to be part of a family, knowing you were going back to a warm house, a well-tuned piano, a decent, ordered existence. Didn't married men stand less chance of getting heart attacks than bachelors?

Let's be reasonable, he told himself, as he followed Elinor and Maisie into the bookshop, you're not going to find another woman anyway. You're one of those people who looked interesting but turned out not to be. You didn't show much early promise, but what promise you showed you didn't fulfil. You're just another little Englishman who gets a laugh at parties. That's what you are. The one interesting thing you've ever done is try and murder your wife. Even if you did end up murdering your doctor and your dentist and –

Oh my God, thought Henry, I'm a murderer. I am actually a murderer. He felt suddenly very cold. Why? Why did he feel something that was almost guilt but not quite? As he stood watching Elinor and Maisie he realized it was something very simple. It was the urge to tell someone what had happened, coupled with the realization that he would never be able to do so. That what he had done was a totally private act, that it condemned him to an awful isolation, a world in which every remark or approach, however natural-seeming, was false. 'You are a poisoner!' an unpleasant, small voice in his head began to say.

And this was worse than anything he had felt before. It was worse, precisely because he now knew that he didn't want to poison his wife. With that realization came an inexpressible relief. He felt like a man who has just been told his brain scan is clear. He wanted to rush up to her and tell her the good news (although in that negative way women had she would probably brood over the implications of his original intention). But at the same time as this relief came this stinging, nagging ache. This feeling of isolation that threatened to overwhelm him, and lead him to shout out the truth here, in the shop, on a cold October afternoon.

Hang on, hang on, Henry. This is England, not Russia. For Christ's sake! You've tried to poison your wife. It was something people did. In the heat of the moment. No jury would convict. You had a tiff – you went out and got a shotgun or some strychnine and let off steam. You couldn't have love without hate as that man on *Stars on Sunday* had pointed out. Think positive, Henry.

I have become tougher, he said to himself, I have become more independent. I am better read. I know a lot more about chemistry. Yes, I have lost a valued friend and several neighbours, but for God's sake, if people can't learn from their mistakes and become useful citizens once more, what is the hope for any of us? Crime does not necessarily imply punishment these days – if it ever did. We are more, not less Christian than we were in Dostoevsky's day.

As they approached number 54, he linked his arm into hers. She started at first. Elinor was not used to him touching her. Her therapy group had apparently decided that Henry had something called 'touch taboo'. And, indeed, the pressure of her arm on his felt, at first, a little alarming. But as they turned in through the gateway Henry realized, to his surprise, that he was not actually gritting his teeth. She felt warm and, yes, comforting.

It was amazing how, when you had decided not to poison a person who probably deserved it, the world suddenly seemed a better, more decent, cleaner place. Maybe that was it. Maybe he had been suffering from whatever it was Raskolnikov had had, and hadn't realized it. He had had bad thoughts. He had acted on them. He had been mean and small-minded and thought only about himself and his problems. And look what had happened to him as a result! Years of negative thinking had turned him into a quadruple murderer. But, thought Henry as he let them in to the hall, he wasn't going to lie down under that stereotype. No sirree!

He had been full of spite and bitterness towards the world that lay outside Wimbledon. But now he was going to learn to be generous. Some people flew all over the world and had themselves profiled in colour magazines and had hundreds of women and as much Jack Daniels as they could drink while other people were fat and lived in Wimbledon. That was life! Some people sat up till four in the morning talking about the imagination and the sunset on the north face of the Eiger, while other people watched *News at Ten* and went to bed. That was life. The people with yachts and penthouses and as much sex as they wanted and shares and private beaches and planes constantly at their disposal and suntans and fantastic digestions were not, most of them, happy. Were they! Oh no. Happiness was a more complex emotion than that.

Would he, for example, when it came down to it, swap Maisie and Elinor and 54 Maple Drive for some villa with a swimming pool in Marbella complete with leggy blonde with a first in physics and an insatiable appetite for sex in strange positions with Henry? Would he?

Henry felt a momentary twinge of doubt and pushed it aside. He wouldn't.

Would he exchange his life of struggle, of patient, unrewarded research on a subject that was, possibly, of no interest to anyone anyway? Would he swap his *Complete History of Wimbledon* for some quick, easy, Nobel Prize-winning piece of crap about the state of play in Third World jails? Would he exchange all that lived experience, the forty years of actually being Henry Farr for the cushy way out – I mean, said Henry to himself, who do you want to be? Henry Farr or Graham Greene?

For the briefest of brief moments he thought he was going to scream 'GRAHAM FUCKING GREENE!' and, running from the room, sink the coal shovel into Elinor's neck, but such was the power of positive thinking that the moment

166

passed. He looked round at the sitting room and, his heart growing bigger and bigger, more and more human with each glance, he reached for a pencil and paper. He found himself writing:

Pluses
1. *I have not been found out.*
2. *I have not killed anyone on purpose.*
3. *I have come to terms with my marriage.*

Minuses

But, when it came to it, he could not think of any minuses. From where Henry was sitting, poisoning had been a challenging, bracing way of getting to grips with a mid-life crisis. The *Reader's Digest* would have been proud of him. He was already thinking of Henry the Murderer in the past tense. Something along the lines of 'When I Tried my Hand at Poisoning . . .' or 'My Wife-murdering Phase'. He was entering a new world in which he might learn all those basic skills that had for so long been denied him. For Christ's sake, thought Henry, women are just people. People have problems, don't they?

The awesome thought came to him that, on his own, without any artificial aids or any money changing hands, he, Henry Farr, was experiencing Therapy.

'Open up, Henry,' said a voice within him, 'you are not all bad! You are businessman, father, cook, raconteur! You are murderer, socialite, good neighbour. A murderer is, in many ways, a very positive thing to be. Quite a lot of people would like to be in your shoes. Go with the flow, Henry. Accept the changes in your life! Be well, husband, commuter, solicitor, unapprehended poisoner!'

He was actually grinning to himself when Elinor came into the room. She looked, he thought, almost triumphant.

'John Rush!' she said, in the tones of a butler announcing a celebrity at a party. Then she flung the door wide open. 'He says he wants to see you about something!'

Henry goggled at her as Rush came into the room, bowing slightly as if to acknowledge the importance of his appearance. Before she retired, Elinor, still in larky mood, waved her hand towards him, as if she was proud to have a representative of Law and Order on the premises.

'Detective Inspector Rush,' she said, 'all the way from Wimbledon CID!'

PART TWO

Crime and Punishment

'Don't you see that blessed conscience of yours is nothing but other people inside you!'

Luigi Pirandello, *Each in His Own Way*

CHAPTER TWENTY-FIVE

Henry could tell straight away that, when actually on the job, Detective Inspector Rush was one of the most astute and ruthless detectives of the twentieth century.

There was something about the way he fiddled with his pipe, tamping down the tobacco with the back of a matchbox, biting the stem and, from time to time, squinting along it in a knowing sort of way, that suggested a policeman of almost superhuman intelligence.

But Henry could tell, from the man's drabness, his thin, nasal voice, and his resolute disinclination to discuss anything to do with criminology, that he was a very serious customer indeed. Why else was he parking himself in Henry's front room talking about the weather, about Elinor, whom he seemed to know worryingly well, and, indeed, almost anything but the subject that had quite obviously brought him here. He was clever, thought Henry, very, very clever indeed.

'Your wife,' said DI Rush, 'is a remarkable woman!'

'She is!' said Henry.

'You picked a good 'un there!' went on Rush.

'Indeed!' said Henry.

What was it about Elinor that made her so attractive to such widely different social groups? Policemen, doctors . . . where would it end? thought Henry. Was it simply that, without really being aware of it he had, for all these years, been married to a very attractive woman? The thought was, somehow, frightening. If this was the case – how was he going to hang on to her? Rush was talking again, and something about the look in his eyes told Henry he was getting on to the purpose of his visit.

'I'm sorry to trouble you,' he said, eventually, with what

seemed like reluctance, 'but I've been talking to quite a few people in Maple Drive about . . .'

Here he waved his pipe at the window. Once again Henry noted the subtlety with which the subject was being introduced. It was almost as if Rush was broaching it against his will.

'. . . poison . . .'

'What kind of poison?'

The detective inspector seemed to forget, for a moment, which kind. But he also managed to suggest that this very absentmindedness might be some subtle interrogator's ploy. Henry felt an absurd desire to throw himself on the carpet and shout 'I confess! I'm an animal! Take me away!'

'Poison . . .' he said, and paused. Then he gave a short, stagy, little laugh. Henry wished he would stop making gnomic remarks and get on with the real business of the afternoon – alibis, heavy innuendo and possible threats of violence.

'I'm particularly interested in poison,' Rush was saying. 'I look through the local paper and I see someone's been taken ill or found dead somewhere or other and I think . . . I wonder . . . I wonder . . .'

'Yes,' said Henry, 'I expect you do.'

Rush was at the window. He wheeled round, suddenly theatrical, and jabbed his pipe at Henry. 'Three people dead,' he said, 'after a . . .' He paused.

'Drunken spree?' said Henry.

'Precisely,' said DI Rush.

He paced back to the sofa and sat on the arm, looking even more like a man who had been instructed to do all this – walk, sit, tamp down pipe, suck, pause, blow – by a not very good theatre director.

'And of course,' Rush seemed close to laughter, 'there was no inquest. It was simply another party that got out of hand. Three more stiffs.'

'Can I offer you a drink,' said Henry, 'or are you on duty?'

'I'm never off duty!' said Rush. 'I'm always on duty. At

172

four in the morning I wake and I stare into the darkness, thinking about crime and the evil things we do to each other. And about, well, how beastly we can be! I'll have a gin and tonic if you're having one.'

'Surely!' said Henry, trying to keep his voice steady.

He went to the door. Maisie was crouched at the keyhole, eyes round with excitement. She followed him through to the kitchen.

'What have you done?' she said.

'What have *you* done?' said Henry.

'Nothing,' said Maisie, 'I'm a child.'

'Being a child,' said Henry, as he poured the biggest gin and tonic he had ever poured in his life, 'is no excuse.'

He poured one half the size for the detective inspector and, followed by Maisie, went back towards the front room. She installed herself by the crack in the door as he went in. Rush was still standing, staring out at the street, his hands by his side, the pipe now dead to the world. When he heard Henry he wheeled round sharply.

'A nice quiet street,' said Rush in a manner that suggested that it was nothing of the kind, 'in a nice, quiet suburb. Full of nice, quiet houses, and nice, quiet families inside them. And somewhere, in one of them . . .'

His eyes flared dangerously into life. 'A madman. A psychopath. A killer.'

Henry jumped. 'Do you think so?'

'Oh, I know so,' said Rush, 'I know so. I know that somewhere out there, somewhere out there is a man so twisted by hatred and spite, so bent out of shape by life that he couldn't really be called human any more.'

'Golly!' said Henry.

'A man,' said Rush, waving his right arm and pacing up and down on the carpet, 'a man who thinks the world owes him something. A drab little man, obscure, meek and mild, hen-pecked perhaps. Like Crippen, say, with a pathetic pipe dream of his own that will never come to fruition – '

Henry thought of *The Complete History* and gulped. He had

the uncomfortable sensation that this man could see right into him, that unlike almost everyone else with whom he had dealings (including Elinor) he knew what Henry was thinking.

'A man who is probably impotent. Unable to connect. Perhaps homosexual, I don't know. But, above all, a man with a warped, vile, grotesque view of the world. A narrow, twisted little man, a moral cripple, a – '

'A beast?' said Henry, in a high, squeaky voice.

'That's it!' said Rush, amazed at Henry's powers of intuitive understanding. 'A beast!'

Rush's face was pale with righteous fury. Henry could see his knuckles whiten round the pipe.

'Most of us,' he went on, 'rue the day the death penalty was abolished.'

'Indeed,' said Henry, 'indeed!'

Rush was clearly not one of your namby-pamby community policemen. He was a copper out to get his man. The sort of person who would work on a case twenty-four hours a day, seven days a week, until he had brought the guilty one to justice. The sort of policeman of whom, in normal circumstances, Henry thoroughly approved. He was not entirely sure, however, that in this case such zeal was appropriate. There was something, he decided, odd and fanatical about the man.

It was the same with the death penalty. Henry had always been in favour of the death penalty. For other people. In his case he felt it would quite simply be unfair. He deserved something for what he had done of course. Light whipping maybe. But death? For God's sake! Would his death bring Donald back? Wasn't it simply an archaic desire for revenge? He drank deeply of his gin and tonic.

'But,' said Rush, 'you've got me on my hobby horse!'

'What is your hobby horse?' said Henry.

'The Wimbledon Poisoner,' said Rush. He laughed, briefly, and from his top left-hand pocket drew a sheaf of clippings. Henry wasn't quite sure whether he was supposed to look

174

at them, and in order not to offend the man – he had in fact an almost insane desire to stay on the right side of him – he stretched out his hand for them. Rush moved his hand away with a larky little smile. He wagged a reproving finger at Henry.

'Oh, no you don't!' he said. 'You're the same as me!'

'How do you mean?'

'A local historian.'

'Ah . . .'

Certain things about the man's behaviour were becoming clearer.

'You remember at the Wimbledon Society,' went on Rush, 'last year. They were telling us about Everett Maltby!'

'Were they?'

Why was he unable to remember meeting Rush at the Wimbledon Society? Surely something as important as a talk about Everett Maltby (he was beginning, now, to recall it) would have marked the occasion as something special. It struck him that there might be something sinister in this lapse. His notes on Maltby were constantly going astray, weren't they? Perhaps, Henry didn't like this idea at all, there was something paranormal going on.

'All areas of the world,' Rush was saying, 'have their particular crimes, and the same is true of districts of Britain. There are, for example, an awful lot of cases of death due to sudden, unscheduled abdominal pain in Wimbledon.'

Henry coughed. 'How do you mean?'

'I mean,' said Rush, 'that crime isn't always a matter of bashing an old lady over the head and running away. Real crime can be very much more subtle. Real crime is often hidden, beneath the surface of an apparently respectable community. The doctor who raises his hat to you in the High Street may be one of the Bus Station Buggers. The bank manager may have a rather over-liberal attitude to accounting proceedings. You take my meaning?'

'Not really,' said Henry.

'I'm coming to you,' said Rush, in a tone that suggested

the opposite was the case, 'because of course we're both local history fiends. It's difficult. Quite a few people think I'm way off beam on this one. But I had a hunch you might understand.'

'Understand what?'

Rush flung his arms wide. 'We live on the street,' he said, 'we're neighbours. Let's get together. Let's discuss it. You know what I'm talking about, don't you? You know what I think's going on under the oh-so-respectable surface of this oh-so-respectable manor. I'm talking, of course, about poisoning.'

So this was a social, rather than a business call. Or was it? Was Rush here to frighten him? Or had he some even darker purpose?

'It's just a barmy theory of mine,' he was saying. 'I'm a voice in the wilderness, but I'm convinced, absolutely convinced that there is a poisoner at work in the borough. Here and now!' He gave an enigmatic smile. 'My colleagues think I'm crazy,' said Rush, 'they don't want to know. With them, it's clamp this, clamp that, traffic flow . . . football hooligans . . .' He snorted. 'Football hooligans.'

Then, 'When I first got on to the poisoner, I told a few people, and they were, I have to say, unsympathetic to a degree. But that, if you don't mind me saying so, is the mark of a modern police officer. The door-to-door slog, the house-to-house search, the repetitive, mechanical labour of collecting evidence. Look at the Yorkshire Ripper.'

'Well, indeed,' said Henry, 'indeed, he – '

But Rush ignored him. 'There was no one there who trusted his judgement. Who went out on a limb. Who stood up and said "Look, I have a theory. A crazy theory." Because the psychopath is only to be tracked down by an intuitive guess. He's somebody who otherwise doesn't read as a criminal. He's you!'

He pointed directly at Henry. Henry gave a low squeak.

'He's me! This is the story we're looking at. The Wimbledon Poisoner is out there OK. He's there. He's anyone. He is you and me. He is the dark part of ourselves. You know?'

'Fascinating,' said Henry, 'and . . . er . . . when did you first notice this . . . er . . . pattern of abdominal disorders?'

Rush screwed up his face, paced across to the patch of carpet nearest to the fire, which seemed to be his favourite spot for significant remarks and, wheeling round, did his best bit of pipe work so far, a double lunge, with parry in quarte and passage of waltz-time conducting, followed by a bit of invisible cross-hatching above his ear.

'It clicked,' he said, 'it all fell into place a week or so ago. When I saw you at Donald Templeton's funeral.'

'Let me,' said Henry, 'get you another gin and tonic.'

CHAPTER TWENTY-SIX

It was horrible. The man was playing some elaborate game with him, waiting for him to crack. He might even be lying about the Maltby talk. Oh Jesus, thought Henry, I am very sorry about the poisoning. I really do apologize. If you get me out of this one I will never ever do anything like it again. I will not think unpleasant things about people. I will not . . .

He poured a gin and tonic about twice the size of his first one, drank it and then poured one twice the size of that for Rush. Important to have the man on your side.

Maisie was still crouched by the door.

'You could bring me a drink!' she said.

'Shut up!' hissed Henry.

'It's very interesting,' she said, 'about the poisoner. Who is it, do you think?'

'You shouldn't be listening to this,' said Henry.

When he had been served with his drink, Rush started pacing the carpet once more. 'But I really started,' he said, 'a long, long time ago. You see evidence, in a case like this, has a habit of disappearing. What looks like a normal death . . .'

He took a fairly pristine-looking cutting from the file and thrust it at Henry.

TEMPLETON, Donald [it read]. At his home in Maple Drive after a brief illness. Much loved father of Arfur, and devoted husband to Billykins. 'FOR GOD'S SAKE WHY?'

'She was very upset,' said Henry. 'It's not the best-worded announcement of a death I've ever read.'

Rush snickered. 'It seems pretty carefully worded to me,' he said, ' "brief illness". Not, you notice, "sudden and inexplicable gastric attack", not "after severe abdominal pains". No no no. People aren't interested in that sort of thing. They like to draw a veil over it, don't they?'

He stopped at his favourite patch of carpet and then, as if conscious that he had used this as a base before, moved off towards the window. 'And then,' he went on, 'actually at the funeral, three more deaths! Extraordinary coincidence, don't you think? Extraordinary! But of course no one remarks on it, do they? No one puts two and two together, do they? In the paper we read – '

He handed Henry another cutting. Henry read:

COVENEY, *Rufus. Beloved son of George and Myfanwy. Novelist and critic of note, at Maple Drive after a seizure. 'Go not behind for all is dark before!'*

Henry was studying this quotation and finding it vaguely suggestive when, below it, he saw:

SPROTT, *David. David died peacefully at a social gathering of friends last Tuesday. His funeral will be held at Putney Vale Crematorium, where anyone who wishes a last chance to see him will be most welcome, and afterwards at the family home. Good man, good dentist, good, good, good. 'Farewell.'*

He was beginning to sweat.

'All just slips by, doesn't it?' said Rush. 'Another corpse. Why bother? It is only someone who looks carefully, who studies the evidence, who can put facts together and say "Hang on a tick! There's more here than meets the eye." That's police work, Mr Farr. Constant vigilance. Constant suspicion. It's like having a little man inside who asks nasty questions. I've got a nasty little man inside me and he won't go away. Look at this – '

Rush pushed a much older-looking clipping towards Henry. It read:

PURVIS, *Alan. At Parkside Hospital after a collapse in the Cat o'Nine Tails Bar and Brasserie. O Death where is thy sting? Mourned by Mum, Dad and all at the folkclub.*

'There are others,' said Rush. 'Manning, last September. Severe intestinal pains after an outdoor buffet lunch with a group of salesmen from White's garage, Wimbledon. Pedersen, collapse and subsequent death after ingesting a hamburger at Putney Show. Annabel Lee Evans, only twenty-two, vomiting, diarrhoea and death in May of this year four hours after attending a disco and Bar-B-Q at Southlands College where she ate a meal of curried chicken and coleslaw . . .' He spread his arms wide. 'We're dealing with a maniac. A clever, unscrupulous maniac.'

Henry was inclined to agree with him. He had never met such a maniac in all his life. The man should not be allowed out. But, as Rush continued to pace the carpet, stab the air with his pipe and talk rubbish, Henry wondered whether he might not be misjudging him. He recalled a phrase of Keith Simpson's: 'Almost every event in life is consequent upon a meal.' Just as poisoning was, therefore, hard to detect, it was, by the same token, all the more possible. And once you had fallen under its sway, as Rush had, it offered a hideous but plausible explanation for so many things! In a way, of course, he and Rush were not unalike. Other people would have found them dull. They were dull. They both knew that they were dull. But that didn't stop them.

'A maniac,' said Rush, 'someone who roams the streets, waits his moment, and then, bingo, injects the hamburger, the chocolates, the ham and tomato sandwich, the chicken vindaloo. Lays his little trap and passes on. The poisoner's reward is reading about himself – reading about deaths that *he* made happen. He has a power that no one knows about. *He* made all this happen. He's playing God, don't you agree, Mr Farr?'

Here Rush snaked his head forward at Henry, seeking his interlocutor's eyes, and then, heading back to his favourite bit of carpet, looked around the room for applause. For a moment Henry thought, How does he know? and then, as quickly, realized that he had better not start feeling guilty about poisonings in which he had no involvement. This was taking social responsibility a little too far. He was off the hook, wasn't he? He didn't fit into this guy's theory. Or did he? If he didn't, why was Rush looking at him like that, in that knowing way? Maisie's head appeared round the door.

'Mummy says do you want sandwiches?' she said.

'That would be most kind!' said Rush.

'Chicken mayonnaise or liver sausage?' she said.

'Anything,' said Rush, 'so long as it doesn't contain a registered poison!'

He laughed. A jolly, companionable laugh.

'I'll tell her!' said Maisie.

'It was the deaths in Maple Drive that confirmed my theory,' went on Rush. 'Before then I thought I saw a pattern. And the pattern would evade me. You know? I'd think to myself sometimes, "Rush, you're barmy." No way is there any connection between Julia Neve, who died of quote polyneuritis unquote last February, and Martin Crump the railway worker who died in agony in Roehampton only five hours after eating a meal of peaches, risotto and Continental cheese.'

Elinor appeared at the door, wiping her hands on her apron. Rush looked up at her, sharply, and for a brief moment her eyes met his. *There is one not very far from here who admires me!* thought Henry. He looked across at Elinor as she shook the black hair away from her forehead, and he had to acknowledge that his wife was a very attractive woman. How was he going to keep her? How was he going to put Neighbourhood Watch off the track?

'Are you all right, Henry?' said Elinor.

'Fine, love,' said Henry, 'fine.'

Inspector Rush was looking at him oddly. 'All this talk of poisoning,' he said, 'has put you off your food!'

'Not at all,' said Henry.

181

'Actually,' said Elinor, 'Henry is very interested in poisoning. He's got a whole lot of books about it upstairs.'

Henry decided it was time to intervene. 'Actually,' he said, 'I am very interested in poisoning. I'm thinking of writing a book about it. The . . . er . . . Everett Maltby case got me started. I thought . . . you know . . . I'd look into poisoners as a breed. They're a fascinating bunch. Fascinating!'

Rush's eyes watched him. 'Indeed!' said Rush.

Did he suspect the truth or not?

CHAPTER TWENTY-SEVEN

It was worst of all when he talked about Donald.

'What I don't get,' he would say, his eyes on Henry's face, 'is how the poisoner got to that chicken!'

For there was no doubt in Rush's mind that the chicken that had been Donald Templeton's last meal was in the same category as the tubful of beef satay at the Wimbledon Council's Bring and Buy Sale in Aid of Bangladesh; it had been got at.

'Perhaps,' Henry would say, sweating, 'he got at it in Waitrose.'

'How do you mean?' said Rush, a little smile curling at the edge of his lips. *Pull the other one, squire, it's got bells on it! Come on, Farr! Own up, why don't you, eh? Eh?*

'He could have . . . er . . . injected it through the polythene cover. Or else made up a simulated free-range chicken in his own home and smuggled it into Waitrose.'

Rush would look at Henry. A man who could think up something as perverted as this was quite clearly in the running as a suspect.

'Yes,' he would say, 'ye-es. Or possibly he could have introduced some substance into a batch of saucepans. Easy to do. Smear a little carbon tetrachloride round the edge and next time you cook sprouts it's headache and vomiting and bysey-bye to your renal functions.'

'Except,' Henry replied, 'we were all right.'

'Yes,' Rush said, 'you were all fine and dandy. Weren't you?'

And his little detective's eyes travelled up and down Henry's face, and he smiled that smile again, that bleak little policeman's gesture to levity that said *You better watch your step, sunshine.*

'Ah me,' he continued, 'maybe there is another explanation!'

And he laughed, lightly.

He seemed to be constantly round at the house. One night he was in the front room when Henry returned late from a meeting with his divorce in Aldershot (the woman, it transpired, could only make love to her husband with the dog in the room, 'which,' Henry pointed out, 'might or might not be favourable to her case, depending on the kind of involvement required of the creature'). He invited the two of them out for meals at a fashionable bistro in Wimbledon Village, during which he made several off-colour jokes about poisons. Elinor seemed to find them funny, but Rush's eyes, Henry noted, never left Henry's face.

'It would have been so simple,' said Henry at one point, 'if you could have pushed for an autopsy on . . . er . . . the Maple Drive contingent!'

'Wouldn't it?' he said in a quiet voice.

If Henry had had a soul, Rush would probably have been looking straight into it.

'I pushed for an autopsy on Ellen Wilcox of South Wales Road, New Malden,' he said, 'and my, there was a fuss. I'd showed my hand too early. We found nothing. Since when my . . . superiors have been running scared of me. Never mind if a psychopath gets away. Just don't rock the boat. Eh?'

'Indeed!' said Henry.

'We'll get our autopsy,' said Rush quietly; 'one day he'll overplay his hand. He's crazy. He's bound to. And in the meanwhile, maybe we'll get lucky – '

Here he gave a professionally ghoulish laugh. 'Maybe someone'll forget to bury a body!'

Elinor was staring across the table at him, her eyes bright with the wine. 'Your job,' she said, 'must be fascinating!'

'It is!' said Rush, and he looked levelly at Henry. 'There's nothing more interesting than stalking a criminal. Waiting,

184

watching, listening, and then, suddenly, when he's made his mistake – '

Here he leaned forward and rapped the table sharply with a bread roll.

'Pouncing!'

Henry jumped.

'All we need,' said Rush, 'is a body!'

It was almost November, the week before Hallowe'en, when someone told someone in the street who told someone else in the street who almost immediately told someone who told Elinor who told Henry that Mrs David Sprott, widow of the highly insured dentist, David Sprott, forty-two, kept his mortal remains in a small glass jar on a shelf in their bedroom. She also kept, in a drawer in a dresser in the same bedroom, Sprott's false teeth (one of the most closely guarded secrets in world dentistry), his wire glasses and a small fragment of his beard. It was, as Henry said when he heard, almost as bad as having Sprott himself around.

'His trousers,' said Edwina Sprott in her deep, bass voice, 'are still in the cupboard. His boots are still in the hall.'

Bits of Sprott himself! Powdered dentist! Powdered dentist that might contain traces of Finish 'Em, of bleach, of Shine and Zappiton and whatever else he had put into the punch. The trouble was, Henry didn't know whether such things remained in the ashes of a cremated victim. The police had certainly identified traces of thallium in one of Graham Young's victims. Was the same true for bleach? And how much bleach had they drunk anyway?

'Suppose,' he said to Rush one afternoon, 'one had drunk a fair amount of corrosive fluid . . .'

'Yes . . .'

'And suppose . . .'

'Oh, for God's sake!' said Elinor. 'Can't you two talk about anything but poisoning? There are other things in life, you know. There are healthy, normal things! Things that nourish and sustain!'

Although Elinor had given up her therapy class she still

185

retained traces of their style in her speech. The woman in charge had told her, apparently, that she was cured. She was, Elinor told Henry, a fully rounded human being. She was in no further need of therapy.

At first Henry assumed that this meant the therapy class had finally had enough of her. But on close examination he found his wife to be a perfectly pleasant woman in early middle age, with whom he could not, however hard he tried, find any fault. She had had her hair cut, and started to sing as she went about the house. She began to eat normally. She developed an obsession with television programmes involving American policemen shooting at each other. And she dressed in gayer colours, like a woman who wanted to please a man.

Which man, though? That was the problem.

By the night of Maisie's Hallowe'en party the little bits of Sprott on Mrs Sprott's mantelpiece had become a major talking point in Wimbledon. Almost the only person in the street who had not discussed the issue with Henry and Elinor was Detective Inspector Rush. Rush, Henry decided, was waiting for Henry to make his mistake.

'She's got Sprott in a vase!' he said, as he arrived for Maisie's party, carrying, as he often did when visiting the house, a large bunch of flowers for Elinor. 'The remains of Sprott,' he went on, 'are less than a hundred yards from where we are standing.' And he looked hungrily over in the direction of the dentist's house.

Henry coughed. 'I . . . er . . . know!' he said.

Why was the man mentioning this fairly well-known piece of local gossip now? Because, presumably, he felt sure that Henry was about to make that 'fatal mistake' to which the policeman was always referring. If Rush thought he was about to make a fatal mistake, thought Henry, he had better go right ahead and make one. In the end it would probably be simpler.

Maisie was wearing fangs and a black cloak. Henry had a rubber hammer sticking out of his head and a highly realistic bloodstain across his temple. Elinor was looking, Henry thought, rather ravishing, in a kind of black silk bodystocking. He was looking at her back when Rush approached, and trying to decide whether he had made the right move by resolving not to poison her. She had been showing signs, lately, of a reawakened interest in sex, which Henry was not entirely sure was a good thing. Only last night she had made a number of arch references which Henry thought seemed to imply that they had had anal intercourse in the lavatory of a train between Margate and Ramsgate. He could not remember ever going to Ramsgate let alone buggering his wife on public transport in that area of the country.

'Sprott,' said Rush, his eyes on Henry's face, 'in a vase! Makes you think, doesn't it?'

'Come on!' said Elinor gaily. 'We're going to frighten people!'

The other thing about post-thallium Elinor was that she seemed to have become almost relentlessly cheerful. Especially when in the company of Detective Inspector Rush. This, thought Henry, is probably Her Moment. He would have liked to have had a Moment. Unemployed Journalist with Punk Hairstyle, from 194, was always talking about His Moment which, apparently, occurred in something called The Seventies. Younger people talked about The Seventies as if they were something that actually happened, and not, as they were for Henry, a sort of ghastly blur punctuated by requests for money from the National Westminster Bank's Home Loans Service.

Maybe this was her moment. She was flowering, just as he, Henry, was about to fall into whatever trap it was the detective inspector had set for him. He looked across at Rush, who was wearing a brown trilby and had on a battered, rather dated suit, very different from his usual neat blue outfit. He was also, Henry noted, sporting a small false moustache.

'Who are you supposed to be?' said Henry with just a trace of irritation.

Rush smiled enigmatically. 'I should have thought you would have recognized the allusion,' he said, allowing his smile to curl upwards like paper in a furnace, 'being a keen student of poisoners!'

Henry started to shake.

'Would you?' he said, more than ever convinced that the man was trying to frighten him into doing something foolish.

'I'm Hawley Harvey Crippen,' said Rush, 'of Hilldrop Crescent. The meek little man who wanted to murder his wife. And so bought five grams of hyoscine which he gave her.'

Elinor and Maisie were now some yards ahead of them. Henry found he was talking in a whisper. 'People,' he said, 'do murder their wives, don't they?'

'They do,' said Rush, 'and if they do . . . we often find they're capable of anything. Now – shall we talk about how to get hold of Sprott? For the purposes of analysis.'

CHAPTER TWENTY-EIGHT

'Who shall we frighten first?' said Maisie. 'Let's frighten someone who doesn't like me.' She laughed ghoulishly. 'Gives us a lot of scope!' she added.

'I know,' said Elinor, 'let's frighten Accountant Who Talks a Lot!'

She had recently taken to attempting to follow Henry's re-christening of the neighbourhood, without noticeable success. She lacked malice, thought Henry, looking at her and remembering vaguely why it was he had wanted to kill her.

'Let's!' he said.

'The trouble is,' said Rush, 'because that bloody doctor did what he did I'll have a devil of a job to get a look at him officially.' He chewed his lip. 'Evidence, evidence, evidence,' he muttered. 'All I want's a body!'

'Come on, Maisie!' said Elinor.

Maisie made a farting noise with her lips and followed her mother.

'We could ask to borrow his ashes,' said Rush, 'for senti-mental reasons.'

'You're a policeman,' said Henry. 'For God's sake! Can't you impound him? Or subpoena him or something?'

Why had he said this?

'I'm afraid,' said Rush darkly, 'there are not many who think as we do. To some the poisoner is a fanciful notion!'

Henry thought he could understand the reasons for this.

'I'm regarded,' said Rush, 'as a bit of a joke!' And he gave Henry that intimate glance, as if to imply that only the two of them knew the real secret. Yes, thought Henry, he knows, but is never going to tell. He's going to amuse himself with me, torment me with this shared secret until one day I can't stand it any more and I find myself screaming to anyone who'll listen – 'I DID IT! I DID IT! TAKE ME AWAY!' This, of course, had happened to Raskolny-whatever-his-name-was, hadn't it?

Maisie was now running ahead of the group. In her right hand she was carrying a bright red apple. Henry tried to break away from Rush who, without apparent effort, seemed to be able to stay about a yard from his left elbow. Police training presumably.

They were at the corner of Maple Drive. The garden of the house in front of them, piled high with builder's rubbish, looked dark and threatening to Henry. Hallowe'en was quite frightening enough without dressing up as a monster with an axe in your head. Saying the word, hearing the shrieks of the children in the neighbouring streets . . . Over to the right a group of rowdy little girls was approaching, decked out in black hats and coats and rather fetching little broomsticks. 'Trick or treat, trick or treat?' they were singing. 'We have slime that you must eat!'

'What's the apple for, Maisie?' asked Henry.

'I thought somebody might bob for it,' she said. Maisie looked at the apple as if surprised at the fact that she was holding it. It was improbably large and shiny, a fairy-tale apple. Had she had it with her when she came out?

'Where did you get it?'

Maisie looked at it, puzzled. 'I'm not sure,' she said, 'I just got it.'

That was the other thing about children. Just as they had started to stun you into silence with their maturity, their knowledge of sex relations or the IRA they hit you with cluelessness and infantile jokes or a bewildering ignorance about something on which you had assumed they would be well informed. If only, thought Henry, people would be one thing and stick to it. If wives would be nice or nasty, if . . . oh, his trouble was easy to spot. He wanted the world to stay the way it was.

Rush was giving him one of those looks again. Henry tried to move away from him, and went in pursuit of Maisie.

'Who,' she said to him as he drew level with her, 'are we going to frighten?'

'We are going to frighten Jungian Analyst with Winebox,' said Henry, 'and we are going to terrify his wife, Lingalonga Boccherini, not to mention Birdwatching Child Viola Player and Sensationally Articulate Twelve-Year-Old!'

Jungian Analyst with Winebox was a man called Gordon, who for some reason always insisted on being called Gord. He was married to an immensely tall, thin woman with huge eyes and a mournful manner, who for no very good reason was known to Henry as Lingalonga Boccherini. The other two were their children, Caedmon and Wulfstan. Elinor, who was an old friend of Lingalonga Boccherini, had never heard this name before, although she seemed to know to whom Henry was referring.

'Do you mean,' she said edgily, 'Gord and Julia?'

'I do!'

'I don't think,' she said, 'that is a funny or clever way of describing them.'

'They can take it,' said Henry, 'they're psychiatrists.'

'I don't think we should frighten them,' said Elinor.

'Why not?' said Henry. 'Why should psychiatrists be exempt from being frightened! They dish it out all the time, don't they? They tell you you're regressive and introverted and immature and God knows what. They're always going on about the importance of ceremonies, aren't they? Why shouldn't we scare the arse off them?'

'Because,' said Elinor, 'they'll be out frightening someone else.'

Henry began to find this conversation bracing. Gord and Julia were, of course, Elinor's friends. All Elinor's friends belonged to Elinor, although it was understood that if Henry ever acquired anyone interesting (the nearest he had ever got to it was Donald, which was not, Henry felt, very near) then Elinor had rights of trespass on them.

'It's very important,' Elinor was saying, 'for them to

express anger. That's why you're such a mess, Henry. Because you don't express your anger.'

Henry felt his neck thicken in his collar and wondered whether not poisoning Elinor might be bad for his health. Gord and Julia didn't need to express anger as far as he was concerned. What they all too clearly felt was that it was a public disgrace that someone as disgusting as Henry should be allowed to stalk about the place unanalysed. But Henry had seen them *get* angry at him. He had seen their lips tighten when he referred to all psychiatrists as 'shrinks' and to all psychiatric theories as 'bollocks'.

Henry did not like analysts. He was frightened of them. The idea of lying on a couch and telling someone everything that was in your mind! Everything in Henry's mind! That 'open sewer' as Elinor, in one of her less charitable moments, had called it. Where would he start? With the poisoning? The incessant masturbation? The feelings of hatred towards absolutely everyone?The total lack of moral scruple? The compulsive eating? The lack of talent? And what would he be left with if all this were taken away?

'Jungian Analyst with Winebox,' said Henry, 'deserves frightening. Him and his mane of white hair. Walking around, conducting imaginary orchestras. He deserves frightening right out of his sensible, caring, cord trousers.'

'He won't be *in!*' wailed Elinor.

'He'll be in,' said Henry; 'he broke his leg!'

Maisie finally decided the matter. She wanted to frighten Caedmon and Wulfstan. They would not, thought Henry, be difficult to frighten.

Jungian Analyst with Winebox and his family lived in a small cottage on the edge of the common. Here, surrounded by clavichords, violas and books about dreams, they looked out at the south side of the common as the dusk came in through the beech trees.

The party went up through Belvedere Avenue and into Church Road, then left towards the village High Street. Here expensive cars, parked nose to tail, waited for their owners.

The village itself wore, as usual, the air of some carefully designed exhibition at Olympia, and Henry, looking at the wooden shopfronts and the come-hither graphics in the windows, the resolutely phoney atmosphere of the antique, saw, the way some people saw skulls under skin and hair, the plaster, the rotten beams, the real, ugly history that held the suburb together.

Everett Maltby had started to frighten him. Perhaps it was the night, perhaps it was Rush, trotting behind him like some apparently biddable dog, perhaps it was the disturbing power his career as a murderer seemed to have given him, but as they crossed on to the damp grass Henry felt haunted by something. This was how Maltby felt, wasn't it? When he watched his wife die? And wasn't that another set of footsteps he could hear behind him on the cold pavement? The footsteps of a man with a pale face and a high wing collar and a handshake as clammy as the evening.

Henry walked ahead of Elinor, and seizing Maisie by the hand ran forward towards the cottage that stood, alone, at the edge of the grass. In a sudden hurry to get this over, he raised his hand to beat out a rhythm on the door, but before he could do so, just as Maisie was preparing to screech a witch's curse, it was flung open from the other side and from the darkness came a howl like a hungry wolf's.

CHAPTER TWENTY-NINE

'GO AWAY!' shouted Gordon Macrae. 'AWAY! AWAYA-WAY!' He had clearly been at the winebox. He did not turn on the light but stood in the shadows, his mane of white hair shaking this way and that. Maisie stepped back, whimpering. Macrae's voice seemed to have been amplified in some curious way.

'It's Hallowe'en!' he shouted, in the same ghostly voice. 'It's Hallowe'en. There are spirits abroad. Away! Away! The damned are out tonight! There is Evil in the air! I feel it!'

All this was fairly standard with Macrae. As the author of a bestselling book about the significance of gesture and a brief but telling study of death and exorcism, he waved a mean arm, and, when he chose, frightened pretty good. Tonight, however, perhaps prompted by the season, he was almost worryingly effective. Behind him, in the pale hall, the even paler figure of Lingalonga Boccherini emerged. She looked, thought Henry, like a crofter's wife, caught at a nasty moment in the Clearances. She was wearing a brown shawl, a brown headdress and stout brown shoes and, as if to emphasize her resemblance to something out of a diorama in the Folk Museum, Aberdeen, she stretched out her hand towards Gordon and began to keen.

'Oh no . . .' said Lingalonga Boccherini. 'Oh no-oo-oo . . .'

Maisie cowered behind Henry. She had clearly not expected resistance. At Hallowe'en you went round and scared people and they gave you sweets. They didn't rush out at you with plasters on their legs, howling and keening.

Jungian Analyst with Winebox produced from behind his back a knobbed walking stick and began to wave it. 'There is a curse out tonight!' he went on. 'A curse! Away! Away foul fiends! Away!'

Then he laughed. Maisie clearly found the laugh the most frightening thing about him. She ran into Henry's coat, as in the remote distances of the hall two figures in pyjamas, of the kind Henry could remember from his childhood, striped flannel jobs with white string cords, crept towards Lingalonga Boccherini. Caedmon and Wulfstan.

Caedmon (or was it Wulfstan?) was saying something. 'Please mother,' he was saying, 'just one more two-part canzonetta before bedtime!'

Lingalonga Boccherini did not hit him hard in the pit of the stomach for this remark. She continued to keen in the direction of her husband.

'Yaaargh!' said Elinor, rather lamely.

Nobody seemed very frightened.

'Hullo, Julia!' she said.

Maisie stepped out from behind Henry's coat. 'Oooowaaieeeiou!' she howled, and then, 'Eaaaargh!'

Lingalonga Boccherini smiled sweetly at her. 'Oh, Maisie . . .' she said, 'lovely!'

And then, from the shadows, came Inspector Rush. He had been standing in the long grass, a little out of sight of the Macrae family, but in two steps he was caught in the yellow light of a street lamp, his neat mackintosh pulled up round his face, his trilby well down over his eyes. He had sucked in his cheeks and stroked his moustache. His attempt to seem sinister was undermined, however, by his voice. Rush was quite simply unable to stop sounding like a man asking you whether you were aware that you were travelling in a bus lane with out-of-date tax disc on display.

'Name's Crippen! Hawley Harvey Crippen. Hilldrop Crescent. Would the kiddies care for a cup of hot, sweet tea?'

Birdwatching Child Viola Player burst into tears. 'Who's that horrid man, Mummy?' he wailed.

'It's Crippen!' said Henry, ghoulishly. 'We found him on the common. He's a poisoner!'

Macrae cackled. He seemed pleased by the sight of his own children's mental collapse. 'Jolly good!' he cackled. 'Jolly good! Crippen! Hawley Harvey Crippen, of course! The man who loved his wife!' He winked broadly at Elinor.

'Poisoners,' said Macrae, not asking them to come in, or to come any nearer his winebox than was absolutely necessary, 'poisoners love their subjects. It's their way of saying "I want you and I don't want anyone else to have you." Julia is writing a paper on it, aren't you Julia?'

Lingalonga Boccherini looked up from Caedmon. Her face had moved, as so often, from melancholy gladness, to sudden, irrational terror. 'Yes,' she said, 'poison is nourishment!'

Rush gazed at her with some respect.

'Poison is all the bad things we think about anyone expressed in chemical form, isn't it? And it's nearly always served with love and attention, to turn the loved one into a victim, the way in which the possessive mother – '

Here Jungian Analyst with Winebox pointed at his wife's head.

'Which of course, as Gordon says, I am – the possessive mother seeks to control her child, of course, very much in the way the doctor controls the patient. Because motherhood, like murder, is controlling. And we say, don't we, that motherhood is "murder". Or that the children have been "murder" today. And that is because, of course, we want to kill them because we love them and because our love is, literally, murder, which is why we want to put arsenic on their fish fingers or whatever!'

Wulfstan started to howl. Jungian Analyst with Winebox laughed and went back into the darkened hall after his son. Lingalonga Boccherini shrank back with the boy in her arms.

'And chop them up!' her husband added. 'And fry them and serve them to the neighbours the way they do in Polynesia! Best thing to do with your wife and your children, in my opinion! Eat them before they eat you! Ha ha ha!'

Caedmon was also looking on the verge of tears. As indeed, thought Henry, will I be if he doesn't let us in and at the Côtes de Nuit fairly soon. But Jungian Analyst with

Winebox showed no signs of letting them past his front porch. He paced around in the darkened hallway, waving his arms frantically, free associating, free of charge, into the dank November night.

'The Manichees,' he went on, 'believed that virtue and evil are locked up in certain foods. Rather like saying, if you grasp this, that bananas are immoral!'

'Or toast and marmalade is good!' said Henry, brightly. Macrae looked at him suspiciously.

'Evil dwelleth in the frankfurter!' went on Henry. But this remark only made matters worse.

Macrae gripped him by the collar and, with undisguised dislike, said, 'Food. Don't you see? Food *is* morality. Why do you think we lay such emphasis on "table manners"? Why do we need to control our eating?'

'Because,' said Henry, hoping that Macrae would put him down soon, 'we don't want to get fat!'

'Listen to the words we use about food,' replied Macrae, slackening his grip, 'we offer someone a drink and say "what's your poison"?'

'I'll have a Côtes de Nuit!' said Henry.

'We want, of course, to kill our friend, to punish him for his greed because, of course, the irony of food is that it is a hunger for spirit, as in the communion wafer for example, the sacrament of married life, say, in which we eat each other and no one gets the leftovers. And the irony of poison is that it is a hunger not for death, but for life, for the spirit that quickens! It is a way of bringing the loved one in direct contact with the Almighty.'

Rush goggled at him from out of the darkness. He had clearly never met anyone like Jungian Analyst with Winebox before. The Wimbledon CID, thought Henry, probably used a much tamer species of psychiatrist. But Maisie, who was now clearly out of her depth and anxious to restore some kind of festive quality to this encounter, stepped forward with the apple in her hand. Perhaps, Henry thought later, she was going to offer it to him as a reward for shutting up;

197

in fact it provoked a new torrent of speculation on Macrae's part.

'The apple!' he said. 'Of course! The apple! The apple that we bob for at Hallowe'en is of course the same apple offered to Snow White in the fairytale! What is it? The apple of death in life. The apple of desire that Eve forced Adam to eat in the Garden of Eden. The apple of the female principle. The feminists understand this, don't they? The male poisons the apple to kill his mother, of course!'

'Oh, yes,' chimed in Lingalonga Boccherini, 'because this aspect of nourishment is perceived of as threatening by the male, isn't it?'

Macrae was nodding vigorously. When on this course the Macraes could keep up a kind of antiphonal exchange that, in Henry's experience, could last hours. He began to peer past them in the direction of the kitchen where lay the wine-box of Côtes de Nuit.

'But in the folktale, of course,' went on Lingalonga Boccherini, in the dreamy, hypnotic voice that had been largely responsible for her nickname, 'after she has eaten the poisoned apple, poisoned by the wicked possessive mother, who is someone like me really, I suppose, she falls into a faint and she can only be wakened by a kiss from a male, that is to say, a prince, which isn't really a kiss of course but the male urge to rape and violate and explain away the contradictions of the female, very much as you, Gordon, of course try and destroy me sexually!'

'Absolutely!' said Macrae, nodding.

He took the apple from Maisie and held it up high, shaking his white hair out behind him. 'The apple of good and evil, of the carnal and uncarnal knowledge of others! Why else do we bob for it at Hallowe'en? Because of course it represents the evil spirits that are around tonight. Here, even as we speak! And yet of course, we must not, as Adam in the garden did or Snow White at the gate of the cottage, bite into this round, red juicy thing, for it is, of course, tainted. It is the apple of death!'

Here he suited his actions to the words and gnawed a chunk of the fruit away. It had crisp, white flesh and that treasured, sour smell of apples that Henry remembered from his childhood, when his mother . . . Why was he thinking about his mother?

'If we bite into it and chew it we go blue! And choke! And whirl around like this!'

Here he performed what was, even for Macrae, a fantastically good impression of someone dying of prussic acid poisoning. He leapt up in the air, tugged at his collar, gave a ghastly choking sound and, his face blue, fell forward on to the path in front of the house.

It was only when he failed to rise that Henry stooped down beside him and discovered that the psychiatrist was stone dead.

CHAPTER THIRTY

The worst thing about being a serial killer, Henry reflected in the weeks after the demise of Gordon Macrae, was that you might not know you were a serial killer. You might think you were jogging along with the occasional regrettable lapse, such as the poisoning of a few people in the road, but by and large, you might suppose, you were a decent enough citizen. And then, one day, you might wake up and discover that when you thought you had been watching the television or mowing the lawn you had, in fact, been out garrotting people on towpaths.

Christ, Henry could not even remember the names of people with whom he had had dinner the night before. He had for years of their marriage offered Elinor both tea and coffee, forgetting she did not like either, and these days was unable to remember talks he had given on (oh, my Christ!) the Wimbledon Poisoner. Suppose he was *the* Wimbledon Poisoner? Not the half-hearted creature he knew himself to be but a real, top-level psychopath.

Because on the inquest on Gordon Macrae it was revealed by a very senior police forensic scientist that the apple contained enough prussic acid to wipe out half the Jungians in Wimbledon. 'And thereby,' said Henry to Elinor, 'saving the neurotics of the district a large amount of valuable time and money.'

Everyone wanted to know where Maisie had got the apple. She couldn't remember. The more they asked her the more she couldn't remember. She didn't seem distressed by their questions, remarking to one particularly insistent WPC, 'I didn't kill him! I didn't like him but I didn't kill him!'

For a time Henry thought she might be following in his footsteps. But even Maisie was not up to the purchase of prussic acid, let alone injecting it into an apple. The more he thought about it, the more Henry became certain – along with all the national and local press – that there was such a person as the Wimbledon Poisoner. And that he was it.

'MADMAN ON LOOSE IN WIMBLEDON!' they said in the London *Standard*. And 'IS THERE A POISONER IN YOUR ROAD?' They published artists' impressions of a man people had seen behaving suspiciously near the scene of the crime (which looked, as Elinor remarked, exactly like Henry). They published analyses of him by eminent psychiatrists, who were more than usually censorious about the unknown assassin. All the sketches of the poisoner's character sounded, to Henry, like Henry.

When, he wondered, as he rattled in to Harris, Harris and Overdene, would he strike again? A client of his in Epsom threatened suicide if contracts were not exchanged on his house by Christmas. But Henry could not concentrate on work. He sat staring out at Ludgate Circus, waiting for the red mist that would send him off down the road, in a deep trance, for another kilo of antimony.

At times he wondered whether he might not only be the Wimbledon Poisoner but a few other psychopaths into the bargain. His guilt knew no bounds and, if there was any consolation, it was that Donald, Sprott, Coveney and Loomis no longer caused him any pain. They were simply a step along the road for the poisoner, an episode when, for some inexplicable reason, he had remained fully conscious while perpetrating his despicable acts.

'WHO IS HE?' asked the local paper. 'CHECK YOUR SUPERMARKET TROLLEY. HE MAY HAVE GOT THERE FIRST!'

In Waitrose plain-clothes policemen loitered ostentatiously near the shelves full of chicken legs, pre-packed meatballs and pork chops. They folded their arms and whistled near the cereal packets and the spaghetti and were seen browsing through Smoked Meats with the thoroughness of a bibliophile in an antiquarian bookstore. But no lunatic, syringe in one hand, packet of poison in the other, was spotted. At dinner parties – although as the poisoner scare went on there were less and less dinner parties – people made hearty jokes about bringing their tasters along with them, but it was noticeable that even people like Surveyor With Huge Gut and Fondness for Potatoes (24b) toyed with their food in a way that they would not have once done. Tins were popular, although one paper published an account of how someone with a little technical knowledge had been able to inject noxious substances into three cans of Heinz Beans and Burger Bites.

Rush was interviewed everywhere. He even appeared on television news, smiling enigmatically. 'What,' said the interviewer, 'is the poisoner like?' There was a pause and Rush leaned slightly towards camera. Then he said, in a low, serious voice, 'He is, in my professional opinion – a monster.' Several papers profiled him; one, which referred to him as 'superhumanly dedicated to his job', titled its piece 'NO RUSH TO JUDGEMENT'.

He was suddenly a star, and his colleagues and superiors, some of whom trudged with him on his house-to-house searches, clearly resented the fact. They responded by looking at each other significantly every time Rush played with his pipe, narrowed his eyes or in room after room (Henry was actually allowed to accompany him because of what was termed his 'special local knowledge') he made for exactly the same spot of carpet and made exactly the same speech.

There could be only one reason why Rush wanted Henry to accompany him, of course. He wanted Henry to see how close he was getting, to join in at every stage of the game, to watch each clue unroll, to stand helplessly by as the trail that led to Henry and only to Henry was uncovered. But he had no choice in the matter.

The first thing Rush did was to track down those suspected poisoner victims who had been buried and start digging them up as fast as he could. There was, everyone agreed, not much time. The editorial in the *New Statesman* announced that poison was 'well and truly ensconced in the bloodstream of our national life', blamed the low wages paid to employees of supermarkets and demanded swift action. The *Sun* ('GIVE HIM A DOSE OF HIS OWN MEDICINE') led the call for a new, possibly chemically based method of execution for dealing with this kind of pervert. An enterprising youth set up a stall in the High Street, selling Poisoner Products (T-shirts, plastic syringes and Poisoner Peppermints – 'Suck them and you do feel queer!') before he was moved on by a policeman who had somehow got left out of the house-to-house search.

At first, Rush did not have great success with his autopsies. Patricia Leigh Smith who collapsed and died five hours after eating a tuna fish salad at a whist drive in Merton in 1986 had her bones ground up and sifted, but nothing was revealed. But then Hugh Padworth, who collapsed and died six hours after consuming a Bakewell tart at a fête in Putney, was found to contain traces of arsenic ('HE'S A POISONER VICTIM – IT'S OFFICIAL!' *Wimbledon News*). But Rush, like many dedicated detectives, had nothing but an ever-increasing list of suspects to offer an increasingly disturbed public, and his investigations, apart from worrying everyone a good deal more than they were already, did not seem to be leading anywhere.

Maisie was very excited by the poisoner. She had proposed a project at school on Poisons and Poisoning. She had composed a short song, which she sang constantly, the chorus of which went, 'It's good for you! Take it down! Take it down!' Elinor, too, developed a passionate interest in the case. It eclipsed feminism, Nicaragua; even whales, it appeared, were a poor second to the poisoner. She announced that she was starting work on a monograph, provisionally entitled 'The Politics of Poisoning', which, she told Henry, would deal with everything, from prussic acid to salmonella in eggs. 'It is,' she told him, embracing an issue that seemed to give a new dimension to his hobby, 'an additive issue. It's a statement about us because we are defined by what we eat.' But, while all around him were united by their fear of the person who, according to which newspaper you read, stalked or lurked or smouldered through the quiet borough of Wimbledon, Henry grew more and more isolated, more and more frightened by each knock at the door, each ring at the bell. It wouldn't be long now, he told himself, before Rush tired of his game. With each new piece of hard evidence Rush's smile grew wider, until, thought Henry, he was almost nudging and winking at him.

When he finally came to call, one afternoon in late November, when all the leaves had gone from the trees and cyclists and pedestrians walked hunched against the cold east wind that people said would blow till Christmas, it came as a relief. Henry knew, he thought, as he saw him walk up to the house, that he was in the last phase of the game he was playing. He was steady-eyed as he pressed the bell and when Henry answered it he didn't speak or move to come in, just stood on the threshold, the street behind him, his eyes full of enigmatic mockery. Henry took him into the kitchen and offered him a drink.

'Why do you think he does it?' he said, when the silence was becoming unbearable.

'Who knows?' said Rush. 'Resentment against society?'

'It's funny,' said Henry, 'I've got a lot of . . . resentments. Against society.'

'Really,' said Rush, 'and you such a quiet chap.'

It was curiously easy to talk about all this to Rush. Perhaps this, thought Henry, was what it was like talking to a psychiatrist. His words seemed to fall like coins down a well, into a silence that went on and on, waiting for a distant impact.

'Oh yes,' said Henry, 'I mean Gordon Macrae . . . for example . . .'

Jungian Analyst with Winebox! That's what you called him, you callous bastard, didn't you? Eh? Eh?

'And who are these . . . resentments . . . directed against?' said Rush.

He seemed to be speaking very, very gently, his voice no more than breath on a pane of glass. It disturbed Henry's train of thought no more than a small animal might disturb the undergrowth on one of its tracks.

'Oh . . . everyone . . .' said Henry. 'I think . . . people have got it in for me. I think they're out to get me. I think they're all doing better than me.'

Rush's face was not the pinched mask it usually seemed. His skin seemed paper thin, the way Henry's father's had before his heart attack; he had that dried-out vulnerability you sometimes see in old men.

'I mean,' said Henry, 'I might be . . . I might . . .'

Rush leaned forward. 'Might be what?'

'I might be the bloody poisoner! You know!'

Rush nodded slowly. 'Yes,' he said, 'yes.'

Was this it? Was this the beginning of the long journey to the Old Bailey, the endless dashing in and out of police stations with a blanket over one's head? Could he go the whole way now? And confess? He wanted, suddenly, to confess. He wanted to own up to those ghastly thoughts that floated into his head, that, in some awful way, sustained him, the things he didn't speak about even to himself. Because if he confessed he might be like other people once again. He might end this awful, nightmarish isolation.

Henry looked back into Rush's eyes and thought, He understands. He knows about people like me. But could not, for some reason, say the words he wanted to say. He let his head droop and found himself staring at the carpet, at an irregular brown stain to the left of the sofa. Rush was saying something, in that quiet, gentle voice of his.

'I think . . .' he said softly, 'we should get hold of Sprott's ashes. Don't you?'

CHAPTER THIRTY-ONE

What Henry didn't understand was why Rush didn't pull him in. He was by now under considerable pressure. Any large-scale murder investigation, as Sam Baker QC (almost) reminded Henry at dinner, made a star out of a detective. It also brought him into what could be uncomfortable public prominence.

'WHAT ARE THEY DOING ABOUT THE POISONER?' a story in the local paper asked. Keen-eyed young men in glasses paced the pavement outside the All England Lawn Tennis Club and asked the camera keen-eyed questions to which it did not respond. Rush was interviewed outside Wimbledon police station, where his acting style came in handy. But he was still unable to provide the Great British Public with hard evidence.

'WHEN WILL HE STRIKE AGAIN?' the newspapers asked. And Henry, quivering in front of the television, wondered when he would.

Come on Rush! Make it safe to go into the supermarket!

'Of course,' said Lustgarten, 'Detective Inspector Rush, that keen-eyed and conscientious policeman, had not yet proof in the one case where he thought he might be able to lay an offence directly at the door of the morally maimed creature who lived at 54 Maple Drive. He bound himself closer and closer to Farr, waiting for the sociopath to let slip a remark that might bring him to the modern equivalent of the gallows. And Farr himself, whose conscious apprehension of his inner, murderous self had only arisen in relation to his wife, the feminist, Elinor, could not but accede to the detective's wily request to be "in" on the murder investigation! A cruel irony! As his love burgeoned again for Mrs Farr, it burgeoned, as it so often does, too late! He was doomed! But Fate does not deal kindly with those who step into that no man's land where dwell the lost and hapless souls who bear the Mark of Cain!'

Lustgarten, like Rush, like everyone, was getting rather hysterical.

And it was, as Lustgarten said, ironically true that, as the affair of the Wimbledon Poisoner became first local, then national, then international news, Elinor seemed to grow sweeter and more reasonable with each day that passed. Over supper they would discuss the case and feel genuine retrospective sorrow for (say) Loris Kemp, now alleged to have been poisoned after ingesting a lamb korma at a tandoori restaurant in Wimbledon in March 1987. They often had sex after these discussions. Their congress seemed to grow out of the case. In the middle of a sentence ('But how did he get the stuff into the pickle? If it was the pickle? Did he –?') they would break off and find themselves eating each other over the ruins of the supper table. They did it in ways that were only hinted at in sex manuals. They whipped each other with towels and leather belts. They did it on the floor, surrounded by Maisie's crisps and the remains of their evening meal. They pulled off their clothes as they climbed the stairs and copulated on the landing. They enjoyed long sessions in which physical release was preceded by pleasurable verbal abuse ('You're fat!' 'I know!' 'You're a fat bitch!' 'Yes yes yes, I'm a fat bitch.' 'I'm going to fuck you because you're fat!' 'Yes, oh yes, yes oh, I'm fat!' 'It's *because* you're fat that I'm fucking you!' 'Yes yes yes, oh yes, fuck me, I'm fat!' '*I'm* fat too!' 'Yes yes yes, you're fat!' 'I'm fat and I'm fucking you!' 'Oh God yes. Oh God yes, you are so fat and you're fucking me, oh God!' 'Oh my darling, we're both fat and we're fucking each other and it's so good!' 'Oh yes, we're both fat and we're fucking and it's so good, it's so fucking good and fat!' etc., etc.). In the week in which Rush announced that the deaths of an Irish family of eight in Southfields ('HE KILLS OFF HIS BEAT') were traceable to a kebab served to them by the proprietor of a Greek restaurant in

Raynes Park, Elinor and Henry climaxed, simultaneously, a staggering twelve times.

Partly, of course, Henry told himself, this was due to the fact that, at long last, people were beginning to take an interest in Wimbledon. 'Interest' was putting it mildly. Journalists moved into hotels near the village. They wrote long colour pieces about the fear that stalked the borough, and even, in some cases, went into the history of the place at some length. They got drunk in the Dog and Fox and tried to persuade the barmaid to pose for a saucy snap, holding a cheese roll to her lips. And on 10 December, after a particularly gruelling interview with a man from the *Sunday Times*, Rush showed Henry the following letter:

Dear Detective Inspector Rush,

I am writing to you, at a time when I realize you must be under great pressure, to ask if I could possibly take some minutes of your time. I am engaged in commissioning a book about the Wimbledon Poisoner, to be written by Jonathan Freemantle, who has written several highly praised books about mass murderers. As Jonathan is away in India at the moment, interviewing researchers, I have promised him that I would approach you to see if you would be able to co-operate with us in the planned work.

I shall be staying in Wimbledon for a few days in the week after next and wondered if I could buy you lunch and discuss the case with you? I would stress that we do not contemplate a sensational piece but a serious study of some of the sociological issues involved in the Wimbledon poisonings.

Yours sincerely,

Karim Jackson

Editorial Director

Brawl Books, London N1.

'A Pakistani gentleman, I imagine,' said Rush darkly, 'with, I have no doubt, negative views of the force!'

'Seems a fairly inoffensive letter to me!' said Henry.

'I'll put the word out he's coming down!' said Rush. 'He sounds like a troublemaker to me.'

Henry smiled weakly. He could no longer feel as angry as he once had about Jackson. The trouble was, once you had started being charitable, it was very hard to stop. Some of Rush's expressions struck him as grotesquely out of place, until he realized that, once, he had thought and spoken exactly like that. He recognized his old self in Rush and did not much care for it. Involved in all of this was also plain, straightforward fear. He felt about the detective inspector the way snakes are reported to feel about mongooses. As usual with Rush, he was fairly sure that what the man was actually confiding to him was in a kind of code. Was he trying to let Henry know that yes, he knew about Henry's book, about Henry's racism, about yet another unhealed sore? Since his first suggestion that they get hold of Sprott's ashes, he had not mentioned the subject, except very indirectly, and then only as a response to a question of Henry's. In order to get an autopsy, said Rush, he would have to have an inquest; this would create 'bad feeling in the street'. Mrs Sprott didn't want to be bothered with such things.

Of course, thought Henry, an inquest would only prove that Sprott had an unusually large amount of bleach inside him. And Rush wanted more than that. He wanted the only thing that would get him a conviction – a confession. And Henry knew all about confessions. The police used any and every method of extorting them from suspects. Once the detective inspector had declared his hand, all Henry had to do was deny. He was being cleverer than that. He was making friends with Henry. He was slowly and surely creating an atmosphere in which Henry wanted to tell him things, to confide in him. And what better atmosphere than one in which the two of them became partners in a kind of crime. It was as if Rush was a kind of accessory to Henry's guilt.

The policeman's very panic at the thought of not catching the poisoner (already people were suggesting wild and fantastic suspects, from the star of a current TV soap opera to a member of the royal family) had communicated itself to

Henry, so that at times, in the way one finishes a sentence for an old friend, he wanted to see Rush's uncertainty resolved.

The other thing that made the advent of Advent more than usually unpleasant was the thought that, somehow or other, Everett Maltby was responsible for all of this. In the days after Gordon Macrae's death Henry went, two or three times, to *The Complete History* to refresh his memory about the Maltby case. On one occasion he got as far as looking out his notes on the poisoner; but when he had got within five or six pages of what he now thought of as the danger area, the paper seemed to weigh on his fingers. It was rather like recalling a party at which one had misbehaved or, more nearly, staying away from a dark room in which something (what?) could be heard moving. It woke in Henry all sorts of fears and anxieties that made him set down the manuscript and stare out of the study window at the bald suburban garden for hour after hour.

It was at such moments that Henry could see himself doing the ghastly things the poisoner was supposed to do. And he found the only company that seemed able to relieve him, the only person with whom he felt able to share anything was Inspector Rush. He was almost getting to like Rush. They spent long hours walking across the common, whole afternoons sitting in Henry's front room, neither of them speaking. If Henry went to the pub, Rush accompanied him; and sometimes the detective would share information about the latest news on the case.

What no one had been able to discover was a pattern in the case. The poisoner seemed to murder (where murder was verifiable) in an entirely random manner. His victims were not exclusively male or female (although, Henry was relieved to note, there were no children); the only thing that united them, as far as anyone could see, was that all the crimes occurred in Wimbledon. Rush was of the opinion that there was no pattern, although plenty of people had identified what they described as his 'target group'. The most popular theory was that he was a man with a grudge against

Wimbledon itself, possibly an unsuccessful trader. But no one – to Henry's relief – had, so far anyway, come any closer than that.

'Of course,' said Elinor one afternoon, 'there might be a pattern. But he' (everyone called the poisoner 'he') 'might be deliberately obscuring it.'

Rush leaned forward in the armchair that he now designated his. He looked across at Henry, as he said, 'How do you mean?'

'Well,' said Elinor, 'he might have a real target in mind. And he might not want us to know who that target is.'

'So you mean,' said Rush, 'he goes about poisoning people as a blind?'

'It's possible.'

Henry coughed. 'Sounds a bit cumbersome,' he said. 'If I wanted to murder someone I'd get right in there and do it. Get my hands dirty.'

'You wouldn't, Henry,' said Elinor, with unusual prescience, 'you'd gibber around with all sorts of schemes and make a complete hash of it. Actually – ' here she gave her booming laugh – 'it's such a far-fetched idea of mine it's the sort of thing you'd go for. You never deal directly with anything.'

Henry managed a jovial laugh. 'Oh,' he said, 'so I'm the suspect, am I? I'm the chappie who goes around tampering with the groceries!'

Rush, he noticed, wasn't laughing.

'I'm not saying that!' said Elinor. 'All I'm saying is – it's possible the poisoner isn't a psychopath who kills at random, but a man who wants to kill someone desperately, so desperately that he deliberately kills an arbitrary selection of people in order to conceal his true target. Maybe even from himself!'

Henry gulped. 'How do you mean . . . from himself?' he said.

'I mean,' said Elinor, 'he can't face up to the fact that he really wants to kill the person he wants to kill, so that he kills, almost unconsciously, not simply to lay a false trail,

211

people that he sees as "in his way". He might not even know he's doing it!'

Henry looked briefly across at Rush to see if the detective was watching him. To his relief, he wasn't. Henry's heart was making an eerily amplified noise inside his ribs. He folded his arms judiciously and tried to look as if he was just another wally discussing the poisoner.

'It still sounds a bit . . . complicated to me,' he said; 'what gave you the idea?'

'Everett Maltby,' said Elinor.

The room had gone very quiet.

'Tell us,' said Rush, 'do!'

CHAPTER THIRTY-TWO

'It was the apple that gave me the idea,' said Elinor.

'How come?' said Henry.

'Well,' said Elinor, 'I like apples.'

Rush stroked his chin reflectively. Of all his Great Detective mannerisms, this was the one Henry found most irritating. Elinor, however, seemed oblivious of him.

'No one knows how Maisie got hold of the apple, do they?'

'They don't!' said Henry.

'Well,' here Elinor sighed deeply, 'I gave it to her.'

Rush shifted in his chair.

'I know I should have said,' she went on, 'but I just couldn't bear to. And what I had to say wouldn't have helped much. And a bit of me – it's really stupid – felt guilty. I felt I was somehow responsible.'

'And where,' said Rush, 'did you . . . obtain the er . . . apple?'

'That's the point,' said Elinor. 'It was just . . . there. On the bowl. I couldn't work out how it had got there.'

Henry was thinking back to the night on which Jungian Analyst with Winebox gave what was positively his last consultation. Had he had time to go out, buy an apple, inject it with prussic acid and leave it on the fruit bowl for Elinor? Probably, was the answer.

'But I can't resist apples. Especially big, red juicy ones. Henry knows I can't!'

Henry wondered whether to admit this was true. As she talked he tried to work out whether being a solicitor would give him less or more rights when he was arrested. Would he only be allowed, for example, one phone call to himself? He wouldn't be any use, though, would he? He couldn't do conveyancing, let alone murder. But Rush wasn't looking at him. His piggy little eyes were fixed on Elinor's face.

'And then I remembered,' she went on, 'about Everett Maltby. That man Henry was always going on about. It was the apple, you see, that reminded me. So I went and looked him up. There's an awful lot written about him.'

'Actually,' said Henry, 'in *The Complete History* I try to – '

What did he try to do? Why had he so thoroughly and completely blacked out on the subject of Maltby? His entire mental processes, these days, could be described as the physiological equivalent of the dot dot dots in *The Murder of Roger Ackroyd*.

'There's a particularly good book,' said Elinor, 'called *A Woman's Weapon*, which is a sort of feminist study of domestic murder in the nineteenth century.'

'Proving,' said Henry, 'that it was a response to male chauvinism, presumably. *Lizzie Borden: Pioneer Worker in the Field of Sexual Politics.* I think – '

'Shut up, Henry!' said Elinor sharply, 'I'm talking!'

Rush was looking at her with a kind of adoration. Why was it, Henry wondered, that his wife was able to inspire uncritical appreciation in so many people who weren't him? If he had been able to look at her like Rush, all this would never have started.

'Actually,' she continued, 'it studies men who killed women and women who killed men. But it's most interested in men who killed, or tried to kill, their wives. And by far the best bit of the book is about Everett Maltby.'

'Maltby,' said Rush, 'didn't only kill his wife. He killed – '

'Norman Le Bone, the butcher,' Henry heard himself saying, 'Genevieve Strong, a neighbour, and – '

'I'm telling this, Henry!' said Elinor. 'Shut up!'

Henry had grasped a new and potentially sensational fact about his memory. It only seemed to function in close proximity to his wife. Maybe Elinor, who had always seemed to know where his tie, socks, shirt or clean trousers were located, had begun to usurp other functions of his brain.

Perhaps his little store of knowledge had leaked across to her circuits. Perhaps there was an instruction in his cerebellum that said: COPY FILE TO WIFE.

'And of course,' she said, 'Maltby was born in this very street!'

That was something Henry knew he didn't know. He had never known that. This was something completely and utterly new. Or was it? The trouble was, once you had forgotten something it was pretty hard to remember whether you had ever known it. The best thing to do was to behave as if you were with one of Elinor's intellectual friends, nodding sagely at the titles of books you had never read, films you were never going to see . . .

'Don't tell me,' he said, 'he had a daughter called Maisie!'

'Actually,' said Elinor, 'he did!'

Rush let out a long slow sigh, like a deflating lilo, and taking out his pipe started to do some rather overdone listening, of the kind that suggested he was waiting for a chance to interrupt.

'And his shop,' said Elinor, 'was just off the bottom of the hill. In one of those roads whose name you never can remember. You know? Like Bolsover Street or Atlantis. It's one of those streets you can never find consciously. The only way back to it is to let your mind go blank and hope your feet get you there. I think the chemist's shop is still – '

'He was a chemist,' Henry was saying, 'of course he was a chemist!'

Elinor ignored this interruption. 'Maltby's wife seems to have had some kind of nervous breakdown, and in the spring of 1888, as far as we can tell from her journal – '

Journal? Journal? This was typical of feminist history. Who could have known Mrs Maltby kept a journal? Of course, in his study of the Maltby case Henry had more or less concentrated on the Wimbledon angle; but he had no recollection of where the man lived. He would have remembered that, surely?

'She went off sex anyway. Became very difficult, and

215

Maltby, who in many ways was a very advanced husband –
he did most of the cooking, for example, most unusual in a
Victorian marriage – decided to do away with her. It seems to
have been that he saw no other way out of his relationship.'

Henry looked at the floor. He found, somewhat to his
surprise, that he was clenching and unclenching his hands.

'In truth,' Elinor said, 'I see no other way forward, for all
sides oppress me like a wall that faces the humblest prisoner
in a jail and strong poison is my only helpmeet!'

Maybe she was possessed by the soul of a Victorian
poisoner. This certainly wasn't how she normally carried on.
Then Henry saw that Elinor was reading from a paperback
book.

'You see,' she said, putting the book down, 'I got this
ridiculous, ridiculous idea that Henry was trying to poison
me!'

'My God!' said Henry, 'surely you didn't!'

He decided to try this line again. He still sounded unbelievably unconvincing. 'Me?' he said desperately, trying to
kick start his credibility. 'Me? Poison you? Darling!' He tried
a little laugh here ('No, love, no!' from Rush's invisible
director).

'Because, you see, Maltby hit on a most ingenious way of
getting rid of Helena. He began to poison people in the
locality, rather in the way William Palmer did, but, as was
argued at his trial, he murdered the butcher, the clerk in the
house opposite and a family of five simply to cloak his real
intentions.'

'I still don't see,' said Henry, 'what this has got to do with
our poisoner.'

He stopped.

'Unless of course,' he said, 'you think I'm sort of . . .' he
laughed again, 'possessed! Or something!'

By way of answer Elinor got to her feet. Henry had never
heard her talk for so long on any subject not directly concerned either with Maisie's education, her personal therapy
or a domestic appliance. He felt vaguely as if his interest in

216

the subject had been hijacked and, looking across at Rush, hoped to see the man yawning or shaking his head sadly. He wasn't. He was looking at Elinor with what could only be described as rapture.

> 'The cup he hands you and the wine
> Are tainted with the hate he bears
> Yet drink it down and ye yield up
> All of your present woes and cares!
> Pour on! Pour on! Drink deeply now!
> Since Faith and Hope and Love are gone,
> Let us drink all with Him they call
> The Poisoner of Wimbledon!'

This, Henry realized, from the uncomfortable silence that accompanied it, was poetry. He didn't like poetry. He didn't know much about it but he knew he didn't like it. Elinor, perhaps sensing this, gave him some more.

> 'Since Memory and Reason are
> But dust in th'Historic Wind,
> Since Love and Justice are alike,
> Both impotent and vain and blind,
> Let us take meat and share our board
> Yea! Let Him feed us and begone!
> We have forgot our need to live
> Brave Poisoner of Wimbledon!'

Elinor gave no clue as to where this poem might have come from or, indeed, why she was reciting it, but that was fairly typical of poetry lovers. They shoved it down your throat at every opportunity, declaiming it in buses or quoting it with relish at you when you were trying to do something else. A bit like people who insisted you had an alcoholic drink, or the worst type of jazz *aficionado*.

Rush didn't seem interested in the poem. 'And where,' he said, 'did you find the apple?'

'In the bowl,' said Elinor, 'by the window. But then anyone could have got in. It wasn't that that spooked me about it.

You see poison is a spooky thing, as Gordon was saying. It's to do with . . . I don't know . . . it sounds stupid . . . with . . . loving someone in a way. And I thought . . . that poem, it's by Edwina Cousins, a Victorian lady poet who got quite obsessed with Maltby, what it's saying is . . . poison is to do with obsession. And you see this person, who's doing all this, now, I mean, I think they got it all from Maltby.'

'Why?' said Henry. 'Whatever gave you that idea?'

'Well,' said Elinor, 'all the people the poisoner has killed, I mean *our* poisoner, live in exactly the same streets lived in by Maltby's victims.'

Rush gave a little gasp.

'And when Maltby did finally kill his wife, he did it with a poisoned apple. Laced with prussic acid. He was a keen amateur photographer you see!'

She looked across at Henry with a smile. 'That's why I didn't tell the Law,' she said, 'I thought it was Henry! Doing his bit for local history!'

Henry bit back a sob. 'Extraordinary!' he said. 'And then, I suppose you thought . . . how absurd! Henry wouldn't . . . er . . . do anything like that. Did you? Is that what you thought?'

CHAPTER THIRTY-THREE

If the poisoner's intention, as a woman on the *New Statesman* had opined, was 'to destabilize bourgeois society' – he had not really succeeded. Bourgeois society, even in Wimbledon, went right on being bourgeois. People washed their cars and read quality newspapers and worried about their shares as if there wasn't anyone sneaking around Belvedere Drive and Pine Grove waiting to make their diet even more high risk than it already was.

The poisoner had, however, had considerable impact on lunch. People didn't walk into San Lorenzo di Fuoriporta, at the bottom of Wimbledon Hill, with quite the same *élan*. The waiters didn't greet you with the same style, and somehow there wasn't quite the same thrill as you sat at the white tablecloth, toyed with an aperitif and wondered whether to have *linguine alla vongole* or *carpaccio* for your first course. For a start, you couldn't see the kitchens. And this fact that, previously, had made lunch such an entrancing prospect for the bourgeoisie of the borough, rendered it, now, almost unbearable. Who knew what was happening behind those double doors that flew apart and slammed shut behind the sallow waiters as, humming rather effortfully, they made their way from kitchen to table? *He* could have got to the *radicchio* before you did. *He* could have done a thorough job on the *gnocchi*. *He* could have coated the *vitello* with something a bit more lively than a *salsa tonnata*.

Businessmen still gamely went through with the ritual. Many of them said that the British economy would collapse without lunch. The more honest of them said that they didn't know about the British economy but for sure they would collapse without lunch. But you could see from their nervous glances about them, their anxious inquiries about where

Luigi was buying his stuff these days ('Don' worry sah – we go alla way to Keeng's Cross! An' we got double locks on alla da doors!) that the pleasure of dining out, that exquisite combination of helplessness and dominance, that highly formalized return to the nursery had lost, both literally and metaphorically, its savour.

The most popular restaurant in Wimbledon, since the poisoner scare had started, was a small Turkish taverna. For a start you could see what the chef was cooking. And the very simplicity of the cuisine – grilled meat and salads – militated against the poisoner's techniques. The restaurant bought its meat from Smithfield, brought it, under lock and key, to Wimbledon, and invited the diners to compose their own salads. BRING YOUR OWN VINAIGRETTE said a sign in the window, DON'T LET YOU KNOW WHO HAVE A HAND IN YOUR LUNCH! Alone of the eateries in the district, they seemed to make a virtue out of the crisis, perhaps because of the healthy tradition of poisoning that had always existed under the Ottoman Empire. When they brought your doner kebab to the table there was always a little joke ('This should finish you off nicely!') and always, in a gesture that was both charming and did genuinely inspire confidence, the proprietor tasted the offered dish before serving. As Henry observed to Elinor one of the great thrills about eating in Mehemet's Cave of Pleasures, as the place was known, was wondering whether Mehemet would keel over and drop dead immediately after nibbling a bit of your shashlik.

It was to Mehemet's restaurant that Henry went, one day in December, to meet Detective Inspector Rush and Karim Jackson of Brawl Books. It was fairly clear, Henry thought, that the policeman had asked him to the occasion in order to tempt him into making one last, fatal mistake. Jackson was, after all, the man who had turned down *The Complete History of Wimbledon*, and Henry had quite often made abusive remarks about him in the detective's presence. It might be true that, when possessed by the soul of the poisoner, Henry was so fiendishly clever that even this mistake would prove fatal only to those who shared his meal. But this thought was no longer of much comfort. Henry wanted to be discovered. He wanted it all to finish. If he was found slipping something into the publisher's humus, so much the better.

Elinor and Maisie seemed pleased that he was going out to lunch with someone from the media. Maisie asked him if he could get Michael Jackson's autograph, and Elinor hinted that a casual mention of her upcoming monograph on 'The Politics of Poison' might earn Henry unspecified sexual favours. But Henry's heart, as he pushed open the restaurant door, was heavy. He did not want to kill again. 'I must not,' he muttered to himself as he scanned the shabby tables, 'bear hatred. I must not feel angry. This man has a right to reject my work. I do not want to kill Karim Jackson.'

'Hi!' said a voice from a table in the corner, and Henry found himself looking at the first man to send back the most detailed account of a suburb ever put together in the English language. 'Henry Farr?'

To Henry's surprise the only concession that Karim Jackson appeared to have made to the Third World was to be ever so slightly biscuit-coloured. In dress, manner, frame of cultural reference and physical appearance he seemed completely English. He was, also to Henry's surprise, really rather charming. Henry waited in vain for him to sneer or boast. When he was told that Henry was the same Henry Farr who had offered him *The Complete History of Wimbledon* he seemed overjoyed. He spoke warmly of 'the vast scale of the book's ambition' and explained that, although it wasn't something they wanted for 'their list' (at which, in spite of Jackson's extreme diffidence of manner, Henry felt a prickle of hostility) he thought it was a splendid piece of work and one which should, in time, find a proper home.

What made all this much worse was that, at any moment, Henry knew he might try to slip something in Jackson's food. Although he had searched himself thoroughly before leaving Maple Drive, Henry knew enough about the workings of the unconscious to know that he might have secreted Jackson's quietus, without his being aware of the fact, anywhere about his person. He might even, thought Henry, have got up in the middle of last night, broken into Mehemet's Cave of Pleasures and doctored a fragment of doner which he might then, by a process so subtle he himself would not even be aware of it, manage to steer in the direction of the publisher. The whole trouble with therapy, he reflected glumly, acknowledging that he was in the middle of some crude, stone age, do-it-yourself version of the activity, was that it stirred up things you never even knew were there. You got to know quite what a bastard you were, exactly how far you were in the grip of things that made you, to use Elinor's phrase, 'stunningly peculiar'.

He had even started reading books on therapy – although there didn't seem to be many of them aimed at middle-aged men – and wondering whether he was something called an anal regressive. He was – Henry took another mouthful of cabbage – obsessed with farting and bottoms. This was something (according to one of the books he had read) you were supposed to have got out of your system by the age of five. Might his poisoning activity be a way of compensating for the unsatisfactory nature of his mother's attempts to breast-feed him (he assumed from everything about himself that they were unsatisfactory, although he would never have dared to broach the subject with Mrs Farr Senior). Was he, in stalking about the place tipping solanaceous alkaloids into vats of rice salad, trying to provide nourishment for the dark impulses that, as Elinor was always pointing out, he had nourished for so long?

'Is your wife green?' Jackson was saying to Henry.

Ah ha, thought Henry, at last the insult, carefully led up to by a show of politeness to put you off your guard. *No, she's blue with pink spots. What colour is yours?*

'Because,' went on Jackson, chewing his chicken kebab very slowly and thoroughly, 'I rather go along with the eco-logical aspect to the poisoning case. Poisoning as a way of controlling the environment, say, of purging it of the things that one sees as unhealthy. But purging it, of course, by making it, as we would say, "worse". Do you take my meaning?'

'Not really,' said Rush, who was looking white and strained.

'Well,' said Jackson, 'what's healthy to us, a lively society, say, one that's mixed racially – '

Henry tried not to think about racism. Racism brought back memories of Donald. It brought back, too, the disquieting thought that this man had a point. Wasn't it rather absurd to be obsessed with a few square miles of suburb, when one's society offered someone so puzzling, picturesque and likeable as Karim Jackson.

'One in which things are growing and changing, not staying static, is one that someone else might say was "sick". The human ecology of our society actually depends on change and growth, just as the . . . whale needs the plankton, say . . . we need . . .'

He grinned rather charmingly. 'Paki bastards like me.'

Please, thought Henry, please don't talk about racism. Please don't talk about the loss of the British Empire and multi-culturalism and the need for change. I'm sure those things have their place, but it isn't, I'm afraid, in Wimbledon. Yes, I know I shouldn't think these things. I know it's backward of me. It may be why I seem to do these monstrous things. Elinor is always going on about what she calls the 'monster of racism' that lurks in me. But it's how I am. I am trying to be better. I am trying as hard as I can not to murder people, not to think the awful, shameful thoughts that seem to lead on to murder. But it seems that I can't stop. And if you start going on about the British Empire, for whose excesses I was not personally responsible –

'The Amritsar Massacre, for example,' Karim Jackson was saying, 'is an interesting example. Like all of the other show-piece horrors of British Imperialism, it was carried out by decent quiet, home-loving Englishmen, who weren't aware of how racist, how savagely, murderously hostile they actually were to the world outside the world they knew. And our poisoner is a hangover from the imperial past. He kills to forget the horrors he is heir to.'

Henry could feel the hostility rise in him. Make him stop! he prayed. Don't let him go on about Thatcherism and the danger of Little Englandism! Deep down, he intoned in his head, over and over again, Karim Jackson is a nice bloke. He may have a funny name and be the colour of underdone toffee but *au fond* he is, like me, an Englishman. I am not a racist psychopath, I am – hang on, that's wrong. I *am* a racist psychopath but I am trying not to be one. *And this bastard is not helping me any by going on about Imperialism and Thatcherism!*

Henry noticed he was gripping the table hard with his hands. Jackson was now, to Henry's horror, talking about the Boxer Rebellion. He folded his hands over his ears, then, to try and stop them shaking, held them on to the table. Out of the corner of his eye he saw Rush. The policeman was looking at him with that mocking, enigmatic smile of his. 'Go on!' he seemed to be saying, 'go on! All I need is the evidence of my eyes. An inquest, and then you'll be neatly sewn up, won't you, sunshine?' Henry looked down at his hands. There was something in them. A piece of paper from his pocket? What was it? His hands did not seem to be able to keep still. They were sliding nearer and nearer to Jackson's food. And Jackson was talking again. Henry must concentrate on his face. Then he wouldn't be able to see what his hands were doing. What the eye doesn't see the heart doesn't grieve about. He'll stop me, won't he? The Law wouldn't let a man die, would they? Or would they? Evidence. They want evidence. These days you've got to have evidence. Henry stared at Jackson, willing the man not to say anything Marxist or anti-Imperialist.

'The poisoner,' he was saying, 'is a perfect metaphor for the way we are now. Our fear, our narrowness, our obstinate refusal to see ourselves as anything other than the centre of the world. It's the perfect Marxist paradox. England's very littleness has made her universally relevant. You've no idea of the interest I've had from American publishers and media people about this story. They see it as absolutely central. And yet, in a sense, begging your pardon, Henry, but if it weren't for this who, really, would give a stuff about Wimbledon? I mean it's a nightmare really, isn't it? Wimbledon? It's dead from the neck up. It takes a psychopath to make it interesting, right?'

Henry could not see clearly. The room in front of him was going in and out of focus and Jackson's voice that had, a minute ago, seemed pleasant, cultivated, was booming, echoing, as if they were in some cellar or underground cavern. Jackson's face too was a brown blur and his teeth had gone as white and sharp as a tiger's. All Henry could hear was '. . . Wimbledon . . . not interesting . . . psychopath . . . not interesting . . . Wimbledon . . . not interesting . . . psychopath.' I must get out, he told himself, before I do something awful. I must get out . . . Wimbledon . . . not interesting . . . psychopath . . . not . . .

'Must have a pee!' he heard himself say. Had he actually said that out loud? Or had he said Mustapha Pee the well-known Turkish lavatory attendant, ha ha ha. Foreigners, as Frank Richards said to George Orwell, are funny ha ha ha. Turks and Pakis and Jews and *Oh my God, Henry, what are you saying? Is this the inside of your mind?* And don't be stupid, Henry, just take it calmly, remember the murder of Roger Ackroyd, this isn't that, is it, *dot dot dot* . . . ? Oh dot fucking dot, where am I? Could I have put some poison up my arse like they do with cannabis at airports? I am a bit obsessed with my arse. *Oh my God, Henry, this is the inside of your mind, Henry, this is what you are actually like, is it?* . . . *dot dot dot* where are we? Where are we, are we all right there, are we? Are we all right? What am I doing? Am I all right?

'Are you,' Rush was saying solicitously, 'all right, Henry?'

They were in the lavatory. As far as Henry could see he was not sexually assaulting the policeman. He seemed to be urinating in an orderly fashion, with Rush next to him, doing likewise. But how had he got here? And what had he done in between the table and the lavatory?

'Don't blame you for getting out,' said Rush. 'You probably didn't like listening to our friend from overseas, did you?'

Rush's voice was sweetly insinuating. Of course he was expert at interrogations. He would know how to conjure up the racist, psychopathic monster that was somewhere inside Henry Farr. Maybe this was all part of a ploy to do more than merely convict him. Thirty years in Broadmoor wasn't enough. Henry looked down at the policeman. He realized, with some surprise, that he disliked Rush intensely. That of the two men he would far rather spend time with Karim Jackson. Karim Jackson was better looking, better read, better dressed and far, far better company than Rush would ever be. And yet, such were the appalling limitations of being white and English and living in Wimbledon, he, Henry, was doomed to spend the rest of his life with people like Rush, had indeed, just attempted, or indeed, succeeded, in poisoning a man whose only crime would appear to be that his parents came from somewhere a bit more interesting than Wimbledon.

His fingers stiff and weary, he buttoned his penis back into his trousers and followed the detective inspector out of the Gentlemen's.

At the door, Rush stopped and looked up at him knowingly. 'What disgusts you,' he said, 'is that people like that, black uppity bastards like that come over here, get good jobs and probably white women and plenty of them into the bargain. Isn't that what you can't stand?'

Henry reflected that Karim Jackson had probably an altogether prior claim on white women than he and Rush, on the grounds of hygiene alone. But he did not say that. He stood, listening to the dripping cistern, the door half open, looking down at the inspector's knowing smile, thinking, now the awful rage had passed, How does he know the worst things I'm thinking? Why doesn't he just arrest me? What does he want to make me do?

'He might even,' said Rush, 'try a poke at Elinor! Imagine that! A black man humping your wife!'

These days Elinor's increased libidinous activity had left him so mentally and physically exhausted that such a prospect would come as something of a relief to Henry. But Rush seemed to think it highly likely that Karim Jackson would want to have sex relations with Mrs Elinor Farr, although in Henry's opinion the publisher would probably have to be offered money before he consented to do such a thing.

'Elinor,' said Rush, 'is a treasure!' He sounded, thought Henry, depressingly like Donald. 'I used to see her in the street, long before we even met,' went on Rush, 'and think, "there's an English Rose! There's a perfect specimen of English Womanhood! There's a woman a man could really love!" '

He looked at Henry, the vaguely critical glance with which Henry was familiar from fans of his wife's. 'How,' the expression seemed to say, 'did this fat, badly groomed bastard get hold of such a pearl!' Had Rush been watching him and Elinor long before their fateful encounter at the Everett Maltby talk? Somehow the prospect was even more depressing than the thought that he, Henry, had just poisoned a major force in world publishing, but it might explain why the detective had not yet moved to arrest him. He was Elinor's lover, and he (maybe she as well) was, were playing with him, enjoying the spectacle of his wriggling on the end of the hook. Weren't all policemen sadists anyway? The pleasure of the job was, for them, not the righting of a wrong but the sight of the punishment of the guilty. And my God, was he guilty! As the two men came back into the restaurant, Henry found his lip was twitching out of control. In the mirror above the bar he caught sight of an ill-looking, pale-faced Henry and, his mind a jumble of half-therapized impulses, poisoned apples and sheer confusion at what might be going on in his soul (if he had one), he sat down opposite Jackson.

Jackson was eating a salad and seemed, for the moment

anyway, to be in good health. Maybe I didn't do it, thought Henry, maybe . . . Jackson smiled warmly at him, and Henry, his anger quite evaporated, found himself smiling back.

'This salad,' said Jackson, 'is delicious! It tastes really sweet! I wonder what they put in the dressing!'

'I can't think!' said Henry, lightly. And breathed deeply again. Just to check, he tasted his salad, very carefully. But as he had feared, it did not taste sweet at all. If anything, it was sharply flavoured. Henry chewed it and as Jackson began to talk once again about the poisoner, he reflected that it was possible that the media person's research might be about to prove a little more intensive than he had anticipated.

CHAPTER THIRTY-FOUR

Of the three people round the table at Mehemet's restaurant, it was almost certain that Karim Jackson was the only one unfamiliar with the symptoms of strychnine poisoning.

There were those who said, after the incident at Mehemet's Cave of Pleasures (nicknamed, in the few months the business lasted after the December incident, 'Mehemet's Hole of Horrors'), that the fatal kebab was not, as Mehemet maintained, of chicken but of guinea fowl, or game of some kind, that had run up against a farmer who was with callous disregard for his fellow men ignoring the Animals (Cruel Poisons) Act of 1962.

But, as Detective Inspector Rush pointed out, his eyes on Henry's face, Jackson had absorbed the poison in a quantity that suggested that the poisoner had been at work.

'Basically,' Jackson said, as the others sat down, 'I'd like to do a book which looks at the suburb and the poisoner together. There's a sense in which this is Sunday supplement country, you know, three hundred words on Gewürztraminer for God's sake, but I'd like to do a book about a locale, maybe even using some of your ideas, Henry, and about a case, an issue – my God, I feel most peculiar!'

Henry looked at the publisher open-mouthed. He ought, he knew, to get on the phone and order some gastric lavage for the man, as soon as possible, but could not think how to do so without incriminating himself. Who would believe a story about 'blacking out' for God's sake, any more than they had believed poor Everett Maltby? It seemed such a shame this man had to die. He was, as Henry had already observed, a little over-impressed with America, but this was a common fault among British people. He was politically naïve, and unhealthily obsessed with his obviously complex racial origins, but beside that, Henry could really find not much wrong with the man. Added to which he seemed to be offering to publish Henry's book, albeit in a mutilated and over-sensational form. It was a cruel irony, thought Henry, that the one man he was ever likely to meet who took a genuine interest in his life's work was also one of the people whom his baser, unreconstructed, untherapized, unconscious self should have chosen to murder. Did this mean that, fundamentally, deep down, he didn't want his book published? Or was it yet another illustration of the little known law of nature which decreed that if Henry Farr looked like he was getting a break, God would take it away from him?

'You see,' Jackson was saying, 'the movie, which obviously is what I have in mind, has very universal appeal. Englishness is about our only durable export, and this is a sort of hard study of attitudes in the eighties. What I want to do is stay down here.'

'Down here'? What did he mean, 'down here'? thought Henry, forgetting temporarily that the man had only a few minutes to live. Wimbledon wasn't the end of the world, for God's sake.

'I might stay at the Cannizaro Hotel,' went on Jackson, 'named, as I'm sure you know, Henry, after the Duke of Cannizaro, who was also the basis for one of the characters in the *Ingoldsby Legends*, and really get to know Wimbledon. Soak myself in its atmosphere so that I can get it on the page, make people feel that they are there with me and I might – my chest feels a bit funny – '

Henry gazed in baffled compassion at the only man he had ever met who knew the little-recorded fact that Karim Jackson had just confided across the lunch table. It was at that moment that he knew that somehow or other he must have laid his hands on the cursed alkaloid that comes from nux vomica. Jackson appeared to be grinning broadly at him.

Quite suddenly a rigid stiffening of the body takes place, the back becoming arched (opoisthotonus) and the chest more or less fixed so that cyanosis sets in. It is this fixation of the chest which serves best to distinguish strychnine convulsions from those of tetanus.

Cyanosis or no cyanosis, Karim Jackson continued to make his pitch. In the early stages of strychnine poisoning he yet managed to talk of deals, of percentages of the gross profits, of the paperback rights, the mini-series rights, of the intellectual integrity and honesty of the project he was adumbrating as well as its colossal commercial appeal. He spoke – admittedly with some difficulty – of the *Sunday Times Colour Supplement*, of the sharp political relevance the Wimbledon Poisoner had to British society and thereby to the world. He spoke of agents and development deals and full-colour glossy pictures and of the enormous interest already expressed by television producers in the story he was about to try and tell. British publishing would have been proud of him.

'The story has to be told and it has to be . . .'

He seemed to be grinning.

Tetanus spasm is most pronounced in the jaw. The face is fixed in a grim, sardonic smile, risus sardonicus.

'Christ, the deal would be . . .'

After a minute or two the whole body relaxes and the wretched subject lies exhausted, gasping for breath.

'I'm not feeling . . .'

Some minutes later the seizure grips the body again, often fired off by some trivial stimulus. The mind remains clear until death from exhaustion follows a few hours later.

'Look, this is a really interesting . . . Christ All-bloody-mighty . . .'

Treatment is difficult if convulsions are already established. It is hopeless to try and introduce a stomach tube, assuming one can be easily located, for any such attempt will immediately excite another convulsion.

231

'Wimbledon . . .'

It was, thought Henry afterwards, eerily appropriate that the last word on Karim Jackson's lips should have been 'Wimbledon'. For Wimbledon, that unregarded quarter of southwest London that he had once sneered at, then discovered, and finally, almost embraced, had, in the end, been the death of him. He passed away spectacularly, with the style and flair for catching the attention of the public that had characterized his brief but successful career in publishing. Juddering like a car trying to accelerate in low gear, he jerked forward into the table like a robot and, *risus sardonicus* in full flower (which only increased his nightmarish resemblance to some elegant creature from the metropolis, in the middle of assessing a colleague's reputation), he breathed his last, with twitchy bravura, into Detective Inspector Rush's doner kebab with salad.

'Oh my God!' said Rush. 'Oh, my bloody Christ!' And he looked across at Henry, eyes mute with misery. Rush, you could tell, had had enough of murder. He had had enough of poison. He wanted to go back to traffic control, which was where, unless Henry gave himself up pretty quickly, he was going to be headed. But as well as the misery, Henry saw something else in his face, and it was no longer the superior, enigmatic expression he had feared ever since Donald's funeral. It was pure, unmixed hatred. He knows, Henry thought, he knows what's wrong with me. He led me up to it, made me do it, and still he won't give me the pleasure, yes, the pleasure of arresting me. Because it would, by now, have been nothing but a relief to be able to say, out loud, to someone, even if it was only a policeman, what he was thinking and feeling. He's in love with Elinor, thought Henry, and that's why he's letting me do these things! He fought for the words that would implicate him, and found, to his horror, that they would not come.

Karim Jackson's funeral, which neither Rush nor Henry attended, was a very fashionable affair. Edwina Lush, the fashionable lesbian novelist, author of *Boy's Games* and *The*

Fearing, gave a dignified, simple address that, those present agreed, enhanced her already considerable reputation as a fashionable lesbian novelist. 'She looked,' said Meryl Johnson, an unfashionable lesbian novelist, 'very boyish. Karim would have been proud of her.' It emerged during the proceedings that his name wasn't Karim at all, but Dave, and that he had adopted his first name at the age of fifteen, on learning that his mother's first husband (not his father) hailed from Rawalpindi. He was biscuit-coloured because he was biscuit-coloured. There was, his closest relatives revealed, absolutely no racial significance in his colour.

There was another headline, the usual rash of comment, and then people forgot about Karim Jackson. Or at least Henry did. He was no longer aware of what people, or indeed journalists, thought. He was scarcely aware of Elinor or Maisie. Only when Rush came to call, which seemed to be every other day, did he take notice of his wife, watching the way she smiled when Rush told one of his endless anecdotes, nearly all of which seemed to deal with the fatal mistakes made by over-confident criminals.

'Your murderer,' he would say, watching Henry keenly over his gin and tonic, 'is a man living in the hell of guilt. He knows – as we know – that one vital piece of evidence will send him to the Old Bailey, and that somewhere in the trail of misery he leaves behind him the one piece of fabric or trace of chemical that will tie him to the crime lies in wait for the observant member of the force! Let's take Sprott, for example!'

'He died!' said Maisie, watching Rush with huge eyes. When he has finally finished playing with me, thought Henry, and married Elinor, he will make a good father to Maisie. Perhaps the three of them will come and see me in Broadmoor.

'I know,' laughed Rush lightly, 'but you see at the time people didn't take kindly to my theories about the poisoner. They thought your Uncle John was barking mad!'

Elinor flushed. 'If people had listened to you,' she said, 'none of this need have happened.'

Rush shrugged. 'No hard feelings!' he said, and bent down to Maisie. He'll bath her, thought Henry, when I'm in Broadmoor he'll bath her and tell her stories. They'll all have a good laugh about me. My God, why don't I do away with him now? One more won't make any difference, will it?

Elinor was looking at him oddly. 'What's the matter with you, Henry?' she said. 'Is something worrying you?'

'Nothing darling.'

I'm a mass killer, that's all! And that man knows it and is waiting for me to crack! Is enjoying the spectacle of my guilt! Wants to make it last!

'So you see,' Rush was saying to Maisie, 'I couldn't get an inquest at the time. I was a voice in the wilderness. But you see, our murderer – ' here he looked straight at Henry – 'probably knows that there is some chemical in the ashes of David Sprott that ties the murder to him!'

Finish 'Em, thought Henry. They probably had people down at Wimbledon police station who could not only spot traces of Finish 'Em in a corpse, but say something pretty authoritative about when and where it was bought. Why, though, did Rush want to hang the death of the dentist on him? After all there were plenty of other bodies around for which he seemed to be responsible – psychiatrists, publishers, Boy Scouts, too, as far as he could tell, and . . .

Henry stopped, and found he was staring at Rush. A terrifying thought had occurred to him. Suppose there really was a maniac on the loose, and the maniac wasn't him. Suppose Rush *knew* it wasn't him. Suppose the man had simply been waiting, all this time, for the moment when he could tie Henry to one murder, and thereby to all the others. That would explain his insistence that Jackson and Macrae had been the victims of random attack, and the reason for his waiting until now before moving in on the remains of David Sprott.

'It's Sprott we need to look at,' Rush was saying, 'and if

it takes too long to get the paperwork sorted we shall just have to nip over the garden wall and take the matter into our own hands. Eh, Henry?'

Henry whimpered slightly. 'Yes,' he croaked, 'yes, of course.'

As Elinor went past the policeman to fetch a tray of cakes from the kitchen, he put his arm round her waist with offensive familiarity. She stopped and looked down at him, beaming maternally.

'You picked a good 'un here, Henry!' said Detective Inspector Rush. 'You better watch your back or I'll have her away from you!'

'Don't do that!' Henry said in a voice whose pitch surprised and displeased him.

Rush looked into his eyes and smiled. 'May the best man win!' he said.

And both Maisie and Elinor laughed.

CHAPTER THIRTY-FIVE

There was only one way out of Henry's dilemma, and that was to get hold of the remains of Sprott before the policeman. Rush had been making several references to the paperwork involved in exhumations, in the week before Christmas, and one night, without really planning the business very carefully, Henry added breaking and entering to his list of crimes.

The night he became a burglar began with another of his attempts to talk to Elinor about what he was now fairly sure was a raging affair with a senior member of the Metropolitan Police. He started as he usually did by pretending to discuss Rush the Policeman, rather than Rush the Great Lover.

'Old Rush,' he said, 'has obviously got a theory of who the poisoner is, hasn't he?'

This thought seemed to excite Elinor unnaturally. As she turned towards him, her eyes bright, it occurred to Henry that she and Rush might be working together, the two of them pushing him closer and closer to the edge, until . . .

'Who is it, do you think?' she said. 'Who do you think?'

'Mmm.'

'No, who though? I mean . . .' She propped herself up on one elbow. 'Do you know, Henry, I really did think . . . at one time . . . it might be you!'

Henry's eyes popped open in the dark.

'Well,' she said, 'you are pretty repressed. You are interested in poisons. And you know a bit about Maltby.'

'The Maltby theory is crazy,' said Henry, 'it doesn't . . .'

'But,' said Elinor, falling back on to the pillow, 'I decided you couldn't possibly be the poisoner.'

Henry closed his eyes again.

'The only person you'd want to poison,' she said, in a smallish voice, 'is me.'

Henry stiffened. 'Why should I want to poison you, darling?' he said.

'I don't know,' said Elinor, 'I'm the only person who's nice
to you.'

Henry found this curiously touching. 'Would you be nice
to me,' he said, 'even if I was trying to poison you?'

'Don't be stupid,' said Elinor, 'how could I be nice to
someone who was trying to poison me?'

'I might,' said Henry, 'be trying to poison you in a nice
way. Isn't poison an acceptable brand of oral sadism?'

Elinor sat up again, and flailed her left hand in the direction
of the bedside lamp. It collided with something that slithered
on to the floor. When the light came on, Henry recognized
it as a copy of a magazine called *Lifestyle Design*, that was for
some reason pushed through their letterbox every month. It
was, as Henry recalled, full of articles about how to make
brik à l'oeuf and which rosé to drink at parties. It was probably
all written by Karim Jackson under false names. Oh my God.
Karim Jackson! He burrowed back under the duvet.

'If you tried to kill me,' said Elinor, in a warning tone, 'I'd
jolly well try to kill you back.'

'I know,' said Henry, 'but you might not know!' He could
hear Elinor thinking about this. If she didn't go to sleep soon
the dawn would be printing itself on the sky behind the red
roofs of Maple Drive, old Mr Grade from 37 would be taking
his dog for a walk . . .

'You don't try to poison someone because you love them,'
said Elinor, 'it isn't a branch of sado-masochism. It's a sneaky
way of doing someone in, that's all. You aren't really trying
to poison me, are you Henry?'

'Switch the light off,' said Henry. 'I'm trying to get to
sleep.'

'I won't switch the light off,' said Elinor, leaning over him,
'until you tell me.'

'Switch the light off,' said Henry, 'and then I'll tell you.'

He peered up through a crack in the duvet. Her big white
face was just above him. She looked fairly serious. There was

a pause and then she moved out of his line of vision; a crash as another two magazines hit the floor to join the puddle of glossy pages already there, and then the room was once more in darkness. To Henry's surprise, she did not speak. And, to his surprise, he heard himself saying, 'Of course I'm not trying to poison you. I . . .'

'You what?'

'I love you.'

This sounded, even in the dark, incredibly insincere. She sounded surprised to hear this news.

'Do you?'

'Yes. Yes, I do!'

He heard the sound of her moving towards him under the duvet, like some large animal lost in the underbrush. When she got to the end of her duvet (the Farrs slept under separate duvets 'in order', Elinor used to tell their friends 'to avoid unnecessary body contact at night') she grunted slightly as she moved through the cold patch into his territory. When she reached him, her right hand groped for his body and landed on his stomach. It felt large. Henry wondered, with some apprehension, where it was going to next.

'I mean,' he said, 'I may have thought about poisoning you . . .'

'You what?'

'Well. I mean . . . this last year . . . you haven't been . . . we haven't been . . .'

'I've been awful,' said Elinor.

Henry tried not to sound as if he took this as an offer of submission. 'Well I've been . . . pretty awful . . .' he said.

'You've been dreadful.'

This struck Henry as unfair.

'I don't believe you really have,' said Elinor, 'not really thought about poisoning me.'

'I suppose,' said Henry slowly, 'thinking about doing it is as bad as doing it. Or . . . trying to do it and failing!'

Elinor guffawed suddenly. 'That's pathetic!' she said. 'That's what you'd do, Henry!'

Well, thought Henry, I think I have had rather an alarming success rate actually. I don't call a body count of five too bad for a first-time poisoner. It's just that none of them happened to be you, darling. In fact I may well have murdered thousands of people . . .

'I love you,' Elinor was saying, sounding, Henry thought, a good deal more sincere than him.

'Even though you are a psychopath.'

'Am I a psychopath?'

'A bit of a psychopath.'

Her large hand slid down and landed on his penis. Henry was not sure what to do about this, so he did nothing. By way of response, Elinor made a farting noise with her lips, a gesture that Henry found curiously comforting. Henry propped himself up on his elbow.

'Do you think I could be the Wimbledon Poisoner? And . . . not know I was sort of thing?'

'God knows, Henry,' said Elinor, as she started to move off with elephantine slowness to her own duvet. She had received the comfort she needed. She was ready for sleep. Henry was now wide awake.

'If I was . . . you would sort of . . . stand by me, wouldn't you?'

'Don't be stupid,' said Elinor drowsily, 'of course I wouldn't. Poisoning people is wrong. Especially poisoning complete strangers.'

Henry thought he saw a glimmer of hope for himself here.

'Do you mean . . . poisoning your wife . . . or husband, of course . . . is OK?'

'I don't mean that. But it's . . . understandable. If there's . . . provocation . . .'

Like . . . feminism, possibly?

'Anyone can murder really, can't they? And it could be someone they then realize they love. Like Othello.'

Henry could not think of anyone more unlike him in any of world literature.

'Love is funny. It's mixed up with really horrible feelings,

239

isn't it? If it's any good or it's going to survive children and people dying and your parents and so on, it must be full of the most awful . . . well, poison. But taste sweet, like that poor man's salad.'

Henry did not want to think about Karim Jackson. But Elinor was now wide awake too.

'Actually,' she said, 'it's an awful thing to say. But all that business with Donald somehow got me through depression. I don't know.'

Thanks, Donald, thought Henry, thanks a lot, mate. Donald didn't answer. Perhaps Donald was beginning to have second thoughts about his earlier, generous attitude to being poisoned by Henry. Perhaps he had been talking to Loomis, Coveney, Sprott, Macrae and Jackson.

'I do love you, Henry. Although you're absolutely horrible.'

'Could you ever . . .' said Henry, 'love anyone else?'

'How do you mean?' said Elinor.

'Well,' said Henry, cautiously, 'you must be attracted to other people. Maybe you have . . . you know . . . secret admirers!'

If he was honest with himself, one of the things he had at first liked then disliked about Elinor was the thought that she would not, could not be drawn to anyone else. But now, the very thing that was pulling him back to her was his suspicion that she and Rush were up to something. Was it wickedness and weakness that people liked to see in other people?

'Yes . . .' he said, 'I think . . . you see old Rush is in my view no ordinary policeman. He is someone who has a mind that must make him very attractive to women. Women like you, who are . . .'

He stopped. Elinor was snoring, loudly. Her full-blooded snores were echoed, from upstairs, by a shriller version of the same from Maisie. It was, thought Henry, as if mother and daughter were calling to each other. As she snored, she moved, or rather flailed her left arm in his direction. Henry kicked her hard in the leg. This usually stopped her. But instead of answering with a grunt and a retreat to the edge of her side of the mattress, this time she carried on both snoring and thrashing the duvet with her left arm. Henry got up, went to her side of the bed and, pulling her by the foot, got her as far away from him as possible, so that she was lying diagonally across the corner that was at the opposite end of their bed's rectangle. Her head lolled over the side awkwardly and her right foot protruded from the grubby linen. She looked, even in sleep, uncomfortable. But at least she wasn't snoring.

Henry stumped miserably back to his side of the bed. It had started to rain outside. Oh my God, thought Henry, poor old Donald. It would seem that poisoning the bastard was the most positive marital move he had made in fifteen years. It seemed to have cheered Elinor up no end. Of course, when it came down to it, people wanted other people to die. It made sound ecological sense. Death and money, these days, were the only way of telling how well you were doing.

'Donald, old son,' he said, 'you didn't die in vain.'

'Absolutely not,' said Donald. 'I look on it as being a kind of kidney donor, really. I go over the top but show you guys the way.'

'Donald,' said Henry, 'I'm really sorry. I'm really, really sorry.'

'For Christ's sake, mate,' said Donald, 'don't apologize!'

The rain was harder now. He was going to have to get up in a minute and go down to the street and when he was finished with the night's work there would be nothing left to link him with the Wimbledon Poisoner. That was all he had to do. And then he could forget about it. Because he wasn't going to kill again. Somehow he was sure of that. It had just been something he did, an illness really, like influenza or jaundice. With the last of the evidence would go the last of his guilt. Come on, Henry. Up you get. Up you get.

Elinor was muttering something in her sleep. Something in the elaborate chemistry of her brain sent a signal along a nerve that moved her tongue, and her voice, though not her conscious self, started to say . . . 'He's a poisonous little man . . .' Henry looked over to see if she was awake. She wasn't. Without her knowledge, polypeptides and neurons hummed and wriggled inside her and she said, again in a bass, mechanical voice . . . 'Poisoning a poisonous person isn't poisonous . . .' Henry looked more closely at her. She still wasn't asleep. But her voice was fading slightly . . . 'Poison a poison . . .' she said and again, 'It's poison . . . poison . . . poison . . .' Then she spoke no more.

All we are is chemistry, thought Henry, as he struggled into his trousers, socks and shoes, that is all we are. But if only we were something more! If only! Perhaps then mankind wouldn't be such a horrible, self-seeking, blind, greedy, poisonous little bunch of bastards. And with that uncomforting, not totally original thought he crept down the stairs, opened the door and tiptoed towards David Sprott's house.

CHAPTER THIRTY-SIX

David Sprott's dustbins were legendary. 'You could,' as he once told a man from Teamwaste, who was flinching at the sight of what he thought was a maggot, 'eat your dinner off my dustbins.' They seemed to Henry, as he crossed Maple Drive, to be a touching memorial to the man, arranged as they were, like soldiers, facing the street, inscribed, in white painted letters a foot high, SPROTT: 69 MAPLE DRIVE WIMBLEDON. (Who did Sprott think was after his dustbins?) Sooner or later, thought Henry, the rubbish men will come for me. They will take me out in a van or a skip and, like everything else in the suburb, the bedsprings, the cardboard boxes, the Pentel pens, the old cassette cases, the buckled cans of lager, the potato peelings, the floor tiles nobody wanted, the stacks of wet newspaper and the empty, grease-stained bottles of Soave, I will be carried out towards the great ocean of junk.

He started down the side passage; the door, neatly painted and labelled, was closed and locked, but under a brick on the windowsill to his left was a Yale key. Henry eased it into the lock, pushed open the door and, holding his breath, moved forward along the rough concrete of the passage, above him, to his right, the red-brick cliff of the building. Somewhere away to his left a dog barked, and on the hill he heard the sound of a single car.

The window that was usually unlocked was on the far side of the back of the house. To get to it, he would have to cross the french windows, and to his horror, he saw that from within the dining room behind them there was a dim, single light. Surely she couldn't be up? Not at this time? Henry flattened himself against the wall and wriggled round towards the french windows; he must try and blend into the background; he mustn't even breathe; he must move one step at a time and between each step, stop, look, listen.

He stopped. At the far end of the rear wall of the house, screened from him by one of the thick bushes that fringed the fences of the garden, there was a figure. Oh no, thought Henry, please no! For an instant he thought he could make out the shape of Sprott's head, the beard, the glasses, and, as he froze into the wall, he waited for the sound of the dentist's voice, that mocking northern intonation . . . 'Hullo there, Henry? All right, are yer?' But then the figure moved out from the bush towards the window to which Henry was moving, as slowly and cautiously as Henry himself. The moon made the garden, as neat as the fences, the doors, the dustbins, and the thick, empty lilac bushes into a bold, clear woodcut, and the face of the other stranger, in dramatic relief, was a thing of frightening contrasts. The nose twitched and sniffed, like some animal after its quarry, and the mouth was half open, with excitement or fear or both. But it was the eyes that Henry noticed most. The eyes were fixed ahead in a rapture of concentration, as if something in the house was sucking them in, as if the light from the french windows exerted some horrible, unavoidable pull on Detective Inspector Rush.

There could be only one thing he was after, thought Henry. And he could not be allowed to get his hands on it. He stepped out into the moonlit patio and hissed a greeting.

'Rush – ' he heard himself say, 'Rush – it's me!'

The detective stopped and turned towards him. As soon as he saw Henry his face split into a smile, all teeth and lips, that reminded Henry of the *risus sardonicus* printed on Jackson's face, a week or so ago. He knows, thought Henry again, he knows all about me. He even knew I was coming here tonight. That's why he's here. He knows all of the ghastly things I think and feel and don't tell anyone about. And he knows them without me having to explain. He knows all the things only the detective knows about the criminal.

'Well,' said Rush, 'well, well, well!'

Sometimes Henry wondered whether Rush might not be a bit of his own genetic material that had somehow sloped off on its own to some lab and got a dodgy biochemist to set it up as a freelance individual. If he was a cutting off Henry, though, he was probably grafted from the toenail or somewhere up the rectal passage.

Rush continued to smile. 'Are you looking for what I'm looking for?' he said.

Why don't I tell him ? Why don't I just say: 'Fair's fair. Between you and me and the gatepost and Sprott's lilac bush, I did it. Now go ahead and prove it!' What was unbearable, as always with Rush, was the urge to confess, because only with this man was what Henry had done actually thinkable. When with Elinor, Maisie, people from the office or the street, it seemed to have nothing to do with Henry at all. But here, in the moonlight, looking at the policeman, tugging at his upper lip, Henry knew he had killed five people, none of whom, with the possible exception of Sprott and Coveney, deserved to die. Henry decided to face it out.

'Well,' he heard himself say, 'I thought I'd . . .'

'Get hold of the ashes,' said Rush, as if he were referring to the cricket trophy, as if this were the most normal thing to do in the world, 'of course!'

Without speaking, Henry went towards the window and, in silence, began to slide up the sash. It rattled as it rose. The silence between Henry and the policeman became, as he worked, not silence. A car came up Maple Drive. You could hear it from a long way away, falling in pitch and gaining in volume in a graceful curve until it shouldered its way past them, directly outside, with a muted 'pop', followed by the long, slow slide to absence and somewhere else.

Had Rush seen him? Leapt out of bed, taken an alternative route, some secret tunnel perhaps known only to members of the Wimbledon CID that led to Sprott's back garden? Was he intending to confront Henry with the granulated dentist,

245

waving the urn around in a challenging fashion? 'See! Here he is! This is what you've done, you bastard!'

Henry got one leg over the sill. Inside, the house was silent. Rush, who followed him in, led the way across the carpet. As they came out into the hall it occurred to Henry that all this might be some ghastly mistake, that Edwina Sprott might not, after all, have gone on her weekly visit to her sister. If that were the case, however, Rush had clearly got hold of the same inaccurate information for, as they reached the stairs, he spoke again in clear, almost relaxed tones.

'It's a funny thing about poisoners,' he said. 'Most of them want to get caught. It's a club, do you know what I mean? They have to show their cleverness to the world.'

He looked straight at Henry. 'I've studied poisoners,' he said, 'all my life. They're . . .' Here he gave an awkward little laugh, to show that he was making a joke. '. . . meat and drink to me.'

Perhaps Rush was going to drug him and take him back to some private Black Museum of his own. Perhaps Henry was of too great scientific interest to be just chucked over to the boys from legal aid and then sent off to Parkhurst for twenty years. Perhaps he would be taken into Rush's garden shed and nameless experiments would be performed on him. Henry thought he would probably prefer Parkhurst.

'Is there something you want to say to me, Henry?'

'No!' said Henry, rather sharply.

'Are you sure?'

'Yes,' said Henry, 'I'm sure.'

Rush stroked his upper lip.

'It's the loneliness, I think,' he said, 'I think they must have spent night after night wondering . . . is there anyone like me out there? Someone who shares my . . .' Here he laughed again, dry, perfunctory. '. . . enthusiasms. Cream, Young, Crippen, Palmer. The only time they come together is as waxworks. Know what I mean? And what they wanted was probably to just be with someone who would understand. Who'd say the names with them, you know? Hyoscine, gelsemium, aconite . . . You know?'

Henry was sweating. 'I think,' he said, 'we should go on up the stairs.'

Rush smiled. 'Of course, Henry,' he said, 'of course!'

He became suddenly practical when they reached the bedroom. The door was open and, facing them, above the mantelpiece was a 12" by 10" portrait picture of Sprott in his dentist's uniform. He was standing in his surgery with a drill in his right hand, trying, unsuccessfully, to look relaxed. Below his image, in a blue vase, was what remained of him, corporeally speaking, and on either side of the vase were two blue candles, burned halfway down. Say what you like about Sprott, thought Henry, he was a damned good dentist.

'Wait there!' said Rush.

The detective sank to his knees. Henry backed away nervously, while Rush flopped forward on his belly into the Sprotts' bedroom, indicating to Henry that he should do the same.

'Photo cell alarm!' he said, indicating a point about halfway up the side of the door. Henry wondered whether these precautions had been taken before Mrs Sprott's husband had swallowed a litre or so of bleach; in a sense, of course, people's value only became clear when they were dead. When alive Dave Sprott had been treated with amused condescension, now he was getting the treatment handed out to a more than usually influential local saint in Mrs Sprott's church (Edwina was reputed to be a devout Anglo-Catholic).

It didn't take Rush long to check the mantelpiece. He straightened up and from his left-hand pocket took a polythene bag. He slipped the neck of the vase into the bag, and, making sure not a drop of dentist was spilled, upended Henry's neighbour's remains into it. Then from his other jacket pocket he took an envelope and shook its contents into the vase.

He turned to Henry. 'Two rabbits,' he said, 'she should be quite happy with that.'

Then he held up the polythene bag. 'One dentist!' he said. 'Just add water and stir and he'll be back on the job in no time!'

Henry thought this remark was in rather dubious taste, and said so.

Rush's only response was to flash him a crooked grin. 'When you're dead,' he said, 'you're dead. And that's all there is to it. There's nothing else to say.'

Rush seemed able to alter Henry's opinions more drastically than anyone he had ever known. He very much, for once, wanted this remark not to be true. He wanted a flash of light to break in at the window and for Sprott to rear up, twenty feet tall, tearing at Rush's throat with his hands.

'What,' said Henry, 'are you going . . . to . . . do with . . . him?'

Rush smiled slightly. 'What were you going to do with him?'

'I was . . .'

The policeman was still holding the ashes aloft. He looked up at them, as a Chancellor might look at his briefcase on Budget Day.

'I think,' he said, 'the poisoner wants to get caught. I think being caught is the only thing that would relieve the awful, awful loneliness he must feel. The dreadful sense that everything that happens is happening in his head. That there isn't a real world at all, just his own consciousness. And that his consciousness . . .'

Henry gulped.

'. . . is hell. That he's reduced someone to this. That he's brought a man who could walk, talk, be any number of things, to something you could fit into a jumbo matchbox. And the reason he's done it? Shall I tell you the reason he's done it?'

No, thought Henry, please don't!

'Because he can't feel,' said Rush, in a crooning voice, 'he can't feel anything at all. He's dead inside. And to make himself feel, he has to do the most frightful things. He has to kill and kill and kill again and each time he kills he thinks it will be better but it isn't, and so, in shame and disgust, he goes out to kill again, to heal himself, but after the next killing there is still the same emptiness.'

Henry thought it was about time they left. Interesting as this conversation was, this did not seem the time or place to be having it. Somewhat to his surprise, Rush's technique was not having much effect on him. Perhaps he was so hardened a psychopath that he didn't even realize that he wasn't feeling. He was so much of a loony that he thought he *was* having feelings. Tremendous, strong, violent, real feelings. About therapy groups and being made to go to Waitrose and –

'He has to go back to his victims and dig them up and examine them and go through their ashes and test that what he did to them did actually kill them. Because to him, life is a kind of experiment. He has to go back to it and back to it to try and understand it but he never will understand it and that's what cuts him off from normal human feeling and why he never will be human at all!'

This, thought Henry, was a little unfair. He had always hoped that, one day, be might become, if not completely human, at least partially so. He was only forty, for Christ's sake. There was a way to go, he knew that, but in ten or fifteen years he might have acquired the odd natural response. 'Steady on, Rush!' he wanted to say, 'this isn't Russia. This is Wimbledon.'

But Rush was staring into his face with that same, glittering intensity. 'You know that poem about Maltby,' he said, 'don't you?'

'I think,' said Henry, 'I heard a car outside. I – '

'Death has no terrors for me now,
My heart's heavy; let's begone!
And dine with He who heals all grief,
The Poisoner of Wimbledon!'

Henry wasn't, for once, lying or exaggerating. He had

heard a car outside. And the sound of its engine was familiar. And – oh my God, no, say it isn't so – the door was slamming and he could hear familiar footsteps and –

> 'Let's feast on all his sides of beef
> Let's slaver over cottage pies,
> For he who dines with Maltby, boys,
> Dines marvellously, ere he dies!
>
> O hurry Southward, didst thou think
> That Phoebus' brightness ever shone?
> No no! The evening comes and brings
> The Poisoner of Wimbledon!'

It wasn't, thought Henry, only his sense of guilt that made this performance so unnerving. Rush's hands shook as he came to the last verse and his mouth, never a very attractive thing at the best of times, wriggled across his face like a snake in a bag. He looks, thought Henry, about as crazy as I must be.

Down below the front door opened. Henry heard what was almost certainly Edwina Sprott's step in the hall. No one could mistake that slow, tombstone tread of hers, the creak and thud of her Doc Martins hitting the stripped pine floor, reminiscent of the opening sequence of *Feet of Frankenstein*, and then the deep boom of her voice, calling up the stairs – 'I'm back, darling!'

CHAPTER THIRTY-SEVEN

Henry's first thought was that Mrs Sprott had a toy boy concealed somewhere about the house. Women in Wimbledon, Elinor included, were always moaning on about toy boys, perhaps because if their husbands had one thing in common it was a lack of ludic quality. Accountant's Wife with Over-developed Breasts and New Sierra had, people said, actually got a toy boy, although when finally sighted he was reported to be quite as fat and old and boring as everybody else. Certainly number 12b had had a black toy boy, who had come to investigate her soakaway drain and stayed, but he had only stayed three days and, people said, had left with her television, compact-disc player and fifty-three pounds in cash.

It was only when the widow was halfway up the stairs that Henry realized. She was talking to the late David Sprott.

'I couldn't stand Nelly any more,' she was saying, as she dropped what sounded like a case, 'so I left and came straight on back. I just felt sort of wild and crazy and desperate to get back home. Do you know what I mean?'

Henry thought he did. He started to tiptoe, at speed, towards the large cupboard in the corner of the room. Rush, polythene bag in hand, followed him.

'She was going on about how marvellous she was was Nelly,' said the relict of the man known to some as 'Cap 'em' Sprott, 'and if I have to hear one more time how marvellously that stupid little cow Monica is doing at St Paul's, I shall spit. She reckons she has an IQ of 184 or something – I said "come off it" – and plays the violin without music. I don't condone that myself.'

This conversation brought a new dimension to all those wise words about death being but a brief interruption in our conversation with our fellow pilgrims. It also served to remind us, in Henry's view, how, very often, those conversations should never even have been started, let alone continued across the Great Divide. Death and taxation might be the only certain things, but Mrs Sprott's version of snobbery was probably immune to both.

'Mozart this and Mozart that, I let her know how well Timmy was doing anyway, and why she won't have Mother for Christmas I don't know, it suited me to have her on Boxing Day but oh no, it had to be Christmas Eve. Anyone would think her husband was something interesting. He's only a monkey who reads the news!'

In amongst his second victim's suits, Henry remembered that Mrs Sprott's brother-in-law read the local news somewhere or other; it was a source of mild satisfaction to him that she should be subjected to the incomprehensible, bottomless vanity of this species of person.

'I said had they seen the results of the Lossiemouth by-election but it was pretty clear that they had no interest. I tried them on Nicaragua but they didn't seem to have formulated a view on it. And one of them didn't seem to have any idea of who the member for Bristol East was!'

Sprott, of course, had been kept abreast of politics by his wife, whose capacity to consume weekly journals, TV programmes and even live conferences concerned with political issues was legendary. It was clear that even his death was not going to stand between him and political enlightenment.

'And I heard Kinnock on the radio. That man has no conception of how to orchestrate his power base. He needs to confront Conference!'

Through a chink in the cupboard door, Henry observed her pull the lid off the vase and peer down at whatever Rush had put in it. If it was rabbits she was presumably looking at a whole colony. Whatever it was it seemed to satisfy her, for she replaced the lid with a little smile.

'It's nice to be home, darling,' she said, 'it's nice to know you're there on the mantelpiece.'

Henry looked down. Rush was squatting on the floor, clutching the polythene bag close to him. He looked back out into the room and, to his horror, saw that Mrs Sprott was starting to undress.

She slipped her dress over her shoulders and allowed it to fall to her knees. She was wearing a black bra and black silk knickers that Henry recognized, with a thrill, as coming from Marks and Spencer's. Elinor had a pair exactly the same. She crossed to the full-length mirror in the corner of the room, and looked at herself. Henry heard Rush give a little wheeze of excitement next to him, as Mrs Sprott lowered her knickers. The two men gazed out from her cupboard at something no man other than the late David Sprott had ever seen, the naked, white buttocks, tapering down to a fuzz of black pubic hair and a pair of no-nonsense, meaty, muscular thighs.

Next to Henry, Rush continued to wheeze. Was the detective, Henry wondered, stimulating himself in some way? He looked down and saw Rush, on his knees, eyes fixed to the crack in the cupboard door. His hands, as far as Henry could see, were nowhere near his trousers. The widow Sprott started to unhook her bra, in an extremely sensual manner. She shook it over her breasts, while making little rowing motions with her upper arms, and as it fell to the floor she gave a little twitch of the hips, causing Rush to leak what sounded like a whimper.

Did this, thought Henry, go on every night in the Sprott bedroom? And what about other bedrooms in Maple Drive? Did Mrs Is-the-Mitsubishi-Scratched-Yet, after she had drawn the bedroom curtains, switched on the light in the hall, come down in her dressing gown and gone up in her dressing gown, carry on like this? Was this the reason Mr Is-the-Mitsubishi-Scratched-Yet leapt up the stairs each night, two at a time, minutes after she had gone upstairs? And if this was the case, if things like this, or things even more spectacular than this even, were happening in front bedrooms the length of the street, wasn't it time Henry got a

253

pair of infra-red binoculars and some kind of hide in the front garden?

She turned to them, naked and humming to herself went towards the cassette deck by the bed. She had one of those deep, architectural, solid navels, Henry noted, and large brown nipples. Elinor's were pink. But before he had time to compare and contrast the two women (another aspect, he presumed, of his cold, calculating, psychopathic nature) Mrs Sprott had turned on the machine and the strains of 'Guantanamera' filled the room. It was a song Henry had always enjoyed and, even under these somewhat awkward circumstances, he found himself nodding his head in time to it, and trying, once again, to work out what the hell those words were that immediately followed the opening.

> Guantanamera
> Akeela (?????)
> Guantana-meeera!

And, one more time –

> Guantanamera
> Ah feel ya (?????)
> Guantana-meeera!

And, surely, this time one would get it? Come on! Here it comes again! This time, surely! Surely!

> Guantanamera
> Tequila (?????)
> Guantana-meeera!

But no. They were on to the bit about his poems being flaming crimson and how he was a truthful man who only wanted to bugger sheep. And Mrs Sprott, who had returned to the mantelpiece, was dancing, naked, in front of the photograph of her late husband. Henry did not dare look to see what Rush was making of this. He almost expected the picture of the dentist to register some emotion (surprise possibly) but, like a holy picture, like Mary or Jesus receiving an act of piety, Sprott continued to grin out at the opposite wall, while his widow rotated her buttocks, bumped and ground and . . . oh my God, she wasn't, was she?

Oh yes she was. Now wildly out of time to the music (the man had finished his translation of the lyric and, having demonstrated to his and everybody else's satisfaction that it was incomprehensible in both Spanish and English, was now singing it all over again, in that same, linguistically secretive style), she rotated her hips faster and faster and her elbow jerked up and down as if she was beating mayonnaise.

> Guantanamera
> Ah steal ya (????)
> Guantana-meeera!

Not feeling that this was something he wanted to watch, Henry concentrated on the picture of Sprott, who continued to look at the camera in what he clearly thought was a confident, solid, reasonable fashion. But his wife (it was impossible to ignore her) was pumping her way towards climax, as the guitars, drums and flutes continued their endless circle. Her left hand snaked round her neck and pulled at her hair, then slid down, past her breasts and buried itself in the flesh of her left buttock. She was moving faster, faster and . . . What happens, thought Henry, if the cassette finishes before she does? But through what was probably long practice, both Mrs Sprott and the Havana All Stars – or whoever they were – came to a conclusion at the same time and, dripping with sweat, she started to cast around for her clothes as the tape hissed on in disapproving silence. My Christ, thought Henry, whoever said Wimbledon was dull?

Eventually she resumed her conversation.

'Well,' she said, as she struggled back into her clothes, 'that was very nice, David. Very nice indeed. Thank you very much. I enjoyed that a lot. I hope you were all right. Were you all right? I was. I was fine. Oh, look, you had a good innings really, didn't you? For God's sake, we none of us live for ever, do we? You could be bloody boring, David, actually. You had no interest in politics. You just – ' Here, she sat on the bed and began to sob violently.

Oh my God, thought Henry. Oh my sweet Jesus Christ. I am sorry. I am very, very, very sorry. This is awful. I didn't mean to. I tried to stop them. I honestly did. I tried to stop him drinking the bloody stuff. I really didn't want him dead. I didn't like him. I admit that. But I didn't want him dead. I mean I may have wanted him dead once or twice. But I didn't mean it. Everyone wants someone or other dead some time or other, don't they? Look, I'm really, really sorry.

'Look, Henry,' said Sprott, 'I was insured. I was very heavily insured as a matter of fact. She's better off now than she was with me alive.'

Mrs Sprott continued to cry on the bed. Fat tears rolled down her face, smudging her make up, blurring the lines on her cheeks, reminding Henry against his will that real actions had real consequences. And it was then, he realized afterwards, watching a lonely woman crying on a rumpled bed, in a deserted house, that he knew, whatever else he was, he wasn't a psychopath. He was pretty fucking close, but not there yet. And the only way he was going to get out of this, the only thing that would stop the dull ache the sight of her caused him, would be if he went out to her now and told her everything. Told Rush too. Told all of them what he had done and why he had done it. Atoned, for Christ's sake. Atoned. Because this feeling wasn't containable. It was like a needle in his side or an unstoppable headache that made him, as he stood there in the cupboard, feel he was about to lose his balance.

He probably would have gone out there too, he thought afterwards (in which case the whole thing would have ended differently). The only thing that stopped him was the near certainty that he would have given her a heart attack. And he didn't, no, he positively did not, you could quote him on that, want to cause any more deaths. Ever. He wanted to be nice to people. He wanted to make children smile. He wanted to gladden the last years of grannies and grandpas. He

256

wanted to be helpful, in an unpatronizing manner, to the disabled. He wanted to be all the things his class, his upbringing and his country seemed to militate against. Generous. He had, in the last few months, got rid of so many hostilities, resentments, spites, perversions and jealousies that he must now, he thought, be the nicest guy in Wimbledon. He was poison free, for Christ's sake! He was as clean as a lanced boil! What he was feeling, here in the cupboard, while Mrs Sprott cried into her sheets for a man who was – let's face it – a pretty nice guy as well, was love. Love for her, and for her husband, yes, don't laugh, for Sprott and for Mr and Mrs Is-the-Mitsubishi-Scratched-Yet and Nazi Who Escaped Justice at Nuremberg and Vera 'Got All the Things There Then?' Loomis and Jungian Analyst with Winebox and Lingalonga Boccherini and Surveyor with Huge Gut and Drink Problem and Surveyor with Huge Gut and Fondness for Potatoes and Published Magical Realist and Unpublished Magical Realist and, oh for God's sake, all of them, the whole hopeless, gargoyle crew of them. Because, this was the fact he had never been able to face, let's face it, he wasn't any better or worse than any of these people. He was one of them. He was Fat Man with Bowler Hat and Unimaginable Feelings of Hostility Towards People. He was –

If only I could roll back time, thought Henry. If only I wasn't a quintuple murderer. How simple, easy and pleasant life would be!

And that thought brought him back to the fact that he couldn't roll back time. That he wasn't just Fat Man with Bowler Hat and Unimaginable Feelings of Hostility Towards People, he was Fat Man with Bowler Hat Who Had Poisoned God Knows How Many Innocent People. And that thought made him feel he was falling, falling, the way he had felt that night he tried to strangle Elinor and, to stop that feeling that he was falling, which of course was unstoppable because once you fall you fall, dead people don't come back to life and time will not, however hard you try, go backwards, he felt for a feeling that would stop the falling feeling and found he was feeling, or rather failing to feel, since he was falling, for something that felt as if it was filling the feeling that perhaps he had been failing to feel, the feeling that –

He was gripping Rush's shoulder, hard, the way he had gripped Maisie's shoulder that night, months, although it felt like years, ago. And Rush was trying to brush him off. And Henry's face was pushed into the dark cloth of one of Dave Sprott's suits. And his brushing against it must have started up dust, because of course the poor bastard hadn't been able to wear them where he was going, and the dust swirled about Henry's nostrils and something in the chemistry between dust and nose set off a reaction that, once started, could not, it seemed, even by a major effort of will, be stopped.

Henry sneezed.

CHAPTER THIRTY-EIGHT

To understand what happened next, it is necessary to appreciate quite what an effect the presence of the Wimbledon Poisoner had had on the local population. It wasn't, as Nazi Who Escaped Justice at Nuremberg pointed out, that people were afraid to go out. They were afraid to stay in as well. You never knew just where or when the poisoner would strike. The folk stories about him, and there were plenty, said that he was able to slip into any house he wanted. That he was a trained locksmith as well as a trained chemist. Some said, of course, that he was a policeman who talked his way into people's kitchens while pretending to warn them about the poisoner. Others maintained he was a member of the judiciary and still others that he was, in fact, a she-poisoner, a motherly woman who worked in some local school, who had looked after children all her life and suddenly, sickened by all that care and nourishment, had turned to food that blighted, not sustained.

A sneeze in a cupboard meant only one thing to Edwina Sprott. It said *poisoner*, loud and clear.

She didn't move. She stayed where she was on the bed and said, in a clear, nervous voice, 'Please don't do anything to me!'

Neither Rush nor Henry knew quite how to respond to this. 'If you're the poisoner,' she went on, 'don't make me eat anything!'

Rush looked up at Henry, his jagged mouth turned down comically. He was mouthing something. Henry leaned down and made out the words 'Fantastic tits!'

Really, thought Henry, Rush wasn't the sort of man with whom one would have wanted to share any kind of space, however large. Being in a cupboard with him was almost completely unacceptable.

Mrs Sprott was talking again. Her delivery was that of a not very good performer in a West End play. Her lines were put over with a kind of emphasis thought needful to get across basic information to elderly people who have come miles by charabanc, and who, as well as being of low intelligence, are halfway through a large box of Cadbury's Milk Tray. This theatrical manner did not, however, manage to conceal her evident embarrassment at having had an audience for her recent performance in front of Sprott's photograph.

'I'm going out now,' she said, 'and I shall leave the door open. I shall not ask any questions of you. You are free to leave. I am going to take refuge with a neighbour. I promise not to look or phone the police.'

Rush looked at Henry, grinning. Henry ignored him.

'In my opinion,' she went on, 'you are in need of psychiatric help. I bear no malice to you for what you did to my late husband. Hating you won't bring David back. I think you are a poor, sick, creature whose mind is disturbed. You probably don't even know what you're doing. Give yourself up! I am going now.'

Henry was going to give himself up. Not now. But soon. He would go somewhere quiet with Detective Inspector Rush and turn himself in. He had had enough.

It wouldn't be too bad. At least he would find out what he had and hadn't done. Whether he was, like the conkers he had played with as a child, a one-er or a two-er, or a three-er or maybe a fifty-eighter. There would be the trial, of course – bad pencil sketches of him on *News at Ten*, yet more profiles, and after the verdict an endless string of articles and photographs of the exterior of Maple Drive. They would write about Elinor too. POISONER'S WIFE DENIED HIM SEX! THERAPY DROVE MASS POISONER FARR TO MURDER FIVE! 'I LOVE HIM STILL' SAYS POISONER'S WOMAN. Then there would be the musicals, the drama documentaries, the serious studies of the case written by people who would not, sadly, be Karim Jackson; and then a long, long time in Broadmoor with all the other loonies.

Oh, Broadmoor wouldn't be too bad. He had seen a film about it a few weeks ago. About the only drawback to the place, as far as Henry could see, was compulsory group therapy. Although at group therapy would be eager-eyed psychiatrists just dying to hear about his guilt, his blackouts, his sense of isolation.

'She's gone!' Rush was whispering. 'Let's go!'

It occurred to Henry that Mrs Sprott might well be lying in wait for them. She hadn't sounded like a woman about to lie in wait. She had sounded like someone en route for dressing room number one and the smelling salts. But she might, possibly, be planning to conceal herself somewhere and spy on them. It was to this end that Henry removed two jackets from the hangers in the cupboard, and indicated to Rush that they should place them over their heads. It would probably, he thought grimly, be good training for his first appearance at Wimbledon Magistrate's Court.

With the late dentist's jackets over their heads, the two men crept out on to the landing. By pinching the lapels together, Henry managed to conceal his face and preserve a narrow field of vision; it meant that he had to move his whole body if he wished to look in another direction, rather as if he were the front end of a pantomime horse, but at least, as he scanned the landing, left, right, fore and aft, and then one 360° turn, like a radar beam sweeping over the night sky, he was able to be sure that Mrs Sprott had been as good as her word. The two men started down the stairs. The front door was open as Henry, head lowered, made for the street, the jacket hugged to his head like a friar's cowl. Ahead he could see a plane tree, empty of leaves, pointing angrily in all directions. But there was no sign of Mrs Sprott. Henry walked slowly out and down the front path, towards the white gate.

He peered left. No one. Then right. No one. With a short,

urgent gesture to Rush Henry started out to the left, along the pavement.

He couldn't see or hear her but perhaps she was on the phone already. Perhaps, in minutes, Maple Drive would be swarming with dog-handlers, meat wagons, forensic experts and all the other things the police liked to drag along to places where they had no hope of solving serious crime. The trouble was, his field of vision was so restricted by the jacket that he was unable to ascertain whether or not it was safe to remove it. He ran, bent double, zig-zagging like a man avoiding machine-gun fire. Behind him he could hear Rush, breathing heavily and occasionally calling out for reassurance: 'Are we OK?'

Henry did not even want to answer. He was vaguely aware that they were passing number 84 (Stockbroker Who Could Turn Nasty) but, since it seemed easier to keep his head down, he had no idea of what might be ahead or behind him. He noted the pavement, marked with cracks and discolorations, a low wall, painted white, then a privet hedge to the left, a tree to the right, a lamp post, then more discoloured pavement. He stopped. He had come to a bumpy section of kerb, north of which was the gutter. Raising his head he saw he was in Belvedere Road. All he had to do was to slip the jacket off and stroll up towards the common. No one knew him in Belvedere Road. He would go on the common, with Rush, and there he would end all this. He would turn himself over to the policeman. He was just about to slip the jacket off his head, and planning the opening stages of his confession ('Have you ever heard of something called Finish 'Em by any chance?') when, from behind, he heard cries. Not only cries. Feet. Feet slapping the pavement. Not just one person's feet. Quite a lot of feet. Henry juddered round, as awkward as a robot and there, jerked into vision, like something slipping into the perspective offered by a periscope, he saw the line of houses that was Maple Drive. About a hundred yards away a door was opening, and beyond that, another door. Someone was shouting something. Was it Mrs Sprott?

Henry did not wait to find out. Burrowing his head into the dentist's jacket he pushed Rush in the back and the two men ran for the common. He had almost forgotten, in the excitement, that he was the Wimbledon Poisoner. If any of the inhabitants of Maple Drive got to him before the police (Fat Man with Loved Alsatian, for example) he would be very lucky to get as far as Broadmoor, and it wouldn't be group therapy he'd be needing but plastic surgery on a large scale.

'Faster!' he hissed to the detective, almost oblivious of the fact that this was the man to whom he was due to make his confession, 'Faster! Faster! Faster!'

CHAPTER THIRTY-NINE

The hue and cry, as Henry had noted in volume seven of *The Complete History of Wimbledon*, was a comparatively rare occurrence in the history of the village. In 1788 a man called Paggett had been pursued from the Dog and Fox towards Putney Hill, because – according to a contemporary diarist – he had shouted revolutionary slogans outside a butcher's shop in the village. Enraged local tradesmen had followed him across the common to the Queen's Mere, where 'they caused him to regret his Enthusiasm for the Queen's enemies by using those appurtenances of honest labour viz their true English Hands, to douse him in one of Her own Ponds!'

If anything, thought Henry, the contemporary inhabitants of Maple Drive were a deal more frightening than a few drunken butchers. There were even, Henry shuddered at the thought, a few bond salesmen at the posher end of the street. If what you read in the newspapers was true, the middle classes in the Britain of the late 1980s made your average pack of ravening wolves look like the *corps de ballet* in *Swan Lake*. He thought he could hear more doors opening, more shouts, more feet on pavement, as he ran, quite blind as to what was ahead of him, up towards the village.

After a hundred yards or so, however, he found his pace had slowed, and was, for the moment, unaware of the pressure of anyone's hand on his back. Perhaps his neighbours were so deeply imbued with the philosophy of self-help that, when actually faced with someone who had taken the law into his own hands, they were unable to stop themselves standing back in admiration. Perhaps murder, like everything else, was now part of Mrs Thatcher's enterprise economy. Or perhaps – this was the most likely explanation – they were all a little too scared. Whatever the reason, when he and Rush reached the village High Street, pulled off their jackets and looked back down the hill, they saw no one, only the quiet suburban streets and the cars, parked with loving neatness under the lamps.

It was then that Henry turned back to the village and, in the window of a shop selling electrical equipment, found himself looking at the face of Everett Maltby. He recognized the big, damp eyes, the side whiskers and the high collar. Next to him, with a little shock of horror, he recognized Maltby's wife, and to one side of the couple a pile of photographic plates. It was one of those cardboard displays, of the kind usually used to advertise something. Surely they couldn't be cashing in on the poisoner? Henry felt a chill of disgust at the thought that his perverted desire to kill was being employed to market electrical goods. Then he saw the slogan: WIMBLEDON TRADERS AGAINST THE POISONER. FIGHT THE BLIGHTER! And underneath this was what looked like a list of signatures. Why did people think that signing your name to a petition affected anything? It might, perhaps, have some minimal impact on politicians, but its effect on murderers was probably to spur them on to greater efforts.

'Hullo there!' A figure who had been staring in at the Maltby display turned to face Henry, who to his horror saw it was smiling at him.

'Mr Bleath, isn't it?'

It was the young man who had sold him the thallium.

'I – '

Henry found he was walking towards him across the empty street. Behind him he could hear Rush's footsteps in a dead patrol – one, two, one, two, we'll get you, Farr, one, two, one, two, I'll marry your wife, we'll get you, Farr, one, two, one, two . . .

'Did you call me Bleath?'

'Isn't it Mr Bleath? Didn't I sell you some – '

'Optical lenses!' said Henry wildly. 'Optical lenses!'

What was this man doing here so late at night? Why was he looking in at that picture of Maltby?

'Your shop . . .' Henry found himself saying, 'is near where Maltby's . . . I mean, your shop is . . .'

'Mr Bleath?'

'Maltby lived here . . .' Henry was saying, 'and now there's a poisoner here and . . .'

'Thallium?' the young man from the chemist's was saying in a wheedling, comforting tone. 'Thallium? Thallium? Thallium?'

Henry looked from the chemist to Maltby and back to the chemist again. Remarkable how similar they looked really. Bland. Innocent. That was why they were using Maltby to sell things of course. Like so many poisons he looked sweet and innocent and attractive. Like so many guilty people he looked respectable. Henry could hear Rush's footsteps behind him. One, two, three, don't try and run, Farr. One, two, three, we're going to get your wife, Farr. One, two, three . . . Why was the man in the window looking at him like that? Could he see into his soul? Why was he looking at him so knowingly?

Later of course, when it was all over, he could see quite clearly that the youth was simply a youth (admittedly a youth with a somewhat over-liberal interpretation of the rules governing the sale of registered poisons) and the picture of Maltby simply a picture. That in the affair of the Wimbledon Poisoner everything was precisely as it seemed and that dreams, hauntings, reincarnations and all the other junk beloved of such people as Unpublished Magical Realist were precisely that – junk. But at the time, with the racket in his head and the racket behind him, as he stared at the man who knew him as Alan Bleath, when all this pretence had started, Henry felt himself letting go of everything he had taken for reality. And that falling feeling started again, so that the youth's face zoomed in to his, as it had that day he had taken off his glasses and a voice that seemed like his but was, of course only in Henry's head, started up and he found he was saying, not thinking, the magic words that would release him from all of this.

'I am the Wimbledon Poisoner!'

The youth did not seem very impressed with this remark. Henry tried again.

'I,' he said, 'am the Wimbledon Poisoner. My name is Henry Farr and I am the Wimbledon Poisoner.'

There was, as there always is at moments of crisis, a great deal of time. I must, he thought, be saying it wrong. He started towards the youth and tried out the sentence again, in a calm, I-have-got-to-live-with-this voice. They probably got a lot of basket cases coming up to them and trying to tell them they were the Wimbledon Poisoner.

'I,' said Henry, stooping down towards the youth and gripping his arm, 'am the man who did the poisonings!'

Perhaps this new construction would get the message across. It didn't. The youth was looking at him as if Henry was a rather puzzling piece of modern sculpture or a German expressionist play.

'Look – ' said Henry.

And then time, as time always does, started again, and Henry heard Rush right behind him, heard the policeman's heavy breath and wondered – Why don't you do it now? Why don't you arrest me and get it over with?

'And so it was,' said Lustgarten, 'that the poisoner, Farr, met his end at the hands of the very man who he had feared for so long! At the sight of the innocent chemist who had sold him the thallium a whole host of memories came flooding back and he saw that some evil spirit was working its way through him as it had through Everett Maltby all those years ago. For Justice has a way of finding out the guilty and, in the end, making them confess, very much as Henry Farr the solicitor did, simply to be rid of the intolerable pain of their conscience!'

'Listen!' Henry shouted. 'I am the Wimbledon Poisoner!'

The young man didn't seem at all interested. He was turning from the Maltby display and, with what looked like some urgency, moving away up towards Putney. It seemed to Henry as if he didn't want to hear him.

'I killed them!' he shouted at the retreating chemist. 'I killed them all!'

The man did not even turn round. Christ, thought Henry, what do I have to do to get attention? Steal a nuclear bomb or what?

'I'm a bastard!' he shrieked. 'I am! I put thallium on Donald Templeton's chicken! I did! For God's sake, I did!'

It did sound, he had to admit, pretty improbable. For a moment he found himself wondering whether it was even true, and then, like a man determined to see through a difficult, dull, unlooked-for task, he went on with his confession. It would have sounded a lot better if there had been music on the soundtrack, or if he could manage something a bit more Grand Guignol in the delivery; as it was it seemed, in spite of the sensational nature of its content, a fairly low-grade affair.

'I put bleach in the punch!' he shouted again. 'I get blackouts! I forget things!'

But by now the chemist was running. Perhaps he thought Henry was trying to implicate him in the affair of the Chicken Thallium. Or perhaps, given his carefree way with scheduled poisons, this was always happening to him.

'I inject apples with prussic acid!' yelled Henry. 'I slip strychnine into salad dressing! I hang round supermarkets, for Christ's sake, and I smear aconite on to wholewheat loaves! I'm poison! Hear me! I'm a dreadful, cruel, greedy, stupid, mad thoughtless person! I'm the fucking Wimbledon Poisoner, for Christ's sake! That has to be worth something, doesn't it, you bastard?'

No one, of course, had ever really sat down and listened to Henry. If they had, they tended to get up and walk away halfway through whatever it was he was trying to say. At school, however high he lifted his hand, he seemed to be one of those boys the masters never saw. The least he could have hoped for, he felt, was for people to listen to his confessing to multiple murder. I mean, Christ, he thought miserably, what do they want from me? Some people go on television

268

and talk about absolutely nothing at all and people listen with their tongues hanging out. OK. I'm the quiet little man in the corner. I read a few books and then forgot them. I'm the man who looked like he might do something and then didn't. I'm a . . . well . . . I'm a solicitor, for Christ's sake, but surely, when in a lull in the pub conversation I lean forward and in a piping voice just happen to mention that I chopped up my wife and left her in a bath of acid, people might say 'Hey! There's something going on here!'

'LISTEN!' he shrieked, as the chemist disappeared into the gloom, 'LISTEN! I HAVE MURDERED FIVE PEOPLE! AND A WHOLE LOT MORE PROBABLY! I'M SICK! CAN'T YOU UNDERSTAND? I NEED HELP! I'M A CRAZY! PLEASE! LISTEN! I'M THE FUCKING WIMBLEDON POISONER, YOU STUPID, GREEDY, IGNORANT BASTARDS!'

He was alone in the street. The man had gone. No one was left to listen to him. Only the man who he had started to think of as his conscience, as someone inside him nagging at him, indistinguishable from his very self. It was, of course, as it always had been, to Rush that he would have to talk. Rush who wanted all of Henry – his wife, his confession, his very soul. For the first time in forty years, as Henry turned to face his tormentor he really felt that there was such a thing as a soul. What else could be giving him such a non-corporeal ache? What else could be singing in his head like blood pressure, blocking out the here and now, forcing him to say things he had never thought he could say?

But there was a kind of insufferable complacency about Detective Inspector Rush, and his expression, too, suggested that if he had heard Henry's confession he did not find it particularly interesting or believable.

'So,' he said, 'you're the Wimbledon Poisoner, are you?'

'I – '

Henry found his voice faltering.

'I've . . .'

'You've what?'

'I've killed people!' said Henry. And now, for the first

269

time, his crimes sounded real. Prosaic, flat, but terrifyingly real.

Rush smirked. 'Tell me about it!' he said. 'Tell me! Tell me! Do!'

CHAPTER FORTY

The two men, as if by some pre-arranged signal, began to walk up towards Putney. Henry tried to concentrate on his confession. This was, he knew, a very important moment for him. Ideally he would have liked a ring of admiring listeners, a log fire and a policeman who wasn't trying to steal his wife. But he would have to do the best he could. It was going to be difficult, he could see, to get across the pity and the terror of it all. He felt rather as a relative of Aeschylus must have felt, when trying to tell someone about how the great playwright died: 'Well . . . it's like this . . . he was walking along and . . . a tortoise fell on his head!'

'First of all,' he said, 'I put some thallium on her chicken.'

'Pull the other one,' said Rush, 'it's got bells on it!'

Was he, wondered Henry, trapped in some ghastly reworking of *The Trial* by Franz Kafka, in which he was doomed to wander around London trying, unsuccessfully, to convince people of his guilt?

'And then,' said Henry, 'I put a whole load of Finish 'Em in the punch at Donald's funeral.'

This still failed to capture the detective inspector's interest. Perhaps he wasn't saying it right. Perhaps he wasn't expressing enough remorse. The trouble was, although he had felt remorse, remorse wasn't something you could go around feeling for long. Henry was perfectly capable of feeling randy or envious for phenomenally long periods of time, but remorse was, in his experience anyway, something that sneaked up on you, like indigestion.

'Why did I do it? What made me do it? How could I have done it? It seems incredible, doesn't it?'

'Yes,' said Rush, in a small, mean voice, 'it seems completely incredible.'

Far away to their right a pair of headlights raked the darkness of the common and swung away north up towards town.

'I think,' said Henry, 'that I am losing my mind.'

Rush speeded up his pace. To Henry's horror he realized the man was trying to get away from him. Henry stumbled after him through the long grass.

'I'm a bloody psychopath,' he said again, 'I'm a bloody psychopath, man. I'm a crazy. I should be put away somewhere before I do any more damage. I don't know how I got this way but . . .'

Rush turned to him. 'But what?' he said. 'But what?'

'But I have the blood of five people on my hands!'

The trouble was, the more he went over his confession, the more improbable it sounded. Had he really done all the things he thought he had done in the three months since he sat in his office and thought about disposing of Elinor? Or was the whole thing a mirage, a thought experiment?

'You see,' he said, 'Everett Maltby – '

Rush rounded on him again. This time the detective grabbed Henry, and Henry found, to his surprise, that the man had an extraordinarily strong grip.

'What about Everett Maltby?' he said.

'Do you believe,' said Henry, 'that people can possess you? That you can find yourself doing things and not know you're doing them? Like Jekyll and Hyde?'

Rush declined to answer any of these questions.

'Because,' Henry continued, 'maybe the poisoner is someone who's full of . . . I don't know . . . bitterness, bad emotion . . . and maybe this . . . maybe Maltby sort of . . . acts through him . . . or maybe he, I mean maybe I, without knowing it, am acting out what Maltby did. You see? Do you see? Maybe I'm sort of going through what he did, like a puppet . . . like . . .'

Rush's lower lip was working furiously. 'You don't know anything about Everett Maltby,' he said. 'You don't know anything about anything.'

Then he paused. As if the thought had just occurred to him, he said, 'Were you really trying to poison your wife?'

For the first time since the beginning of this conversation Henry felt an important question was being asked. He felt, too, that when he answered it, his answer would count for something. That it really would describe the long years of bitterness and frustration, go some way to explain what Elinor and he had become, how once, perhaps, they had loved each other, but now, whether through time or lack of imagination or weakness on one or other of their parts, they had, quite literally, forgotten what that love meant. And perhaps, in trying to kill her, he had been trying to make that love come alive again, that forgotten feeling, forgotten like so many other things, that was, if it was like anything, like a kind of certainty or a memory of a place he had once visited, oh probably Switzerland, for Christ's sake, who the hell knew?

'Yes,' he said, clearly, simply, 'I wanted her dead. I really did want her dead.'

With a kind of eldritch screech Rush ran at him, his talon-like hands out in front of him. Henry stepped back, fell against a tussock of grass and the detective landed on him, his hands groping for Henry's neck.

This was a bit more like it. At least, thought Henry, we're getting some reaction here.

'There are times,' he said, as they grappled together in the long grass, 'when I'd like to take a fucking pickaxe to her. When she drives me so fucking crazy I'd like to tie her up in a sack and drop her over Hammersmith Bridge. When I'd like to tie her up and throw darts at her. When I'd like to drop her out of an aeroplane.'

Rush was kneeing upwards into Henry's crotch. By leaning forward Henry managed to absorb the blow in his stomach. He pushed out his right hand and clawed at Rush's face, getting a fair bit of cheek and quite a lot of thick, rubbery nose.

'Cunt,' said Rush, 'fucking horrible bastard cunt!'

273

This, Henry thought, was manly and straightforward talk. At least we all now knew where we stood.

'Don't tell me,' he said, 'you haven't felt like murdering your wife. Not that you've got a wife. But if you had one you'd feel like murdering her. Everybody does. They just haven't got the nerve to go through with it, that's all. They quarrel about property or the children or they destroy each other slowly, over years, when what they really want to do is get their hands round the old rat's throat and squeeze. Everyone wants to murder their wife. It's fair enough!'

Rush, who had not yet managed to make much headway with Henry's throat, was screaming obscenities at him.

'She's owed a crack at me, probably,' went on Henry. 'Why not? What's all this big deal about killing people? At least it's over and done and you can get on with your lives! Christ, it's better than rowing all the time, isn't it? It's better than niggle niggle niggle. Get right on in there and wrap the whole thing up. For Christ's sake, lots of people murder people they really and truly love, for God's sake. Because they don't want anyone else to have them! And they walk out of the courts free men! You can get more for robbing a train than for killing someone! Why is it supposed to be the worst thing in the world to try and top someone?'

Rush was kicking Henry in the shins. He seemed to be trying to say something but Henry wasn't particularly interested in listening to it. What he really wanted to do, he realized, was not to confess but to explain, to justify. In order to shut Rush up he got his hands over the man's mouth and started to bang his head into the ground.

'I don't see,' he went on, 'what Elinor and I want to do to each other is anybody's business but ours. It certainly isn't anything to do with you, you grubby little bastard!'

The policeman's face was turning crimson. Saliva was oozing out of the corner of his mouth. In a few minutes, thought Henry, I shall be up to victim number six. How appropriate that it should be an officer of the law!

'President Nixon and Henry Kissinger,' he said, 'killed

hundreds and thousands of people. I know they were only Vietnamese and Cambodians, but they were all fully paid up members of the human race. They do all right, don't they? They get honorary degrees from American universities, for fuck's sake! All I have tried to do is tried to murder a very difficult woman to whom I have been married for twenty years. We're talking about self-defence!'

Rush managed to get one of Henry's hands off his throat. 'Elinor – ' he started to say.

'You don't know Elinor,' said Henry, 'you don't know what she can be like. And in my view nobody who hasn't been married to her for as long as I have has the right to say anything about her. Or just casually condemn me for putting a bit of thallium on her chicken or a touch of bleach in a festive potion. I know Elinor, OK?'

Rush was staring up at him in something like horror. He was no longer attempting to kick, strangle or scratch Henry.

'Sometimes I love her,' said Henry, 'sometimes I hate her and sometimes I want to kill her.'

He realized he had left something out. 'And sometimes,' he added, slightly lamely, 'I do actually try to kill her!'

He now loosened his hands from Rush's throat. 'But I . . . er . . . don't succeed. I seem to succeed in poisoning everyone in the street apart from her. Which is . . . right . . . depressing. I mean I had nothing against Donald Templeton. I had no legitimate grievance against Sprott or Coveney or Loomis or any of them. I didn't know Donald was going to eat the bloody chicken or that that punch at the funeral would be quite so bloody lethal. You knew then, didn't you? That's when you knew, didn't you? And you've been playing with me ever since, haven't you, you bastard? I mean, I didn't want Karim Jackson to die. Well, I may have wanted him to have a nasty accident but . . .'

He wished Rush would stop looking at him quite like that. One thing, he realized, was that he would never be able to explain quite what he felt about Elinor to anyone. He thought they were probably too close, now, even to use a word like

275

'love'. He hadn't fallen in love or out of love with Elinor and what was between them was a lot more frightening and complicated and, probably, durable, than the meanings associated with that overused and under-explained word. There was no one else in the world quite real to him. That was it. She was the only person associated in his mind with any sort of feeling, and even though quite a lot of the feelings were of the more unpleasant kind, it was probably true that bad feelings were better than no feelings at all. He probably wanted to be a psychopath and she wouldn't let him, that was why he had tried to kill her. But he was as much a disaster at assassination as he was at being wholeheartedly without scruple.

Henry let his arms hang loose by his sides. He rocked back on his haunches and looked up at the moon.

'Anyway,' he said in a rather sulky voice, 'you'd better clap the handcuffs on or whatever you do. Or caution me or something. Because, hard though this may be to believe, I am the Wimbledon Poisoner!'

Rush looked at him. His lip curled slightly, and he said, 'No, you're not.'

He paused.

'I am.'

CHAPTER FORTY-ONE

As the French poisoner Eustachy said at his trial, 'It was all a joke!' And Henry, too, as he looked down at Detective Inspector Rush, realized that he had never been fundamentally serious about poisoning. He was not, would not, could not be in the premier league of those who seek to administer toxic substances to persons without their prior knowledge or consent. And, as he scrambled to his feet, it was obvious that if there was to be competition between himself and the detective for what the late Gordon Macrae would have called 'the role of Wimbledon Poisoner', then Rush had the edge on him. He was, to coin a phrase, quite clearly desperate for the part.

'Look,' said Henry, who was rapidly losing his grip on this conversation, 'you may be a poisoner, I don't know. You may be *a* poisoner who happens to live in Wimbledon. But I am *the* Wimbledon Poisoner. I know when I've put poison in something and – '

'Poisoner!' said Rush. 'You don't know anything about poison. You couldn't poison a fucking fruit cake!'

'I think I could actually . . .' Henry started to say. Then he stopped. Rush was walking away from him again, deeper into the darkness of the common, so far from the road now that you could not even see the distant lights in the houses on Parkside. Ahead of them the bare trees lifted their branches out towards each other, touching at the tips in a dead, pleasureless embrace.

'I am the Wimbledon Poisoner,' said Rush, 'and there are no other poisoners worth their salt operating in the district. I am the Wimbledon Poisoner!'

This, thought Henry, was getting like one of those dreary demarcation disputes of the early 1960s. But before he could start rehearsing his life of crime once more, Rush had started to talk again, in a crooning voice, his head rocking from side to side as he spoke.

'Poison is a passion,' he was saying, 'there are so many poisons! So many things that can change the way your body is! When I was ten, you see, I got a chemistry set and – '

'Look,' said Henry, 'I put thallium, got it? Thallium on a piece of chicken that my wife was supposed to eat but didn't! And I put Finish 'Em, got it? Finish 'Em in a punch that my wife was supposed to drink. I'm a poisoner, OK?'

Rush snorted. 'Templeton died, what, four hours afterwards?'

'Yes . . .'

'You don't know anything about poisons,' said Rush. 'You know fuck-all about poisons. If you knew anything at all about poisons you would know that his symptoms were nothing like the symptoms of thallium poisoning. And that the speed of action of the poison was nothing like that of thallium. Christ Jesus, Jesus, Jesus! Stupid, ignorant little man! Stupid, stupid, little amateur cunt! Where was the depilation? Eh? Where was the stomatitis, eh? Loss of energy and weight? Polyneuritis, eh? AND ALL THESE ARE DELAYED, YOU IGNORANT LITTLE BASTARD!'

Henry watched Rush's face very carefully.

'How much did you give him?'

'I don't know exactly,' said Henry, feeling piqued by this mode of questioning, 'a few grams, I . . .'

'A FEW GRAMS, EH? IS THAT IT? A FEW GRAMS? AND HOW MUCH FINISH 'EM DID YOU GIVE 'EM, EH?'

'Well, er . . .' said Henry, with an increasing sense of irritation, 'a bottle, basically . . .'

'A bottle, eh?' said Rush, who had gone suddenly quiet after his outburst. 'A bottle of Finish 'Em. I know the stuff. In dilute solution. Yes? About thirty bottles of Yugoslav Riesling, right? Do you know what's in Finish 'Em? Have you even looked at the make-up of the stuff? It's only a brand name. Do you know what's in it, Mr Wimbledon Poisoner?'

'Well,' said Henry, now definitely annoyed at this series of slurs on his poisoning record, 'it's got . . .'

'Mild alkali NaKOH, or something along those lines. Milder than that. You'd need 80 to a 100 grams neat to finish you off, work out the odds on a few glasses of a dilute solution, try and remember how they died, you stupid, stupid, stupid little man.'

Henry was trying, admittedly not very hard, to remember how they died. He did remember David Sprott talking, rather over-enthusiastically, about teeth.

'The symptoms of atropine poisoning,' said Rush, 'are primarily excitative: restlessness, mental excitement, incoherence, even mania, flushing and dry skin, pupils dilated . . . think back, think back!'

Henry thought back. And he remembered all these things. Looking across at Rush he remembered seeing the man at the edge of the punch-bowl. Could it be possible that . . .

'You don't know anything about poisons,' said Rush. 'If you've read any books on the subject you certainly haven't absorbed the information in them. You've just let your eyes travel over the page for a few minutes and then closed it under the illusion you've actually acquired some knowledge.'

This, thought Henry, was entirely probable. It seemed indeed a fairly accurate description of his normal method of reading. But if thallium hadn't killed Donald Templeton, then what had?

Rush answered his thoughts. 'I wasn't able to get as much atropine into the chicken,' he said, dreamily. 'You see I injected quite a few things at random, and I didn't get much time. They're always watching you. I had to tear the stupid wrapping off. And it would have taken about four hours, I reckon, with the amount I'd managed to get into it.'

The wrapping, of course. He had forgotten that. Did this mean that Henry hadn't killed anyone? He was about to ask Rush about Karim Jackson and Gordon Macrae but, once again, the little man was there before him.

'The trouble about poisoning,' he said, 'the real trouble

with it is not how difficult it is to conceal, but how impossible it is to detect. Every day, in every part of the country, people are being poisoned. But nobody cares. Poison is part of our diet. We encourage it. I couldn't get anyone to understand, you see. I'd put something in the food and no one would notice. They wouldn't believe me. The food's all poisoned anyway. It's all poisoned. England's poisoned now. There's filth in the water supply, there's salmonella in the eggs, listeria in the cheese, there's caesium fall-out in the milk and lamb and – '

Here Rush pressed his face close to Henry's. His breath, Henry noted, smelt strongly of onions. He had, too, a large and worryingly mobile Adam's apple. Henry tried to look away but the policeman's eyes found his.

'There's the Paki poison, isn't there? There's the Jew poison and the Arab poison and all the other poisons that flood in and change the chemistry of the country. So that Wimbledon isn't Wimbledon any more but somewhere else. And England isn't England. It isn't a green and pleasant land any more. It's a brown and pleasant land, isn't it? It's do you want a chapati, isn't it? It's where's my poppadum? Eh? Eh?'

Henry was beginning to suspect that he might be uninvolved in the placing of strychnine in Karim Jackson's green salad. That he might not be the person who had left around a red apple full of hydrocyanic acid for his wife to find, only to have it consumed by a Jungian analyst. He might – this thought was almost too surprising to contemplate – have not poisoned anyone at all. What did you get for attempted poisoning? Six months? If that. They wouldn't be interested in Henry anyway, not with a twenty-four-carat fruit cake like Rush on the stand. He was clearly going to sell a lot of newspapers, thought Henry, provided he could be got to the Old Bailey in one piece.

'What about Gordon Macrae?'

Rush sniggered. 'Macrae got the apple. Isn't that funny? Macrae got the apple. He wasn't supposed to get the apple, of course. But he did. But by then I almost didn't care who got the apple. It was doing it, you see. It was seeing how they died. It was so . . . interesting.'

There was a long silence. Henry didn't feel like talking at all.

'A psychopath,' said Rush, very quietly. 'is someone who doesn't feel anything. You're not like that. You feel a lot of things. I can see it in your face. You're full of feelings. Bad and good, I don't know. I have no feeling. None. Can you imagine that? Can you imagine what it's like to be me? It's like being locked in an empty room day after day after day. Can you imagine what that's like?'

Henry moved away from him slightly. 'Actually,' he said in a shaky voice, 'I think I can.'

Rush didn't seem to have heard this. 'I got the idea from Everett Maltby,' he said, 'that's what gave me the idea. You could poison a lot of people and then you could poison the one person you wanted to kill and people wouldn't think it was you. They'd think, they'd think it was . . . a . . . maniac!'

He started to laugh. His laugh erupted across his face, shaken out of his body, like nausea, rippling across his shoulders, rising in pitch like an operatic soprano and then, suddenly, cutting out, dead.

'It's funny,' he said, 'you can have a fantasy about something. You can think "What would it be like *if* . . ." You know? And then, one day you can decide to put the fantasy into practice. To see what happens. I used to go to prostitutes.'

I'm not surprised, thought Henry. I can only hope the poor things were adequately rewarded for their trouble.

'They were boys mainly . . .' said Rush.

It's a wonder they weren't fucking alligators, thought Henry, who faced by this creature was coming, to himself anyway, to seem more and more like a pretty regular guy.

'It was like it was with the prostitutes,' said Rush, 'it was like a dream, really. It was so easy and slow and curious. And the more I did it the more I wanted to do it. Because I wanted to see what it was like, you see. Because I hadn't really done it. Not really. Because nothing is real to me, you see. I can't feel anything at all. I'm dead inside. Quite, quite dead.'

And, much to Henry's distaste, the little man put his head into his hands and started to cry. He wondered whether he should say something along the lines of 'there there' or 'pull yourself together' or even 'cheer up – it isn't as bad as all that' but, thinking about it, he decided Rush should probably not cheer up because it was quite as bad as all that. It was probably a great deal worse. More to stop the man's tears than anything, he heard himself say, 'Er . . . did you want to kill anyone specific?'

Rush looked up from between his hands, his face grubby with tears.

'I mean . . . did you have anyone in particular in mind? Or was it just . . . anyone?'

Suddenly the detective became angry. 'Of course I fucking did, you stupid, ignorant little cunt,' he said. 'Of course I fucking did. Didn't I tell you I got the idea from Maltby? Didn't I? Didn't I?'

There was a long silence. Henry did not speak. Over in the bushes to their left a small animal of the night moved cautiously through the dead leaves.

'It was Elinor I wanted to die,' Rush said, dreamily. 'I didn't want her to live, you see. I couldn't bear her to be alive. I couldn't bear it.'

Henry might have been expected to feel some vague stirrings of kinship with the man at this point. But if anything could have convinced him that murdering Elinor was the reverse of a good idea it was the news that someone who was not him should have embarked on the project.

'Why?' he asked, somewhat unreasonably given his circumstances, 'should you want to murder Elinor?'

Rush did not answer this. The two men stood some yards apart in the moonlight, a little way away from the black trees. Then, still without speaking, Rush turned again and walked off north, where, against the black and silver sky, they could see the clear, surprising outline of the windmill, its sails like the blades of some infernal machine, poised to deliver just or unjust punishment.

CHAPTER FORTY-TWO

Rush was mumbling to himself as, the polythene bag containing Sprott in his right hand, he trudged on about ten or fifteen yards in front of Henry. They had found one of those paths that run across the common and were walking on black cinders; their shoes crackled, out of time with each other. It was very cold.

Rush appeared to be talking about love.

'If you want someone,' Henry heard him say, 'if you want them, really want them, want them to be all yours, then . . . then . . .'

Henry decided not to join in this one.

'Love,' said Rush, 'love . . .'

And then again, 'Elinor. Elinor . . .'

His voice, still addressed to no one in particular, became suddenly quite perky and chatty. 'I first saw her,' he said, 'in the street. And I thought what I thought. She was so pure. So good and pure and sweet. I didn't understand how she could be with you, do you understand? I didn't understand how anyone so pure and patient and sweet and honest and gentle could even dream of loving someone like you. Because you're evil. You're a rotten little compromiser. There's no soul in you, there's only a little snigger about the beautiful things in the world. Oh Elinor! You're so beautiful! And so gentle and so sweet!'

The one thing Henry had never had about Elinor was romantic illusions. She had always been, since the first day he met her, simply Elinor. She had an unavoidable quality. Partly because, even then, she was a fairly wide girl. Henry had met her on the towpath up near Kew Gardens and, from what he now remembered of the encounter, she had, quite literally, been blocking his way. At first he had been rather irritated by this. But on closer inspection there had been something he rather fancied about her.

'What are you looking at?' she had squawked.

'You!' Henry had replied.

Their early courtship had been nearly all on that level.

'Do you want to come out?'

'Well, I'm not bothered . . .'

'Well I'm not bothered either!'

'That's nice!'

'Is it?'

Why was he recalling all this so clearly now? And why had it been hidden from him for the last few months? Memory was so closely related to will, wasn't it? Henry could not, still, recall how he had met the shambling figure walking ahead of him. Rush was someone who had come over him quietly, like a virus. He tried to block out the man's voice and think, think again, what it was about Elinor . . .

They had both known in those early days that something was going to happen. But neither knew quite what it might be. Sometimes it appeared that it was going to be a fist fight. At other times Henry thought they were both waiting for some other person to come along and get them out of whatever it was that they had started. But, somehow, no one else did come along, did they? And so, presumably, they can't have been looking very hard.

'Like a jewel . . .' he heard Rush say, 'like a jewel and that fat bastard crawling all over her and if you could stop . . . if you could stop it . . . if you could make it so that no one, no one . . . ever . . .'

Then a low moan, 'Elinor . . .'

Henry had always found romantic love a demeaning spectacle, and Rush seemed to exemplify the final stages of the disease. The ideal lover worshipped his or her partner without much reference to his or her behaviour; the only way to get the love object to collaborate unquestioningly in the fantasy was to stop it moving, permanently. True lovers didn't fart like Henry or Elinor (actually very few people farted

285

quite as much as Henry or Elinor); they didn't argue about who was going to do the shopping or clean the floor, they went around feeling big, beautiful emotions and making people like Henry feel like vermin.

But who, these days, could afford big, beautiful emotions? And why was it people were such suckers for things that came on grand? At least he had been honest about what he felt.

The more he thought about it, the only thing he regretted about his attempts to murder Elinor was their underhand nature. He should have come at her with a pickaxe that first Saturday. She would have understood. She would have lowered her head, gone for his midriff, nutted upwards into his neck . . . it would have been OK.

'Call yourself a fucking poisoner . . . you couldn't . . . no, you couldn't . . .'

In fact, thought Henry, the level of his incompetence had reached the stage where it was a definite asset. If he went on like this he was going to end up President of the United States. He wondered, idly, how many other people Rush had poisoned in the course of the winding road that had brought him to 54 Maple Drive and the poisoned apple for Elinor Farr.

'We will never know,' said Lustgarten, right on cue. 'Was Rush the man who introduced four grains of veratrine into a selection of speciality rolls at Marks and Spencer's, Lee Lane, in June 1985? Was it the disordered representative of order who made free with the picutoxin on Albert de la Fissolies's first course of chargrilled polenta with chicken livers at a restaurant in Barnes in August 1987? The answer to these questions will never be known. Rush took them with him to the grave, just as he took the secret of the origin of his perverted passion for the lawful wife of Henry Ian Farr, or the precise pathology of his obsession with the case of the celebrated Victorian poisoner, Everett Maltby. Was Maltby in some way haunting the detective, as he had, in his own way, haunted Farr? Only one thing is certain – it is unwise'

286

– here Lustgarten, aware that he was about to deliver a *bon mot* to the camera, smirked – '. . . to interfere between husband and wife, even when they are trying to kill each other.'

Henry stopped. Lustgarten was, as he seemed to be doing more and more these days, anticipating events. What was even more worrying was that very often he seemed to be absolutely right. He was becoming a kind of Tiresias for the media age. Even if he wasn't right about this one, it was certainly true that Henry was in close proximity to a very deranged customer indeed. Rush certainly looked as if he was about to kill someone and, if it wasn't himself, it was probably fairly sure to be Henry.

Just as Henry thought this, Rush turned to him and, as if noticing him for the first time, said, 'I should have killed you first!'

'Do you think?' said Henry, as politely as he could.

'I should have killed you,' said Rush, 'that day I put the atropine in the punch. It would have been easy.'

'I'm sure,' said Henry, not wishing to antagonize the man, 'that for you it would have been no problem at all. You obviously . . . know your stuff when it comes to poisons!'

Rush looked at him narrowly. 'Don't patronize me!' he said.

'I'm not patronizing you,' said Henry, 'I just think that . . . well . . . when it comes to poisoning people you're . . . first class! Obviously!'

Rush sniffed. No one, thought Henry, not even a deranged psychopathic mass poisoner, is immune to flattery. As Rush walked on closer to the hedge that fringes the Wimbledon Windmill, Henry tried a bit more of it.

'Christ,' he said, 'I thought I was a poisoner! I fancied myself at it. I can see now I was a complete amateur. I didn't have a clue!'

Rush was starting to scowl. Henry decided to change the subject. Get his mind off whatever his mind is on. Talk about something that will absorb him. 'I was thinking the other day,' he said, 'about Charles Bravo, you remember the one? Who died on . . .'

'Friday, 21 April 1876,' snapped Rush, 'after being in constant agony since the previous Tuesday, when he had consumed a dinner of whiting, roast lamb and anchovy eggs on toast.' His lip curled slightly, 'Don't try and change the subject,' he said. 'We were talking about how I should have killed you.'

Holding Sprott's ashes high up above his head he moved towards Henry. Henry smelt once again that sour smell of onions on his breath, noticed the folds of skin on the neck, the ill-fitting collar, the watery blue eyes and that awful, yearning expression that seemed to be looking way, way beyond them, but was in fact looking only inside at the mess within him. He judged it best not to back away, but to stand his ground as one might with a dog that seemed threatening.

'And how I still might,' said Rush, 'how I still might! You've had murderous thoughts in you, haven't you? You deserve to die! Don't you? Don't you? Don't you?'

Henry coughed. 'I think,' he said, sounding rather pompous, 'I could learn to be a useful member of society!'

Rush put one clawlike hand on Henry's shirt. He shook his head. Once again Henry had that uncomfortable feeling that this man, only this man, knew precisely what he was feeling, knew the worst things about him, the things he never told anybody, the things he couldn't start to put into words.

'Oh no,' said Rush, 'oh no, no, no. It's too late for that caper. You're going to die, Henry Farr. You're going to die, die, die!'

CHAPTER FORTY-THREE

One of the chief drawbacks of poison as a murder weapon is that it does require the collaboration of the victim. Short of forcing a tomato sandwich down Henry's throat or suddenly breaking off to suggest a visit to a nearby Thai restaurant, Rush did not really have much going for him. He could, Henry supposed, try and jab a syringe in him and, indeed, he was waiting for him to make a sudden movement; but the detective, seemingly exhausted by his monologue, stood quite still in the damp grass, the ashes of his victim in his right hand. And then, slowly, wearily, he groped in his pocket and produced his pipe.

Henry backed away a little. It might, conceivably, be a dual-purpose pipe, a blow as well as a suck job. From his inside pocket Rush was taking something from a square box and he was squeezing it into the bowl and . . .

He was putting tobacco in it. He was lighting the tobacco. He was smoking it. Henry breathed out slowly. He looked up at the windmill – the rear end of it, lit from below, looked like a space capsule, the small, rear sail resembling a propeller rather than anything else. The light only faintly touched the four larger sails, waiting in the black sky for some signal that would never come.

'I,' said Rush, in one of those abrupt changes of mood that seemed to accompany his overtly lunatic side, 'am a member of the Wimbledon and Putney Commons Conservation Society!'

'Really?' said Henry, trying to sound interested.

'Oh yes,' said Rush, 'I'm in and out of the Ranger's office. I'm in and out of the windmill.'

He seemed to have completely forgotten about poisoning

for the moment, and if the extermination of Henry was high on his list of priorities he gave no sign of the fact.

'It was in a house next to this windmill,' said Rush, 'that, in 1907, Lord Baden-Powell began writing his book *Scouting for Boys!*'

Henry, of course, knew this. Just as he also knew that in 1840 Lord Cardigan fought a duel just below where they were now standing, watched by miller Thomas Dann, his wife, Sarah, and their fourteen-year-old son, Sebastian. Just as he knew that Lord Spencer, the evil bastard who tried to sell off Wimbledon Common for building land in 1864, converted the mill into six small cottages, or –

It was curious, thought Henry. In a way Karim Jackson had a point. There was nothing, at first sight, more fascinating than local history. 'Oh,' you said to yourself, 'just here, in 1846, so and so was beheaded, or just there, over where they've put the new telephone box, there was a pitched battle between some Jutes in 389! Fascinating!' But it wasn't. It was actually completely and totally boring. Who, really, when you came down to it, gave a stuff about local history? Or Wimbledon for that matter?

He gazed at Rush (who was still droning on about the windmill), almost grateful to the man. This, thought Henry, is how I look to other people. How absolutely appalling!

'In 1893 the miller, John Saunderson,' Rush went on, 'was empowered to carry out repairs. He completely rebuilt the roof of the – '

'SHUT UP!' said Henry.

Rush stopped. His lower lip began to tremble.

'I'm not interested,' said Henry, 'I'm not interested. I've had it. I've had it up to here. What do you expect me to *do* with all this information? I'm not interested. Any more than I'm interested in you telling me about my wife and prancing around as if it's clever and funny to go round poisoning people. Well it isn't. Anyone can stick a bit of prussic acid in an apple. A child of two could do it. It's boring and stupid and useless. And it's also wrong. It's inadvisable. It's something that on the whole we should try and avoid. And it's dull, Rush, it's very dull! No one thinks it's clever or funny! It's dull!'

Rush was beginning to look a little like Billykins on the day of Donald's funeral. But Henry, who was beginning to discover the bracing effects of morality on the system, continued in almost sadistic tones, 'I'm not sure I believe you, anyway. Any of this stuff. Isn't it some sick fantasy? I can't see you or anyone else really doing all the things you claim. I think this is just a pathetic way of trying to make yourself interesting. The Wimbledon Poisoner? Come on! It'll never do. There are real and horrible things in the world and you and I are nothing to do with them. The Wimbledon Poisoner? Come on! Come on! Come on!'

He stopped.

From his trousers Rush had taken a small, glass phial. Henry was not sure what it was but, bearing in mind the man's recent testimony, it was a fair assumption that it was not likely to be particularly good for you. Henry's nervousness must have showed in his face, and the policeman, clearly convinced that he was at an advantage, held it as high as the bag of powdered dentist, and began to wave it in Henry's face.

'See!' he hissed. 'See!'

'Yes,' said Henry, 'I see!' Then he said, 'I think you ought to see someone. A psychiatrist.'

So long as he wasn't a Jungian, Henry felt sure he would be sympathetic. Mind you, from the way Rush was carrying on it would probably not be long before he was crossing over to the Other Side, where he could, were he so minded, have chats about his dreams with Jungian Analyst with Winebox, not to mention Sprott, Loomis, Coveney and all the other people he had helped to speed to eternal bliss.

'See!' said Rush again. 'See! See what I have here!'

Actually, thought Henry, Rush was not reachable by any method of analysis yet known in the Western world. He was in the grip of the kind of dementia that could only really be assuaged by hiring Earl's Court and getting a few hundred thousand people together to clap and cheer at every remark made by the sufferer.

'We have so many English poisons,' he was saying, 'yew, yew, yew. Yew with its toxic alkaloid, taxine. And laburnum bark. Laburnum bark. And do you know what the country people call aconitum napellus, which is the flower that makes your pupils dilate and your chest ache and ache . . . they call it monkshood. And they call hyoscyamine henbane. Henbane, henbane, henbane.'

His little eyes were bloodshot. All around them on the darkened common was silent. And his voice, now, seemed to be coming from inside Henry's head. If Rush was part of him he was the authentically evil part. Was he now going to come even closer, to sidle up to Henry's mouth, and press himself close to him, put those wrinkled middle-aged lips on his and climb into him, as an astronaut might clamber into a space suit?

'The anemone is poisonous when fresh,' crooned Rush, 'and water dropwort, they call it oenanthe crocata, that's poisonous too. Nature has made it look like the plant they call sweet flag. Some children ate it and died in 1947. Why did Mother Nature do that? Why do you think? I think because she is very cruel, like all mothers, and she plants in her garden things that heal us and things that hurt us and we don't know any more what will heal and what will hurt us. We are living off poison. We have poison in our bloodstream; it has got into our bloodstream and we must drive it out.'

His voice was rising in pitch and his mouth, working this way and that, was dribbling freely. 'I wanted to save Elinor from the poison. You're poisonous, you are, you are poison. I wanted her to be free, I gave her the antidote, we have no antidotes now, we have sold our antidotes, we have no English poisons, we have Paki poison and Jew poison and Nigger poison and you're not listening to me, are you?'

Henry was trying not to listen. But it was proving difficult.

Rush's voice suddenly changed tone completely. 'The earliest form of windmill in England,' he said, sounding rather bright and cheerful, 'was the post mill, which first appeared in 1180!'

Windmills, Henry decided, were much safer territory than the English Naturalist's Guide to Poisons of the Hedgerows. In the interests of keeping this conversation as alive as conversations of this nature could ever be, he said, 'Really?'

'Don't pretend to be interested,' said Rush, 'when you're not! Don't fake it! I can spot fakes!'

He looked across at Henry in a sullen manner. 'Do you think God is a windmill?' he said. 'I think God is a windmill. Worm drive and rack and pinion. Fantail and sailblade. I am His Miller you know. I am God's Miller. He came to me last night and asked me to grind up the bad people in Wimbledon. All of the bad people. Do you think I should grind them up, Henry?'

Henry found this a completely unanswerable remark. Once, years ago, a boy at his school had, in the middle of a history lesson, informed him that all the clocks and watches in Wimbledon were being shipped out at night in furniture vans. What, he asked Henry, who was only fourteen, was he going to do about this? He goggled then, as he goggled now, at a loss to know what to say.

'Jesus Christ,' said Rush, 'died for us, and he broke bread for us but it isn't wholewheat you see, it's processed. It's full of poisons. They put the list of the poisons on the side and God is angry. So I am going to give everyone an antidote to the poisons. Truth casts out falsehood, right? Sodium thiosulphate casts out hydrocyanic acid, that would have done your shrink friend more good than talk talk talk about his dreams, there are no dreams. There are laudanum dreams, what would you give for laudanum? Potassium permanganate. We must cast out the devils in the bread!'

'I see . . .' said Henry, thinking he had found a way of giving this conversation some direction. If he could bring it round to additives in food he felt he was on safe ground.

But Rush was looking at him as if he, Henry, was the one who was barking mad. Insanity of course, is very proud of its rules, it doesn't want just anyone to join its club. What was strange about Rush was the easy commerce between the apparently normal and the transparently crazy, and the fact that the building bricks of the edifice Rush was constructing, the words, the phrases, the sentences, some of the ideas, were the currency of the normal, the everyday. Just as poisons were chains of chemicals, which, linked in another order, might create, and not destroy life, so Henry saw cliché, comedy, real pain and even rational intelligence glimmer fitfully in his speech, promise the great human achievement, coherence, only to see them, seconds later, gutter out in the wind and the rain that blew through his skull.

'I am going up into the mill now,' said Rush, 'because my mother is there. She knows all about Maltby of course. She's good with Maltby. There's a man in CID Wimbledon called Maltby and a man called Miller. That's when I knew I was God's Miller and I had to grind him up the way we used to grind the bread so I ground glass in his beef daube, you can see through glass, I could see right into his stomach and in his stomach I saw all this poison, all this poison we read and see and think and feel and never own up to because we are supposed to be so fucking squeaky clean, I am going in now!'

'OK, then . . .' said Henry.

And walking like a man in a dream, clutching the remains of Sprott in his right hand and the phial of whatever it was in his left, Detective Inspector Rush walked towards the Wimbledon Windmill to talk to God.

CHAPTER FORTY-FOUR

Henry did not attempt to follow him.

Not that he believed God was in the windmill, although, if He was, Henry did not think he was, yet, in a fit state to see Him. What he did feel was that Rush was quite capable of leaping out at him from behind a wooden pillar or a display case of nineteenth-century artefacts.

The trouble was, after Rush had gone and Henry was alone, he suddenly felt exposed, like a man standing under the walls of a medieval castle waiting for the defenders to tip out boiling oil, or an archer to appear somewhere high up on the battlements, his arrow aimed at Henry's heart. The windmill was so still! So quiet!

Perhaps he should go after him. He cut through the wicket gate in the privet hedge and made for the open door. As far as he remembered there was a steep staircase to the left, leading up to a landing. But it was possible that Rush might be waiting for him on the stairs. It would be best to wait below until the policeman made a move.

The trouble was, once he was inside the door, it seemed quite as frightening to stay where he was as to continue up the dark stairs. The only light came from the illumination outside, which from the interior gave one the illusion of being behind the footlights of a *son et lumière*. Henry felt on display, caught, like an escaping prisoner in a searchlight, but in spite of the alarmingly public nature of the place, everything round it was silent. He stood listening for a moment. There was someone on the floor above him. Creak. Creak. Creak.

'Er . . .' Henry craned his neck upwards. 'Rush?'

There was no answer.

'Look . . . Rush . . . if you're hiding up there . . .'

If you're hiding up there what?

'If you are . . . you can't hide for ever . . .'

There was a scurry of feet on the boards of the museum above and the sound of something being dragged across the floor. Was Rush barricading himself in? Henry imagined the noise growing in volume, the creaks, thumps and rattles coalescing, fusing, until in the dawn Rush would, as he had promised, start to grind. The great spur wheel would turn, the governors start to clatter and the unseen hand of some miller open the shutters of the sails through the striking rod and the great stones would start to grind the corn, only it wouldn't be the corn of course, but the suburb itself, sucked into the machine, like smoke from a pipe, squeezed and bruised through the bed stone and the runner stone, shaken out through the hoppers, mounted on the framework they called the horse, shaken by the spindle they called the damsel because it made so much noise, and then poured like liquid meal through the holes into the floor to be bagged up for market. Reaping the sinners!

'Rush?'

Henry was now round the turn of the stairs. In time to see the policeman's legs disappear from the end of a ladder placed against the trap door that leads to the upper part of the mill. Once, in Maltby's day, there was an external staircase up to the fantail stage – now Rush was climbing up through the interior to . . . to what?

With a new confidence, Henry started to follow him. He was on the third or the fourth rung of the ladder when he heard a voice, booming round in the upper chamber – 'Come along, Mother!'

Henry stopped. Then he called up into the darkness above him. 'Rush? Rush?'

He heard what sounded like an old woman's voice: 'I'm tired, Everett!'

Then Rush's voice: 'Not much further, Mother . . .'

'Everett! . . . I'm tired . . .'

Henry climbed further up the ladder and put one hand on the edge of the trap door.

'Everett!' he called. 'Everett! Are you there?'

There was a silence.

Then, Rush's voice: 'They hanged me at Wandsworth in 1888. They put a rope round my neck and dropped me through the floor. Can you imagine that?'

Another silence. Then – 'The answer to all this is Maltby. He's the answer to all this. Nobody understands, you see. Nobody cares about what happened. Nobody cares about the past. That's what they've done to this country. They've stopped caring about the past. And so we have to go over it and over it. Over and over and over – '

Rush's voice was coming nearer.

'And over and over and – '

'CHRIST!'

This last ejaculation was caused by Rush's slamming down the trap door on Henry's fingers. He heard the policeman cackle as, pushing aside the trap door, he shouldered his way to the upper chamber, in time to see Rush scrambling up the steps that led out to the fantail stage. Henry followed him.

When he got out on to the wooden platform, the thick white sails of the fantail straight ahead of him, like one of those child's toys designed to turn and rattle in the wind, Rush was nowhere to be seen. Down below Henry could see the top of the two yew trees, from this angle and in the theatrical light as dense and sculptured as a cumulus. He looked around him in the cold December night and then, cautiously, went towards the edge of the platform, shielded from the drop by only one whitened spar, at above chest height. Had the man jumped? Then as he came to the edge he heard a laugh above him and, turning, he looked up to see the detective sitting on the edge of the windmill's cap.

'Look at it!' said Rush. 'Look at it!'

He gestured out towards Parkside and the village. From up here you could see the lights, and beyond them the dark incline of the hill; beyond that the far south of the city, spread out into Surrey, Merton, Mitcham, Wallingford, Epsom . . .

'Look at what?' said Henry.

'Wimbledon!' shrieked Rush. 'Wimbledon! Wimbledon! Wimbledon!'

And, unsteadily, he climbed to his feet. He began to walk across the curved cap of the windmill towards the floodlit sails. Away down to Henry's right he heard voices. Someone had been alerted.

'I don't like Wimbledon,' Rush was saying, 'I don't like it.'

This, thought Henry, was in some ways a promising development. If he could get him to talk about –

'I don't like the people!' Rush went on. 'I don't like them!'

Henry decided not to respond to this.

'I don't like the roads or the trees or the houses or the pets or the gardens or the shops or the cars or the – '

He stopped and looked down at Henry.

'Why do you think you're so perfect?' he said. 'Why do you think you're so squeaky clean? Every single thing you do helps to kill someone. Every time you make a plan or buy a drink or phone a friend, you're helping to kill them. Life is a disease, my friend. And how do you know what you put in that food didn't kill? It helped to kill, didn't it? It all helped to kill.'

He held up the polythene bag containing Sprott. 'What counts,' he said, 'is our intention. What counts is our secret thoughts. People put on smart coats and ties and go out to lunch and look almost human, but inside . . . oh, inside . . . And if we do look at the intention, you see, if we do look at the soul, and we judge the soul, how many times a day do we kill or murder or torture or betray or behave obscenely? Everyone is guilty in their secret thoughts. Don't think you're any better than me because you aren't. You're a hypocrite. And your Justice, your dear old Blind Justice is just a way of reassuring yourself that you can see. Well, you can't. You're stumbling along in the dark, groping your way home and you don't know anything about anything.'

The voices below were getting louder. Someone was telling someone else that there were vandals. But as yet, it seemed, no one could locate the source of the voices. Henry should have called out to them but he didn't. He stood looking up at Rush.

'Morality,' said the policeman, 'morality! What's your morality? Your morality is poison. And you swig it down and roll it round your tongue and you say "that did me good" because someone smacked your bottom when you were a baby and said "now you're better" and you were better. It's a matter of habit, your morality, and you're going to have to acquire some new habits, little man in the bowler hat, because your world is changing and with it your morality. And you're all going to have to get used to the taste of poison. There's poison in Ireland and poison in Africa and poison in Latin America and there's poison right here in Wimbledon and every day you drink it up like a good little man in a bowler hat and you say "My, that feels better! My, that's good poison!" Don't you? Don't you? Don't you?'

Henry felt this required some response. 'I – '

But Rush, waving the polythene bag around his head, silenced him with a scream. 'In here,' he shouted, 'I've got a dentist!'

He shook the bag violently. Sprott's ashes rattled against the transparent, plastic walls of the container.

'Forty-odd years – ' went on Rush, 'of being a dentist! Of being a good little dentist! Of doing his bit for people's teeth! Good boy! Well done! Forty years of standing up and drilling away and thinking you were being some use! And at the end of forty years? What at the end of forty years, eh?'

Here he shook the bag again. Little bits of Sprott dashed against the polythene. There was the possibility, thought Henry, that he would evacuate the man's remains all over the cap of the windmill. But, instead, Rush opened the neck of the bag and looked down into it. What he saw seemed to please him.

'There, there,' he said, 'there, there, there!' And started to shake the contents of the phial in his left hand into the bag. Henry watched. Was Rush, he wondered, extending the range of his poisoning operations to include those already dead? What else would explain the fierce look of concentration on his face as he kneaded the colourless liquid into the ashes of Henry's neighbour? The policeman stirred and poked the dark grains and, as Henry watched, the remnants of a married man of forty-two soaked up the transparent juice in Rush's left hand. As Rush stroked it into the surface of the ashes, the liquid molecules bumped and rolled into the solid molecules, and the dead oral surgeon changed shape, until he was closer to yeast or dough than chaff or meal. This seemed unnatural. When we die, thought Henry, we do not rise again. We are not put in the oven to prove. We are dust, aren't we? Dust on the wind . . .

But Sprott was yeast, flour and water. Sprott was living bread again, and as Rush kneaded him he acquired that eerie, plastic life that dough, plasticine or clay have in them; he was God's raw material and Rush, the mad miller, the crazy baker, was pushing and pulling him into human form once again. He was a ball now, a dense, rubbery ball, and Rush was rolling him between his fingers, holding him as high as he could, like the communion host, shown to the loyal congregation.

'Take,' said Rush, 'take! Eat! This is Thy Body!'

He started to giggle.

'This is Thy Blood and Body! This is Thy Spirit and Flesh! This Nourisheth and Sustaineth! This is the staff of life, O Jesus!'

His voice rose to a scream. 'This is the Body of God! This is strong poison! This is the acid of the Lord God of Hosts! Bow down! Bow down! This is the Body of Jesus Christ! Eat him for his Burthen is easy! And his . . .'

He started to giggle again. A hideous, unrestrained canter up the scale, operatic, alien . . .

'His Choke is Light!'

And as Henry watched, Detective Inspector Rush began

to masticate the paste. He chewed it with elaborate ceremony and seemed to savour whatever it was that had bound the fragments of Sprott together again. Were they, Henry wondered, afterwards, the alkaloids of aconite, were they brucine or emetine or quebracho or yohimbine or cotarnine or curare or colchicum or cantharidine or laudexium, its salts or dyflos? Whatever they were they were the staff of death. They were part of Detective Inspector Rush's last meal on earth, and from the ecstatic expression on his face you would have thought he was swallowing life its very self. Poison was always his favourite flavour and to eat it à la resident must have been the ultimate experience, the equivalent, for a gourmet, of a meal at the Tour d'Argent. How quick acting it was Henry never knew, for the policeman gagged on his former neighbour, slipped and fell forward on to the huge white sail that sloped away from the cap down to the dark garden. There was a scream, a sound of slithering Rush, and then, somewhere out of sight, the dull crunch of a body hitting the earth below. Then, for as long as Henry waited, no sound.

Rush was dead. But he was a psychopathic poisoner. As well as a psychopathic poisoner he was one of the most boring people Henry had ever met. So that was OK. Wasn't it?

Henry stumped down the stairs towards the body.

CHAPTER FORTY-FIVE

In Rush's home they found, among other things, a detailed account of his poisoning activities. It was this diary, made available to the coroner's inquest, that closed the affair of the Wimbledon Poisoner. When it was published a few years later (to form the basis of a very successful stage play called, simply, *D. I. Rush*) it caused something of a sensation. People talked about the banality of evil, about the lessons for all of us in Rush's ramblings and Henry read bits of it, out loud, to Elinor, when the more decent parts of it were published in the Sunday papers.

November 3rd 1987
Morning overcast. In the afternoon it rained. I put 0.2 grains of
gelsemium in a bun and tried to feed it to the fish. They didn't seem
to want it. In evening hoovered spare bedroom.

It was hard, from the papers, to work out which crimes of Rush's were fantasy. Even a year after his death no one was quite sure how many people he had killed. The natural tendency, of course, was to give him credit for every abdominal disturbance, polyneuritis, seizure, fit and remotely questionable disease in the Wimbledon area for the past few years. He had drawn pictures of some of his victims, and in the downstairs broom cupboard was an electoral roll with a skull and crossbones by the names of at least half of the inhabitants of Maple Drive – which proved, as Henry pointed out to Elinor, that he wasn't all bad. His mother, it transpired, was a schizophrenic who, by a coincidence that turned out to be just that, lived very near to Henry's mother.

Rush was, of course, a monster, but in the course of time he became another sort of monster. A more graphic creature altogether. People who had known him spoke of the strange look in his eyes, of the aura of evil that surrounded him, and many said he had for some years been practising devil-worship. He was said to have heard voices, to have stalked and raped young women and, in the words of one profile, 'to have always been alone'. Nobody, for some reason, asked Henry about him. Nobody ever mentioned the fact that he was incredibly boring. Being boring didn't, somehow, go with being a mass poisoner and psychopath.

In the course of time people forgot about the Wimbledon Poisoner. He went into history, along with Maltby and Seddon and Maybrick and Lafarge and the rest of them. And they forgot about Henry; it seemed extraordinary, really, that they had ever been able to remember him. He was quoted, briefly, in one paper, on the subject of Rush, but the newspapers, to Henry's surprise, were remarkably ill-informed about the true facts of the case. The journalists who hung around Maple Drive and drank in the Dog and Fox were, almost to a man, highly incurious people.

And in the course of time Henry, too, forgot. He forgot more things than he had already forgotten. He forgot about poisoning, or not poisoning, his doctor, his dentist, his wife's psychiatrist, his ninety-two-year-old neighbour, his publisher (he had come now to think of Karim Jackson as his publisher, and even boasted to neighbours about 'going up to London for a chat with his editor') and he forgot not only whether he had or had not poisoned any of these people but even whether he knew who they were or where they had come from. He lived very, very quietly.

He forgot about Wimbledon too, although he continued to live there. He forgot about Everett Maltby and Everett Maltby's wife and Everett Maltby's trial. He forgot about world affairs and local affairs. He forgot about the seasons and the stars and the winds and the rains and almost everything that he didn't absolutely have to remember in order to pay his mortgage, feed and clothe his wife and daughter and get reasonably drunk three nights out of four.

But he did not forget about the time he tried to murder his wife.

It was, of course, about the most interesting thing he had done. Or, to be more precise, nearly the most interesting thing he had done, since he had never actually done it. It was in his mind when they went to bed and when they rose in the morning and it coloured every individual way he looked at her. Because, of course, now he was not burdened with the intolerable weight of having to go through with it, it was, once again, a delightful possibility. If she showed signs of interest in a holiday with Club Mediterranée, for example, or an ill-thought-out fondness for the work of some young radical playwright, there was the possibility, close to hand, of dropping into the Fulham Armoury, buying a hand gun, and simply blowing her head off, one Saturday morning, just before he departed for Waitrose. The more he entertained this possibility, the better behaved she seemed to be, until about a year or so after he had first decided to kill her he realized, with dumb wonder, that they hardly ever argued, that their friends (they seemed to have acquired quite a lot of friends) were pointing them out as a model couple. And it was then that he thought quite seriously of telling her about the time he tried to give her Chicken Thallium. But he never did. Somehow saying the thing out loud would have had a quite unreasonably large impact on their marriage and, as certain adulterers go quietly to their graves with a secret, so Henry Farr hugged his to himself.

One night, about a year after everyone had been talking about the Wimbledon Poisoner, when he was long forgotten, when Maisie had suddenly grown miraculously taller and thinner, when Henry's office had become an almost restful, neutral place of pilgrimage, when Elinor had acquired a whole new range of obsessions and phrases and Henry hadn't even noticed them, they were lying in bed, under their separate duvets, when she suddenly said to him, 'Did you ever try to kill me?'

Henry did not reply.

'There was a time,' she went on, 'when I really thought you might be . . .'

'Really?' said Henry in what was almost genuine surprise.

'Oh yes!'

'When was that?'

She stirred under the duvet. He hoped she wasn't going to come over to his side of the bed. Henry liked his side of the bed. It felt safe and warm. He heard her click her teeth, a sure sign that she was thinking.

'Oh ages ago . . . I don't remember . . .'

'Was it . . . when the poisoning . . . started?'

'No,' said Elinor, 'it was just before all that. One Saturday. Here. There was such a bad feeling in the house.'

'Yes . . .'

'And then poor old Donald . . .'

Henry coughed. He didn't want to think about Donald. 'How was I going to do it?'

'I don't remember.'

Henry turned over and listened to the wind on Wimbledon Hill.

'Well,' he said, 'suppose . . .'

'Suppose what?'

'Well . . . suppose the balance of my mind was disturbed sort of thing . . . and suppose . . .'

'Suppose what?'

'Suppose I did . . . well . . . only once, of course . . . get this . . . mad urge . . . to . . . do away with you . . .'

Elinor sat up in bed. Henry stayed very still.

'How do you mean?'

'Well . . . I don't know . . . suppose . . . well, say we'd been having a row and then we were walking . . . well, near a cliff, say . . . and I had this urge to . . . push you off . . . say . . .'

'And what then?'

'Well . . . suppose . . . you know . . . I . . . had a go sort of thing . . . you know? What would you . . . er . . . do?'

305

'I'd divorce you,' said Elinor, 'and I'd phone the police and have you sent to prison.'

'Fine!' said Henry.

There was another pause. Eventually she slid down to a supine position in the bed. But he could tell from the tense quality of her stillness that she was not asleep.

'I just wondered!' he said, brightly.

'Because you don't want to kill me, do you Henry?' she said.

'Oh no!'

Elinor coughed. 'Good,' she said.

He heard her snuggle further down into her duvet.

'You couldn't really say anything else, could you?' she said.

'No,' said Henry.

Then she stirred in a lazy way and yawned. 'I'm very strict about things like that!'

'I know,' said Henry.

The silence was of a different quality now. It was restful, autumnal, like the season, like the leaves on the plane tree outside, that were turning, as they had turned a year ago when they were both different people, as they would be tomorrow.

'You can't go round murdering people!' said Henry. 'It's just not on!'

Elinor chose not to answer this uncontentious remark. The pause between them lengthened, and then, in the last moments that preceded sleep she spoke again: 'You think I'm stupid,' she said, 'but I'm not. I know all about you, Henry. And I'll tell you one thing about us. It's till death us do part. That's the way it is. Right?'

'Right!' said Henry.

She was snoring quite soon after that, but Henry lay awake for a long time, staring into the darkness, waiting for sleep that would not come. He thought about Elinor, and why he was still with her and what it would be like in the weeks and months and years to come. If there was one single thing that she had that was worth something, it was her mysterious quality. She was so hard to explain. He still didn't quite know what she would do next in any given situation. He still wasn't sure what she did or didn't know about him and what she was planning to do with whatever information she had picked up about him. Killing her would have been a very stupid thing to have done. There was, he decided, as he turned over to address himself to sleep, quite a lot of mileage in her yet.